TRAVELERS

IMBRIFEX.
BOOKS

Also by Brett Riley

The Subtle Dance of Impulse and Light

Comanche

Lord of Order

Freaks

TRAVELERS

A FREAKS NOVEL

BRETT RILEY

IMBRIFEX BOOKS

IMBRIFEX BOOKS
8275 S. Eastern Avenue, Suite 200
Las Vegas, NV 89123
Imbrifex.com

Travelers, a Freaks novel

Library of Congress Cataloging-in-Publication Data

Names: Riley, Brett, 1970- author.
Title: Travelers : a Freaks novel / Brett Riley.
Description: First edition. | Las Vegas : Imbrifex Books, 2022. | Series:
    Freaks ; vol. 2 | Audience: Ages 13-20. | Audience: Grades 10-12. |
    Summary: Now high school sophomores, the Freaks are determined to evade
    the federal agents intent on their capture, while the mysterious Baltar
    offers the group his wisdom, and in the woods outside town, a trickster
    god awakens from his long rest.
Identifiers: LCCN 2021043619 (print) | LCCN 2021043620 (ebook) | ISBN
    9781945501470 (hardcover) | ISBN 9781945501753 (epub)
Subjects: CYAC: Ability--Fiction. | Espionage--Fiction. |
    Tricksters--Fiction. | Gods--Fiction. | LCGFT: Novels.
Classification: LCC PZ7.1.R5475 Tr 2022 (print) | LCC PZ7.1.R5475 (ebook)
    | DDC [Fic]--dc23
LC record available at https://lccn.loc.gov/2021043619
LC ebook record available at https://lccn.loc.gov/2021043620

Jacket design: Jason Heuer
Book design: Sue Campbell Book Design
Author photo: Benjamin Hager
Typeset in ITC Berkeley Oldstyle

Printed in the United States of America
Distributed by Publishers Group West
First Edition: August 2022

I do not claim that this book follows in their footsteps. I do not share their heritage. But I was thinking of Louise Erdrich, Joy Harjo, and Leslie Marmon Silko. Thank you for all you've done. For what it's worth, this book is for you.

CHAPTER ONE

I was the last to travel through the hole between worlds, and when I arrived, I filled it in behind me. The children who opened the aperture believe they undid their night's work by closing their book of magic, as if something begun with an ancient dance and a song could be stopped so easily. They were wrong.

On that night, I had been sitting on my green hill by the river of time, feasting on the meat of a deer older than white man's language. A ripping sound, like some shredded heavy cloth, and then the hole burst into being, glowing like a star. I shielded my eyes. The children's song floated through, faint at first, then louder, like the approach of war parties. Shadows danced in circles, spirits perhaps, and then the starlight flared, and the opening churned and swirled—a nexus. Beasts from other worlds appeared and vanished, leaping or being sucked into the land where the children sang. I had encountered these creatures or their kin on my journeys across the omniverse. Some were gentle, some dangerous. Some could devour a civilization, a world, a whole plane. Many, many more were drawn to the light as fire lures certain insects. I knew that, in moments, those beings would reach the nexus and cross over. But still I sat, for this event concerned me not at all. Hardly the first time some brash fool had doomed its fellows.

Then the song's words grew louder, and I recognized the language. Not mine or that of the humans I once walked among, but the tongue of that people's great enemy. The singers came from my native land, or one very like it on the sidereal chain. A pup from an infinite litter that was itself only one of a limitless species. The omniverse was deep and wide and always growing. Even such as I could never see it all.

But *that* world. Its people. Maybe even *my* world and not one of its reflections.

I would not let them die in the mouths of monsters and mad gods. Some other way, yes, as all things must die. But not that way.

And so I hurled myself through, knocking aside the horrors that had not yet passed over. I landed in a tiny lodge filled with trinkets and tools—bladed weapons white people used to tame the land, boxes full of memories. On the ground lay children dressed in long, coarse garments. Two slept. The rest stared into the starlight they had summoned, shielding their eyes. Their terror struck me like a demon wind. In the middle of the lodge, their book lay open, a line of sheer power connecting its pages to the bottomless gap in the fabric of being.

I opened my mouth and spat out half my heart. As the children struggled, I threw it into their aperture, where it grew and grew until it squeezed the killing light out of this reality, diverting that world-crushing power to the end of the sky.

Then, darkness.

One of the lodge's walls had been destroyed from the inside. Splinters and dust lay everywhere. A great force had burst through. One of my fellow travelers.

The children still lay at my feet, dazzled and sluggish. Their raiment was strange, as if they had cut holes in blankets and wore them like skins. Even then, the smallest coals of power glowed inside them. They had taken their first steps down a hard trail from which they would likely not return. Though their book had closed when I destroyed the nexus, it emanated dark power in gusts both intermittent and rank. Where had children found such a tome? And how had no one taught them the sly ways written language can steal your life and send your tribe west into the sunset?

I stepped outside, each movement a war with myself. I had walked the paths between universes, but now, if I had brought a horse, I would have ridden even those few steps. Vomiting out your heart leaves you weary, diminished.

The night air kissed my fur. The grass was cool under my feet. On the wind, an odor like burning hair, the scent of anger mixed with confusion—my fellow travelers.

I needed to see them. I became a falcon and soared high above the trees.

Riding the winds, I found another scent, like that of the kill a bear leaves half buried to season itself with decay. But where was the corpse? Those winds spoke of smoke-choked skies and melting ice, of herds and flocks hunted and butchered until not even the ghosts of their footprints remained, of fouled rivers and misshapen fish and thick forests cut down to the roots.

This *was* my homeland, where I had walked for centuries, tricking the First Peoples and fattening myself on the forest's plenty. But it was not the world as I had left it.

I flew higher, watching those that did not belong here. Each had already gone its own way, as if the presence of the others repelled it.

My eyes grew heavy. Sleep would come soon.

As the travelers moved beyond the borders of the village, I marked them. Down in the stone waterway beneath the city fled a Go'kan, a four-armed blood-drinker bigger than any bear. I knew him. A prince of his people, his name was Na'ul, which, in the Go'kan tongue, means Breaker of Bones. I once spent a few winters in his world, watching his race feed. He even tried to eat *me*, to his sorrow. Now I wished I had killed him instead of driving him away and moving on. Unchecked, he would purge his humiliation through inflicting destruction on my home world.

I could have tracked him and, even in my weakened state, killed him. But if I did that, I would have lost the other travelers. Who knew if I could find them again?

So weary. Perhaps I had given more than half my heart. Even for me, such matters leave much to chance.

Six trails led far away. Two rode the air, two the water, two the forest paths. As long as they did not threaten the land I once loved, I cared nothing for them.

Besides Na'ul's, two other sets of tracks ended nearby. One being had scurried through the human village and splashed into the river beyond its borders, nestling somewhere deep in the muddy bottom, its life force strong and steady like sleeper's breath. Perhaps it felt as I did. Or maybe this was its way. I had not seen its form, so I could not be sure, but evil dripped along the path it traveled like blood from a wounded deer. Hopefully, it would sleep forever. But I marked it anyway—its scent, its dread energy.

The other creature had risen from the children's lodge, growing as it flew. It came to rest deep in the woods between villages. I knew its form, its tribe. Once they roamed this world, this sky, like scaled hawks. Their breath laid waste to whole forests. Their claws could rend a horse or a bear to pieces with one slash. A more dangerous creature had seldom walked the earth. Still, she would likely keep to herself, if allowed. And, like me, she would soon need a long sleep. Her kind dreamed away the colder months.

Three travelers who seemed intent on dwelling here, at least for now. One certain threat, two more possibilities. Na'ul would wake first. His force seemed most vital that night, though he was by far the least of us.

I hoped he would keep. Sleep called to me, gentle but insistent.

I landed in the woods, far from every human village I could sense, and changed back to myself. Then I dug my burrow, crawled inside, and curled up, dreaming of the old days, of scampering amid trees and thickets and fields of sweet clover. Perhaps, before I left this world again, I might play tricks, as I was born to do, as I did for ages here in the place where people still told my stories.

They called me Rabbit. It was not the name I was born with, but it had always seemed as good as any.

✷

Something woke me early—power rippling through the land like water from a dropped stone. Power that burned. The woods' inhabitants felt it, too, as they sense the storm before the lightning strikes. Their paws and hooves struck the ground above me, squirrel and deer and rabbit, a bobcat, boar. Wings beat the air. Insects scurried past. Even the worms fled in their slow, slow manner.

My heart was not yet whole, but another traveler had awakened. Or returned.

I crawled from my burrow and stood, the pulses from the west lapping against me. I closed my eyes and sniffed the air.

Na'ul. Of course.

But not only him. I sensed others, their essences as red as blood where Na'ul's was bright blue, like his skin. The children had discovered their powers, though those energies were still aborning, the merest spark that might grow into an unimaginable fire, power to rend the heavens, to raze the earth.

My eyes can see far along the curve of the land, through the spaces between worlds, but too many objects lay between me and the others. My ears hear more than I sometimes wish—from that battle, roars like a great cat's, splashes, shouts in the odd blunt language of the white men who drove my people west. The odor of burning flesh filled the night.

Against the flow of fleeing animals, I scampered to the village, following the power surges until I found those young warriors charging their adversary, circling him in a death dance of their own making.

Na'ul, prince of the Go'kan, even larger than I remembered.

The children felt unlike any beings I had encountered in my ageless life. Their human selves had mixed with something strange, like the smokes from burning hickory and a cookfire fueled by dung. They likely believed themselves no different at the root, the same people they had always been. But I knew better. No mortal wields power like that without its forging them anew.

Who had they been before they used the book? And who were they now?

One of the males gestured, and Na'ul caught fire. A trail of ice stretched from the child's other hand and bound the prince's feet.

One of the females shot lines of sheer white force out of her hands and drove the prince into the nearby pond.

Another male flew without wings. Such had seldom been possible in this world.

Grown men followed the shoreline and watched the battle. They carried weapons like those their ancestors had brought to these woods: guns and arrogance and a desire to conquer. All but two wore uniforms like the armies of old, and only those two were not afraid. Hatred wafted from them like sweat. The uniformed men trembled, their terror acrid like Na'ul's burning flesh, yet they did not retreat. I admired their bravery, their dedication, if not their intelligence. What could they do against beings like those now battling to the death on that beach?

The two who stank of hate seemed to be the chiefs, and they kept the others back in the trees, probably hoping the battle would weaken the winners. A crafty strategy, if not an honorable one. Strong beings who follow weaker ones have always saddened me. The omniverse would benefit if those servants overthrew their masters, for masters ride servants like beasts until their legs collapse and their hearts burst.

Prince Na'ul emerged from the waters where the children had driven him. He swung his mighty arms as a second female ran faster than any creature I had ever seen. She circled the Go'kan, surrounding him all by herself.

Something about her—I concentrated my senses, sending part of my own spirit to commune with hers. She moved so fast that I could barely touch her, yet even a glancing connection served. Now I could see it, smell it—a faint, diluted echo in her blood.

Before I could ponder what this meant, the last boy, bigger than the others, fought Na'ul hand to hand. How strong the child must have been, to stand before such a force and acquit himself honorably.

The battle splintered trees and churned the waters. Weak as I was, I planned to enter the fight. None of these beings could be trusted, not with power such as I witnessed on that shore. If I have learned one lesson, it is this: power always destroys, and power without conscience or experience destroys indiscriminately. A wildfire cares not whether it eats a family's lodge or a rabbit's warren, a forest or a prairie stretching beyond the horizon. It feeds itself and starves the world.

The strong boy drove the prince to the ground. The girl with the force blasts brought a sharpened stake. The fast girl, moving so quickly I could barely track her, drove it deep into Na'ul's heart. The prince shrieked in pain and outrage. And when he died, his deepest energies burst forth in one great wave that saturated his enemies. They did not know it, could not feel it, but I sensed those coals of terrible power inside them grow brighter, hotter. Some of Na'ul's energy entered me, and the night grew clearer, the forest's sounds crisper. Every leaf the humans treaded on whispered to me.

If only I could have absorbed everything the Go'kan lost, much that happened later might have transpired differently. Perhaps better, perhaps worse. Such truths are hidden from me.

Before I could engage them, the children vanished. The flying boy took one girl in his arms and soared away. The fast girl carried the others to safety.

I sat in the forest, thinking of what I had seen.

The adults searched the grounds. Their anger and frustration could have boiled all the water in the pond, but as the leaders began to shout at the others, I lost interest. Their power lay in their malicious wit and their weapons, but the armaments they had brought to the pond posed little threat to the children, none at all to me.

I slipped past them and bounded through the woods. The breeze wafted through my fur and brought to me the new scents of the young ones, like smoldering oak. I could have followed them to the edges of the earth. Instead, I stopped for a moment and turned, looking past distance and obstruction to see where they burrowed.

The flying boy took his girl to one lodge and then soared to another alone. So they came from different families.

The other girl ran too fast for me to follow in my weakened state, but it seemed likely that she and the other two boys dwelled in this village. Humans of this era seldom took what they owned and moved. They lived only feet away from dozens of others, whether they loved each other or not. I knew all this, having sometimes watched this world's progress from the other lands I walked. Most of white people's progress had seemed more like destruction to me. For every lodge they built, for every life they nurtured, a hundred winked out of existence.

I had never intervened. After all, I had seen whole planes rot. But beings like Na'ul did not belong in this world. Nor did these children anymore. They had to be removed.

I needed more sleep. The sliver of Na'ul's power would help my recovery, but only if I returned to my warren soon.

What to do?

In the end, weariness stole over me. My limbs grew heavy, my breath slow. I crawled back into my burrow and slept, hoping the earth would still be turning when I awoke. The last image in my waking mind: Prince Na'ul on his back, the stake deep in his heart, his mouth open and screaming.

✳

Almost thirteen moons had passed by the time I awoke. So had most of my weakness. I crawled to the surface and shook the dirt from my fur and stretched my limbs. Nearby, a buck watched me. It would make a good meal.

From five separate points in the village, the children's coals glowed and pulsed. After so much time, how hot might their fires burn? Still not at my full strength, my heart not quite whole, I needed to watch and listen and think. Then I could truly hunt.

CHAPTER TWO

The social worker, a million-year-old woman named Mabel Jansen, consulted her notes for what seemed like the fifteenth time. Her dark gray hair frizzed every which way. Was it supposed to look that way, or had she just never seen a brush? Micah Sterne slumped in the uncomfortable, faded red chair, banging his knees against her metal desk for the third time. Mrs. Jansen jerked and nearly dropped the document she was examining. She glanced at Micah over the rims of the reading glasses resting on the end of her nose. Micah shrugged. She half smiled and returned to the file, but Micah's father glared at him. Micah pretended not to notice and looked out the window.

Here in New Everton—the seat of Branson County, Arkansas, also home to Micah's personal hell, Quapaw City—the sun shone on the rectangular patch of yellow and brown grass that ran parallel to the building. Two hickory trees stretched up and up. Someone had raked the leaves. Three squirrels played around the roots and ran up and down the trunks, looking for nuts. Temperatures this fall had hovered in the fifties, but now, in the second week of November, you could feel real winter in the northwest wind. Micah was a Southern boy who hated the cold. When the thermometer dropped below sixty, he felt grumpy and out of sorts. He had never understood those fools who wore shorts on icicle-and-frost mornings. Give Micah a video game and a cup of hot coffee.

And yet if Mrs. Jansen had said, *Micah, I'll let you out of here if you strip naked and chase those squirrels through the trees for an hour,* he would have taken her up on it.

Her office squatted on the first floor of the two-story New Everton

County courthouse, a series of squarish buildings made of weathered red brick. The room's once-white walls looked yellowed, as if a series of heavy smokers had worked here. Mrs. Jansen had decorated those walls with the same goofy motivational posters you saw in freshman dorm rooms in the movies: "Hang in there!" said the little cat, who looked terrified. The desk Micah kept kicking was a brown metal monster that was probably older than his father. The puke-green carpet felt about as soft as concrete and might have last been vacuumed the day Micah was born. Plus, the whole place smelled like dust. Dad had already sneezed three times. Maybe Mrs. Jansen should have handed out respirators at the door.

The social worker set the file on her desktop and smiled at them again. *Nothing to worry about*, that smile said. *I'm your best friend.*

Micah did not trust Mabel Jansen. Not a bit.

"So it's fair to say that your situation hasn't changed since our last meeting," she said, aiming the statement at Dad.

"I reckon so," he said. "We're doing the best we can. It's been hard."

Micah maintained his poker face, but inside, anger boiled in his guts. *Hard. Yeah, right. A four-armed blue vampire from another world tore Mom in half and ate her insides right in front of me. Dad makes it sound like we missed a car payment or some shit.*

"I understand," Mrs. Jansen said, turning to Micah. "But I hope you both appreciate that Micah simply can't stay in your house alone while you're on the road. You're still long-haul trucking, aren't you, Mr. Sterne?"

"Call me Malcolm," Dad said, though he didn't seem really invested in this attempt at friendly connection. He was shifting in his chair and frowning, as if it hurt his back. He looked as if he had aged five years since Mom's death, the wrinkles around his eyes and mouth more pronounced, the gray spreading through his black hair, the bags under his eyes a deeper and deeper purple. "I leave him at the Entmanns', but he wants to stay in his own room. And I get it. He's in tenth grade now.

His mom taught him to cook some, and I give him enough cash for groceries and takeout. He ain't missed no school, either."

"That's all well and good," Mrs. Jansen said, fake-ass sympathy dripping from her tongue like spit. "But an underaged child can't live alone. If you can't make arrangements, the state will have to intervene."

Micah's eyes narrowed. The anger grew five degrees hotter. What would Mrs. Jansen say if she knew he could incinerate her with the flick of a finger? Or freeze her to that chair, preserving in ice whatever stupid expression she happened to have on her ignorant cow face?

"The state should stay outta our lives," Micah said, locking eyes with Mrs. Jansen, whose smile disappeared. "We're doing fine. What do you want, for Dad to quit his job? Y'all gonna pay our mortgage?"

"That's enough," Dad hissed, glowering. But what was he going to do, ground Micah? In a week, he would be back on the road, and Micah would go wherever the hell he wanted.

"No, we won't," said Mrs. Jansen. "And I'm deeply sorry for your loss, Micah. My own mother died in a car accident, too."

That lie again, the one that Homeland Security and the Quapaw City Police Department had fed the town: a hit-and-run that had left poor Doreen Sterne in pieces. Micah understood why they hadn't told the truth—who would believe it?—but it still galled him. And how did this woman expect him to move on when he had to spend so much time at Jamie's or Christian's houses, where his friends crept around him like he might explode and the parents kept telling him how he was always welcome, and they were so sorry, and was there anything in the whole wide world they could do?

Sorrys and welcomes didn't help. Grown-ups should have known that. When they spewed all that bullshit, their platitudes faded behind a whispering, lulling voice from deep inside Micah's mind. It told him to freeze every moron that crossed him, to reshape the town until looking at it didn't hurt anymore, to burn down the world.

But he couldn't say any of that, and none of it would help Dad, who had tried so hard in his own fumbling way over the last thirteen months.

"I'm sorry," Micah said. "But taking me away from my only parent ain't in my best interest either, is it?"

Mrs. Jansen settled back in her chair, which squeaked every time she moved. Somebody needed to oil the stupid thing. "I'd rather it not come to that. Can't you just stay with your friends when your dad's out of town? If you'll just stay put, all of this goes away."

The heat rose a notch or two. *Well, ma'am, I ain't forgiven Jamie and Christian for inviting our old bully into our group. See, my friends and I used a book of magic to open a dimensional portal, which gave us superpowers, but Kenneth the slow-witted thug got them, too. When I tried to pay him back for everything he'd done to us, the cops and some asshat government agents decided I was a terrorist, and then a vampire ate my mom. My so-called buddies expect me to forgive Kenneth when what I really wanna do is cook him like a steak. So no, sometimes I can't stay with my friends as long as I'm supposed to, because I don't know what I might do. Sorry.*

But he couldn't say any of that, either.

"I guess I can try," he mumbled. Anything to get out of this room. It would be weeks before he would have to come back. Maybe by then he would have figured something out.

Mrs. Jansen's smile returned. She really did look sincere. Probably a decent person for a government stooge. Or maybe not. *What if Mossman and those other feds are behind this? What if they're siccing this woman on me just to screw with us?*

"I'll talk to Thom Entmann and Frey Posey," Dad was saying. "Tell 'em not to let Micah leave, even if they have to tie him down. And I've got a couple other ideas. We'll make this work. Just please—*please,* ma'am—don't take my boy away."

Mrs. Jansen watched them for several moments, considering. "All right," she finally said. "But if things don't change, I'll have no choice but to step in."

Dad stood and offered his hand. Mrs. Jansen rose and shook it. She closed the file on the desk and then turned to Micah. He pushed himself out of the chair and shook her hand.

Outside, the squirrels were trying to crack open a hickory nut.

∗✹∗

Later, Micah sat in his room, listening to music on his phone while scrolling through social media. These days, nobody posted anything he gave a shit about. Here was a pic of Jamie and Gabby curled up under a blanket at a football game. They leaned into each other, their heads touching. A sour stew of jealousy and longing bubbled inside Micah, like how your stomach feels just before you puke. At least he felt *something*. Last year, he had been too angry about Kenneth Del Ray to care much about his best friend and his longtime crush getting together. Then his mother's death had nearly wrecked him. For most of his adolescent years, he had seen Mom as little more than an irritant, so after her horrible death, his grief had been overseasoned with guilt.

He had suffered through all these calm months—no more monsters, nothing but surveillance from the feds, no new agents in town after the initial post-Na'ul influx, no contact at all from the police. Hanging with his friends might have distracted him from his shame, but in the wake of the federal team's arrival, the Freaks had agreed to take a break, to spread out the agents, to pretend like they were drifting apart, as friends often do. He had seen them only at school and when Dad dropped him off at their houses, but then he had often been forced to watch Jamie and Gabby suck face. These days, Micah ate lunch by himself more often than not, sometimes with Christian, occasionally with Jamie and Gabby, but God, who could stand *that* for more than ten minutes, with all the lovesick eyes and giggles? Their happiness reminded him of everything he had lost, made him feel even lonelier than when he slept in his empty house. And it wasn't like he could just find a girlfriend of his own. Christian, his only other close female friend, was a lesbian. Every other girl in Quapaw City High still looked at him like he had three heads.

He had been staring out the window without really seeing anything. He looked back at his phone. Here was a picture of Christian and Juana de Leon sitting in the back of somebody's truck, eating McDonald's and laughing. Over the last month, those two seemed to have buddied up. Hell, even Kenneth and Brayden had each other. Nobody really had time for Micah.

When Dad left him with the Entmanns, Micah *wanted* to stay, just to be with other people. He wanted someone to confide in. He was dying to talk shit about Marsha Dickens, who had grown, like, three feet over the summer. But every time Micah looked at Jamie or Christian, he thought of Kenneth, of the harsh words the group had spat at each other last year, of the sound his mother's body had made when the vampire ripped her in half. And when he thought of all that, Micah would sneak out and go home and cry in his room.

Now Mrs. Jansen had presented an ultimatum. He could stay with Jamie or Christian, or else he would—what? Go into foster care? A group home?

Stupid, stupid system. Stupid interfering bitch.

Someone rapped on the door. Micah jerked and pulled out his earbuds. "Come in," he said.

Dad walked in holding a bottle of Bud. He wore a Razorbacks T-shirt and a QCHS ball cap. Back in the day, he had played defensive end. He had seemed bitterly disappointed when Micah (a) showed no interest in sports and (b) developed the body of a Class-A punter. Dad knew nothing about video games or anime. He hunted deer, squirrel, and duck every year. Micah would not have been caught dead traipsing through damp, cold woods with a rifle or shotgun. Hell, he and Dad barely spoke the same language.

Now they were stuck with each other.

"Hey," Dad said.

"Hey," Micah said.

"Listening to music?"

Micah shrugged. "What's up?"

Dad sat on the edge of the bed and sipped his beer. Then he pushed his cap back and scratched his head. "I wanted to talk to you about this social worker thing. It's serious."

"I know. I'll stay at Jamie's next time. For the whole trip."

"I wish I could believe that."

So there it was. Dad thought he was a liar but had never asked *why* Micah had withdrawn from his friends, *why* he had seemed so miserable and angry. *Do you not care about what's wrong, Dad? Or have you not even noticed?*

"I'm not lying," Micah said. "If I say I'll stay, I'll stay."

Malcolm took another swig and eyed Micah as if he expected his son's nose to grow. "I believe you mean it. Now. But something's happened to you and Jamie. You're not as close as you were."

Huh. Okay, so at least you noticed that much. "What's your point?"

"Maybe it's something to do with the Davison girl. She come between you and Jamie? Is that why you keep running off?"

Micah scowled. "She didn't do nothing."

Dad considered this. Then he nodded. "Well. I gotta go back out directly. So what are we gonna do with you?"

Micah laughed and shook his head. "Maybe believe me?"

Now Dad scowled. "Don't sass me, boy. You ain't too big for me to tan your hide."

Not likely, Dad. I'm stronger than I used to be. Plus, I could set you on fire. "Well, what's your solution? I go with you and split the driving?"

Dad ignored that. He stood and walked to the door, putting a hand on the knob. "I got a couple feelers out. But in spite of what you think, you ain't grown yet." He looked at the floor, dejected. "I'm doing the best I can here, kid. I miss Mom, too."

Regret jabbed Micah in the heart. For the first time in years, he wanted to go to his father, hug him, say *I love you, Dad*. But they did not have that kind of relationship.

"I know," Micah said.

Dad nodded. Then he left and shut the door.

His footsteps retreated down the hall. In hell, Na'ul was probably laughing at them, so broken, so separated. After a moment, Micah put his earbuds back in and resumed his bitter tour of his friends' feeds.

CHAPTER THREE

On the second Monday in November, with a cool breeze blowing dust and fallen leaves across the student parking lot, Jamie Entmann walked out of Quapaw City High School and headed for the tomato-red Nissan Altima Gabby's parents had bought her for her sixteenth birthday, two weeks before. Gabby leaned against the ass end, arms crossed over her chest. Her charcoal hair, now long enough to reach her shoulder blades, blew out behind her. She wore a pair of jeans and a red *Wizards vs. Romans II* T-shirt. She saw him and smiled. Her teeth were white and straight, except for one crooked lower primary incisor. Gabby's complexion, smooth and light brown, had somehow stayed zit-free, while Jamie's had rebelled, deploying fire teams of pimples to his cheeks, his forehead, even his back. How had he gotten so lucky, falling for a gorgeous girl who actually liked him back?

Gabby met him with open arms. He kissed her on the cheek.

"Hi," she said, brushing hair from her face.

"Hey," Jamie said. "You good?"

"Yeah," she said, looking around. "Seen Christian or Micah? Or Kenneth?"

"Not since lunch," Jamie said. "Well, Kenneth was in World History, sixth period."

"Let's go," Gabby said. She turned and got into the driver's seat. Jamie walked around and climbed in. "I know we can't put a time limit on grief, but Micah's not getting any better. I just don't know what to do for him."

"I was thinking about that. Maybe it's time for a Friday night pizza-and-games session."

As she was backing out of the parking space, Gabby glanced at him. "Really? We ain't had one of them since—"

"Since before Micah's mom died," Jamie said. He thought Gabby knew better than to say anything about the Freaks, but he didn't want to chance it. Maybe interrupting your girlfriend like one of the dickwad Bubbas who lived in this town was part of the price Jamie had to pay for the others having anointed him their leader. Still, he'd have to watch himself. He didn't want to turn into an asshole.

He turned up his hearing. There it was—some kind of subsonic whine, the sound of the cameras and bugs the feds had planted in their houses and cars. The devices were active, as it seemed they always were. At least the agents hadn't discovered the Freaks' enhanced senses. Or so Jamie hoped.

"Anyway," Gabby said as she joined the line of vehicles snaking out of the lot. "I'm in. You wanna hit everybody up, or should I?"

"I'll do it later."

They fell silent, Gabby stopping and starting as kids turned onto Ash Way. When it was finally her turn, a black SUV with deeply tinted windows pulled away from the curb, its hazards first blinking and then shutting off. Jamie watched it in his side mirror. When Gabby turned right a few blocks up and onto Louisiana Road, the SUV turned with them.

Gabby adjusted her own side mirror. "I saw two bats today."

"Dope."

They had agreed to use *bat* as a code word for the federal agents; translation: Gabby had seen two agents in their tail car. Sometimes real bats flitted around at night, looking, as Gabby had once said, for some girl's hair to land in. The word had felt like a good choice—something you actually saw around town, but not anything common enough to make the feds wonder why high school kids would bother bringing it up.

Jamie turned down the radio and concentrated. His hearing spiked, filtered out noise and unwanted input, focused, zeroed in on the SUV until the voices of the men inside coalesced. He wondered what the Team would do if they knew he had identified them, even made a list.

The Federal Interagency Occult, Supernatural, Extraterrestrial, and Otherdimensional Task Force, aka THE TEAM

Chip Mossman, Homeland Security (aka Manticore)
Drew Greenwalt, Little Rock FBI (aka Prince)
Floyd Parker, NSA (aka Doberman)
Quincy Jeffcoat, ATF (aka Canebrake)
Cornelius Vincent, DEA (aka Lancer)
Joe Kragthorpe, CIA (aka Shrike)
Elijah McCreedy (head of the Team; aka Engineer)

Jamie had kept a handwritten log of the agents' comings and goings, cross-referenced by which members of the Freaks they had followed, as well as times and locations. When you could listen in or watch any time the feds followed you around, when you could even learn to recognize them by scent … well, the surveillance went both ways.

Following the rules they had agreed to after killing Na'ul, all five Freaks hadn't gathered in one place all year. They had practiced their powers in small, discreet ways, and only in safe places. But Jamie missed his friends. The feds obviously intended to stick around, so screw them. The Freaks deserved some fun.

Gabby turned onto Sixth Street, where Jamie lived. His was still the only Black family on the block. They had lived there most of his life; he had no memory of the previous house, a dingy two-bedroom place his parents had rented until they saved enough money for the down payment on this spot. He had seen that house a couple of times and couldn't imagine living there. It seemed as if it might fall over in a strong wind, and the yard looked about as smooth as a washboard road. Still, that down payment hadn't been the only price the Entmanns had paid for their move to Sixth Street. Cold expressions, unreturned waves and hellos, even some outright hostility—things had gotten better over the years, but even now, roughly half the residents on this block never spoke to them or invited them to backyard barbecues. People could talk about progress all they wanted, but in places like Quapaw City, change happened slowly.

As Jamie and Gabby pulled into his driveway, he was surprised to see Christian sitting on his porch. Her used bike, which she had bought at a garage sale, stood on its kickstand in the yard.

"Did you know she was coming over?" Gabby asked.

"Nope," Jamie said. Maybe Christian could read minds now. Jamie had once mind-melded with a vampire from another world. Who knew how they would evolve next?

Gabby parked and shut off the engine. She and Jamie got out. He retrieved his backpack, and they walked up to the porch.

Christian had shaved the right side of her head and kept the left side and the back neatly trimmed, but she'd let the locks on top of her skull grow long enough to flip down over the shaved part. Today she wore old combat boots she had bought at a Little Rock Goodwill—she had favored them over sneakers all year, claiming their weight reminded her not to use her super-speed powers—and jeans that frayed at the knees, plus a Tegan and Sara shirt. Yesterday, she had sported a vintage Pink Floyd tee her mom had found somewhere, and, on the first day of school, she had been forced to go home and change out of a Pussy Riot shirt. When Jamie asked her why she had even bothered trying to get away with it, she had told him that the patriarchy had to be dismantled one brick at a time.

"Sup?" Jamie said, lifting his chin.

Christian sat cross-legged, leaning against the house. She ran a hand through the long part of her hair. "Got an idea," she said, flicking her eyes toward a second black SUV idling on the curb two houses down.

"Okay." Jamie glanced at the SUV. His and Gabby's tail car had stopped parallel to the other one. The feds clearly knew they had been made long ago. They weren't even really trying to hide.

"Let's get together this Friday," Christian said. "Like old times. I'm sick of this shit."

Huh. Maybe she really can *read minds.*

"We were just talking about that," Gabby said. "We're in."

"Straight fire," Christian said, grinning. "Think Micah will come?"

"He's supposed to stay with us this weekend, so I'm pretty sure," Jamie said.

Gabby cleared her throat. "I think we should invite Kenneth."

Everyone got quiet. Christian frowned and turned away. Gabby was looking at Jamie, but he didn't meet her gaze. He was thinking back on everything that had happened with Kenneth, even beyond all the bullying—the way Kenneth had jumped them in Micah's shed, which had caused their game-turned-serious-as-shit spell to go even more haywire than it already had; how Micah had attacked Kenneth on the football practice field; how Kenneth had returned the favor in the middle of class; how his strength had been crucial in killing Na'ul. Over the last year, everyone but Micah had reached out to Kenneth, and he had occasionally hung with one or two of them. Mostly, though, he had begged off. Now over a year had passed, yet the group seemed no closer to Kenneth than they had been at the end of the Na'ul affair.

"Well," Jamie said, finally looking at Gabby, "I—"

"No," she said. Her firm, assured expression returned—the one few people had seen before ninth grade, the one she had worn in the final battle against Na'ul, the one that had retreated over these last months so that now it looked out of place. "When we all got shook over Micah's mom, Kenneth stepped up. We said we'd try to move past all the old BS, but none of us have done enough. Him included. It's time."

Christian watched the SUVs down the road. If she had thoughts on this subject, she kept them to herself.

"If Kenneth comes, Micah might bail again," Jamie said. "What will we do then?"

"He can't bail," Gabby said. "Not with social services on his ass. Anyway, him and Kenneth ain't fought in a long time."

"Because they ain't been in the same room together, except at school."

"They used to fight at school. That's progress."

The SUVs idled on the street between the Newses' and the Hickses' houses. These past months, Jamie had seldom looked out a window or down a road without seeing at least one of those cars. Even if they never saw another monster like Na'ul, they still had enemies. The Freaks needed each other.

"We can try," he said. "But if Micah bugs out, you get to tackle him."

Christian snorted. "Ain't we evolved and shit?"

"You know that Kenneth will probably bring Brayden?" Jamie asked Gabby.

Now Christian did speak up. "God. When did we agree to make him our mascot?"

Gabby elbowed her, frowning. "Ever since Gavin died, Brayden's seemed pretty harmless."

"Yeah, but he'll probably eat all the pizza."

Jamie laughed. "Okay. Speaking of pizza, who's buying?"

✳✳✳

Kenneth Del Ray lay on the twin bed his parents had bought him months ago to replace the one with the broken rail. Mom and Dad still brought up that bed from time to time, as if it had collapsed just because Kenneth had been careless. And, he supposed, that probably nailed their take on it. What other explanation might work—metal fatigue?

He had drawn his white curtains as the sun set. His closet door, now sporting a Motorhead poster he had found in a Monroe memorabilia shop, was halfway open, the handle end of a new Louisville

Slugger protruding. After Kenneth had announced he was quitting the football team last year, and that someone had swiped his old bat from the park—a lie, of course, since Christian had carved it into the stake they had used to kill Na'ul—Dad had bought the new one, hoping Kenneth might stick with baseball over the summer. He hadn't. When you were strong enough to literally knock the cover off the ball and send the innards over the fence and the trees and the Quapaw River and the state line, you tended to attract attention.

Brayden sat on the coarse, faded brown carpet playing *Sanity Wars* on the Xbox. He had gotten a haircut the day before, so his blond hair looked more like a wispy fuzz with his pink scalp shining through. The muscles in his broad back pulsed as he worked the controller. His shirt, with Kylo Ren on the front, was one he would not have been caught dead in a year ago. Hanging out with the rest of the Freaks, even just here and there, apparently rubbed off on you.

Brayden paused the game and scooted around to face Kenneth. "You wanna get in on this?"

"Nah," Kenneth said.

"You heard from Jamie and them?"

Kenneth sat up, drawing his knees to his chest. "Not in a few days."

"Y'all have a fight?"

"Bro. We're not dating."

"You know what I mean."

Kenneth sighed. Yes, he knew. He had been forced to work with the Freaks because, just like them, he had gotten superpowers. For some reason—Entmann said it was because Kenneth was the biggest and strongest—Na'ul had focused on him. After the final battle, the Freaks had invited him to join their little group. Kenneth had agreed to help fight any other monstrosities, to help them keep tabs on the federal agents. But the geeks wanted more. They wanted him to hang, to join their nerd games and all that shit. And, because he didn't want to be alone, he had tried, bringing Brayden along. *No Brayden, no me,* he had told Entmann, and again, all of them had agreed. Well, all except for Sterne. So Kenneth had hung out with them here and there, had even encouraged Brayden to get closer to them. After all, everybody else in town either hated the six of them or simply didn't give a shit either way. A Black nerd, a half-breed, a dyke, and Micah Sterne, the geekiest geek who ever read a comic book—everything Kenneth had learned from living in this town, everything he had believed for the first fourteen years of his life resisted the whole idea of hanging with the Freaks.

But still. Nobody deserved to be alone.

"We're good," he told Brayden. "Or as good as we were the last time I hung with 'em."

"Huh." Brayden popped his clenched right fist into his open left hand, as he often did when he needed to work something out in his mind. "Well, you ever wonder if, like, *we* should invite *them* to do something?"

"Just finish your game," Kenneth said, scooting back until he could lean against the wall.

"But—"

"Seriously, bro. Leave it alone."

Brayden watched him for a few moments. Several times, he seemed on the verge of speaking. But in the end, he turned around and picked up the controller.

Outside, headlights splashed across Kenneth's window, grew brighter, faded. On the TV, Brayden's avatar stalked the halls of a gothic asylum, searching for the force driving the patients to acts of brutal violence. An eerie, insistent narrator spoke of slaughter and the freedom you could find in giving in to evil.

CHAPTER FOUR

At eleven thirty that night, Christian Allen followed the protocol she had come to think of as Going Dark. She lay in bed, all the lights off and her new blackout curtains drawn, a towel stuffed into the crack under her door, and she concentrated, blocking out the night's noises, picturing the cells in her body, all of them bursting with energy. The power built and built inside her, pulsing with her heartbeat like electric current, then outstripping it. At that moment, between breaths, between thoughts, she zoomed out of bed, arranged the pillows so they looked like a sleeping body, covered the camera the feds had hidden in her air vent with a black cloth she tacked to the wall, grabbed her go bag from beneath her bed, and zipped out her window, pushing her screen off the outer sill to climb out, then sliding the pane back down and replacing the screen.

It all took perhaps two seconds. She just kept getting faster. That was pretty cool, especially given this past year's embargo on using their powers in big, showy ways. These runs to the Team's HQ were the only times she had really gotten to stretch her muscles, but they were all the same—out the window, down the road, into the woods near the old farmhouse where the feds lived. The ache to run free sometimes nearly took her breath away.

Another second, perhaps less, and she had dressed and stashed the duffel bag behind the hickory tree in her backyard. A weathered, rotting six-foot privacy fence—Mom had always said it came with the house—concealed her from the street, where, if she recognized the voice correctly, Jeffcoat sat in his SUV, reporting that everything was quiet.

Sucker, Christian thought. *I really hope I can shove that phone up your ass someday.*

She wore her costume over the outfit that served as her bed clothes—an old, flimsy pair of shorts and a plain white T-shirt. Over the last year, she had learned to sew using online tutorials. It was amazing how quickly you could learn when super-speed meant you could cram a shitload of practice into a small window. Since then, she had altered the Freaks' dark, coarse robes, trimming the heavy fabric that had fallen all the way to the tops of their feet and turning it into legs. She even managed to make the costumes form-fitting. Jamie had suggested they wear identical shoes, so Christian had zipped through Wal-Mart and stolen five new pairs.

You swiped these? Gabby had said, holding the shoes at arm's length, like they might be radioactive.

Well, if I bought 'em in front of everybody, it wouldn't be secret, would it?

So Christian had done all the sewing, all the gathering. If they ever had to fight again, it would be nice not to have all that extra cloth flapping around and threatening to trip them or catch on branches and shit, but she wished the others could do more to help. Sometimes it felt like most of the work fell to her. On top of the sewing, she and Jamie had conducted all the countersurveillance on the feds. Maybe Gabby could contribute now that she had a car. Still, Christian often felt like a full-time Freak and a part-time human being. She hadn't even gotten to spend much time with Juana.

Six or seven weeks ago, Juana de Leon had surprised her by walking up and saying, "Cool shirt. I love Black Sabbath and all that old stuff. You must like Pizza of Mind, since they've got all those posters and concert notices and shit on the walls. You wanna go with me after school?"

Christian had looked around, sure that Juana was talking to someone else. Grabbing pizza with a classmate wasn't Freaks business, and straight girls in Quapaw City didn't exactly trip over themselves to grab a slice with the lesbian.

In fact, though she had known Juana since kindergarten, they hadn't hung out since they were both in Brownies. Christian had quit the scouts after third grade; Juana had stuck with it for another year or two before deciding it was lame. By then, Christian had started "dressing like a boy," as Quapaw City's parents apparently put it, whereas Juana loved makeup and hair products and brand names. She had never participated in the bullying Christian had suffered, but she hadn't stepped up to stop it, either. She had become just another face at school, so when Juana asked her to Pizza of Mind that day, Christian had felt suspicious, as if she was being set up.

Yet something inside her had stirred and stretched. She hadn't been able to articulate it at the time, but now, after years of spending all her time with the same three people and all these months of reducing even that number to throw off the feds, Christian needed a break. Juana de Leon lived so far outside the world of portals and supernatural killers and shadowy government agents that spending time with her felt like another life altogether, one that Christian hadn't truly been a part of ever since coming out.

Now, standing behind the hickory tree, she shook these thoughts from her mind. She had business.

Christian inhaled deeply, then sprinted around the tree and over the fence and down the street and out of her neighborhood in one second, perhaps two. The SUV that had been sitting outside her house didn't follow. It never did.

They've been here over a year, and they're still just watching. I mean, they've got cameras and bugs in our houses and cars, but they don't do anything. What are they waiting for?

Mossman and Greenwalt had stayed at the Arkansas Scenic Hotel last year, but once their buddies began to arrive, they had moved to the old Gilchrist farmhouse on Grisham's Loop, east of town. Micah's dad had told him that nobody had grown anything on the farm in probably thirty years. Even the big two-story house had been vacant as long as

Christian could remember. She supposed the government had bought or leased or just plain seized it. Townsfolk whispered about the agents with their dark vehicles and darker glasses, how they seldom bothered to speak to anyone, what they might be doing out there now that the murders had stopped. Christian could have enlightened them. The feds sat at their monitors, watching and listening to a bunch of teenagers. They were, in other words, spying on American citizens.

The Freaks had given them little to work with, but still, the question remained: What were they waiting for?

Jamie had been the first to learn that the Team didn't surveil each Freak twenty-four/seven/three sixty-five. With only seven agents and five kids to watch, it would have been impossible. Instead, they kept at least one guy stationed at the farmhouse monitors, while the others followed the Freaks in patterns that still seemed random. McCreedy, the leader, seldom seemed to go farther than the front porch. Christian supposed she should have been grateful. A shadowy strike team would probably have a much harder time calling in reinforcements.

Tonight, five of the seven Team SUVs were parked in a neat line beside the house. Another one was watching her place. Where was the last one?

The Team hadn't bothered with landscaping, so the knee-high weeds and grasses, now yellowing as fall deepened, rustled in the light breeze. Beyond the farmhouse, the fallow acres stretched back into the night. A hulking, unpainted barn loomed twenty or thirty yards from the main structure. As far as Christian knew, the Team didn't use it.

Maybe we ought to set up a spy nest of our own in there, if they ain't got it wired. She could probably listen past the farmhouse and check the barn, but she didn't want to stay out too long tonight. It was colder than she'd thought. As they had done for months, she sat against a pine tree trunk twelve yards deep in the wood across Grisham's Loop. Once she had settled, she closed her eyes and concentrated, turning up the world's volume.

Then she filtered.

The wind roared past, sounding more like a hurricane than a light breeze.

She tuned it out.

Now that electronic whine—the motion detectors facing the road along the property line.

She tuned it out.

Bugs chirped and buzzed. The grass rustled. More whining—the security cameras the Team had posted on the house itself.

She tuned it all out.

Now inside—the thuds of footfalls on wooden floors, more whining and buzzing from computers and monitors and whatever else they had in there, inhalations and exhalations and mutterings from sleeping Team members.

And, finally, the voices.

Christian focused, focused. The world shrank. Nothing existed but the words.

"If I hadn't seen the evidence myself, I'd believe you two made much ado about nothing," said a harsh, raspy voice full of irritation—Elijah McCreedy, the Engineer. "After a year, we've got nothing but a few marginally suspicious comments. Frankly, gentlemen, it's hard for me to credit a bunch of teenagers with this level of caution."

"But you *did* see the evidence, sir," said a deepish voice with Massachusetts inflections—Chip Mossman of Homeland Security, also known as Manticore. "And remember that these kids stayed hidden from two trained agents. For weeks, Prince and I thought we had only one perp."

"We also have to consider the possibility that more than one bogey came through with the Go'kan," said a third voice, this one higher than Mossman's but just as determined—Drew Greenwalt, aka Prince. "I think that's the bigger concern."

"Bullshit," said Mossman. "We should prioritize the kids. They're the ones that fooled us. And the five of them add up to at least a Class Four threat. I mean, they killed a Class Five on their own."

"But they're still kids," Greenwalt said. "*American* kids."

"They've mutated," Mossman spat. "And given their levels of patience and discipline, they're also *extraordinary* teenagers. We should get proactive. A nice strike on one or two should be enough to make them reveal themselves."

"Kids," Greenwalt said again. "If this were another Go'kan, I'd be right there with you, Chip. But children? Come on."

"Jesus, Drew. Are you going soft, or are you just a chickenshit?"

"Look, motherf—"

"*Enough*," McCreedy growled. "Agent Mossman, you've proposed this before. I don't need a reprise."

"But sir—" Mossman began.

"Agent Greenwalt is correct. These are American children, not bloodsuckers or slime-dripping aliens. That makes this situation different than any we've dealt with before. While we will always do what is necessary, I would rather wait to move against them after you've found enough evidence to prove they are a threat to national security. If we're ever called to testify before Congress, doing so might keep us out of prison."

"What about that dead Go'kan?" Mossman said, a sharp edge in his voice. "Or the 'American child' who attacked those other kids last year?"

"And what would we say about that?" McCreedy asked. "That they did this nation a service by killing a murderous monster? Or that they fought each other like teenagers do everywhere? Think about it. Who else did they really hurt? Principal Hoon, who might have needed a heating pad for his injured back?"

"Sir—"

"*No*, Agent Mossman. Last year's events do not justify wetworks. Not against Americans. You want to move on them? Find the evidence."

No one spoke for several moments. Then Mossman said, "Yes, sir." More footfalls, probably as he walked away.

"He's not going to let this go," Greenwalt said.

"No," McCreedy said. "I'll expect you to keep him in line."

"Yes, sir."

McCreedy lowered his voice. "Frankly, he's not wrong. Powers like those you've described pose a threat to this nation. Sooner or later, we'll have to deal with these kids, even if we risk our own freedom."

A long pause. "Yes, sir. I understand."

Christian turned down the volume and stood. Usually she or Jamie stayed at least an hour, school night or not, but she had heard enough. The Team would keep watching. A fight was coming.

After securing her mask, Christian sped away, the darkened streets flying by like the seconds.

CHAPTER FIVE

Lying in bed with her sheet and down coverlet wrapped tightly around her, Gabby Davison stared at the ceiling, unable to sleep. It had been hours since she'd texted Kenneth:

> Game night this Friday
> All of us
> U in

He hadn't replied. Gabby had considered following up, maybe even calling him, but something had stopped her. Too much pressure might scare him away or piss him off, or even make him think she was interested in being more than friends. Gabby loved Jamie and wasn't about to jeopardize that. Deep down, though, Gabby didn't really think either of those things would have happened. They didn't feel right.

The truth reached back to the simple fact of her personality. Kenneth didn't care about her invitation. Who would? Despite Jamie's love, despite how she had overcome her self-doubts and played a key role in stopping Na'ul, she had discovered that healing didn't travel in one smooth direction. For her, at least, it was like trying to walk against a hurricane-strength wind. Even if you dug in, leaned into it, forced yourself forward two or three steps, it blew you backward. After hours of marching, you could still see where you had begun.

Stop it. Just quit.

But she couldn't just stop. God, how good she had felt that night at the pond, using her force beams to drive a four-armed, eight-foot-tall interdimensional vampire to his knees. How cool to be part of a group, to belong. And then, less than a week after those highs, Steve Whitehead, ninth-grade quarterback, had sent her spiraling right back into her old self-image.

That day, Mr. Singh, her and Jamie's Algebra I teacher, had called her to the board and asked her to solve a problem that had stumped most of the class. Her face had felt flushed, her stomach fluttery. When nobody else could find the answer, the teachers usually called on Jamie. Gabby spent most of her classroom time listening and taking notes and doodling, secure in the knowledge that her teachers generally treated her like a piece of furniture—present, solid, but just part of the scene. But as it happened, she and Jamie had worked that problem together the night before, going over it until they both understood it.

She had walked to the whiteboard and, in her looping script, completed the equation.

"Good work, Gabby," Mr. Singh had said, beaming.

Jamie had gently, almost surreptitiously pumped his fist and winked.

Then, as she sat at her desk and turned to the next problem, Steve Whitehead whispered, "Shocker. Sister Gabby's a try-hard."

Someone tittered.

Gabby's face had flushed again. She gripped her desk, all that embarrassment and shame rising from the deepest part of her until she felt nauseated. Sister Gabby, the nickname with which she had been saddled because her mother was Catholic in a heavily protestant town—made even more ridiculous by the fact that her father was Jewish—the nickname people like Steve had thrown at her whenever she had the temerity to exist in public.

She knew she shouldn't let it bother her, not anymore. Religious intolerance equaled bigotry, and the opinions of bigots shouldn't matter. Besides, if she had wanted to, she could have blasted Steve through a wall. He didn't know that, but she did, and knowing should have allowed her to feel strong, confident. But it hadn't.

And now Kenneth had ghosted her. God, why was she so pathetic?

Why did she set herself up for so much disappointment? Better just to stay silent, in the shadows. Better not to try.

Her eyes filled with tears.

Then she sat up and threw off her covers and picked up her phone from the nightstand, wiping her eyes. Because screw that. People might shit on her for the rest of her life, but she didn't have to take it.

She texted Kenneth:

U dont have to come if u dont want to but you could at least respond
Asshole

She sent him five middle-finger emojis. Then she turned off her phone, lay down, and pulled her covers up. She lay awake for a long time.

∗✳∗

Kenneth stared at Gabby's messages. He had typed at least a dozen replies, trying a new tone and approach each time—

screw you you halfbreed bitch
idk more later
what does micah say

—and on and on, but he always erased them. Nothing seemed adequate to both express his feelings and keep from detonating a bomb in the fragile relationships they had all built. God, he was too young to worry about shit like this. He felt like a politician, where everything he said consisted of one part honesty and three parts fake-ass smiles.

He turned off his phone, set it on his nightstand, and lay back, feeling as lonely as he ever had.

CHAPTER SIX

The next morning, Gabby rolled over, yawned, stretched, and turned on her phone. Her notifications tone, a chirpy electronic version of the *Dr. Who* theme song, rang out as she sat on the edge of the bed and ran her fingers through her tangled hair. She had several DMs, but no text from Kenneth. Anger flashed inside her like heat lightning, but she put down the phone and stood, because, again, screw that. And screw Kenneth. She had tried. Nobody could say she hadn't. Let him live in a cave with Brayden if he wanted to.

Outside, the day was cool, the sun blazing through the increasingly bare trees. Golden, red, and brown leaves lay piled in everyone's yards. Across the way, Mr. Meddars, retired and gray-haired, wore a Razorbacks windbreaker and thick glasses as he raked his lawn. He had cleared half the front and dumped the leaves into two piles. When he spotted Gabby, he waved. She raised a hand as she dug her keys out of her pocket.

As she drove down Mississippi Street, the usual black SUV—she had never cared about cars, but Kenneth had told her this one was a Suburban—pulled away from the curb and followed six or eight lengths behind her.

Wonder who's in there today. Probably Vincent again. Vincent was DEA, code name Lancer. *I wonder if they think I got junkie tendencies?*

Gabby laughed. That couldn't be it. Surely, after a year, they knew better. From what she had gleaned from old movies, her grandparents' generation might have called her a "square." That McCreedy guy could probably relate.

She turned up the volume on her stereo and drummed her steering wheel. At the next intersection, she glanced in her rearview mirror. The Suburban crept along. Why did they even bother with the distance? She knew they were there, and they knew she knew.

Just for the hell of it, she sat at the stop sign for a while. They slowed down even more. Gabby laughed again. Then, from the corner of Mississippi and Poplar Avenue, a black sedan pulled out. It maneuvered between Gabby and the SUV. She positioned the mirror until she could see the symbol on the grille—a Lexus? The car's sheen, its flawless paint job, suggested it was new. The tinting on the Lexus's windows seemed even darker than that of the feds' cars.

She drove away, cranking the volume.

At Jamie's house on Sixth Street, she parked behind his parents' car and honked. After a moment, Jamie appeared. His arms, honed over the last year, strained against the fabric of his button-down shirt as he shifted his books from one hand to the other. His jawline had gotten more pronounced. Wisps of hair grew on his chin and upper lip; occasionally he even had to shave them. He smiled, revealing his strong and even teeth, and waved, flexing those muscles again.

He is fine, Gabby thought. *If the other girls in this town—well, straight girls, anyway—had any damn sense, I'd have to beat 'em away with a stick.*

Jamie opened the passenger door, slid in, and slammed it shut, balancing the books and notebooks on his lap as he fastened his seatbelt. "Morning," he said, leaning over and kissing her cheek.

"Hey," Gabby said. She put the car in reverse and backed out. The SUV followed her. But—huh, that was weird—a black sedan now crept along behind the feds. That same Lexus? The three cars trundled along the residential streets like a sad parade. She cleared her throat. "I saw another bat this morning."

Jamie started. "Different from the one that's been flitting around your street?"

Gabby nodded. She couldn't tell Jamie about the Lexus yet, given that the Team monitored her car's interior.

"Smaller than the others. The bat, I mean. First time I've seen it."

"Huh," Jamie said, and now he did check his side mirror. Whether he saw the Lexus, Gabby didn't know. "Oh, I meant to hit you up last night. Pops gave in. They're getting me that Bug." A few months back, Jamie's mother had found an orange 1970 Volkswagen Beetle for sale on one of the backroads outside of town—two thousand dollars, refurbished. She had mentioned it at supper one night, and Jamie had fixated on it ever since. He'd be sixteen on December fifth, and he'd spent weeks bugging his parents about it, promising he would take care of it, learn to do routine maintenance, never let his friends drive it, and on and on. His dad had said no. Jamie didn't need a car. His girlfriend had one, and in Quapaw City you could bike to most places you wanted to go, which was healthier anyway, and then Mr. Entmann wouldn't have to worry about his only child getting T-boned in some intersection by some irresponsible shithead, and so forth. But Jamie had constructed and employed a lot of persuasive arguments—*I won't need rides to school or my friends' houses. I can run errands. The car won't take up much room in the driveway because you can almost pick it up and carry it away.* Mrs. Entmann had agreed with Jamie, probably because most of the chauffeuring had fallen to her.

"That's great," Gabby said. "I guess we'll start meeting in the parking lot every morning?"

"Or we could take turns driving each other," Jamie said. He glanced in the mirror again. "You ever wonder how people can see when they get that really dark tint?"

"Yeah. I thought it was illegal."

"Guess some folks don't care."

They looked at each other for a moment and laughed. Then Gabby checked the rearview again. The Suburban and the Lexus inched along.

After parking in the student lot, they walked toward the school's side entrance, a pair of red doors with meshed windows. As Gabby kept checking her phone, Jamie wondered yet again what had happened to the various beings that had spilled from the hole they had torn in reality. After all this time, he struggled to remember what any of them had looked like, as if his brain didn't want him to know. Where had they gone? Had they died? He had spent a lot of time scouring the Internet for any weird local news, but he had found nothing. Because there was nothing to find? Because the feds had stopped it or covered it up? Or because those monsters lay in wait, ready to obey some kind of starting signal Jamie could not even imagine?

The hell of it is, I don't even know if I'm doing the right kind of research. Everybody's gonna look to me, especially if something else happens. And I'm as lost as a damn goose.

Inside, their classmates opened lockers and traded out supplies. Up ahead, Mrs. Figueroa shooed kids into her Spanish classroom, muttering *"Date prisa y entra. Date prisa y entra."* When Jamie and Gabby reached the hallway with the sophomore lockers, Jamie stopped at his and took off his combination lock, while Gabby continued down the way. As Jamie dug out his English II notebook, Christian walked up and leaned against the locker doors. She had dyed the longer parts of her hair purple. She wore a plain black tee, baggy black jeans, her favorite combat boots, and three piercings in each ear.

"Looking good," Jamie said.

She elbowed him, grinning. "You look okay yourself. Gabby says you're getting that Bug."

Jamie closed his locker and refitted the lock. "Yeah, but not till after my birthday. The guy said he'd hold it for us."

"Straight fire. Oh, yeah, I almost forgot. Last night, Mom and me went into Larry's. Kenneth was stocking shelves."

Jamie raised his eyebrows. Larry's was Quapaw City's local grocery store, the only competition to a small Piggly Wiggly that everyone called the Pig. "Huh. I didn't know he had a job."

"Me neither. I stopped and talked to him. His birthday's not till February, but he's working to buy a truck."

Jamie closed his locker door. The energy in the hall increased as the student body hurried toward their classes, everyone sensing the approach of the first bell. Assuming he wasn't sick, Kenneth would be walking somewhere among the cliques, probably with Brayden. If he really got a truck, then by March, only Micah and Christian wouldn't have wheels. Could Micah stomach driving his mother's car? Since her death, it had sat mostly unused. He'd only need gas money.

Would cars bring the group closer? Or would they carry each Freak in a different direction?

Stomach fluttering with nerves, Jamie took a deep breath. *Cool out. You don't know what'll happen. Hell, the Freaks might have been a one-time thing, if those other monsters we saw don't come back. Then the worst that would happen is we don't hang like we used to. That'd suck, but at least we'd live. And I wouldn't have to take everybody's life in my hands.*

"How about you?" Jamie asked. "You got plans to find yourself a ride?"

Christian winked. "Well, I can get where I need to go pretty good. But yeah. I've been thinking of looking for a job."

"Fire," Jamie said, unable to think of anything else. He wanted to be happy for her. Getting a job and a car meant Christian was growing up, like any normal kid. But jobs also made it harder to get everyone together, for games or movies or monster-hunting or whatever.

The first bell rang. Jamie and Christian moved down the hall, joining the general flow. "Oh," she said. "Game night. Micah's in."

Jamie stopped short and grabbed her by the arm. She looked at him with raised eyebrows. "Seriously?" he asked. "Did you tell him Kenneth's coming? And probably Brayden too?"

"Yep," she said as Jamie let her go. "I mean, we did this through DM, so I don't know if he threw a fit or made a voodoo doll of me or what. He just said, 'I'll be there.'"

"Huh."

Since everything went down last year, Micah and Kenneth had rarely gotten close enough to read each other's facial expressions, much less talk, chill, play. Now Micah had agreed to stay in the same room with him for several hours? And Brayden, too? Weird.

"Gotta get to class," Christian said, trotting away.

"Me too," Jamie muttered. *But I don't know how I'm gonna learn anything with my mind blown out my ears.*

"No running in the hall," Mrs. Figueroa called. Christian slowed down.

CHAPTER SEVEN

Later, in World History, Christian sat in front of Micah, who wore a QCHS Buffaloes hoodie. Where had he gotten that thing? Micah had about as much school spirit as the gum stuck under Christian's desk, and he liked sports the same way he'd like crotch rot. Hell, he hated Quapaw City on general principle. He seemed to have somehow shrunk into the cloth, as if it had more depth than it appeared, like the Tardis. She could barely see his features. Most teachers wouldn't let you keep your hood up these days—who knew what you might be hiding?—but Mrs. Broom said nothing.

"Y'all turn to page 287," the teacher said, adjusting her thick glasses. She was writing something on the whiteboard about the religious conflicts in Ireland.

"I'm glad you're coming on Friday," Christian whispered to Micah. "I know you don't want Kenneth there, but it's good you're trying."

Micah grunted and bent over his textbook.

Someone knocked on the door. Mrs. Broom set her marker in the tray under the board and made a "come forward" gesture. The door opened.

Principal Hoon walked in. His graying brown hair had grown longer than Christian had ever seen it, nearly over his collar. He whispered something to Mrs. Broom. Then he walked out.

Someone else entered. And Christian sat forward, gripping the edge of her desk.

The newcomer wore her caramel-colored hair in an undercut, revealing three piercings in each ear, just like Christian's. Her complexion matched her hair. Christian enhanced her vision. The girl's eyes were chocolate brown. A thin, barely discernible scar crossed the bridge of her nose. She sported a black *Wizards vs. Romans II* tee, black cargo shorts, and what looked like motorcycle boots. A black denim jacket was slung over one shoulder. As Mrs. Broom shut the door, the girl looked over the class and half smiled, as new kids tended to do. You didn't trust the new faces enough to give them all your pearly whites, but you probably shouldn't look too aloof, either.

New girl's brave, looking like that. The many homophobes wandering QCHS's halls would almost certainly target her.

That tee hugged her torso. Like Christian, she had skipped the makeup.

She seemed to catch Christian's eye. The smile grew, just a little.

"Wow," Micah whispered. Christian looked at him. He was openly staring.

Maybe she was looking at him, Christian thought. *Or neither of us.*

Mrs. Broom said something to the girl and turned to the class. "Everybody, this is Rebecca Villalobos. I understand that their pronouns are they, their, and them. Let's all make them feel welcome. Rebecca, you can sit here." Mrs. Broom indicated an empty desk two up and one row to the left of Christian's.

"Call me Bec," Bec said as they sat and arranged their materials.

"Oh gawd," Steve Whitehead muttered. *"Them."*

Christian whirled. "Don't you got a football game to lose?"

Steve gave her the finger. She gave it back.

"Quiet back there," Mrs. Broom said.

Halfway through the lecture, Bec Villalobos glanced back Christian's way, lingered, then turned around. Christian's face grew hot.

When the bell rang, Bec stood and gathered their things. Christian snatched up her own materials, but before she could move, someone rushed by her, bumping her shoulder—Micah.

"Need some help finding your next class?" he asked Bec, sounding more alive, more present, than he had all year.

Bec glanced at him. "Sure, I guess."

"Cool. I'm Micah Sterne." He held out his hand.

As Bec shook it, Christian threw an arm around Micah and looked into Bec's eyes. "I see you've met Micah. One of my best friends. I'm Christian."

Micah frowned, but Bec smiled. "Bec. I've got English II next."

"We'll walk you," Christian said, pulling Micah back and taking the lead as they made their way around the desks and out the door. They joined the students flowing down the right side of the hallway. Christian could barely hear Bec over the noise of a hundred conversations and the slamming of locker doors.

When the three of them reached Bec's classroom, they paused. Micah gestured at the open door. "This is you. Mrs. Coopersmith teaches English I and II, plus some advanced composition. She's okay."

Bec ducked their head into the room, looked around, straightened. "Good to know. Thanks for walking with me."

"Our pleasure," Christian said, making eye contact. The two of them held each other's gazes for a moment while Micah shuffled his feet and looked uncomfortable. Other students brushed by and took their seats. Mrs. Coopersmith was writing something on the whiteboard—probably her Mystery Quote of the Day. The first student who identified the author without googling got five extra points. "By the way, tell the teacher that quote's from Emily Dickinson."

"Cool," Bec said. They winked.

Micah cleared his throat. "Hey. Me and Christian and a few other friends are getting together on Friday night. Gonna play some video games, eat some pizza, maybe watch a movie. You can come if you want."

You slick son of a bitch, Christian thought with admiration. She could run faster than anything on Earth, but when it came to making a first impression on the hot new kid, Micah had lapped her. *Of course, they may not be interested in either one of us. But if they like him, well, maybe he'll have a reason to come back out of that shell he's built.*

"That sounds like fun," Bec said. "I'll find one of you and get the deets."

"Really nice meeting you," Christian said.

Bec lingered for a moment. Then they said, "You, too. Later."

Micah and Christian watched them go. Christian checked her phone—one minute till the tardy bell. "You know we won't be able to talk about powers practice or the bats if the new kid's there, right?"

Micah smiled. For the first time since his mother died, it looked genuine. "A small price to pay."

Christian dug her elbow into his ribs. "Come on, bro. We're gonna be late."

They set off up the hall together. When the bell rang a moment later, they sped up and ducked into their rooms just before the teachers closed the doors.

✸

After eating lunch under a pine tree near the edge of campus, Kenneth and Brayden sat against its trunk. The sun winked through the needle-filled branches as a cold wind blew in from the northeast, nicking their faces and hands. Soon, everyone would be wearing jackets every day, then winter coats. The woods would fill with hunters, and about eighty percent of the town would wear camouflage.

Huh, Kenneth thought. *When me and Dad go hunting, will those agents follow us? I doubt they'll put on their orange and set up a stand.*

Brayden sat back against the tree trunk, his chin on his chest. The breeze picked up a little. A candy bar wrapper cartwheeled past a squirrel sitting on its hind legs and nibbling an acorn. Kenneth nudged Brayden.

"Huh?" Brayden said, starting. "What?"

"Gabby Davison DMed me. She wants us to come to their stupid-ass game night this Friday."

Brayden rubbed his eyes. Apparently he wasn't sleeping well. Kenneth could relate. Yawning, Brayden said, "I'd have to come by after the game."

There was a home game this week against Pine Bluff Dollarway. Brayden played defensive end. Kenneth had played defensive tackle and offensive guard, but after he got his powers, he had quit the team, afraid he would lose control and literally drive someone into the ground. Every time he thought about football, his stomach dropped, and he forced himself to close his eyes and picture a bright blue sky with a cloud shaped like a bass boat. It helped him get past the deep resentment he still felt when he thought of all the ways his life had changed—almost no social life, no sports. And, of course, the four geeks to whom he now felt attached at the hip.

"I don't know if I'm going," Kenneth said.

"Why not?" Brayden asked, stifling another yawn. "I mean, are you off?"

"Not until nine."

"But you could drop by. I bet your parents would ease up on your curfew, if they knew you were hanging at a friend's house."

"They're not my damn friends," Kenneth spat. "What am I gonna do, go to Entmann's place and eat chitlins and greens? Or grow a Jewfro so Gabby's dad will like me?"

"Dude. You don't really believe that racist shit, do you? I thought that was Gavin's trip. Besides, who else do we got to hang with? At least we'd get some free pizza." Brayden gave Kenneth side-eye. "If you don't put your foot in your mouth or punch somebody, that is."

Kenneth snorted. "I've been a good little boy all year. The only way I'd punch somebody is if Micah Sterne runs his mouth."

He was surprised to find that he meant it. Even when he was talking shit about Jamie or Gabby or Christian, he realized it felt more like playing an old role than anything true to who he was now. Maybe the fight with Na'ul had burned through most of his anger. The rage he had felt after Gavin's murder, his contempt for the Freaks, his need to rip Sterne a new asshole and prove he was the apex predator, his low-grade dislike for Jamie and Gabby, his disgust over Christian's sexuality—most of the time now when he tried to access those feelings, he couldn't. Attending your best friend's funeral, watching his father cry like a baby, hearing his mother's wails, and staring at a casket that was closed because the body was too maimed to look at tended to give you perspective.

Plus, only the Freaks had reached out—not his old teammates, not any of the kids he used to joke around with after school. The Freaks had tried to mend all the fences he had torn down over the years. Maybe Brayden was right. Goddamn it.

"Well," Brayden said, "if they're still playing after the game, I'll stop by. You should, too."

"Maybe."

"Yeah? You'll go?"

"I'll think about it."

Surprisingly, he meant that, too.

CHAPTER EIGHT

That afternoon, Micah rode his bike home to the saddest-looking house on MacArthur Road—maybe fifteen hundred square feet and covered in stained aluminum siding, the roof more ramshackle every month, the yard unraked. A strange car sat in the driveway beside his mother's black Escort, which hadn't moved since the night she died. Covered in pollen and dust, the tires slowly going flat, it looked abandoned compared to the sleek black car Micah didn't recognize. Its windows were tinted so dark that he wondered how the driver could see at night. Micah dropped his bike in the yard and examined the car.

Why would anyone who could afford a Lexus come here?

Dad's truck cab sat against the curb. He must have washed it, because its white paint looked almost as clean and shiny as the Lexus. A terrible thought occurred to Micah: What if the Lexus belonged to a woman? Was Dad *dating*?

Jesus, let it be anybody but a girlfriend.

Micah walked inside. From the front door, you could look through the den into the kitchen, where stacked dirty dishes moldered on the counters. The old shit-brown carpet in this part of the house hadn't been vacuumed in—well, maybe not since Mom died. The place smelled like dirty socks. Micah had gotten used to all that, as well as the emotional inertia that had prevented him from doing anything about it. Dad had never been much of a housekeeper, but then, he had also mostly lived on the road. Micah had spent more time here, and he hadn't done anything besides mowing the lawn every now and then. Yet the house's condition surprised him today, as if he were seeing it for the first time. Part of him realized that it might have something to do with the new

57

kid in school—Bec Villalobos. Something about their hair, their skin, their scratchy voice … it was like parts of him that had been sleeping were suddenly wide awake.

The rest of him, though, acknowledged the greater surprise of that afternoon—the strange man sitting on the sofa beside Dad.

This person was wiry and a head taller than Dad, who stood around five eleven. He wore black slacks and a black shirt buttoned all the way to his throat. His hands and slender fingers looked wrinkled but strong, his nails long and pointed and polished black. Micah had no idea how old he was—fifty or sixty or eighty, the pale blue eyes bright and aware, the crows' feet deep. When he smiled, his gums looked blood-red, his teeth strong but gray, and pointed, as if he had grown only incisors.

"You must be Micah," this man said, his voice a deep baritone like Darth Vader's. Strange to hear that voice coming from such a skinny frame.

"I reckon so," Micah said, looking at his father with raised eyebrows.

Dad seemed distracted. His eyes were open but glassy, as if he hadn't slept well in days. His hands lay palms up on the sofa cushions. "This is your great-uncle Baltar," Dad said. He sounded far away.

"Um. Okay," Micah said. "I, uh, thought Baltar died. Like, a long time ago."

Dad just looked at him.

Baltar stood, walked over to Micah, and stuck out his hand. "Who told you such a thing?"

"Uh. Maybe I just assumed, since I've never met you?"

Micah shook Baltar's hand. His skin was cool and smooth, like he was wearing rubber gloves.

This was where Dad would interject in his gruffest, Dad-est voice, something about respecting old people. But he said nothing. He stared, mouth closed, breathing evenly. Weird.

"I've long been estranged from my family," Baltar said, letting go of Micah's hand and returning to the couch. He gestured at Dad's easy chair. *Thanks for inviting me to sit in my own house*, Micah thought, but he took the chair anyway. "Imagine my surprise when Malcolm called and asked me to watch over you."

Micah fidgeted. In his mind, an alarm rang. Dad hadn't mentioned Baltar that often in Micah's hearing, but when he had, it had been to warn Micah away. *Don't touch that trunk full of Baltar's junk. Aw, you don't wanna hear about Baltar. He was just a weirdo. Never mind about Baltar; we don't really talk about him.* Now Dad had called him and entrusted Micah to his care? That didn't make sense.

"I know I ain't always been kind to Baltar," Dad said, his voice hollow and monotone, as if he were stoned. "But he's family. The state will let you stay with him."

"Okay," Micah said again. He wasn't sure what else he should say in front of Baltar, but he didn't like the way Dad looked, the way Dad was acting.

"I've cleared my calendar," Baltar said. "And I've sent for my things. I'm grateful for the chance to reconnect."

"Okay."

"You don't have to worry anymore, Micah," Baltar said. "You'll never be alone again. I guarantee it."

"I wasn't worried in the first place."

"Of course not," Baltar said, smiling. There was something reptilian about that smile. After a moment, Micah realized he was thinking of the Gentlemen from that old *Buffy* episode. Those wide eyes, the lips that pulled far back from the sharp teeth and bloody gums. "But still. You are in good hands."

Baltar's eyes shone in the diffused light. Micah looked into them.

He could not look away.

They seemed to widen, to deepen. To pulse. They wavered like heat off a desert road.

The sounds of the world faded, and Micah's alarm dried up like a dead leaf. He felt sleepy, warm. And then he heard that voice again, the one that had whispered to him in Mrs. Jansen's office. It spoke with such certainty that Micah had no choice but to listen.

Trust him. He will prepare you for what is to come. Trust him. Trust him.

I trust him, Micah thought. *It's weird but true.*

"You believe me, right?" Dad said.

"Yeah," Micah said. He yawned.

"Excellent," Baltar said. He rose again, stepped across the room, and laid a hand on Micah's. "I think we'll get along well. And I would love to meet your interesting friends."

"Sure," Micah said. His eyelids had grown so heavy. A nap would *rule*. Right here in Dad's chair. He could recline, close his eyes, let the little patch of sun shining through the drawn curtains lie across his face. "Yeah, we can make that happen. They're awesome, even if they do like Kenneth Del Ray."

Huh. Did he mean that? These past months, anger had smoldered in his belly like coals the slightest breeze might coax into a blaze. But having said it, he thought it felt true. Beyond his anger lived a lifelong affection that often felt like love. Maybe that was why their betrayal hurt so much.

"Sleep now," Baltar said from a million miles away. "Both of you. As long and as deeply as you wish. I will take care of everything."

Micah forced his eyes open. Dad had slumped sideways. His head rested on the arm of the couch. His chest rose and fell, rose and fell. The exhausted expression had vanished.

What did Baltar do to us? Micah wondered, but he pulled the lever on the side of the chair. The footrest extended. He closed his eyes.

CHAPTER NINE

That Friday evening at five thirty, Micah sat in the Lexus's passenger seat, watching the town scroll by. Streetlights burned in bright halos against the sky. Micah sighed. Game night had officially started at five, but Baltar, who drove with both hands on the wheel and never seemed to blink, had puttered around the house, wiping down the counters, putting away a glass Micah had left on an end table. When Micah suggested that perhaps Baltar might hurry up, the old fart hadn't even looked at him.

"They say cleanliness is next to godliness," the old man had said. "And we should all strive to be near our gods."

Micah hadn't asked just whom those gods might be. It had seemed like a dangerous question, and Baltar might have answered.

Now they crept along at the posted thirty-five miles per hour. Micah tried not to scream or bang his head against the window. He wanted out of this car, away from Baltar. Ever since the old guy had shown up, Micah had spent most of his home time crashed in Dad's easy chair or lying in bed, deep in dreams about swirling mists and running water and a voice that whispered of power, of dominion, of righting all the wrongs that anyone had ever done. He didn't believe some guy could walk into his house and change his sleep patterns or what went on in his head, but stuck in the Lexus as it crept across town, sitting only inches from Baltar, Micah wanted out.

Quit it. He's just some guy, and he's old. What's he gonna do, take out his dentures and gum you to death?

Then Micah remembered that creepy grin and shivered.

"Before I came here," Baltar said, "I researched this town. You suffered much last year."

Suffered? Two dead teenagers, two dead cops, Micah's mom ripped apart, several serious injuries. *Suffered* didn't begin to cover it. Micah had no interest in discussing it with Baltar, though. "Yeah," he said, looking out the window.

"I know you don't know or trust me," Baltar said, modulating his tone so that he sounded soothing, not intimidating. Not that Micah would have ever admitted to feeling intimidated. "But I hope to change that. You will find, in time, that you can talk to me about anything. I will not judge. I will not tell your father. I will not share your thoughts with your social worker, or your friends, or your enemies. I came here for you, Micah. Only you."

When Baltar spoke softly like this—a low thrumming, like a cat's purr—Micah's eyelids grew heavy. The old man could probably talk him to sleep every night. Riding on the swells and ebbs of that voice, he would not dream.

Now, though, Micah shook his head, trying to clear the cobwebs, and sat up straighter. "Good to know," he said. He concentrated on the passing houses—the slow strobe of the streetlights, the yards that hadn't been raked. He counted cars parked on the street as opposed to under carports or in driveways.

"Is there anything you would like to share now?" Baltar asked.

Micah would not look at him. He had come to believe—irrationally, stupidly—that Baltar could hypnotize him with a glance, or, if he saw that smile, terrify him badly enough to piss his pants. "Nah," Micah said. "I'm good."

Baltar swerved and parked in front of a house, a small, boxy place with white paint and fading dark trim. A blue kiddie pool sat in the front yard on top of a ring of yellow grass. A mud-encrusted pickup on tires nearly as tall as Micah loomed in the drive. The curtains were drawn. Decorative blue shutters adorned them.

Look at the house. Think about the details. Don't fall asleep, no matter how tired you are.

"I know you and your friends found my trunk, and I know what you took from it," Baltar said.

Now Micah started and turned to him. Baltar gazed through the windshield at who knew what—taillights up ahead, maybe. His hands remained on the steering wheel, ten and two o'clock. His lips were pressed together.

"I don't know what you're talking about," Micah said, trying to sound assertive and harsh, afraid that he only came across as defensive.

"I think you do," Baltar said. "Most of my robes have vanished, and many of my old and priceless tomes now reside under your bed, along with three old socks, the baseball your father bought you years ago, and your journal."

"You went through my room?" Micah asked, now truly angry. "You read my damn *journal*?" Fury pulsed through him, reddening the edges of his vision. With the rage came energy, the kind that built and built until he expelled it through his hands in the form of fire or ice.

"Yes and no, respectively," Baltar said. "Every man should familiarize himself with his surroundings. But I would never violate your privacy. The sanctity of your thoughts. They are yours and yours alone. I'm not your father, Micah. I'm on your side."

Part of Micah wanted to protest. Dad could be an asshole, but he did the best he could. Yet when Micah tried to say that, he felt exhausted again, all those months of poor sleep weighing down his eyelids and limbs like physical bonds. Had Baltar really found the journal and refused to read it? How could Micah know, one way or another?

"Well," he said, turning back toward the house, forcing his eyelids open, "me and my friends borrowed some of your old stuff for a LARP— you know, live-action role play. That's it. No big secret."

Baltar *tsked*. "Oh, Micah. I do hope you'll trust me more than this, sooner or later."

"Whatever."

"Yes. Whatever. Your generation uses that word as a catch-all, don't you?"

"I guess."

Baltar sighed and put the Lexus in drive. "All right. I can see you aren't ready. But know this. A man like me can tell when his belongings have been used. Especially when they have invoked, confronted, and taken great power. I know you used *Bēstiae Barathrī*. I know you opened a portal. And I know what came through."

Shock radiated through Micah like electricity. His jaw clenched so tightly his teeth hurt. "I don't know what you're talking about," he said again.

"I can feel the power within you. I can feel it in your friends, even from a distance. And if I can, so can others. *Murderous* others. Beings that will make Na'ul of the Go'kan seem as dangerous as—well, say, as dangerous as a high-school bully. A lunkheaded, ignorant, barbaric, vicious, pathetic, miserable troll."

Micah swallowed hard. *Control yourself. Don't freak out.*

"What's a Na'ul of the Go'kan?" he asked.

"I should think you would remember the creature that tore your mother in half. The same creature you immolated."

That rage in Micah's chest intensified. He glared at Baltar. "Don't talk about my mom. Just freaking don't."

Baltar looked him in the eye for a moment and then pulled back onto the street. "All right. Just know that I know and that I understand."

No one spoke for a while. Micah's anger cooled into frustration and the same simmering hatred he had nursed since Na'ul murdered his mother. "Monsters. Supernatural shit. It got my mom killed. I freaking hate it."

"And what do you plan to do about them? These beings?"

"Hell if I know."

"What do you *wish* to do?"

Micah glared at the dashboard. The rage was already returning. "If any of 'em come around here, I'm gonna kill 'em. And nobody's gonna get in my way. Nobody."

Then a thought struck Micah, shining like a flashlight in a dark room. *The feds. If they're listening to this, they'll have evidence that me and the others are Freaks. Maybe even enough to come for us. Oh, hell. Oh, shit.* He closed his eyes and turned up his hearing, listening for the telltale whine of the Team's electronics.

"If you are worried about the government agents," Baltar said, "don't be. This car is clean. They will not even know that they can't see or hear us."

Micah's mouth fell open. "What the—how—?"

Baltar glanced at him with a hint of a smile. "They depend too much on technology. Their own and what they have stolen from their enemies. As powerful as technology can be, magic is stronger."

Micah started to say something, stopped, tried again. Nothing came out. He sat there for a while, taking all this in. Then he turned and looked through the back windshield. In the darkness and with all the tint, he could not be sure, but given the frame and distance of the headlights behind them, the next car back might have been an SUV.

"I think they're still back there," he said.

Baltar checked the rearview mirror. "Oh, most certainly. At this point, I have had no reason to make this car undetectable to human senses. But they cannot hear or see *inside* it."

Micah had no idea what to do with this new information. They had left the house only a few minutes ago, but a lot had happened since then. His head spun.

On Mississippi Street, Baltar stopped in front of the Davisons' driveway, where Mr. and Mrs. Davison's and Gabby's cars glistened in the moonlight. Jamie's bike lay on the lawn.

"Well," Micah said. "Thanks for the ride." He didn't know what else to say.

Baltar watched the rearview mirror. Micah looked back again. Sure enough, a black SUV melted into the shadows between streetlights.

"I can help you," Baltar said. His eyes possessed their own mild glow, like a softer version of the red Go'kan eyes you could see across a dark street. Later, Micah would realize that he had never actually told Baltar where Gabby lived.

Now Micah gripped the door handle. "I'll see you around ten thirty, unless you want me to walk back."

"All right," Baltar said. "When you change your mind, you only need to say so. You and your friends know very little about the road you walk, while I have traversed it for decades."

"Sure," Micah said. He opened the door and stepped out and, feeling antsy, watched Baltar drive away. Energy swirled through him, practically demanding to be released. He stood still for several moments, breathing deeply, clearing his mind, calming himself. When he felt in control again, he turned to the SUV, pondering his options. Then, despite the alarmed voice in his head warning him not to do it—a voice that sounded just like Jamie's—he headed for the Suburban.

Micah knocked on the passenger-side window. No one answered. He knocked again. This time, the Suburban's engine turned over and the window scrolled down, revealing Cornelius Vincent's face. The DEA agent had come to Quapaw City in the wake of the Na'ul affair. Micah had memorized his features—likely in his fifties, wrinkles on the forehead and around the eyes and mouth, gray sprinkled in his short brown hair and full beard. One night, Jamie had reported hearing a conversation in which Vincent explained to the Team where each of his six bullet wounds had come from. Micah had never seen these wounds himself—he had never seen any member of the team without what he assumed were their government-issue dark suits—but he had no doubt that the scars existed. They came from a brutal firefight with members of some New York–based Russian gang that had been moving enough heroin to supply the entire eastern seaboard. Agent Vincent was a legit tough guy, so Micah wasn't surprised when he showed absolutely no emotion now.

"Help you?" Vincent said. Jamie had decided the man came from Alabama, maybe Tennessee, but Micah didn't know or care.

"Ain't you sick of this?" Micah asked, leaning his elbows on the window and looking into Vincent's mirrored sunglasses. "I mean, it's gotta be boring, following a bunch of kids around a cruddy town like this."

"I'm not sure what you're talking about, son," Vincent said, expressionless. "I'm just waiting on a friend."

"Uh-huh. Well, I figure we'll knock off around ten thirty. Feel free to take a break and come back later."

Vincent's face still betrayed nothing. "Like I said, son. I'm waiting."

Micah pretended to look around. "Which house does your friend live in?"

"Maybe you ought to go inside before it gets dark. I hear awful things happen to kids in this town after dark."

Micah smiled and slapped the hood of the Suburban. "Okay. If you feel a cramp, maybe get out and stretch. I hear you ain't supposed to sit too long, especially if you're older'n hell."

He turned and walked back to Gabby's house. Mr. Davison answered the door, saying hello and directing Micah down the hallway to Gabby's room. Micah's jaw ached with tension. He forced himself to unclench his fists. Those feds. After all this time, they still wouldn't leave him alone. Would burning down the farmhouse or freezing all their stupid cars discourage them? If not, maybe—

Bec Villalobos sat on the tan carpet in front of Gabby's bed.

All thoughts of the federal agents vanished. Micah's mouth went dry. His legs felt rubbery. Bec wore a Super Mario tee, dark jeans, those boots. The black denim jacket had been tossed onto Gabby's purple bedspread. As Bec played on their phone, they glanced at him and raised their chin. Micah waved, feeling stupid, somehow exposed.

The folding table Gabby used for a desk held her laptop, a dozen or so Funko Pop figures from various video-game and movie franchises, and Gabby's phone and charger. The varnished wooden side table next to the bed held a glowing lamp, a handful of paperbacks with the spines turned toward the wall, and Gabby's school notebooks. Her TV, which her parents had mounted to the wall, blared the sounds of the game—*Wizards vs. Romans II*, which Jamie was playing with a tall glass of Coke braced between his legs.

Micah had seen all this a million times, but Bec's presence changed things. The purple bedspread seemed both deep and bright, like on that old Prince record Christian listened to all the time. The light seemed clearer, the off-white walls purer.

Quit it. You sound like a character in one of Mom's shitty romance novels.

That thought shocked him, and the illusion vanished. It was just Gabby's room, same as it ever was. Still, at least his rising anger had cooled.

"Hi," he said.

Everyone greeted him. "Sup?" Bec said, glancing at him again.

Micah sat a foot or so away from them and leaned against the bed. Christian hadn't arrived, but, so far, neither had Kenneth and Brayden. Maybe this night would turn out to be fun.

"Who's got next?" Micah asked.

✳✳✳

After Jamie's turn ended, he handed the controller to Bec and caught Micah's eye. "Any bats tonight?"

"Just one." Micah was concentrating on the game, or pretending to.

"Good," Jamie said. "I'll be right back."

He stood and walked down the hall and out the front door. On the porch, he leaned against the house and pretended to look something up on his phone while he increased his hearing, focusing it on the Suburban.

McCreedy: "Anything?" The quality of his voice suggested he was on speaker.

Vincent: "Boring as hell. They go to school, they go for pizza or sodas, they go home."

McCreedy: "So the situation remains the same."

Vincent: "Jesus, does it ever. The other night, I was so bored I spent ten minutes figuring out where the hell Allen's mother got a name like Fry. Turns out it's Frey—F-R-E-Y. Her actual first name's Glenn Frey. Glenn Frey Posey. No wonder she's a hippie. Her parents named their baby girl after one of the Eagles."

Parker: "You're shitting me. Who does that?"

Vincent: "Hippies, that's who." Both men laughed. "Hey, Doberman, you hear from the missus yet?"

Parker: "Yep. The oldest pup just got into Brandeis and UMass. She's got her heart set on Brandeis, but my wallet disagrees."

Vincent: "Y'all must be proud."

Parker: "I'm gonna have to add a wing to the house just to store my wife's swollen head."

McCreedy: "Gentlemen, this is riveting, but let's stay focused."

Vincent: "Yes, sir. The Allen girl and the Del Ray kid haven't shown."

McCreedy: "And the Sterne kid definitely made you."

Vincent: "Walked right up and knocked on the window. Told me I ought to take the night off."

Dammit, Micah, you idiot, Jamie thought. *Kid's got the brains of a jack-o'-lantern.*

Parker: "Well, we haven't exactly tried to be inconspicuous."

McCreedy: "No, I suppose it's not much of a surprise. But it does confirm that they're on alert."

Vincent: "I reckon. The brat's got a point, though. Nothing's happening."

McCreedy: "Their patience is astounding. What kind of teenagers *are* they?"

Vincent: "Careful ones."

McCreedy: "Manticore believes we should move on them regardless."

Vincent: "Manticore's definitely got a hard-on for these kids, but that doesn't mean he's wrong. If they won't give us cause, we may have to manufacture it."

Jamie tried to keep his body language casual, but inside, his nerves hummed. The Freaks would have to deal with the federal presence in Quapaw City. But how the hell could they do that without winding up dead or in jail? Not for the first time, he wished he and Gabby could just fly away.

McCreedy: "One more thing. I've had Shrike working on Baltar Sterne's background. The man is a ghost. If you spot his Lexus, report immediately. Do not engage him. Repeat, do *not* engage."

Vincent: "He dropped Micah off less than half an hour ago."

McCreedy: "What?"

Vincent: "Yeah. Nothing else to report. He didn't even get out of the car."

McCreedy: "All right. Report immediately if he comes back."

Vincent: "Copy. Doberman, tell the missus I said hello. Over and out."

Jamie lowered his hearing levels and stayed put for another couple of minutes, pretending to play with his phone. Then he walked back inside. The Davisons were watching some reality show about dancing. In Gabby's room, Bec Villalobos sat on their knees, plunking buttons while Micah and Gabby shouted advice. Jamie scooted behind them and sat on the bed. He stared at the screen without really seeing it, thinking of the Gilchrist farmhouse, the fleet of vehicles, the men in suits, and the weapons they had undoubtedly stashed in their headquarters.

The others would, as usual, expect him to make the plan.

And what about Great-Uncle Baltar? Jamie had been under the impression that the dude was dead. If that was his Lexus they had seen around town, why hadn't Micah said anything? What the hell was going on?

✷✹✷

When Kenneth's mother arrived to pick him up from work around nine thirty, he was leaning against the front wall of Larry's Grocery. He wore his work shirt—a khaki long-sleeve with "Larry's" written in curlicue script on the right breast. Mom stopped near him, and he climbed into her Kia Forte. She was listening to some kind of wimpy folk music shit.

"How was it?" Mom asked, U-turning in the empty lot.

"Okay," Kenneth said. What else was he supposed to say? *I rocked those shelves tonight. If it wasn't for me, those cans of sweet peas would still be in the box. And you should have seen the way I stacked bags into Mrs. Redd's minivan! Pro-level stuff, Ma. Your boy's going places.*

"You want to swing by your friend's house?" Mom asked.

Kenneth turned the heating vent so that it blew onto his face. "Nah. They'll quit around ten or ten thirty. You'd just have to come straight back."

She glanced at him, frowning. "I don't mind."

"I'm good. Really."

Mom gave him side-eye. "Ever since Gavin, you spend most of your time in your room. You need more friends than just Brayden."

He stifled a groan. "Says who?"

"Says me." They stopped at a red light. Mom turned to him and laid a hand on his forearm. "Your dad and me, we're worried about you. We'd feel a lot better if you got out more."

"God, Mom, I'm *tired.* I just wanna go home."

"You're young. You've got lots of energy. Like you said, you'll be there only an hour. You can text me when you're ready to leave."

"But I—"

She squeezed his arm. "Please. For me." Her eyes were full of hope.

"Fine," he said, sighing. "Whatever."

"I've got a fresh shirt for you in the back," she said as the light turned green.

Minutes later, on Mississippi Street, Kenneth spotted the black Suburban. No one had tailed him today. Apparently watching a teenager stock shelves scored a lower priority than staring at a house. Kenneth considered listening in but decided not to. The Freaks probably already knew about the SUV.

After Mom dropped him off and he knocked on the Davisons' door, Gabby's dad answered. He looked Kenneth over, his lips pressed tightly together. "Hello," said Mr. Davison.

"Hey," Kenneth said. "I'm here for game night."

"Ground rules: Gabby's door stays open. No touching."

"Yes, sir," Kenneth said. Like he wanted to touch any of them. *I don't even wanna be here*, he would have said, but that would lead to more conversation.

Mr. Davison stepped aside and gestured for Kenneth to enter. After offering to take Kenneth's windbreaker, he pointed down the hall. One door stood open, a wedge of light spilling into the dark hallway. Kenneth nodded, told Mr. Davison he'd keep his jacket, and headed toward Gabby's room. He stood in the doorway, taking in the place— what had changed since the last time he had been here, what hadn't. Gabby and that new girl, Bec, were playing some game and talking shit while Jamie and Micah cheered them on and discussed a movie they wanted to see. Micah seemed different tonight. He had moped around all year, a lot quieter than usual. Now he almost seemed like he was having fun.

Jamie spotted Kenneth. "Hey, man," he said.

Gabby glanced up and paused the game. Bec set down her controller. When Micah saw Kenneth, his grin disappeared. He didn't scowl or say anything nasty, but his face took on that blank expression it had worn since his mom died. As if Kenneth's very presence obliterated happiness. His old anger and contempt for Micah stirred and stretched as it awakened. *I haven't done or said shit to this kid. I've tried to work with him. And he looks at me like that? I should smack him upside his thick head.*

Then Kenneth took a deep breath and mentally counted to five. *If anybody starts shit, let it be Sterne. You promised everybody. You promised Mom.*

"Hey," Kenneth said. He even smiled a little.

Gabby nudged Bec and scooted over a couple of feet. Bec did the same. "Come on in," Gabby said. "Glad you could make it."

"Yeah, well," Kenneth said. He nodded at Bec. She nodded back.

"You can have next," Jamie said. "When Bec's done, use their controller."

Oh God, that they *shit,* Kenneth thought. *Folks like her gotta throw their weirdness in your face. She's got boobs; she's a damn girl.*

Bec patted the carpet. "Have a seat. I don't bite."

Kenneth sat. Micah looked away, still silent. Tension filled the room. *Oh, yeah, Mom. This was a* great *idea.*

Gabby and Bec took up their controllers again. On screen, their wizards blasted away at Roman foot soldiers. Gradually the conversations resumed, and some of that bad energy faded. Still, Kenneth could feel Micah's gaze boring into the back of his head.

After a few minutes, Jamie said, "Anybody heard from Christian?"

"Nope," Kenneth said.

"Huh. She ain't answering my texts."

Gabby threw a spell that melted a rock wall and revealed a treasure room. Bec ran inside and found a bunch of equipment and power-ups. "You think we need to go hunt for her?" Gabby asked.

"Maybe, if she don't show up soon."

"She's probably out with Juana," Micah said. He seemed to glance at Bec. "They've gotten awful close. Maybe even close-close."

"I think we'd know if she was macking on somebody," Jamie said.

Bec, still playing like a pro, said, "You must be tight. None of my old friends would have looked for me if somebody had dropped ten gallons of my blood on their heads."

"Well," said Jamie, "sometimes Quapaw City can be dangerous. And it ain't like her to miss game night without hollering at somebody."

Bec laughed. "Of all the words to describe this town, I wouldn't have picked 'dangerous.' But y'all know it a lot better than me. I can help you look for her."

Jamie cleared his throat. "That's okay. I mean, you wouldn't really know where to go."

"I can pair up with one of you," she said.

"Okay."

Kenneth pretended to stretch his back and caught Jamie's eye. Entmann looked concerned. How could they talk about what really scared them with an outsider hanging around?

CHAPTER TEN

According to the note left on the counter for Christian, her mom, a nurse at the county hospital in New Everton, had gotten called in to work. Mom had apologized for not being able to drive her to Gabby's. Well, no big deal. Christian would just bike over and leave early enough to make curfew, in case Mom called the landline.

Bike, she thought, frowning. *It's like walking with both feet chained together. God, I wish I could just run.*

With over an hour to kill, Christian lay on her bed and fell asleep in two minutes. It had been a long week. When she woke, the light was too dim. She looked at her phone—5:24 p.m. Shit, she had overslept. Game night had already started.

Her yard-sale bike with its rusting frame and its back tire that simply would not hold air for more than a week lay where she had left it in the yard. She still missed the awesome bike she'd had until the first night they opened the portal. She'd wrecked it as she discovered her speed power and had left it lying in the road, too dazed to think about it. When she went to look for it later, someone had taken it. She picked up the pathetic replacement and got on, ready to ride away.

Near the driveway's mouth, a rabbit sat on all fours, watching her.

"Hey, little guy," Christian said. The rabbit was super cute: brown, long-eared, and tiny, maybe six inches long. She easily could have missed it in the dark. "Somebody might run over you if you hang out near the road."

The rabbit just sat there. Its body expanded and contracted with each quick breath.

Christian walked the bike to the street, passing only a few feet from the critter, which turned and watched her go.

Okay, then. Weird.

She started pedaling. Two houses down, another rabbit nibbled something in the yard. This bunny seemed to be watching her, too. Christian laughed and waved. Maybe some neighbor had scattered a bunch of baby carrots or something.

Three more houses down and on the other side of the street, a larger, fatter rabbit waited on its hind legs, forelegs dangling. As she passed, its head swiveled with her progress.

What the actual hell?

She rode across town, spotting more rabbits in darkened yards or in parked cars' shadows, though two or three stood in the road. Dread crept up her spine like encroaching frost. She had never seen so many rabbits, especially spread out like this.

I ain't scared. They're only little bitty rabbits, and I can outrun anything on earth. But good God. I guess anything stops being cute when it's stalking you.

One last bunny stood on the corner of Mississippi Street and Beech Road. Just hanging out on the sidewalk, observing a teenage girl on a bike.

Jamie stood in Gabby's yard, arms dangling at his sides. Was he waiting for her? Seemed like a silly thing to do when you could just stay in the warm house and check your phone. Had everything in Quapaw City gone nuts?

She rode into the yard, slowed, stopped. Jamie watched her in silence. She leaned her bike against the oak tree. "What are you doing out here?" she asked.

"I was waiting for you," he said.

Huh. Something about his voice—he sounds, what, formal? Like he's giving a speech. "What's up? You sound weird."

Another pause. "I do not know what you mean. But I would like you to come with me. To the park. For a special ... meeting."

She cocked her head. "Oh, you 'do not know'? You 'would like me to come with you'? Seriously, man. You sound like you've got a stick up your ass."

Another two-second pause. "No need to be frightened. We just have … things … to discuss."

Frightened? Had she ever heard him use that word? "Did you get hit in the head?"

"No."

"No? Just no?"

"Yes."

Christian glanced at the Suburban parked up the street. Maybe Jamie thought the Team was listening. How else to explain … whatever this was?

"Where's Gabby? And Micah?"

Pause. "They are waiting for us in the park. We should leave now."

She turned to the house. Lights glowed in the living room windows. Shadows moved behind Gabby's curtains.

"Who's in Gabby's room?"

Pause. "Everything will be explained in the park."

"Maybe we should go in and ask Mr. and Mrs. Davison about it."

Pause. "That would not be a good idea. We should go now."

Christian turned toward the house. She took one tentative step toward it. Jamie didn't move. Then she looked back at the SUV. "Is it a bat? Is that what's bothering you?"

Pause. "No. Not a bat."

Christian hesitated. Something in her gut screamed *Danger! Wrong! Bad!* But hadn't they all been just a tad paranoid ever since they realized the Team was following them? Every stranger had become a potential federal agent, every car they didn't recognize, government issue. Maybe she was feeling some of that now. This was Jamie, after all. One of her best and oldest friends. A fellow Freak. Their leader.

Danger, hissed her gut. *Peril.*

Shut up. Besides, I'm supposed to be the fearless one around here. No way I'm gonna freak out just because Jamie's got something on his mind.

Christian patted her bike's seat. "Let's ride double. We going to the pavilion?"

Jamie walked over and studied the bike for a few moments, as if he had never seen one before. Then he slid onto the seat. "Yes," he said. "The pavilion."

She straddled the bike, one foot on a pedal, getting her balance. Jamie's arms slid around her waist. He felt warm and somehow soft, like he was wearing a down bodysuit. Had he always felt that way? Surely she would have noticed.

But it was Jamie, so she wobbled out of the yard and down the street, heading for the park. Her control of the bike improved as she got used to the extra weight. When she reached the nearest intersection, headlights painted the road. An engine turned over and purred into life. The Team's representative had decided to follow them. Maybe that meant the other Freaks really had gone to the pavilion.

Of course that's what it means. Why would Jamie lie?

They dodged cars and the occasional pedestrian until they reached the park. It closed at sunset, but that hadn't stopped the Freaks before, so Christian bumped over the curb and onto the sidewalk. Jamie kept silent. The headlamps that had followed them now cut out, leaving them with only moonlight. Somebody would have to stand guard, make sure the Team couldn't hear whatever they discussed.

Soon, they reached the pavilion. The first few feet of it were visible in the moonlight. The rest stretched back into the dark, just a shape among shapes. The old slide and creaky swing set and rusting monkey bars stood against the night sky like bones jutting out of the earth. The pond looked like a sinkhole, despite the moonlight sparkling on its waters.

Christian stopped on the walk and let Jamie off. Then she rode the bike across the grounds, crunching over pine straw and leaves and twigs. When she reached the pavilion, she leaned the bike against one of the pillars and increased her hearing. The familiar low hum told her that the Team's surveillance devices were still active. They would have to talk near the water. But where were the others?

Jamie stood in the middle of the clearing, arms at his sides, watching her.

"Okay, bro," she said, approaching him. "You've been acting goofy as hell, and you said Gabby and Micah would be here. What's *really* up? Are you worried about the bat?"

For several moments, Jamie said nothing. Unease crept up Christian's spine again. Then he turned, slowly, until he faced the pond. "From here, it is possible to see the place where you fought and destroyed Prince Na'ul."

Christian squinted. Yes, you could see a piece of that beach. "I reckon so," she said. "What's your point? What are we *doing* here?"

Another pause. "I watched it, you know."

"Well, yeah, because *you were there.*"

Now Jamie turned back to her. When he smiled, the corners of his mouth stretched back and back, nearly to his ears. His upper front teeth jutted from it. His eyes had grown farther apart.

Cold fear clutched Christian's guts, her heart.

"Indeed I was," Jamie said. His voice had deepened. "And it was on that night that I knew you must be destroyed."

Christian started to back away, but then she made herself stop. *No. Don't back down.*

She moved forward and grabbed Jamie by the shirt. She had planned to yank him toward her, to ask him what the hell he was talking about, but when she pulled, his whole upper torso shifted. As if the cloth had stuck to his skin. As if it *was* his skin.

Christian stumbled backward. "Who are you?"

Jamie's body *rippled*, like water where someone dropped a rock. He grew taller, thicker. The smooth lines of his body blurred and shifted and separated. As he rose into the moonlight, it seemed like he had grown fur.

Run, Christian thought. *What the hell are you waiting for?* But her feet wouldn't move, like she was stuck to the spot. Despite herself, she screamed.

People burst forth from the trees. Christian looked around wildly. The newcomers held objects of various shapes, most pointed at the Jamie-thing, a couple aimed at her.

"Freeze, both of you!" someone shouted. It sounded like Chip Mossman.

"Get outta here," Christian cried. "You don't know what you're stepping into!"

"Make a move, and you'll be stepping into a coffin," said another voice. Kragthorpe?

"Jamie Entmann," called a third voice. Parker, if Christian wasn't mistaken. "Don't take another step, son."

"You don't get it," Christian said. *"That ain't Jamie Entmann."*

The men stopped where they were. "Manticore," one of them said. Greenwalt, she believed. "What the hell's she talking about?"

The Jamie-thing threw its arms back and roared. More of that rippling effect, and now something like long, pointed ears jutted from its head. Thick muscles bubbled and bunched all over its body.

"Good God," Kragthorpe said.

"Kill it," Mossman barked, fitting the gun he carried against his shoulder. A bright pink beam of light sizzled through the air and struck the Jamie-thing, which staggered backward and roared again. The beam's glow revealed the monster's long, sharp teeth, chocolate-brown fur, thick claws that looked as if they could tear steel. The monster dropped forward onto on all fours and tensed, as if about to leap.

Christian's paralysis finally broke, and she backed away. When she reached the pavilion, she stepped onto the slab and picked her way through the picnic tables. The four men in the clearing fired their weapons—more of that pink light, something that sizzled and zigzagged like lightning, a thick and foul-smelling ball of gloop that glowed green and blurped past the creature and sizzled into the pond. The fourth rifle fired pure sound, a high-pitched screeching that set Christian's teeth on edge and made her shudder hard enough to hurt.

Run like hell, or stay and help them? Make a decision, but don't just freaking stand here.

Before she could move again, the Jamie-thing jumped straight up. Four discharges converged on the spot where it had been and collided, the resulting explosion blasting dirt and shrapnel everywhere. When not-Jamie landed, it ran straight at the man Christian believed to be Greenwalt, the one who had fired the sound weapon, and grabbed him.

Then it yanked his pants and underwear down around his ankles.

Greenwalt lost his balance, cried out, and fell on his face.

The Jamie-thing disappeared into the woods.

"Prince!" Mossman cried, running to Greenwalt.

That's my cue, Christian thought, and sure enough, her legs finally worked. She trotted fifteen or twenty yards into the dark woods. One of the feds was trying to follow not-Jamie some distance away. Christian upgraded her vision, planning to track him, but when he passed by a forked tree, it *shimmered*. The fed kept on moving, apparently having noticed nothing. Had she imagined it? Had her enhanced vision gone wonky? Before she could ponder it much, the forked tree shimmered again, faster this time. The forks became human arms; the trunk turned into legs.

A tall bald man in dark clothing now stood there, watching the Team flounder around the woods. After a moment, this man turned and looked straight at Christian. He winked. Then he bent to the forest floor and shimmered into near invisibility again.

Who the hell is that guy? Was that the Jamie-thing? If it was, how come he ain't attacking?

Too damn much had happened tonight. Christian needed to talk to her friends. And if all this didn't qualify as a good reason to use her super-speed in public and outside of her spy route, she didn't know what would. Looking around to make sure the Team couldn't see her, she took a deep breath, tensed, and sped off.

The landscape flew by, first the thick woods and then the park proper and then the streets, all in seconds. As she ran on paths she had been denied for so long, faster and more urgent and more spontaneous than her route to the farmhouse, that long-suppressed feeling of elation rose inside her, from her toes to the top of her head, the sheer ecstasy of moving wherever her own will took her. Every molecule of her body felt charged with electricity. Her mind worked faster than her legs. Not for the first time, she wondered whether this was what it felt like to get high. She ran faster, lapping the town once, twice, her muscles stretching, strengthening. God, she had missed this.

After a third lap, she forced herself toward Mississippi Street. The Team cars were gone, so she zipped into Gabby's front yard, opening and closing the door and zooming down the hall in a fraction of a second, stripping off her costume on the way and stuffing it behind the towels in the restroom.

"You feel a breeze?" Mr. Davison asked from the living room.

"Yeah," Mrs. Davison said. "Did you leave a window open?"

Christian ducked into Gabby's room. "Y'all, we got big problems. Jamie—"

Jamie sat on the floor, controller in hand. Beside him, Bec Villalobos leaned against the bed. Gabby and Micah sat on the mattress, looking at Christian. Kenneth had taken Gabby's desk chair.

"Jamie what?" asked Jamie.

"Nothing," she said. Her cheeks burned. "Y'all been here all night?"

"Yep," Jamie said, raising his eyebrows.

"I feel like I missed something," Bec said.

"Me too," Gabby muttered.

It wouldn't have been safe to talk in the house even if Bec hadn't been there. "Never mind," Christian said. "So everybody's been here."

"Not Juana de Leon," Micah said. "What, is she too good for us?"

Gabby shot Micah a dirty look, but she seemed to be trying to figure out Christian's punch line. "Well, Micah was a little late, and Kenneth had to come after he got off work. But once they got here, nobody's left the room unless they had to pee."

Christian stared at Gabby. Then she sat against the wall and ran a hand through her hair. "Okay."

Gabby came over and sat beside her, leaning her head on Christian's shoulder. "We should talk about this tomorrow, right?" Gabby whispered. "Maybe in the park."

Christian shuddered. "No. Not in the park." Then she slapped a hand to her forehead. "Dammit, I just realized. I left my bike. With my luck, the T—somebody will steal it."

Micah and Gabby looked at each other and burst into laughter. Kenneth grinned and shook his head.

CHAPTER ELEVEN

No one asked about what had happened to Christian, and not just because of the surveillance devices planted in the house. Bec Villalobos had slipped into their group dynamic easily, had sat beside Micah for much of the night, the two of them laughing and teasing each other over the games—and God, had it been good to see Micah back to normal for a little while—but Bec's eyes had practically sparkled when Christian walked in. No one had stayed for long after that, though. Jamie's dad had picked him up, and Christian caught a ride with them. Bec had left just before Micah, who sat with Gabby until his phone buzzed and he said goodbye. She had looked out the window, knowing Micah's dad had gone back on the road. Who was driving him home? Was he staying with a friend or relative she didn't know about?

He had crossed the street, where a black car idled.

Is that the same Lexus that followed me and Jamie to school Tuesday?

Now she sat on her bed, pretending to read an old western paperback she had found in the bathroom magazine rack. The good thing about old-school books? No fed could hack the feed. Not that she was actually reading. She just turned the page every now and then. Instead, she had turned up her hearing, wondering who might be monitoring the house. She filtered out the various noises that didn't interest her and, sure enough, recognized the voices of Mossman and Greenwalt.

"You think Engineer will greenlight us?" Greenwalt was saying.

"He damn well ought to," Mossman said. He sounded impatient and tired. "The Allen girl just disappeared."

"She's not even my main concern. What the devil happened to Entmann?"

"No idea. But if whatever changed these kids has turned him into some kind of monster, we need to put him down, sooner rather than later."

"The girl said it wasn't even him."

"And we're supposed to let one mutated terrorist vouch for another?"

"If they *are* terrorists. In any case, I'd like a chat with that thing from the park. And by 'chat,' I mean I want to kill it."

Some kind of loud crunching. Gabby winced. One of them was probably eating Life Savers, that sound a regular hazard of the Freaks' counterintelligence operations.

"Well," Mossman said, "maybe it's time for an extraordinary rendition."

Nothing for some time. Then Greenwalt said, "We're still talking about a kid. An American citizen."

"That line's getting old. Timothy McVeigh was an American citizen. So were Stephen Paddock and Dylan Roof and a hundred others."

"We've got no evidence these kids have been radicalized."

Mossman snorted. "Well, they aren't sweet, fresh-faced kids, either. They're threats to national security. And when Engineer finally pulls the trigger, we're going to put them down. Hard."

Gabby had heard enough. She returned her hearing to normal levels and got ready for bed. She turned off her lights and crawled under the covers. The feds had seen something in the park. So had Christian, and it had scared her. She had always been the toughest Freak. Whatever it was would probably make Gabby piss her britches.

Stop trying to buy trouble. You don't even know what happened yet. And you don't have to freak out every time some problem pops up.

Tough talk, but Gabby didn't fall asleep for a long time.

✷✸✷

Christian didn't even wait for her mom to crash for the night before she locked herself in her room and scanned the street. Every car and

truck out there belonged to a neighbor. For whatever reason, no one
from the Team was watching her tonight. *Probably out at the farmhouse,
freaking out. I don't really blame 'em, but in the park, they were after me.
Can't let that go.* She slipped on her costume and mask, zipped out the
window, and sped out to Grisham's Loop. Once she was sitting against
her favorite tree, she focused her vision and hearing on the house. The
Team's voices sounded excited, almost giddy ... or maybe just scared.

Mossman, a bit tinny, like he was on speaker: "They were arguing.
Then Entmann ... changed."

McCreedy: "And the nature of this change?"

Mossman: "He grew. Expanded. Like this average, skinny kid was
turning into a giant werewolf."

McCreedy: "You saw lupine features."

Mossman: "No, sir. I'm just using the werewolf metaphor to describe
the change. I'm not sure what he was turning into."

McCreedy: "And no one else got a clear view."

A chorus of voices replied with some version of *No, sir.*

Christian sighed. She wasn't sure what she had seen, either. *I told
you it wasn't Jamie, you dicks. And I don't think it was a werewolf. I mean, it
looked like Jamie, and it sounded like him, too, except formal. Stiff. Like he
knew what he wanted to say but had to think hard about the words.*

McCreedy: "Prince?"

Also sounding like he was phoning in, Greenwalt: "Nothing in all
our months here suggests why Entmann might lure one of his friends
to a remote location and attack her. We should consider the possibility
that we've got a shape-shifter."

Kragthorpe: "I don't know, guys. After I worked that one shifter case
a few years back, I studied the files. All known shifters can change only
into people or objects close to their own size. That's how Parker and I
spotted the one in Calexico. It tried to pass as this guy a foot shorter
than it was. This thing in the park, though—it *grew.*"

Christian suppressed a giggle. Kragthorpe sounded like the turtle in *Finding Nemo*—so California Surfer that every sentence might as well be punctuated with "brah" or "awesome."

Parker: "I agree with Shrike. If Entmann's a shifter, he's a new breed." *Shiftah*, in Parker's Boston accent.

Greenwalt: "Or, like the girl said, it wasn't Entmann at all. Could have been something that took Entmann's shape and lured her there."

That's right, y'all. Not unless Jamie went insane, got a new power, and figured out how to be in two places at once. I don't know what that thing was, but it was smart, and powerful enough to tear me apart. I could feel it.

Now that she had slowed down long enough to think, the anger she might have felt toward not-Jamie started to catch up. *You came for me, but you missed.* She picked up a stick and began to strip off its bark, to flick each bit in the direction of the farmhouse. *You shouldn't have done that. It doesn't matter what your real name is or where you land on the Team's stupid "class" scale. I'm gonna kick your ass and send you to hell, just like Na'ul. You're deader than shit. You just don't know it yet.*

Greenwalt interrupted her murderous thoughts. "There's at least one more possibility we should consider. Maybe it's a chimera."

McCreedy grunted. "Nobody's seen one of those for at least a generation."

Greenwalt: "We hadn't seen any mutated humans, either. Not ever. But here we are."

Parker: "God, Prince, I'm so glad you called in. You're so good at cheering us up."

Some laughter. Then McCreedy: "A chimera could do a hell of a lot more damage than any Go'kan. Probably more than the kids."

Mossman, an edge in his voice: "Jesus, how many times do I have to say it? I don't think we can afford to take our eyes off those brats."

McCreedy. "We may be forced to back-burner them. Shrike says a full-force direct hit from the plasma rifle only staggered this bogey. That kind of power may require our full attention. Still, I take your point about the Allen girl. Unless we find the bogey fast, I think we'll need to arrange a chat with her soon."

Mossman, now sounding much happier: "Affirmative, sir."

The meeting began to break up. Christian turned down her hearing and stood, stretching her back. A low ache had settled in just above her hips. Maybe she and Jamie should bring a lawn chair out here, or a stadium cushion, if it turned out that they couldn't use the barn. Anything to keep the damp out of her pants and the roots and branches from poking her spine.

She stood there a while, thinking. The Team believed this new monster was a bigger threat than Na'ul. It had probably come in through the same portal at the same time, which meant they were responsible for whatever damage it did.

On the other hand, hunting it would bring them into direct conflict with the Team again. Who knew what would happen then?

Her phone buzzed. She pulled it out of her pocket. A text from Juana:

wanna hang 2morrow

Christian had already begun to forget what it felt like to be a normal teenager with nothing better to do than chill with friends. She wrote back:

cant got plans maybe next week

Juana:

ok

Christian:

sorry

Juana:

k

Great. Was Juana pissed now?

As she zoomed out of the forest, Christian realized she was starving. Maybe she would stop by the Korner Mart and swipe some junk food.

✳

Jamie lay on his bed, listening to music and thinking about that weird thing with Christian. He wished they could have talked about it, but with the feds listening and Bec in the room, it had been impossible. The first game night in forever had felt okay at best—Christian missing, Micah clearly into this new person who kinda sorta seemed okay with it, Kenneth only there for a little while because of his job.

They needed to talk, to make some decisions. Jamie hit up the group text:

yo looks like another mumpsimus Monday

Soon, everyone replied with their emoji of choice, which just meant "message received and understood."

Months ago, when they first realized that the feds were probably monitoring their phones and social media, they had agreed on *mumpsimus*, a word Jamie had seen in an internet article, as their code for "everybody drop what you're doing and meet at the pavilion right now." If the person sending the message worked in some other geographical or time-related element, the others would ignore "right now." In this case, they'd know that Jamie wanted to meet on Monday, and since he had said nothing about another location, they would default to the pavilion.

Hopefully, nothing would come for them in the meantime. Man, he *hated* making these decisions. Was this even a good way to proceed? Maybe the feds had already cracked their code. Maybe Jamie was leading everybody into a trap.

He plugged his phone into the charger and closed his eyes. He felt much more tired than he should have. Maybe mental stress took more energy than physical work.

Gradually, he relaxed, and sleep stole over him. He drifted down and down, dreaming of an open field hundreds of miles long and filled with long-eared rabbits whose gazes followed him wherever he went.

CHAPTER TWELVE

I soared over the village, my wings stretching out and out. When the cluster of lodges below gave way to thick woods, I set down and assumed my true form and scampered through the forest, my kin emerging from their hideaways and running beside me. At my warren, I squeezed through the entrance, slid down, and landed on my feet in one of the many tunnels I had dug. The forest dwellers rained down and milled about my feet, joining the others who had already forsaken their own warrens. They lay on each other, crawled over their fellows' bodies, ate and defecated where they would. I moved among them, nudging them aside, until I curled up in my favorite spot, the dirt pressed smooth and indented in the shape of my body. The little ones gathered about, some climbing on top of me, others nestling against my coat. They needed whatever feeling of safety and connection I gave.

I had made my first move, separating one of the children by taking the form of her chief. I should have practiced her language, having not spoken it for two centuries, for as we talked, she became more and more suspicious. But she came with me anyway—not to the place where she helped destroy Na'ul, but close. Inside the girl-child, newer, urgent forces boiled like a hot spring, waiting for the moment she would unleash them.

When I had begun to assume my true shape, those forces had surged. My heart sang. The deepest parts of me cried for battle, for a trick well played and a foe well met, and though I faced a child, I felt in my bones that she would prove worthy of such a song.

Then those men came out of the trees, wielding their stolen weapons. I knew those armaments, for I had seen their like on my travels.

The same guns that have been used to lay low villages, nations, worlds. When the pain from the plasma rifle ripped through me, my mind emptied, leaving only the naked desire to survive. I nearly rent the flesh from my attackers, crushing their bones to powder, scattering that dust on the wind. If those men understood the nature of the one they attacked, they would have fallen to their knees and thanked their gods for my strength, which blew away pain's fog and healed me faster than any mortal weapon could hurt me.

I knew the men, too. Not these individuals, but their kind. In the shriveled, rotting fruit they call their hearts, they believe that weapons equal strength, that strength imparts its own right to conquer and rule, that conquering imbues virtue. Beings like them have ever climbed over the torn bodies of the weaker and stood tall on hills made of death. Take away their guns, and they fly apart on the mildest breeze, for they are as hollow as dried gourds. When I walked this land, they came in their thousands and millions, wielding firearms and poison and false promises written on paper that the smallest flame could consume. Their power lay in their totems and their willingness to deceive, not their bodies or minds or spirits. Their promises came bound in the illusion of honor they did not possess and never would. No, these little men were nothing without their toys and their lies. I could have torn them all off the body of the earth. And every other human would have been better off.

But.

These sad, frightened men had come to that clearing to stand against the girl-child. She of the tiny tribe that might one day grind the earth to dust or burn it to ash. She whom I had tricked; she whom I had come to destroy.

Who poses the greatest threat to my people's world: the unwittingly strong, or the desperately weak?

That is why I fled—because I wanted to ponder these matters.

The men did not detect the other presence in those woods, but I did.

As I ran past the girl and the invaders, amid the trees and under the darkened canopy, something fetid and furious lurked. Like a hole in the air that swallowed light and hope. As I scampered, my mind reached for this presence, touched its very edges, recoiled. As if the darkness *burned*, hateful and hungry.

And now, lying snug in my warren, my brethren and sistren nestled against me, their exhalations rhythmic and soothing, I chose my course.

Many forces worked their wills around this village. To know the greatest threat, to stop it, I needed to draw them out. Set them against each other. Whoever survived would face me, and I would send them broken to their gods.

CHAPTER THIRTEEN

After school on Monday, as one of those government SUVs crept along behind him, Micah biked home. At lunch, the Freaks had eaten at their usual picnic table toward the ass end of campus. They had talked about the same old crap—who had gotten how far on which video game, comic-book storylines, upcoming movies they wanted to see. Then everyone had gone back to class. All in all, the day had been duller than dog shit. Now, though, Micah wondered who else had won the Federal Agent Stalker lottery today. If Christian drew a short straw, she could evade the Team easily enough, unless they had developed tech that let them see her while she ran. Jamie could probably ditch them, too, assuming he could gain enough altitude while they were looking somewhere else. Not that either of them would do that, since King Jamie had proclaimed they couldn't use their powers in public. Gabby and Kenneth would struggle to get away, just like Micah, but really, what difference did it make? The Team knew about the pavilion. Sometimes it felt like the group might as well meet on the hood of one of those stupid Suburbans and carve their plans in the paint.

Micah turned onto MacArthur Road. When he reached his house, he left his bike in the yard and walked inside. Ever since Dad had gone back on the road, Micah had ducked and covered any time he heard Baltar coming his way. Other than mealtimes, during which Baltar prepared a surprisingly various and tasty set of meals, the old guy had pretty much left Micah alone. But who knew how long that would last?

Micah peeked out through the living room windows. The street was clear. *Huh. Not that I'm complaining, but it's not like them to follow you home and then just leave.*

Baltar's Lexus was parked in the driveway, but nothing stirred inside the house. Maybe he had fallen asleep. Micah had heard that old people took a lot of naps.

He still hadn't told the others about his great-uncle. What was he supposed to say? *To keep me outta foster care, Dad called the crazy old man who left all that shit in our storage building. The same allegedly dangerous old man I was never even allowed to ask about. Dude makes some mean mac and cheese.*

Still, he would have to tell them *something*, sooner or later. If anyone came over, he couldn't exactly stuff Baltar in a closet.

Micah grabbed a can of Dr Pepper and drank half of it in one long gulp. Then he stuffed an apple in his jacket pocket and walked back outside. As he rode to the park, a strong wind blew out of the northeast. The sky was flawless, a blue so bright and deep it hurt his eyes. Every fourth or fifth house had decorated for Thanksgiving—some decent scarecrows, paper turkeys hanging from porches and low tree limbs, inflatable pilgrims and Native Americans. Seeing these last, Micah cringed. He had never been the most politically sensitive person, but even he knew that some folks would never learn to live in the twenty-first century.

Soon enough, he reached the pavilion. Gabby sat in a swing while Jamie and Kenneth leaned against the frame, which was still lopsided after Micah bent it last year. More proof that nobody really came to this place anymore, not even maintenance workers.

Micah joined the others, standing five or six feet away from the structure with his hands in his jacket pockets. Down at the water's edge, half a dozen ducks floated in the shallows. Occasionally, one would dip its head under and pop back up, working its throat. Micah wondered what they were eating. The wind still blew, kicking up pine straw and leaves. Gabby shivered, but Micah no longer noticed the cold. He wore the jacket only for show.

"Everything cool?" he asked, figuring at least one of them had already scanned to see if the bugs and cameras were active.

Jamie shook his head and cleared his throat. "Seen Christian?"

"No," Micah said. "Not since study hall."

"She said she'd be heading straight over. She should have got here first."

Gabby and Kenneth looked grim, but they said nothing.

Jamie gestured toward the water and led Micah down to the edge. They stood on damp ground, listening to the ducks quack. "What's up?" Micah asked.

"I'm worried, bro," Jamie said, keeping his voice low. "Christian got targeted on Friday night. And she's a no-show today?"

"Maybe she's just late," Micah whispered. "I mean, you told us not to use our powers if we could help it, so it's not like she'd run over here without a good reason. And she lives farther away than the rest of us."

Jamie turned to the pond. Something broke the water fifty yards out—a turtle? A fish? Micah hadn't really looked at the pond since last year and had never thought about it much before Na'ul. It had always been there, like the land itself, just background. Last year had changed it into the place where he had helped kill an interdimensional vampire. Of the Freaks, only Kenneth had any idea how deep the water might be, because Na'ul had knocked him clean into the middle of the pond.

"I don't think so," Jamie said. "She's not answering her texts or DMs. And speaking of. How come you didn't tell us your uncle's in town? Or, you know, alive?"

Micah's face burned. So they knew. Had they spied on him or what? Anger churned his stomach like acid. "I was gonna," he said. "I was just waiting for a good time to bring it up." Gabby said nothing, but she was looking at him with her disappointed-mother expression. The acid churned faster. Micah's mother was dead. He wasn't looking for another one. "What?" he barked at Gabby, who flinched.

"Chill," Jamie said. His voice sounded forceful and authoritative. Like a boss. "You should have told us, man."

Micah had always hated bosses. "I'm telling you now. Get off my ass."

"You need to take the face outta your voice," Jamie said coldly. His eyes had turned to steel.

"You want me to knock a couple of his teeth out?" Kenneth called. He sounded a little giddy at the prospect.

"Try it, motherf—" Micah began.

"Stop it, all of you!" Gabby cried. Then, her voice lowered, she said, "We need to find Christian. We can get into all this other shit later."

Micah opened his mouth to argue. Then he closed it again. He walked closer to the water and leaned against a pine tree, thinking. Jamie joined him. Micah glanced at Gabby and Kenneth as they talked near the pavilion, probably about nothing, just words to keep the feds happy.

"Dude," Micah said. "The bats followed me home. But when I came back outside, they were gone."

Jamie's eyebrows rose. With one hand, he rubbed the back of his neck, grimacing as if he'd slept badly. "Think they took her?"

Micah's stomach sank. The idea had occurred to him, but Jamie's saying it out loud made it seem real. "Maybe. What the hell do we do?"

Jamie put both hands on top of his head and paced along the water line, staring at the ground, his mouth working as if he were talking to himself. Gabby watched him, her forehead wrinkled. Kenneth's face remained neutral. Of course it did. That moron probably didn't even understand what was wrong.

Finally, Jamie paused, fists clenched. "We go get her," he said.

"How do we do that and keep them from knowing it's us?"

"If they've taken Christian, what's the point? We go in costume, but that's just for the town's benefit. If the Team's crossed the line, we're gonna make 'em wish they hadn't."

Micah smiled. "That's what I'm talking about."

Jamie led him back to the others.

"What's up?" Kenneth asked.

"Let's go get your car," Jamie said to Gabby. "I'll fill y'all in on the way."

They got on their bikes and headed out, Jamie leading, Micah bringing up the rear. He stared at the back of Kenneth's head. *Shit's really going down,* he thought. *Maybe Kenneth will get caught in a crossfire. Couldn't happen to a nicer guy.*

CHAPTER FOURTEEN

In bed, covers pulled up to her chin, Christian watched shadows dance on the wall. Cast by the moon and the streetlights, they took the shapes of bare tree limbs and the window's muntins, horizontal lines bisecting jagged, creepy slashes. A deep sense of dread crawled in her guts and rose, inch by inch, into her chest and throat. She tried to turn her head, to close her eyes, but her body refused to obey. The shadows shifted and seemed to vibrate, tossed back and forth as if by a strong wind.

When her muscles unlocked, Christian raised her head and looked toward the foot of her bed. At first, nothing. Then two more or less triangular shapes rose like they were emerging from the footboard. They grew taller and wider. Were they ears? *Rabbit* ears? Soon a head arose, as big as a beach ball, with deep brown eyes that shone with their own light. Black human hair swept back from the forehead and down this being's back. The creature's nose twitched. Framed by long individual whiskers that hung past the neck, its human mouth opened, revealing sharp incisors and buck front teeth. This shape continued to rise, its human torso covered in thick brown fur, human hands with fingers ending in thick, sharp claws good for digging or rending flesh.

This apparition leaped onto the bed; its feet, which landed on either side of Christian's legs, were longer than her torso. Its legs were human down to the knee; after that, they bent backward at the joint. The creature's muscles rippled. The bed groaned under its weight.

For what do you give thanks? it asked. *Do you ever think of the blood you tread through every day of your life?*

What are you? Christian tried to say. *And what are you talking about?* But her mouth had frozen.

I will find you again, it said. *We will find each other.*

Its mouth opened wide. It bent over her, those teeth coming closer, closer.

She screamed.

And awoke, thrashing. As in the dream, she could barely move. Something tight and solid fixed her arms at her sides, forced her legs together from upper thigh to ankle. Everything felt cold. Something covered her mouth, so her struggles to cry out produced only grunts. Despite the cold, sweat dripped into her eyes. Wherever she was, it was pitch black.

Calm down. Just chill the fuck out. Focus.

She stopped struggling and concentrated, closing her eyes and opening her ears.

The familiar whine of the Team's signature electronics. Otherwise, nothing.

She turned up her olfactory system.

Nothing unusual, just metal, some kind of manufactured material, her own perspiration.

Okay. Nothing to see, hear, or smell. My mouth tastes like an old sock. Everything feels freaking cold. So how did I get here? What's the last thing I remember?

School all day. Time had crawled because of Jamie's 911 text. Hard to think about math or some essay when, for all you knew, someone might have died. After school, Mom brought her home and then headed to work, reminding Christian not to leave the house because of the stupid bike, which had been gone when she'd walked back to the pavilion to get it. Maybe the Team took it, though she couldn't imagine why. More likely, some kid or jogger found it. In any case, Mom had grounded her for losing another one. So Christian had waited until Mom had been gone twenty minutes. Then she walked outside, planning to jog to the park. After a year-plus of living with super-speed, Christian could run at a normal human pace as long as she wanted without breaking a sweat, losing her breath, even increasing her heart rate. Jogging from home to the pavilion took as much effort as most people expend sitting on the couch. She had worn a light jacket and a long-sleeved sweatshirt, jeans, some off-brand running shoes Mom had found at the Dollar Store.

What had happened to the jacket, the shoes? She didn't seem to be wearing them now.

What else had happened?

After stepping outside and doing a few cursory stretches for the benefit of anyone who might be watching, Christian had jogged down her driveway, onto Hickory Street, and down to the corner, where … what?

She couldn't remember anything beyond that, but it must have been the Team that had brought her here—them or not-Jamie, and this situation didn't say *supernatural creature* to her.

She felt sluggish, weighed down. Thick fog drifted through her mind. *Focus, damn it. You're in deep shit. Assume nobody's gonna get you out of it.*

In the meantime, slow, deep breaths. Awareness of the environment. Muscles relaxed until whatever dope the Team had used worked its way out, which, Christian hoped, would happen fast, given her super-metabolism.

Someone turned on the lights.

Christian grunted, squinted, and tried to look away, but she could not escape the brightness. She turned her senses back down, and the lights shifted from Full Solar Flare to Plain Old Searing. About the size of a master bedroom in one of Quapaw City's relatively few two-story homes, the whole room had been soundproofed. Long fluorescent light fixtures—the kind you saw in grocery stores, only much more power-ful—lined the ceiling. Spotlights, either hand-held or the sort hunters sometimes mounted on their trucks, had been fixed to stands against the far wall and aimed directly at Christian's face. She was chained to a metal chair that seemed bolted to the floor.

She had to find a way out of here. Maybe she could try that thing the Flash did, where he vibrated—

The door in the far wall opened and she looked up, wincing against the light. A man walked in, just a dark shape against the spotlights at first, but then he placed a metal folding chair in front of Christian, maybe three feet away. Backlit this way, many of his features seemed cast in darkness, but she had seen him before—Joe Kragthorpe of the CIA, also known as Shrike. Maybe five ten in his shoes, Kragthorpe reminded her of the switchblade she had once bought from an older kid—thin and sleek, made of steel, ready to spring. His dark brown hair always seemed freshly trimmed. He had gray eyes and a dimpled chin that reminded Christian of somebody's ass.

"Know who I am?" he asked. Nothing about his voice sounded remarkable, other than that SoCal sound.

She had to be careful here. She knew his name, but they had never been introduced. She knew his employer, though even Chief O'Brien probably didn't. She knew his code name. If she gave any of that away, the Team would probably take it for proof that she was a Freak. They might even theorize that her senses had been enhanced and that her group had been listening in. And if the Team knew any of that, the situation would escalate.

Of course, considering her current position, it already had.

Kragthorpe had brought in a bottle of water dripping with condensation. Christian's parched throat ached. Her mouth felt like a desert. Kragthorpe unscrewed the cap and drank, his Adam's apple working. Then he put the cap back on, crossed his legs, and held the bottle in one hand, casually, as if he had already forgotten it.

"Hi," he said, smiling, as if they were sitting across a table in the school cafeteria.

Christian looked down at her chained hands, as if to say, *I'd shake with you, but I'm kinda tied down.*

"Yeah, sorry about that," Kragthorpe said. "Had to make sure you stayed put long enough to chat a while. You comfortable? Anything I can get you?"

Christian narrowed her eyes, then looked away. *You're hilarious,* she thought. *Get rid of these chains and we'll have some* really *good laughs.*

"My name is Joe Kragthorpe," he said, opening the bottle again, drinking, replacing the cap. "I guess you've probably seen me around."

Christian shrugged.

"Sure you have. You know we've been watching you. And *we* know that *you* know. So let's not bullshit each other."

She kept still.

"I'm with the CIA. Bet you didn't know that."

Christian widened her eyes, glanced to the side, looked back at Kragthorpe. *I hope that makes me look scared. Maybe I should have listened to Mom and tried out for the school play.*

"You're smart to be nervous," Kragthorpe said in a gentle, we're-in-this-mess-together tone. "The United States government suspects you of terrorist activities. Your friends, too."

Keeping her eyes wide, Christian shook her head vigorously.

"Yeah, yeah," Kragthorpe said. "You're no terrorist. You haven't mutated. Why would anybody think so? It's not like you can run a thousand miles per hour. It's not like one of your buddies attacked your own classmates last year. It's not like you killed a monster from another planet after it ate your friend's mother."

Now Christian stared at him for several moments. Then she furrowed her brow and tilted her head, hoping it conveyed confusion.

"I thought we were cutting the bullshit," Kragthorpe said, leaning forward. He held up the water bottle and shook it. "Speaking of which. I happen to know that the tranquilizer we hit you with induces thirst. Miserable, desperate thirst. Your throat constricts till you can barely breathe. Pretty soon, all you can think about is a drink. Something to keep your tongue from sticking to the roof of your mouth. Something that lets you swallow without choking on your own damn near solid spit."

Christian stared at the bottle, her eyes following it as he moved it around. It wasn't part of her act. *Stop it. It's just a dry mouth. You can do this all day and twice on Sunday.*

"But let me guess. You're tougher than that. You won't break just for a drink of cold, clear, sweet water."

She closed her eyes and forced herself to swallow, despite the gluey saliva, the outraged throat.

"It's gonna take a lot more than that. You're the badass in your gang, right?"

He seemed on the verge of saying more, but he paused and looked away. Christian turned up her hearing, pushing past the soundproofing, focusing on the voices from elsewhere.

McCreedy: "Vitals are elevated. She's in distress. Turn up the heat."

Greenwalt: "Sir, using EIT on American soil—"

Mossman: "For God's sake. Stop acting like she's an innocent babe with angels dancing around her head."

Greenwalt: "But—"

McCreedy: "Your concerns have been noted, Prince. Shrike, you have the green light."

Kragthorpe turned back to Christian, so she lowered her volume. Otherwise, his speaking voice might have concussed her. He stood and looked down at her. "I can't take those chains off, because … well, you know. I can remove the gag, though. So we can talk. And believe me, you *will* talk. Sooner or later, everybody does."

He walked behind her and fiddled with something at the back of her head, not taking much care with how often he jabbed her or yanked her around. Kragthorpe ripped off the duct tape that had been wrapped around her head. Then he tinkered with something else back there. After a series of metallic clinks, a metal doohickey fell out of her mouth and into her lap. It looked like a Terminator's jaw piece or part of one of those things they had learned about in history class—what were they called? Scold's bridles? Something men invented to silence women. Typical.

Bruh, women have been dealing with scared little trolls like you ever since the world started turning. Well, you ain't as scared as you're gonna be. I'm gonna make you regret that shit. Count on it.

She worked her aching, creaking jaw. When she tried to spit out some of that thick saliva, it stuck to her chin. She could feel it hanging there like snot. Kragthorpe wiped it away with his finger.

"Thanks," she rasped. "Y'all's hospitality sucks."

Kragthorpe threw back his head and laughed. Then he put his hands on his hips and looked at her with admiration. "Gotta hand it to you. Most kids your age—hell, most adults I've met—would be shitting their pants right now."

"Maybe I'm constipated."

"We'll see." He walked over to the door, opened it, and pulled in a rolling cart covered with a sheet. Something on it rattled as it bumped over the soundproofing. More metal, probably nothing good. Kragthorpe pulled the sheet off with a magician's flourish. The cart was actually a rolling storage box holding a series of drawers with plain brushed-metal knobs.

"Whatcha got there?" Christian asked. "Dim sum?"

"Funny," Kragthorpe muttered as he shuffled through the top drawer. "I hope you can keep your sense of humor once we get started. Huh. Maybe this little number." He pulled out a triangular instrument that looked like a pair of barbecue tongs. Kragthorpe snapped them closed, let them open, snapped them closed, bringing them closer and closer to Christian's face. When the prongs touched, sparks erupted from the ends. A little wave of heat and energy puffed against her cheeks.

Don't move. Don't blink.

"I think you got the wrong thingee outta there, dude," she said, even managing to grin. "I may be a brat, but I'm not a brat*wurst*. Though if you're really into it, me and my friends can probably throw together a barbecue next weekend."

He held the opened tongs near the end of Christian's nose. "We found these, and some other cool shit, after a successful op against something tougher than you. I'd tell you more—"

"But then you'd have to kill me," Christian broke in. "I've seen that movie too, bruh."

"See what happens when I complete the circuit? Feel it? Want to guess what it'll do to you if I put a body part between these leads?"

Christian stared at the tongs for several moments. "You turn me over to see if I'm done?"

Kragthorpe goggled at her. Then he laughed again. "Oh, man. You really *are* a badass. I mean, full-grown, hardened terrorists have sold out their mothers once they saw my little bag of goodies. But you? You barely even flinched."

She shrugged, or did her best to, given the constraints. "Maybe I'm just hard-headed. That's what my Mom says."

He wagged the tongs at her. "I like you, girl. No shit. I'm sorry this has to happen."

"What—" she began.

Kragthorpe positioned the tongs on either side of her left pinkie finger. Then he closed them. When the leads touched either side of her finger, sizzling, buzzing pain like an electric shock ripped through the digit, up her arm, into her brain. Her body jerked. Her head snapped from side to side. Despite herself, she screamed through clenched teeth.

The CIA man opened the tongs. The immediate pain subsided, but that whole side of her body throbbed. She tried to keep her head up, but her chin fell against her chest. Sweat broke out on her back and head. Beads of it formed on the end of her nose and fell onto her lap.

"Still with me?" Kragthorpe said. He was sweating, too. His shirt was already clinging to his body.

Christian panted. "Yeah. Just wish I could scratch my nose."

Kragthorpe laughed. He pulled his chair closer and sat, pushing her head up so he could look her in the eye. "Try moving that finger."

Christian stared at him a moment. Then she tried to raise her left pinkie.

It didn't budge.

Kragthorpe thumped it hard, as if they were back in sixth grade and playing thump-knuckle. It made a loud smack, but Christian felt nothing.

"Huh," she said. Panic rose within her, making her tremble and breathe harder. *Quit it. Don't let him see you're afraid.*

"You'll never use that finger again," Kragthorpe said in a mournful voice, like a doctor delivering news of a terminal illness. He clicked the tongs once, twice, three times. Sparks cascaded onto her face. Waves of energy washed over her. "Now. Imagine what happens if I branch out. I've done it before. I put your nose in here, you never smell your mother's biscuits and possum, or whatever you overall-wearing, barefoot hillbillies eat around here. I touch your eye, you're blind. And I can take other things away from you, too. Things you haven't even gotten to use yet."

Christian watched him—*look at him, not those tongs*—and concentrated on breathing normally. "You said you wanted me to talk. About what?"

Kragthorpe smiled again. "See? That wasn't so hard. You and I, we'll get along just fine as long as you cooperate. Now. Tell me all about yourself and your friends. How you got your powers. Why you attacked your school last year. What's happening to your friend Entmann. And what he's planning next."

She closed her eyes, opened them, nodded. "Okay."

He leaned back in his chair. "Excellent! I really do like you."

"Right." She took a deep breath. "I got my powers when I was working late in my lab one night. Lightning struck my table and doused me with a bunch of chemicals. After that, I could run super-fast."

Kragthorpe frowned. "What?"

"A radioactive spider bit Gabby Davison. Now she shits webbing. When Micah's momma died, he decided to become a bat so he could strike fear into the hearts of criminals. Jamie Entmann's actually an alien. His real parents sent him to Earth just before his planet blew up. And Kenneth Del Ray got caught in a cosmic ray storm. That, or he's just a dick."

All the emotion had drained out of Kragthorpe's face. He looked away, as he had done before, and Christian raised her hearing.

Greenwalt: "This isn't getting us anywhere. Can't you see she won't betray her friends?"

Mossman: "We're just getting started."

The low-grade fear gripping her heart jacked up several levels—the energy that always stirred, then churned, then raged inside her when she ran began to rev up.

Calm down, damn it. Chill.

Vincent: "Her vitals are rising. Instruments detect an energy surge. I can't tell whether it's coming from the girl."

Mossman: "Sir, tell Shrike to terminate her. We've seen what she can do."

Greenwalt: "Jesus Christ, Chip. How many times do I have to say this? She's an American. She's a *kid*."

The panic churned and churned. Christian might have been tough, maybe even as badass as Kragthorpe believed, but she was also fifteen. And as the emotions ramped up, so did her energy.

Chill. Calm down.

McCreedy: "I'm not prepared to terminate. But she needs to understand her position. Shrike?"

Kragthorpe nodded. He kneeled in front of her and fitted the tongs on either side of her left ring finger. "Last chance," he said.

Christian said nothing.

He closed the tongs. Electric fire ripped through her. She babbled against her clenched teeth as her body spasmed. Kragthorpe opened the tongs, and she collapsed against the chains. Now that finger wouldn't move either.

Vincent: "Heart rate's in the danger zone. And that energy surge is off the charts."

It was true. Her hands and feet were vibrating, her body thrumming with a force that demanded to be unleashed.

Mossman: "I'm telling you. We should terminate."

McCreedy: "Negative. Shrike, kill the whole hand."

Christian's hands and feet were shaking. The energy inside her had grown unbearable, and so had her panic. She could barely think.

Kragthorpe maneuvered the opened tongs toward her left hand. "Sorry about this, kid," he said.

Then, from somewhere outside, something roared.

Kragthorpe must have heard it over his com, because he wheeled toward the door. As Christian turned down her hearing to normal levels, cries of surprise and terror rang out. Kragthorpe grimaced and yanked out his earpiece.

"What's up?" Christian wheezed, her heart rate slowing, that red sense of panic easing. As she calmed down, her energy levels dropped. Maybe she wouldn't shake the whole house apart.

From outside the room, more crashes and thumps.

Kragthorpe stepped forward and opened the door.

Something roared again, and Kragthorpe flew back into the room, past Christian. It sounded as if he struck the padded wall and fell to the floor.

A huge, furry form forced its way inside. When it stood to its full height, it had to hunch.

A black bear.

A freaking black bear had burst in and bitchslapped Kragthorpe. It towered over Christian, its deep brown eyes boring into her.

They looked familiar.

Oh, sure. I should have known I'd die in a farmhouse, eaten by a full-grown bear.

The animal lumbered forward, bent, dragged its claws across Christian's chains. Then it hooked those claws between the metal and her body.

The links pulled tighter, squeezing the breath out of her. Black spots danced across her field of vision.

Then the chains broke, releasing all that pressure at once.

The force jostled Christian right out of the chair. She fell to the floor. Blood began to flow back into her limbs in sharp needles.

The bear watched her.

She sat up, pushed the chains away, and backed against the wall next to Kragthorpe, who was unconscious or dead.

What in the ever-loving hell is happening here?

Mossman, Vincent, and Greenwalt burst into the room, their service weapons at the ready. They were shouting as they fired, though Christian could barely understand them over all the noise. The bear staggered and growled. Christian flattened herself on the floor, her ears ringing, gunpowder burning her nostrils.

As the bear turned to the men, she crawled along the wall, trying to reach the door.

Vincent and Greenwalt kept shooting as the bear advanced on them. The bullets struck it in the torso, the face. It stutter-stepped, but it neither bled nor halted. The Team members were still yelling at each other as they backed toward the door—all except for Mossman, who spotted Christian. He sidestepped the bear and leveled his weapon at her head. "See you in hell, freak."

Christian tensed, ready to zoom past him and through the other men.

Then the bear turned, lunged, and bit off Agent Chip Mossman's right hand.

Mossman staggered against the front wall, holding his bleeding stump in front of his eyes as it gushed, spattering the white soundproofing. He shrieked. His gore-covered weapon lay on the floor. Christian crawled over it, still trying to reach the door, which Vincent and Greenwalt were blocking. They stared at Mossman with their mouths hanging open. The bear pivoted toward them and roared. Greenwalt hugged the wall, inching toward Mossman, who was sitting on the floor, his face pale and cheesy. The bear fixated on Vincent, who backed out of the room as he ejected his spent clip and dug another one out while the bear followed him into the hallway. It roared and struck a wall. The whole house trembled. Vincent's gun fired over and over, the muzzle flashes strobing. Other voices were raised out there. Kragthorpe still lay in a heap.

Greenwalt had removed his tie and was making a tourniquet for Mossman, whose eyelids fluttered.

"Is he gonna live?" Christian asked.

Greenwalt glanced at her. "What the hell do you care?"

"Jesus, dude, you think I want somebody to die? That any of us do?"

Greenwalt paused. He looked almost as pale as Mossman, sweaty and disheveled. "Get out of here, kid. While the others are busy. I don't know what they'll do if they survive that bear and you're still here."

She watched him a moment as he resumed his work. He muttered to himself, maybe trying to recall first aid.

From deeper in the farmhouse, more roars, breaking glass, loud crashes like heavy furniture being smashed to pieces, gunshots, voices raised in anger and fright.

Christian stood and stumbled into the hall. The walls had been deeply gouged in parallel lines. Claw marks. She trotted down the corridor. *Don't use your powers, just don't, not yet. This place is probably wired.* The passage opened into a wide living area with a couch, three recliners, a huge television. The couch had been overturned and shredded, as had one of the recliners. Stuffing lay everywhere. To her right lay a dining and kitchen area with droplets of blood cast onto the outdated appliances and the decrepit wooden cabinets. A dining table had been tossed against a wall. Two of the four chairs were overturned, one smashed to bits, one sitting neatly in its place as if nothing had happened. From deeper in the house, more roaring and thumps and unintelligible words.

Christian turned left and trotted out the front door, through the yard and past the Suburbans, and, she realized, a couple of Tahoes. Weird what you noticed when you came so close to dying.

Night had fallen. A chunk of moon rode amid clouds that floated along like dreams. She stumbled through the grass, over the ditch, onto the blacktop of Grisham's Loop. As she slow-jogged in the direction of town, the energy inside her ramped up again, surging with her heartbeat, her breath. It fought against the lingering effects of whatever sedative they had used. Her limbs still felt too heavy, her head fuzzy.

Forget about it. Just run your ass off.

Before she could take off, something crashed behind her. The bear had smashed its way out through the farmhouse door, which hung on one hinge, and had fallen onto all fours. It paused in the middle of the road, looking at her.

Then it lifted one forepaw and waved.

What in—?

Light bathed her. She turned. A car bore down on her. The driver slammed on the brakes, tires squealing. A door opened; the driver got out—Gabby.

"Christian!"

"Yeah. It's me." Christian held her left hand up and tried to flex the fingers. The pinkie and ring finger did not move.

She stumbled forward and collapsed onto the hood. The world went dark. The car shifted beneath her as others opened their doors, got out, grabbed her. They stuffed her inside and got in. Warm bodies on either side, cooing voices. The car reversed, and as the other Freaks talked, Christian let herself drift.

CHAPTER FIFTEEN

As the others drove away, Jamie ducked into the woods and flew a hundred yards deeper than the usual spot. He found a good tree with the least-obstructed view of the farmhouse. Enhancing both his hearing and his vision, he kept one ear on the house and one on the forest in case that bear came back. Speaking of which, why in God's name had a *bear* attacked the farmhouse and freed Christian? Na'ul had been terrifying and bizarre, but that whole incident had more or less played out as a straight-up fight. You could understand it. Na'ul wanted to kill people, especially the Freaks; the Freaks wanted to stop him. Now something seemed to be stalking the Freaks *and* the feds, and Jamie had no idea what it was or what it wanted.

He didn't have long to ponder, though. Greenwalt and Vincent burst from the house, dragging Mossman between them. The Homeland Security agent's head hung. All three were covered in blood. Vincent favored his left arm. As they wrestled Mossman into the back of an SUV, Kragthorpe staggered out and climbed into the car, his clothes ripped, his eyes glassy. Blood trickled from one ear. Once everyone had piled in, the SUV burned out of the driveway and down the road. They were probably heading to the county hospital. Maybe Christian's mom would take care of them. Wouldn't that be some shit?

The rest of the Team filed onto the porch: McCreedy, with his shaved head and air of authority; Jeffcoat, the shortest man on the Team but also the most muscular, his rimless glasses low on his nose; Parker, the Bostonian, with his graying crewcut, thick goatee, and angry eyes. They looked shaken. Jamie didn't blame them. It wasn't every day that you kidnapped a fifteen-year-old girl and then got bum-rushed by a freaking *bear* inside your own house.

McCreedy, Jeffcoat, and Parker watched the SUV's taillights disappear around the curve. Then McCreedy whistled, the sound low and mournful. "Gentlemen," he said. "What the fuck just happened?"

Jeffcoat pushed his glasses to the bridge of his nose. "I don't know, sir. I don't see how we could have anticipated a bear attack." His voice sounded high and shaky for a muscle-headed ATF guy.

"Excuses are like assholes, Canebrake. Everybody's got one. Most of them stink."

Jeffcoat cleared his throat. "Yes, sir."

Parker kept looking at the bend in the road, eyes intense and furious, as if he believed Grisham's Loop had aided and abetted the bear. "It could have been the Entmann kid."

McCreedy harrumphed. "No. Not unless our surveillance equipment has failed. This is something else."

Parker went to the porch rail and picked at the peeling paint. "If this is a shaper and not just a further mutation, we've got a whole host of problems. It could be anyone." He dropped a hammer-fist on the rail. It shuddered, paint flaking onto the grass.

"It knew we took the girl," Jeffcoat said. "It wanted to stop us, and it did."

McCreedy stared into the woods for a while. It seemed the old man was looking directly at Jamie, though that was impossible. "Yes," he said. "This shaper has the advantage. To regain our edge, we need information. The shaper's identity. How it knows us. Its connection to the children. And whether it is coincidence that this new bogey came to town at the same time as Baltar Sterne."

Jamie reeled. The Team knew about Baltar. They knew more than Micah's *friends*.

McCreedy turned and walked back inside. The others followed. The front doorjamb had been vaporized. "Shit," Parker said. "I guess we've got to fix this thing."

"You got this, right?" Kragthorpe said, patting Parker on the back as they entered. "Just pretend it's on Mrs. Doberman's honey-do list."

"Very funny," Parker said.

Jamie listened another five minutes, but the men had moved on to unimportant stuff: Who would go to the hardware store tomorrow, who was sick of having eggs every morning. Jamie returned his senses to everyday levels and flew out of the woods.

✳✳✳

Everyone had to get home soon; they had school tomorrow. But first they needed to figure out what to do with Christian. Gabby wanted to take her straight home, but no one knew Ms. Frey's schedule, and they had no plausible explanation for Christian's condition. Micah had suggested they go to his house. Unsure what else to do, Gabby had agreed.

Kenneth hadn't offered an opinion one way or another. Maybe he didn't care, but Gabby suspected something deeper. Last year, Na'ul had pretty much shattered Kenneth's tough-guy self-image. Twice the monster had sent him into a dead screaming run for his life, and while Kenneth had found his courage and stood toe-to-toe with the vampire in the end, he probably found it hard to shake off the memory of terror. Maybe you got used to living with fear, like what Gabby felt every time she thought about the Team. Maybe your heart got accustomed to a certain elevated rate, your nerves a kind of constant buzzing, the way some people learned not to believe that any overcast or windy day might bring a tornado that would rip their house off its foundation. But when one actually spiraled over the horizon, all that fear came rushing back. Now that the Team had moved against them, Gabby figured Kenneth might be confronting what he had allowed himself to forget—that sooner or later the fight would come, and when it did, it might well end in the Freaks' death or imprisonment.

And what about this new player in town? It had looked enough like Jamie to fool Christian. Then it had become … something else. Christian hadn't been sure what; that night had been too dark, too chaotic. Tonight, as the Freaks had driven up Grisham's Loop with their costumes in the trunk, prepared to hit the farmhouse hard and fast to rescue their captured friend, they had nearly run Christian down in the road, and as they collected her, they had seen what looked like a fully grown black bear smash its way out of the house and trot into the woods. Before it disappeared, it had stopped. Looked at them. Waved.

A *bear.* Had *waved.*

The very ground they walked on seemed like the rubber skin of a Halloween mask. Dig in and you might find some other face, something alien and blood-soaked.

At Micah's house, Gabby parked on the street. Mrs. Sterne's old car still hadn't moved from the driveway. Beside it sat a Lexus that looked out of place in this neighborhood. The same one that had followed her and Jamie that day? *Is that Baltar's car?* she wanted to say in the patient but authoritative voice Jamie used whenever he had to put on his team-leader hat. She had tried it on a few times—nothing major, just a low-stakes insistence that, say, the group make up their minds about whether they should go to Pizza of Mind after school. Every time, it had felt false, like a little kid imitating her parents.

Steve Whitehead still called her Sister Gabby. At school, kids had lain off the half-breed comments, probably because hate speech meant suspension or worse, but she had heard snide whispers that amounted to pretty much the same thing.

Real change, *lasting* change, was pretty hard.

Micah looked guilty. He slung Christian's left arm around his shoulders—when her hand moved, the last two fingers stayed fixed, as if they had been tied together and splinted—and helped Kenneth carry her to the porch. They sat her on the top step. Kenneth moved back into the yard, watching, still silent. Micah stayed with Christian.

Gabby bent over, hands on her knees, and looked into Christian's eyes. "You okay?"

Tears spilled down Christian's face. Gabby recoiled. She had never seen Christian cry. She hadn't even considered that such a thing was possible.

"Peachy," Christian said. She tried to smile but couldn't quite manage it.

If they kicked her ass like this in just a couple of hours, what would they do to me?

"What's up with your hand?" Micah asked. Christian had taken her arm from around his neck. Now she was flexing her fingers. Those same two wouldn't move. Unease burbled in Gabby's stomach.

"Kragthorpe used some kind of fricking torture device on 'em," Christian said, her voice low and shaky. "I couldn't use my powers in front of 'em, so my aura couldn't help."

"What kind of device?"

"Looked like a pair of barbecue tongs, but they generated some kind of power field. I don't think they were from Earth."

"Bullshit," Kenneth said, the first word he had spoken since they had headed for Grisham's Loop.

Gabby expected Christian to bite his head off, but she just looked stunned. "Believe me or don't," she said. "I can't move 'em."

Gabby looked around, half expecting to see a fleet of SUVs peel around the corner, agents hanging out the windows and pointing weird weapons at them. "We should go inside."

Jamie dropped out of the oak tree. Kenneth uttered a high-pitched bark and staggered away. Gabby jumped.

"Jeez, man, how long you been in that tree?" Kenneth said.

"Just flew in," Jamie said, brushing leaves off his clothes and out of his hair. "Figured I probably shouldn't touch down in the middle of MacArthur Road. How is she?"

"She can speak for herself," Christian said. She sounded a bit stronger, more present. "They messed up two of my fingers."

The front door opened. Jamie stepped back into the yard and stared. Kenneth said nothing, but his eyes opened a fraction wider.

A tall, thin, bald man stood in the doorway. He wore black slacks, black work boots, and a black T-shirt that emphasized his ropy arm muscles. His eyes seemed unnaturally bright. When he smiled, his teeth looked gray and sharp, and his powerful hands sported long, pointed nails with black polish. Gabby half expected him to ask why they had come into his woods and where they were going with that basket of goodies. Perhaps to Grandma's house?

"You look as if you could use some hot chocolate," he said. "Come in."

He turned on his heel and walked back into the house.

Everyone looked at Micah, who shrugged. "Uh, yeah. That's Great-Uncle Baltar. But I guess you figured that out."

"Creepy-looking Uncle Fester asshole," Kenneth mumbled.

Micah stared a hole in Kenneth. "You ain't gonna win any beauty contests either."

Christian giggled, then burst into laughter.

"What?" Jamie asked.

"I got tortured by a government strike team until a bear saved my ass," she said, still laughing. "And a wizard's babysitting Micah. These are our lives now."

"What can you tell us about that bear?" Jamie asked.

Christian's laughter tapered off. "Nothing. I met it for only like ten seconds, and then I decided I'd better leave."

The door opened again. Baltar Sterne poked his head out. "The hot chocolate will get cold. You should come inside. Don't worry about your government friends. They can no longer see or hear you inside these walls."

He disappeared. The Freaks stared. Gabby felt like she had been punched in the stomach.

Kenneth said what everyone else was thinking. *"What?"*

CHAPTER SIXTEEN

Kenneth sat on Sterne's ratty green couch and picked at the threads poking out of a hole in the armrest. Beside him, Gabby looked about as comfortable as a geek in detention. Seated to her right, Jamie leaned forward, elbows on his knees, glaring at Sterne like he could barely stop himself from kicking the kid's ass. Christian sat at the far end, a glass of water in her right hand. She still looked shell-shocked. Her left hand flexed and flexed, but those two fingers had not moved. She trembled a little, as if her body wanted to fly apart and she could barely stop it.

Sterne sat in one of the two recliners the old guy had pushed around so they faced the couch. The man himself sat in the other chair, legs crossed, hands laced together and steepled over his chest. He kept smiling, but those bright-ass eyeballs of his hadn't gotten the memo. They looked cold and eager. Like a starving man's if somebody gave him a steak. As for Micah, he had leaned back, chin in the air, seemingly daring anybody to chew out his sorry ass for keeping his uncle's presence a secret.

No one had spoken since they took their seats. Finally, Jamie took charge. "How come you look so young?" he said to Baltar. "If I didn't know better, I'd swear you were only forty or fifty."

"I watch my diet, and I exercise," the old fart said. "If you're looking for a dark secret, I have none."

Jamie grunted. Gabby studied her fingernails. Christian flexed her hand.

Screw it. These pussies won't say it, so I will. "You Sternes seem pretty good at keeping secrets," Kenneth said.

"We don't owe you shit," Micah said.

127

"Yeah," Jamie said. "You do."

Micah made a disgusted noise and looked away.

I could wipe that phony badass look off your ugly bitch face, Kenneth thought. *And I should. Somebody needs to.*

"If I may," Baltar said. "I can help."

Everybody went quiet again. Jamie looked furious. Kenneth rubbed the bridge of his nose. This shit was giving him a headache.

Entmann took a deep breath and let it out. He was doing a good job of controlling himself under the circumstances. "Help with what?" Jamie asked.

"Oh, come, now," Baltar said. "Let's dispense with all that."

"No idea what you're talking about," Jamie said.

Baltar sighed, stood, and left the room.

Kenneth turned to Micah. "You freaking told him."

Micah sneered. "I didn't say shit. Not that I care what you think."

Kenneth started to rise. Gabby grabbed his arm. "Don't," she said. "Especially not now."

He pulled away from her but kept his seat. Micah grinned and winked at him. *Oh, you little turd. I'm so gonna beat your ass one day.*

Baltar returned holding a fistful of leather necklaces. He handed them around, one for each Freak. As he sat, he bent forward, revealing a similar necklace around his own neck. Kenneth examined his. The leather was old and weather-beaten but seemed sturdy. He didn't know much about jewelry, but the circular pendant looked like silver. The rock affixed to the pendant was bright blue shot with white threads.

"Thanks, I guess?" Kenneth said.

"They're real pretty," Gabby said, studying hers. Except for the various patterns of white in blue, the necklaces all looked the same.

"Not just pretty," Baltar said. "Useful."

"Useful how?" Jamie asked.

"The government agents depend far too much on their surveillance. These charms will disrupt it."

Now everybody stared at Baltar.

"Dammit, Micah," Jamie hissed.

"My great-nephew kept your confidence," Baltar said. "I know what I know because I have been watching you, ever since you used my books and robes to open a door between worlds."

Jamie stood and walked behind the couch. He leaned against it, arms folded across his chest, rocking back and forth. *He's freaking pissed, and I don't blame him,* Kenneth thought. *We're half a step from getting clipped or locked up, and some old guy knows all about us.*

"Okay," said Christian. Kenneth hadn't expected her to contribute much after what she had been through. "Let's pretend we know what you're talking about. How do these things help?"

"Much like the spell you used to bring Prince Na'ul of the Go'kan to this town, these charms are magic," Baltar said. He sounded patient and expectant, like a good teacher. "As such, their very existence disrupts technology. I have used a similar glamour on this house, meaning we can move and speak freely even if we take off the charms. If you'd like, I can do the same for your own houses. Everyone deserves sanctuary, do they not?"

"Uh huh," Christian said. "Right."

"I think the feds would notice if their equipment stopped working," Gabby said. Her voice only shook a little.

"Oh, it still works," Baltar said. "But their monitors will show something different than what we actually say and do. Different words, different actions. Something benign."

"How the hell does that work?" Kenneth asked.

"Magic defies explanation," Baltar said, glancing at Kenneth. "As well ask me how much love weighs. Or the temperature of hatred."

Jamie came back around the couch and let the charm dangle from his fist. "And these?"

"These have been specifically geared to human senses. Let them touch your bare skin and repeat a word I shall give you, and the magic will work. If I had to guess, I'd say that the glamour bends light around us, like a cloaking device, and repels sound waves. But the mechanism? That's mystic. Besides, I'm no physicist."

Jamie scratched his head. "Jesus."

"I don't believe a word you're saying," Kenneth said.

Baltar sighed and pulled his own necklace out of his shirt. He gripped the charm and fixed Kenneth with his gaze. "You see? Bare skin. Now watch. *Evanescet.*"

Baltar vanished.

Everyone leaped to their feet, crying out. All except Micah, who sat and watched.

"Where the hell did he go?" Kenneth asked.

Baltar reappeared, still sitting in the chair. "Now do you believe me?"

No one seemed to know what to say. Baltar smiled.

You're awful smug, old man. Could be you need an ass-kicking like your pansy great-nephew.

"These all work the same way?" Micah asked. None of this seemed to bother him.

"Yes. Let your charm touch your bare chest or hold it in your closed fist. Say 'evanescet,' and think of those from whom you would hide. You will then be invisible and inaudible to them, and to them only, until you touch the charm again and say 'videtur.' Or until half an hour has passed, whichever comes first. These are small, harmless glamours, and the magic needs to … recharge, let us say."

Jamie stood there a moment, looking at Baltar. Then he took his seat, his left leg bouncing. "And if somebody had come in and, say, fired a pistol into that chair?"

Baltar spread his hands. "Then I would be dead. The charms do not render you invincible or incorporeal. You can still be touched. And hurt. And killed."

Gabby took Jamie's hand. "Come on, babe. Try to chill."

Christian let her stealth charm dangle from her hand and studied the rock. She flexed her hand over and over, but the injured fingers would not move.

Kenneth walked to the nearest window. The curtains were cracked, and he peered through. Nothing moved on the street, but he hadn't seen Na'ul coming either. The Team had never parked directly in front of anybody's house. Anyone or anything could be out there.

"I am pledged to protect Micah," Baltar was saying. Kenneth turned back to face him. "And I can help all of you. But the choice is yours."

The old dude pushed himself out of the recliner and walked down the hall. He entered a bedroom and closed the door. The Freaks sat in silence for a while. Kenneth took the chair Baltar had vacated and kicked back in it. After a minute, Jamie stood, went to the front door, and opened it. He poked his head out. Then he came back to the couch.

"There's a Tahoe down the road a piece. I guess they're back. One of them, anyway."

Christian's expression went from thoughtful to scared to pissed off in about two seconds. "We ought to go out there and kick their heads in," she said. "Mossman may have lost a hand, but the rest of 'em still got two. I owe 'em at least a couple of fingers."

"Forget them," Jamie said. "For now. What about Baltar? From everything we've heard, he can't be trusted. Then again, if these so-called stealth charms really work, he just did us a major solid. What do y'all think?"

More silence. Then Gabby cleared her throat. "If he can help, I say we let him. Even with our powers, we're still in high school. We could use somebody with experience. Besides, he's Micah's kin, and Micah's our friend."

"How much do we share with him?" Jamie asked. "Everything? Nothing?"

Gabby glanced at everyone in turn. Nobody gave her any help. She cleared her throat again. "Somewhere in the middle, I think."

Christian slipped her stealth charm over her head. The pendant dangled over her shirt between her breasts. "When it comes to our secrets, I only trust y'all. If we let Baltar into our circle, we gotta keep an eye on him."

"Damn straight," Jamie said. "Kenneth?"

"No," he said. "I won't run out on y'all. I don't think any of us can afford to go it alone. But I don't trust that guy."

Jamie nodded. "Micah?"

Looking straight at Kenneth, Micah said, "I vote yes."

Kenneth snorted. "Of course you do."

"Don't start," Christian said. "Either of you."

Sterne leaned forward, elbows on his knees. "Look. I barely know Uncle Baltar, but so far, he's been cool, and he knows more about this shit than any of us ever will. Maybe he could be our Rupert Giles."

"Or Yoda," Gabby said.

"Yeah. And if he gets in our way, well, I'm betting the five of us can take him."

Kenneth wasn't so sure about that. Something about Baltar Sterne made his nerves pulse.

"Christian?" Jamie asked.

"Like I said. I'm gonna watch him close." She nudged Gabby with her elbow. "But I'm pretty sure we're in an 'any port in a storm' situation. I vote yes, for now, but I'm reserving my right to call another vote."

"Fair enough," Jamie said.

"What do *you* think?" Kenneth asked. "You're our fearless leader."

Jamie grimaced. "Okay. Here's the truth. Baltar gives me a bad feeling. If the Team hadn't kidnapped Christian tonight, or if it hadn't become pretty clear there's a new monster in town, I'd say no. But they did, and there is. So I'm with Christian. Trial basis. Nothing more. You okay with that, Micah?"

Sterne held up his hands. "Hey, whatever."

Jamie rubbed his eyes. He seemed worn out. "Let him know he's in. Don't tell him anything else."

"Sure." Micah stood and walked down the hall. He knocked on the bedroom door. When Baltar opened it, Micah whispered something to him. The old dude nodded, clapped Micah on the shoulder, and followed him back into the living room. "So, um. Yeah."

Much as Kenneth liked seeing Sterne tongue-tied and frazzled, he had serious doubts. *Everything about this Baltar dude smells fishy. I don't care who he's related to.*

"We're in," Jamie said.

That creepy-ass smile returned. "Excellent," said Baltar. "And now, a demonstration of my worth. I have been preparing this in anticipation of a happy outcome."

He's supposed to be from around here, but he sure don't talk like it. Maybe he's been gone a hell of a lot longer than we've been told.

Jamie glanced at Kenneth and held his gaze for a moment. Maybe they shared the same suspicions.

Baltar went to the kitchen and rattled around. When he came back, he carried a crude wooden bowl, a little bottle of red liquid, and a book of matches. He showed each of them the bowl. A pile of crushed gunk lay in the bottom. It looked like the mixture of spices Kenneth's mom scattered in her homemade spaghetti sauce. Baltar took the lamp off a side table, carried the table to the center of the room, and set the bowl on it. He opened the bottle.

"What's that?" Christian asked.

"My blood," Baltar said. Gabby and Christian shared a look that suggested they thought Baltar might be crazy, like they were already regretting their votes. "Blood holds great power. Micah tells me you love horror films and books about magic. Surely, even writers of such ephemera understand blood's qualities, its symbolism."

"Yeah," Christian said. "Spike gave a whole speech about it on this old episode of *Buffy*."

Baltar paused. "What is this *Buffy*?"

Christian grimaced. "Dude."

Baltar poured the blood, if the red shit really *was* blood, over the spaghetti spices. "Gabriella, would you be so kind as to look out the window and tell me if your government friends still lie in wait?"

Gabby got up, went to the window, and threw open the curtains. "Yeah. A few houses down."

"Stay there, please." Baltar struck a match and dropped it in the bowl. Flame burst upward in a column two feet high. Sparks flew everywhere, like the old guy had lit a firework. Kenneth jumped, and so did Jamie. Christian grunted. Micah took a step back, caught himself, and returned to his great-uncle's side.

More than ever, Kenneth wanted to punch Micah through a wall.

Baltar passed his hand through the flame and chanted something in a language Kenneth had never heard. Kenneth leaned over to Jamie. "What's he saying? What language?"

Jamie frowned. "How should I know?"

Baltar gestured at the bowl, and the flame died. Bright afterimages played across Kenneth's field of vision. "That language," Baltar said, "is Akkadian. If you could travel back to ancient Mesopotamia, you would hear it. A wizard from those days created this spell to escape his enemies. Why run, he realized, when you can drive your tormentors away? Gabriella, what do you see now?"

Gabby didn't answer for a moment. Then she watched a vehicle pass by. "The feds left," she said.

Micah grinned and pumped his fist. "All right, Uncle Baltar!"

The old man bowed as if he were on stage.

"Well," said Jamie. "Damn."

Gabby came away from the window and sat beside Jamie. Christian seemed mostly unfazed, but she might have been fronting, like Kenneth was. They could never forget that it had been Baltar's old shit, left lying around like a kid's toys, that had started all this.

Jamie looked at his phone. "It's getting late. We should head home.

Gabby, can you give Christian a ride? Even with the feds gone, I don't want her to be alone tonight."

"Bruh, I'm good," Christian said. She continued to flex her left hand. "No freaking way I'm letting those dickbags scare me away from my own house."

"I know," Jamie said. "Just … please? Gabby?"

"Yeah. I can carry all of you home."

They stood. Micah stepped forward and fist-bumped Christian, who used her right hand. "See you tomorrow," he said.

Christian winked. "Not if I see you first."

"Say nothing of all this," Baltar said. He had taken his chair back and crossed his legs, looking satisfied. "If the authorities ask, you know nothing of me. We haven't met."

Jamie snorted. "Mister, we've been keeping our own secrets for years. We don't need to be told when to keep our mouths shut."

"Of course. I meant no disrespect. Together we will determine the nature of this new threat. Together we will stop it."

"Uh huh." Jamie turned to Gabby. "You ready?"

She held up her keys. "Let's roll."

She led the others out of the house. Neither Baltar nor Micah saw them out, so Kenneth pulled the door shut. They piled into Gabby's car, Christian riding shotgun.

CHAPTER SEVENTEEN

Twenty minutes later, Micah lay on his bed scrolling through social media. From the groaning of the rickety floorboards and the occasional closing of a drawer or cabinet, he felt pretty sure Baltar was puttering around the house. Maybe looking for a mouse to sacrifice or something. Micah would never have admitted it in front of his friends, but his great-uncle freaked him out, too. The dude could do freaking magic. *Real* magic, not the bullshit kind you saw at kids' parties or on TV. And the way he smiled—like he had just gotten away with something nasty. Truth be told, if Micah hadn't had powers, he would never have stayed in the house with Baltar. He would have gone into foster care first.

As it was, if the old man tried anything, Micah would boil his balls in their wrinkled sack.

The landline in the kitchen rang. Footsteps thumped down the hall. Micah put his phone down, closed his eyes, and turned up his hearing enough to make out the voice on the other end.

"Sterne residence," Baltar said, his voice like thunder. Micah winced.

"Hey." The other voice belonged to Micah's dad. "How's things?"

"All is well, Malcolm. The boy goes to school and spends time with his friends—lovely young people. He studies and sleeps. No troubles. Ease your mind."

Dude makes it sound like I'm living in paradise and *that I'm boring as hell. Plus, that voice—if a voice could smile, that's what it would sound like.*

"Okay, good," Dad said. He sounded tired.

"And how are you?" Baltar asked.

137

"Just delivered in Atlanta. The boss wants me to make a run from here up to Virginia, but I figured I should probably come home."

A long pause. Then, in soothing tones, Baltar said, "You should accept the job. We don't need you here. Everything is fine."

Another pause.

"But—"

"No, Mal." Yet another long pause. "We don't need you here. Everything is fine."

"Y'all don't need me. Everything's fine."

"That's right. Take that job. Take another after that, and then another. Provide for your son. I will watch over him."

"Okay."

They hung up, and Micah turned down his senses. But what the hell had he just heard? He didn't trust those long pauses, the way his dad had repeated some of the words. Had Baltar whammied Dad?

Well, why would *he? I kinda doubt he loves this babysitting gig so much he'd somehow zap Dad through the phone just to keep it up. I bet he's got plenty of places he'd rather be.*

Still, the question seemed worth asking.

Micah found Baltar in the kitchen, making a cup of hot tea. The old man raised an eyebrow. "What can I do for you?"

"Was that my dad on the phone?" Micah asked.

"Do you always ask people about the content of their conversations?"

"No," Micah said. "But I ain't heard from Dad in a while, so—"

Baltar locked eyes with him. Those deep, bright eyes seemed to pulse, as if every heartbeat sent them an electrical charge. And Micah would have sworn the irises vibrated, a motion that encircled them and counterpointed the pulsing.

No way. It's gotta be another of those glamour things.

And yet Micah felt sleepy.

"Given that tomorrow is a school day," Baltar said in that same soothing voice he had used with Dad, "you should probably get some rest. I have much to do, and I would do it in solitude."

Screw you, Micah thought. *Why won't you answer me?*

"Okay," he heard himself saying. "Goodnight."

Then he turned and walked down the hall and into his room. He closed the door and took off his clothes and slipped under the covers, and now he couldn't think straight, couldn't protest even within his own mind, and his eyes closed, and he fell asleep.

In his dreams, he stood alone on the banks of the Quapaw River. Overhead, a moonless, starless sky stretched into forever. He kneeled in the mud, heedless of the way it oozed through his jeans, and raised his hands to the sky, his head bowed. The placid waters began to churn, to rotate, to spin. A whirlpool stretched from bank to bank, roaring and sucking down every bit of flotsam.

A spectral figure rose from those troubled waters and hovered, waves of dark energy pulsing and pulsing around it. That energy bathed Micah, drowned him, and from deep within it rose that same voice from his previous dreams, eerie and demanding and sure.

Hear me now. Follow me. You will stand beside me. All will fear you. Hear me now. Follow me.

✳

After Gabby dropped him off, Jamie went inside, chatted with his parents for a bit, and announced he was going to bed early. In his room, he turned off the light and looked out the window. No tail tonight. Good. He took off his shirt and tossed it onto the television, hoping it looked like a casual gesture a careless teenager might make. The shirt hung over the corner of the set where the Team's camera had been placed. *That ought to blind 'em. I hope.* He took his costume out of his closet and put it on, holding his ski mask in one hand. Then he opened the window slowly, listening for any sign of parental interference. Detecting nothing, he climbed out, propped the screen against the pane, and trotted into the side yard, where he shinnied up the maple tree with the conveniently low limbs. No movement on the street, no faces at windows.

He took his stealth charm in hand and spoke the magic word. A faint buzzing all around him, like static electricity. He pulled on his mask and floated to the treetop, where he shot high into the air and over town, headed for Grisham's Loop.

He landed without incident in the usual spot. Turning up his hearing but leaving his other senses at normal levels—no one even stood in the yard or on the porch, so there was nothing to see, and surely nothing important to smell or taste or feel—Jamie leaned against the tree trunk and listened.

McCreedy: "You're telling me you abandoned your post, leaving six targets unobserved, because … what are you telling me?"

Jeffcoat, in that shaky voice: "It's the weirdest thing, sir. I had eyes on the house. The surveillance feeds were coming through fine. But then I felt like I had to leave. *Had* to. I can't explain."

McCreedy: "That is unacceptable, Canebrake. If you can't perform in the field, I'll have to pull you out and reconsider your position here."

Jeffcoat, now sounding determined and firm: "It won't happen again, sir."

McCreedy: "Prince?"

Greenwalt: "Manticore's condition has stabilized. If the local quacks don't accidentally kill him, he should recover quickly."

McCreedy: "Good. I have connections in military prosthetics. He'll have the best."

Greenwalt: "Thank you, sir."

A pause, as if McCreedy was gathering his thoughts. Then: "You said Chief O'Brien stopped by the hospital. Did he mention the Allen girl?"

Greenwalt: "No, sir. Not a word. Nothing in his demeanor suggested suspicion. Other than wondering how Manticore lost a hand, which I wouldn't tell him, of course."

McCreedy: "A chief of police wouldn't let the abduction and interrogation of a teenager pass. The girl hasn't reported us. I do believe we're on the right track."

Jamie turned down his volume and flew home. Back in his room, the window closed and locked, his costume stored, the stealth spell expired, he crawled into bed and lay on his side, looking at his shirt hanging off the TV, wondering whether the Team suspected anything. They hadn't said a word about him while he listened in, but who knew what they might have discussed when he first casually covered their camera, or while he flew to and from Grisham's Loop?

I got up this morning and went to school like it was a normal day. But we got no normal days anymore. That thing the feds call a "shaper" … shit's got real again. Plus, Baltar seems about as honest as a politician. Kenneth and Micah back at each other. What the hell's next?

He lay awake thinking and worrying until after midnight, when he finally fell into a shallow, dreamless sleep.

CHAPTER EIGHTEEN

Micah didn't see Christian in the halls the next day. Around eleven a.m., his phone buzzed. She had texted the group, claiming she was sick. Micah asked if she needed anything, but she replied that her mom was home. Micah put his phone away, worried. *She ain't sick. She got her ass kicked for the first time.* It must have messed with her head. He knew the feeling: how the fact that someone could do that made you question your worth as a human being, how it turned the world into a dangerous place where anything might be waiting around any corner.

Maybe he'd stop by her place after school.

As Micah arranged his stuff in Mrs. Broom's class and waited for the lecture to start, Bec Villalobos called his name. "Where's our girl?" they asked, nodding at Christian's desk.

"Sick," Micah said. A weird feeling gripped him, like a bubble had risen in his chest. Man, why did Bec get to him so bad? "I might check on her later."

"Cool," Bec said.

Micah looked away, gripped the edge of his desk, cleared his throat. He hoped he wasn't blushing. "Hey. You wanna go to Mickey D's after school? Grab a Coke and some fries and then head over to Christian's with me?"

Bec's eyes narrowed, as if they were trying to figure out his exact intentions. Then they held out a fist. "Why not?"

Micah bumped it. That bubble in his chest popped. He felt warm all over. "Cool. Meet you at the bike racks?"

"Sure." They turned around as Mrs. Broom walked in and closed the door.

Micah listened to the lecture that followed, but he heard very little of it. He floated through the rest of the day, feeling as if his head had detached from his body.

Dude, it doesn't mean anything. It's not like it's a date. Be cool.

But I asked. And they said yes.

To hanging out. That's it.

Right now, that's enough.

After school, Bec waited for him at the rack, hands in their jeans pockets, the longer parts of their hair blowing in the wind.

Micah's face burned. *WTF? They aren't what you'd call hot in the usual way. But there's something about them.* "Hey," he said, trying to sound casual. *Jesus, is my voice* always *this high?*

"Hi," Bec said.

Micah unlocked his bike. It was a BMX model, though he couldn't do any tricks. Back in eighth grade, Dad had bought it secondhand and fixed up the loose handlebars. Now every ding and dent and patch of rust seemed especially noticeable. Micah freaking *hated* being poor. "Which bike's yours?"

"I don't have one," Bec said. "The parentals pick me up and drop me off. When they can't do it, I just hoof it. I mean, it's not like I've gotta walk across New York."

He laughed. "Well. You can ride my bike. I'll walk beside you."

"Screw that noise. I'll ride behind you."

"Um. Okay."

Still blushing furiously, hyper-aware of how many people could be watching, Micah straddled the bike and tried to hold it steady while Bec got onto the seat. They put their hands on his hips, their feet on the tire's pegs. Micah's mouth went dry, and he felt a stirring in his crotch.

Don't get excited. Just don't. Think of grandmothers. Baseball statistics. Knitting. Kenneth Del Ray's ugly-ass face.

Breathing raggedly, Micah launched the bike forward, standing on the pedals, struggling to balance the extra weight. His awareness of

Bec's hands on his body obliterated every rational thought, so much so that he nearly steamrolled Tyrone Hecht, who swore and flipped him a double bird.

Micah maneuvered onto the sidewalk, keeping to the right edge, calling out to kids who meandered into their path. For the first time since Na'ul had ripped his mother in half, he felt light and free. A cool but not cold breeze in his hair, someone's hands on his hips with their fingers laced in his belt loops, the bike like some powerful engine that was both part of him and something separate, that had to be controlled. Was this what his classmates felt when they liked somebody and that somebody liked them back? Had this part of the world always been there, a fingernail's breadth away? If he had turned his head just so, might he have seen it?

Whoa, boy. You're just giving them a ride to McDonald's. Chill.

But then again, screw that. It was good to feel happy. So what if it didn't last? Nothing did.

Micah had paid little attention to anything other than the sidewalk and the pleasant weight of Bec's hands. And so, as they turned onto Second Street, with the McDonald's Golden Arches in sight, he nearly jumped and overturned the bike when Bec said, "So what's the deal with all the rabbits?"

"Huh?" he said.

"The rabbits," they said in his ear, louder this time. Their breath tickled him. "I've seen a bunch of them in people's yards. Look, there's some more."

They pointed to his right. Sure enough, two rabbits sat in a yard, one brown, one spotted black and white. They crouched on all fours, their noses wiggling. The brown one's left ear twitched.

"I don't know," Micah said. "This town's never had what you'd call a surplus of rabbits."

"Well," Bec said, "maybe they just multiplied."

Micah laughed, braked, and waited for the light to change.

Ten minutes later, he carried a plastic tray filled with two boxes of McNuggets, two orders of fries, one Diet Coke and one regular, and four tubs of hot mustard sauce. Bec had chosen a booth near the restrooms. Only two cars sat in the parking lot beyond the window. The steady wind bent the branches of trees and blew a couple of discarded wrappers across the blacktop. The TV across the aisle and mounted high on the back wall had been set to the news. A couple of angry-looking talking heads faced the camera and blathered nothing but terrible news, death and destruction and hate and misery and people yelling at each other. Micah seldom thought about stuff like this. It was just the way of the world. But today, sitting across from Bec, he wondered if this was really the best people could do.

Before he could start on his McNuggets, the doors opened. Micah recognized two voices he hated: Brayden Sears's and Marla Schott's. Micah stiffened. Couldn't he ever get five minutes of peace? Was that too much to ask?

"What?" Bec asked. They looked at him with open curiosity.

"Nothing," he muttered.

After a moment, Brayden rounded the corner carrying a loaded tray. Marla walked beside him, staring at her phone. Brayden wore his ninth-grade football letter jacket, because of course. Marla wore a deep green jacket over a gray shirt that probably cost more than Micah's bike. Micah gritted his teeth and turned away, grabbing a nugget like it owed him money and ripping into it, not bothering with the hot mustard.

Bec raised their eyebrows. Then they turned and glanced at Brayden and Marla. "Friends of yours?"

"Not in this lifetime." Micah ate another nugget, practically swallowing it whole. The gorgeous day now seemed about ten shades duller.

"Ooookay," Bec said. They ate a few fries, opened some mustard, scarfed a nugget.

Brayden spotted Micah, smiled, lifted his chin. Like they were old buddies or some shit. Like their whole lives prior to last year hadn't happened. Like Micah hadn't become intimately familiar with Brayden's knuckles over eight years of bullying and torment. Did that sack of turds really think they were cool now?

Brayden and Marla took the booth across the aisle and two up. As he slid in and opened his burger, she dropped her little purse-thing on the tabletop and walked up to Micah and Bec. She raised her phone and snapped a pic of them. "Hey, y'all."

She sounds about as sincere as a used-car salesman running for office.

"Marla, right?" Bec asked. "I'm Bec."

"Oh, I know," Marla said, tapping away on her screen. "Sharing. I think this is the first time I've seen Micah with a girl besides Gabby Davison." She smiled in that way mean girls do when they're being bitchy and don't care if you know it.

"Piss off," Micah said.

Bec slapped his hand. "Be nice," they said. "Marla was just sharing an observation, right?"

"Mm-hmm," Marla muttered, still tapping away.

"I mean, what do you expect her to do?" Bec went on. "Mind her own business? Be nice? *Way* too much to ask."

Marla peered at them over her phone, eyes narrowed. Bec presented a fake smile that made Marla's look genuine. Marla huffed. "Whatever." She turned and walked back to her booth, where she slid in across from Brayden, who had already wrecked half his Big Mac. She opened her own sandwich—a regular hamburger—and nibbled it.

Ugh. She can't even eat like a normal person.

Bec winked at Micah. "Mean bitches. They can dish it out, but they can't take it."

Despite how his mood had soured, Micah grinned, hiding his mouth behind his hand so Bec wouldn't spot any food in his teeth.

His phone buzzed: Baltar. "I gotta take this," he said, wiping his mouth with a napkin. "It's my uncle."

"No biggie," Bec said, taking out their own phone.

Micah stood and walked out of the dining area, leaning against the wall next to the front doors. "Kinda busy," he said in lieu of a hello.

"Today we should sit quietly and ponder how we might proceed," Baltar said.

Micah's eyelids gained thirty pounds after the first word. He yawned and rubbed his eyes. What was it about Baltar's voice that made him want to crawl in bed and pull the covers up to his chin and ... dream?

He shook his head, trying to clear the cobwebs. "I can't," he said. "I'm hanging with a friend, and we're gonna check on Christian—"

"Someone else can see to her," Baltar said. His voice sounded loud and echoey, as if he were standing right beside Micah but also speaking from down a long hallway.

Micah shook his head again, hard. The light shining through the windows felt muted and seductively warm. *Is this what being drunk feels like? Or stoned?*

"No," he said. "I'm—"

"Come home," Baltar said. "Now."

Micah's eyes closed. When he opened them, he was standing beside the table. Bec was watching him, confused. He had put away the phone. Had he even hung up?

"I gotta go," he said. His feet moved by themselves, as if the conscious part of his mind had disconnected from the rest of him. As if he were being controlled.

"What?" Bec said. "I thought—"

"Later." He turned and plodded up the aisle past Brayden and Marla. As he opened the doors, beyond which his bike waited, their voices drifted out of the dining room.

"What the hell?" Bec said.

"That kid's always been weird," said Marla. "I tried to warn you."

If Brayden had anything to say, he kept it to himself.

Micah walked outside and got on his bike. As he began to pedal, his eyes closed again, and he drifted in the swirling darkness behind them, listening to that soothing voice from his dreams. It spoke of fellowship and belonging and a day to come when Micah would hold all the power, all the prestige.

CHAPTER NINETEEN

Nestled in my warren, I observed my adversaries through my scouts' eyes. Days ago, I had sent forth the rabbits, reminding them to watch for predators and the village's machines. Since then, they had stood post along trails and roads, outside buildings, on the edge of deep woods, in stands of trees. I shared with them images of the five children I hunted, of their friends, and of the seven government men. In turn, my little kin observed, followed, sent me knowledge. Where my targets went, what they did, sometimes even what they said.

The children called their leader Jamie Entmann, he of wingless flight. The last time I walked the earth, his ancestors wore chains and toiled under threat of the whip and the gun. Now even the white children followed him. And yet, as my emissaries pursued him, I sensed distrust, fear, hatred in some of the whites he passed. Had anything changed after all?

I learned the name of the girl who loved Entmann—Gabriella Davison, called Gabby, who could shoot lines of pure white force from her hands. Lighter-complexioned than Entmann but darker than her friends. Full of power fit to rend her enemies' flesh and bones, yet torn in mind and spirit. Was she a warrior or a mewling foal wobbling on spindly legs? Perhaps even she did not know.

The one whose anger roared inside him like a flooded river, Micah Sterne. Even among his tribe, he stood apart, indignant, his grudges hotter than his fire, colder than his ice. Would all that pain and rage consume him, or others, or both? Of all the humans I planned to trick, he was most worthy of caution, for who seemed more likely to destroy everyone and everything in his path?

151

The fast one, she whom I had lured into the trees, whom I freed from the government men—Christian Allen. In her I sensed the true warrior's spirit that the others had only begun to nurture. Even when terror gripped her, she pried open its claws and walked forward, looking her enemy in the eye. I smashed into the government men's lodge and bit off one's hand to save this girl, telling myself it would quicken the war between the two tribes. But as I lay dreaming in my warren, as I looked through my rabbits' eyes, I began to question my own motivations. Did I *admire* this child who ran faster than the gods? Did I hope to save her? And if I did, what did that mean for her fellows? Or her enemies? Or me?

Something about her—a spark, the whisper of a song in her very blood—called to me. It felt familiar and true, like the faintest echo of voices from the Nations.

The tallest, heaviest child with hair the color of fallen leaves and thick, hunched shoulders, Kenneth Del Ray. Fitting that the power of the portal imbued him with strength the limits of which even he did not suspect. More likely to trudge forward and strike whatever threatened him than to think, this boy might have proven hardest to conquer, for his single-minded aggression had been tempered with a will almost as strong as his limbs. Could I exploit his disdain for his fellows? Set him against the Sterne boy and watch them consume each other, then pick off the others at my leisure?

Soon, I would have to decide. Dark forces worked their wills in the village.

Perhaps the children's allies might prove useful. The boy called Brayden Sears lived somewhere between the world of the village and that of the warrior children. Bigger than all but Del Ray, fair-haired, with a broad forehead and close-set eyes, he lumbered about like a bear cub. The other children distrusted him. I sensed his conflicted feelings for them—an old, stale disdain mixed with a growing affection he did not understand. He liked them despite himself; they wanted to hate him but, except for Micah Sterne, could not manage it. Another crack through which a trick might slip.

The recently arrived child, Bec Villalobos, a name that roughly meant "village of the wolves," if I remembered Earth languages correctly. Here, I sensed a burgeoning desire, and something similar in Micah Sterne and Christian Allen. Whom would young Bec choose, and how might that choice widen the fissures in the tribe?

What would happen if Bec chose both, or neither?

As for the government men, I supposed they could have been worse. At least they came with weapons in plain view and their ill intentions written in every action, unlike the white men who once swarmed these lands waving written promises they would never keep. But this alone would not save this so-called Team if they found themselves in my path, if they threatened this land I once loved or whatever descendants remained of the people who had vanished from these woods to make their life in Oklahoma. The blood I'd tasted the night before was bitter, sour, spoiled by pettiness and fear. But I would taste it again if I had to.

Waking long enough to stretch and turn over, sending my kin tumbling and scurrying, I breathed deeply. The night air was crisp, cold. Soon humans would dash from place to place, seeking the next warm lodge where the wind could not reach them. And on those darker, lonelier nights, I would play my next trick.

CHAPTER TWENTY

After a few uneventful days in which she kept a close eye on the Team cars and, in quieter moments, listened to some unenlightening conversations, Gabby sat alone in her room on the Sunday evening before Thanksgiving, writing an analysis paper on *1984*. Usually these kinds of assignments filled her with dread. She would write a sentence, a paragraph, a whole draft, and then she would read it back, convince herself that her writing stank, that her ideas blew. She'd trash the whole thing and start over, and then do it again, and by the time the assignment came due, she had gone through six or eight increasingly garbage versions, at which point she'd have to turn in the latest, shittiest one because she'd run out of time. *Never again*, she'd tell herself. *Trust yourself more.* And she'd mean it. But she had never been able to do it.

The *1984* paper had gone better, though. Gabby couldn't believe how well the book fit the contemporary world. She doubted her ideas would seem very original, but for the first time in forever, a school project excited her. She had something to say.

In fact, now that she thought about it, Gabby knew more about government overreach than any of her teachers, more than even Orwell. A glance out the window would confirm that. She had seen a Tahoe parked in the usual spot, had listened in long enough to identify the voices of Jeffcoat and Parker. Christian and Micah and Bec were studying at Christian's place on Hickory Street, according to the latest group texts. No one was surveilling them. Meanwhile, Gabby, alone in her room, somehow merited two Team members. Their methodology remained mysterious. Maybe they used a random generator.

Gabby rubbed her eyes. She hadn't slept well since Christian's abduction, but she needed to finish this draft. The paper was due next Monday, and there was no school all week, but who knew what would come along to distract her?

Okay. Quit it. You got two more pages to go. Then you can sleep for as long as you want.

She yawned and placed her fingers back on the keyboard.

Then, outside, something crashed. Gabby jumped, banging her knees on her makeshift desk. Three of her figurines fell over. Shearing metal, glass breaking, raised voices—it had sounded like a head-on collision.

Gabby turned off her lights. Then she went to the window and opened the blinds. Something was happening in the darkness between streetlights. She upgraded her vision.

The Team's SUV lay in two pieces, one heaped in somebody's yard, the other in the street. Jeffcoat and Parker crawled up the road while a familiar figure stood over them, watching.

Kenneth.

Oh my God. He snuck up on them and tore the car in half. What the actual hell, Kenneth?

Jeffcoat picked up something, swiveled, and pointed it at Kenneth. The object looked like a gun, but it emitted only a low coughing sound. Jeffcoat must have used a silencer. He had shot Kenneth, but Kenneth hadn't moved. Had he engaged his powers? Had his aura saved him?

From the living room, Dad said, "What was *that*?"

"Where are you going?" her mother asked, alarmed. "Stay inside."

"I can't," Dad said. "Somebody might be hurt."

Porch lights winked on. Who knew how many brave dumbasses would spill out of those houses? Gabby picked up her phone and texted the other Freaks:

mumpsimus kenneth chasing two bats on my street

She stuck the phone in her pocket and opened her door, and then she dashed down the hall and grabbed her father's arm at the door. "No, Dad. Mom's right."

Dad paused. He glanced back at Mom, who gave him a *how could you even think of it?* look. "I can't just pretend I didn't hear that," Dad said. He turned back to the door.

Gabby squeezed his arm. "Remember Jake Hoeper."

He hesitated. "Mara. Call 911."

Mom was already holding her phone.

Gabby didn't wait to see what would happen. She ran back to her room, shut the door, looked out the window. Kenneth was gone. Parker and Jeffcoat were staggering down the street toward Gabby's house, Jeffcoat on his phone, both of them holding pistols fitted with silencers. Well, that was good. If they had brought a special weapon, Kenneth might be splattered all over the road.

Her phone dinged. A text from Kenneth:

wut r u talking about Im home

Shit. Gabby would have sworn it was him.

Jeffcoat and Parker were passing her house. She turned up her hearing.

"—and tore it in half and dumped our asses on the street," Parker was saying. "Canebrake fired point-blank. No result. Kid didn't even take a step back."

McCreedy on the other end: "Casualties?"

Parker: "Only the Tahoe. But we've got civilian eyes on us. Request extraction."

Gabby turned down her hearing and sent another text:

looked exactly like u sorry still mumpsimus around here

Jamie and Christian sent the series of emojis that meant "on the way." How would they even get out of their houses? Maybe their parents didn't mind them being out a little late, given the holiday. Either way, she couldn't fly or run fast, and she couldn't very well try to leave after she had just talked Dad into staying inside. Her part in tonight's festivities had ended.

She sat on her bed in the dark, leaning on pillows propped against the headboard, and waited for word from her friends.

＊✳＊

When she and Micah got Gabby's 911 text, Christian left Bec and Micah alone in her room. "We're outta Coke," she had said. "I'll bike down to the Korner Mart and grab a two-liter." Mom had an early shift tomorrow morning, so she had already crashed, but with Bec around, Christian couldn't dig her duffel out of the closet and costume up. She would have to be extra careful.

She elected not to take a jacket. She could always get rid of her shirt if someone spotted her, but losing her jacket would bring down the Wrath of Mom. She was already trying to live down losing two bikes. It was cold outside—in the mid-forties, according to her phone—but she would just have to deal. At least her aura would protect her while she ran.

She trotted at normal speed into the side yard, where she edged against the neighbors' house, hopefully too deep in the darkness to be seen. Then she took a deep breath and zipped down the road. A rooster tail of fallen leaves and crud followed in her wake.

On Mississippi Street, half a dozen coat-wearing people had gathered around the wreckage of the SUV. Half of it lay in the middle of the street, the other in somebody's grass. It had been torn more or less down the middle. Christian ran into Gabby's yard and up the oak tree facing the street. A couple of the people glanced in her direction when the branches groaned and bounced, but the wreck took most of their attention.

"What in the hell could have done this?" asked one guy in a tan chore coat. His thick beard and the cowboy hat he wore low on his brow made him look like he'd just stepped off the set of an old western. "I'm pretty sure this used to be a Chevy."

"Oh, Lordy," said an older lady with dark hair as she pulled her puffer coat close. "It's come to our street."

"What has?" somebody asked.

"What happened over on Royal Del Ray," she said, sounding close to tears.

Christian's phone buzzed—thank God she had remembered to put it on vibrate—and she pulled it from her pocket. Another text from Kenneth:

still here havent left all night

He had attached a pic of himself sitting against his headboard, earbud cords snaking from the sides of his head and down his chest. He could have taken it at any time, but Christian couldn't think of a reason he'd lie. Relations within the group had been peaceful. Then, from Jamie:

looking for bats

Christian put the phone back in her pocket, took a deep breath, and climbed out of the tree. When she hit the ground, she zoomed away. The rising wail of sirens suggested somebody had called the cops. No sense hanging around.

She sped through the surrounding streets in a grid pattern, starting with Mississippi and expanding. Four blocks from Gabby's house,

Christian spotted Jeffcoat and Parker getting into a Suburban. The driver floored it, tires squealing, before Jeffcoat could close the door.

Shit. I can't follow them at this speed. They'd see me. And if I get on the roof, they'll hear.

Still, the Freaks needed to know what they were saying. She'd have to keep them in sight and focus her hearing on the SUV without being spotted. She tensed.

Then something in the sky angled toward the car. A human figure, clothes flapping in the wind. It slowed as it reached the SUV and hovered an inch or two above the roof. Jamie.

When the driver made a hard right, laying rubber on the road, Jamie swung wide, possibly visible to the passengers for a moment, but then he course-corrected. As they turned a corner, Christian considered her options. Then she took off, following at what she hoped was a safe distance. If Jamie needed help, she planned to be there.

✳✺✳

Mossman and Greenwalt had picked up Jeffcoat and Parker. Flying above the Team's Suburban, Jamie listened to them with growing unease.

"You're sure it was the Del Ray boy?" Mossman asked.

"What the hell are you even doing here, Manticore?" Parker asked. "You're a week removed from losing a fight to a bear."

"I'm fine," Mossman said.

"Sure he is," Greenwalt said. "That's why he looks so pale and sweaty. And why he's letting me drive."

"Enough about me, goddammit," Mossman said. "Was it the Del Ray kid or not?"

"Damn straight," Parker spat. "The little shit walked right up to us, smashed his hands into the engine block, and tore the whole car apart."

"I shot him in the chest," Jeffcoat said. "On instinct. He just smiled. Then he said he'd meet us in the park, unless we were cowards."

"There's only one problem," Greenwalt said. "Engineer?"

"Yes," said McCreedy, the sound of his voice suggesting he was on speaker. "Kenneth Del Ray hasn't left his house all night. I'm watching him on our monitors right now."

"What?" Parker said.

"So far, he's only threatened himself," McCreedy said. "With eye strain."

Silence for a few moments. The Suburban took a hard left, one hubcap popping loose and bouncing into a yard. An oncoming pickup slammed on its brakes and honked. The driver had probably spotted Jamie. Hopefully he hadn't had time to take any pics or videos. The less visible the Freaks could remain, the safer they would be.

"Well," Mossman finally said. "I guess that confirms we've got a shaper. But why would it take Del Ray's form? Does it know we're after those kids?"

The Suburban stopped at the entrance to the park. Greenwalt killed the lights. Jamie flew vertically twenty or thirty feet, still focusing his hearing on the cabin as he hovered in the branches of a pine. A northern wind brushed the tree limbs. A pinecone bopped him on the head. The Team members exited the vehicle, shut their doors, and met at the rear, where they took out some of those weird-looking comic-book weapons. The rifle types looked like the T-shirt cannons you saw at sporting events, only with high-powered scopes mounted on top and ancillary gadgets along the barrels.

Mossman got out of the vehicle, holding his bandaged stump against his chest, and pulled a weapon from inside his coat. Despite his injuries, the men seemed to be following his lead. Why? Had McCreedy named him second in command? Did he have seniority? Or did he just hate the Freaks and anything supernatural more than the rest of the Team?

"On me," Mossman said. He held a pistol that looked a lot like Han Solo's blaster. "We'll head for that pavilion. Remember that the shaper could be anywhere, looking like anyone or anything."

He led the others over the metal cable separating the parking area from the grounds. They walked in a diamond formation—Mossman in the lead, Greenwalt and Jeffcoat behind him and several feet apart, Parker in back. Greenwalt and Jeffcoat crabwalked sideways, heads on swivels.

That's a good way to step in a hole and break your ankle, Jamie thought. But they, and he, had bigger problems. Mossman and his friends seemed to think the shaper had been hunting Jeffcoat and Parker, but Jamie wondered about that. The bogey's actions felt like a series of probes. Had anybody on the Team thought of that? Or had their past experiences with straight-ahead threats like Na'ul blinded them to other possibilities?

As the men plunged deeper into the park, Jamie floated to the ground. Odd how things changed. As far as he knew, nothing more exciting than a birthday party had ever happened in this park until last year. Parents and kids still visited in daylight, and the QCHS track team trained on the concrete trail that circled the pond, but at night, anything might be lurking in the foliage, the waters. And when the lurker could shape-shift, how could you know what was real?

We need another code word we can use to identify each other, so we know it's really us, not the shaper. We—

Christian appeared next to him. "What's going on?"

Jamie cried out and nearly swung on her. "Jesus! Don't *do* that!"

"Sorry."

He took a second to catch his breath. "Okay. They just moved out. They got some of them special weapons. Hey, you ain't even costumed up. Maybe you should stay—"

From somewhere up ahead, something crashed, and Mossman and the others shouted. One of the Team's weapons blooped, and a purplish glow lit the woods.

"Cease fire!" Mossman shouted. "Everybody sound off!"

The Team yelled to each other. More flashes and weird noises. They had clearly not ceased fire. Jamie turned to Christian. "We should stick close. Should we use these charms?"

"Yeah," she said, eyeing the woods. "I'll follow you. If we get separated, meet me behind McDonald's. No way the shaper could know that plan."

"Okay," he said. "Stay safe. When we do this, remember to think of the Team, so we can still see each other."

"Got it."

They pulled out their charms, held them in their hands, and looked at each other. "One, two, three—"

They both said, "Evanescet." Jamie pictured the Team standing on their porch, suited up and posing with their guns like action heroes. Energy rippled around him and Christian. Then it dissipated.

Christian blinked. "Uh. Did it work?"

"I guess we'll find out."

He floated up and forward, parallel to the ground with his arms stretched out like Superman, heading toward the voices and the snaps and crackles of the Team's footfalls. Gradually, he rose into the lower levels of the tree limbs and increased his vision levels. The moon and the breaks in the canopy allowed enough light to show that only three of the Team remained. They stood back to back, weapons shouldered or, in Mossman's case, leveled at the forest. From the body types and the voices, Jamie felt pretty sure that Parker had vanished.

"Anything?" Mossman asked, his voice tense and strained.

"Nothing," Greenwalt said.

"Same," Jeffcoat said.

"Doberman, sound off," Mossman called.

No response.

Me and Christian will probably have to save his sorry ass, Jamie thought.

"Get out here and face us, you shaper piece of shit," Jeffcoat cried.

"Manticore," Greenwalt said as he swept the barrel of his weapon across the landscape. "We should fall back. Call in the others."

"No," Mossman said.

"A man's down, damn it," Greenwalt hissed. "Engineer needs to know."

"He gave me the com," Mossman said. "We don't leave without Doberman."

"We need backup," Greenwalt said. "We—"

A huge shape, even taller and wider than Na'ul, rose in front of Greenwalt, its body flowing like liquid even as it thrust out some kind of pseudopod and knocked the rifle from Greenwalt's hands. The FBI agent cried out in surprise, maybe pain, as Mossman and Jeffcoat fired. Jeffcoat's weapon burped out a gloopy blob that the shifter dodged, its body contorting. Jamie's mother had an old lava lamp she had bought at a flea market; the shaper's body looked like the junk in that lamp, amorphous and fluid. Another pseudopod flashed outward and struck Jeffcoat in the chest, knocking him onto his ass, even as Mossman fired his blaster. A laser lit the forest, sizzling through the shimmering body of the shaper and striking a tree. Bark exploded; the tree caught fire. The bogey lunged forward, enveloped Mossman like a bubble, and then vomited him out over Jeffcoat's head. He struck the ground and rolled to a stop against a tree.

Greenwalt held his hands up. "Easy. I'm unarmed."

The shaper chuckled as it blurred and morphed and shrank. When it solidified, Kenneth Del Ray stood face to face with Greenwalt as Mossman and Jeffcoat struggled to their feet. Greenwalt eased back until he stood near his friends. The shaper walked past a couple of trees and picked something up—Greenwalt's rifle. It took the gun's barrel and bent it over backward into a U-shape. If it still worked at all, which it probably wouldn't, it would shoot whoever fired it. Or maybe just explode. Like something from a cartoon.

Mossman recovered his pistol. With a shaking hand, he aimed it at the shaper.

"Do that," said the creature, "and I will tear your head from your body and beat your friends with it."

Mossman held his position for a moment. Then he lowered the gun. "Damn you."

"You sought children tonight. Instead, you found me. Do better against them, or you will find me again. One last time."

"Go to hell," Mossman spat. "You think we've forgotten how you broke out the Allen girl? How you did *this*?" He held up the stump of his missing hand.

"And you tore our car apart," Jeffcoat said. He sounded out of breath.

"You don't scare us," Mossman said.

The shaper laughed.

"Where's Doberman?" Jeffcoat rasped. He held one hand to his chest and breathed raggedly.

The shaper said nothing.

Jamie had been hovering in the trees, mesmerized, but he had to get off the sidelines. *Whatever that thing is, it ain't on our side. And at least the Team's human.* Before he could talk himself out of it, he flew toward the shaper at full speed.

He did not see the blow that sent him sailing backward through the air, past tall pines, and straight through a sapling. He hit the ground and skittered ass over teakettle for only God knew how far, coming to rest on his back with his ears ringing. Groaning, he turned down his senses—*Should have done that before I attacked, stupid stupid stupid*—and lay there, looking into the canopy. *Sorry, y'all. Reckon you're on your own.*

"What the hell was that?" Mossman cried. "It just knocked something out of the air!"

"Did *anybody* see?" Jeffcoat asked.

Well, at least we know the charms work, Jamie thought, head spinning. The ground was cold, maybe a little damp. Something with tickly legs jumped on his bare hand and back off again.

More cries and babbled words, and then a crackling sound filled the air, probably Christian running around at super-speed. Jeffcoat's weapon burped again, the muzzle flash bright green. More cries. Jamie tried to sit up. His head swam, so he lay back.

Then the scenery zipped by as strong arms cradled him. When the motion stopped, Christian set him on the park side of the metal cable, thirty or forty yards from the Team's Suburban. "Stay on this side of the tree, and they shouldn't be able to see you when they come back out," she said. From deeper in the park, more flashes and yelling. Something roared.

"They can't see me anyway," he muttered. "The charm worked. We've got another twenty or twenty-five minutes."

"Well, shit," she said, hands on her hips. "We should have hid ourselves from the bogey, too."

"Don't go back," Jamie said. "Everything out there wants to kill you."

She put a hand on his cheek. Her touch was cold. "You just risked your life for those turds. Don't ask me to do any less." And then she was gone.

Jamie scooted against the tree and closed his eyes. "I'll just stay here, then."

✶✳✶

When Christian found the Team again, they were facing each other, talking in low voices as if something might try to listen in. She saw no sign of the shaper—no Kenneth, no bear. No Parker, either. Why didn't they get the hell out of the park and look for Parker in the daylight?

You know why. No man left behind. If Jamie had disappeared, you'd scour every inch of this park.

"Look at this barrel," Greenwalt was saying, holding his ruined weapon. "That thing bent it like it was made of paper, but it didn't break."

"Forget the gun," Mossman growled, though his voice shook. "Doberman's the priority."

"Should we split up?" Jeffcoat asked, trying to see everywhere at once. "Cover more ground?"

"Hell, no," Greenwalt said.

"Well, what about those kids?" Jeffcoat asked. He held his strange scattergun at the ready.

"If we're lucky," Mossman said, "the shaper will eat them."

As the men debated which direction to go, Christian gritted her teeth. She would have loved to turn Mossman's face into spaghetti sauce. Still, she couldn't leave Parker to the shaper. She still had to live with herself. So, as the three government agents walked shoulder to shoulder toward the pond, she turned and ran perpendicular to their path, her vision enhanced so that she could see the darkened shapes in the park before she tripped over them or ran into a low-hanging branch. She ran all the way to the park's border, moved north ten or twelve feet, and headed back the way she had come, scanning the forest floor, hurdling obstacles and holes in the ground. As she began her fourth lap, she spotted something on a bench at the top of a small hill. She veered off and stopped beside the bench. The form lying on it was human—a man in a coat and slacks, his black shoes covered in dirt. He lay on his stomach, face pressed against the wooden slats. Blood dribbled from his right eye. His breathing was even but muffled, as if his nose had been broken. His left arm lay underneath him. The right hung over the side.

"Agent Parker, I presume," Christian muttered. "Sometimes known as Doberman. Looks like you lost this dogfight."

"Indeed," said a deep voice from behind her.

Christian whirled, ready to run or lay some smack down.

She was looking at herself. The same clothes, the same haircut, the same height and weight—everything but her voice. The other Christian moved to the far end of the bench. Its features shimmered, as if it were still perfecting her image. Christian stepped backward, then stopped herself. Her legs shook and her hands trembled, and her breathing had quickened, but she would be damned if she'd let the shaper know she was afraid. If it made a move, she would fight it as hard as she could, run if she had to, kill it if possible. But she would not cower.

"Does my hair really look like that?" she said as Parker snorted and shifted. He didn't wake up.

If her flippant comment bothered the shaper, it gave no sign. "Your friends threaten this land. This world. Yet I sense goodness in you. Loyalty and love."

"Stop. I'm blushing."

"I also sense in you the blood of the people who still tell my stories. Diluted and weak, mere drops in a vast river, but alive. I would not destroy you if I could help it."

Christian had no idea what the shaper meant. What people? What stories? "Well, thanks, I guess. But you're gonna find it harder to destroy us than you think."

The shaper indicated Parker. "I have known men like him. They speak from both sides of their mouths. Their guns and their hatred raze the earth and slaughter everything. You and your friends must end their threat before they end yours."

"Ah," she said, nodding. "So that's what's up. You want the Freaks and the Team to kill each other while you sit back and eat popcorn." On the bench, Parker stirred again, groaning.

The shaper smiled. "I have marked this man. He's mine. As for you, hear my words and know their truth. Your friends' existence puts the earth at hazard. Nor am I eager to let these government dogs run free on this ground I once loved, before the whites slaughtered and exiled my people, before they poisoned the very air and water and then raised their own children in that venom. You, however—just you—might find peace and long life. Join me."

Christian shrugged. "Dude, I don't know what the hell you're talking about."

The shaper stepped forward. Christian stood her ground. A hand that looked exactly like hers fell on her shoulder, heavy and thrumming with heat. "Look to the past. Then come to me. Help me save this world. Do that, and you will live long and long. Do it not, and I will tear the life from you and lay your corpse beside your dead friends."

Christian stepped away from that hand, so much heavier than it should have been. "I'll find you, all right. But like I said, you'll find it harder to drop Freak bodies than you think."

The shaper moved away. In the dark, Christian couldn't be sure, but she thought she saw sadness in its eyes.

Parker sat up, holding his head, groaning. "Oh, God. What happened?"

The shaper's body ran like water, spread over the forest floor, vanished. Christian could not locate it, even with her enhanced vision. She trotted several paces north and looked around, hoping to see a panther or a goat, anything she could chase, fight, kill. She found nothing but trees and ground.

Back on the bench, Parker moaned. "I'm over here," he said, trying to yell but not really succeeding, as if he was struggling to breathe.

Lowering her voice so that, hopefully, Parker couldn't tell she was a girl, Christian said, "Your bogey was just here. It—"

But Parker was still trying to alert the other Team members, like she hadn't spoken.

Yep, she thought. *The charms definitely work.* She considered revealing herself to Parker and trying to explain, but he probably wouldn't be in a mood to listen.

Christian sped to the parking area and found Jamie still sitting against the tree. He looked much better, his eyes clear and alert. He stood and brushed off the seat of his costume.

"How'd it go?" he asked.

"The shaper said some weird shit."

Jamie's eyes widened. "Jesus! Did you actually *talk* to it?"

The Team's voices and footsteps drifted out of the darkness. Looking in that direction, Christian said, "Yeah. It wants us all dead. The Freaks, the Team, God knows who else. Jamie, this thing is smart, and it's ruthless, and I'm pretty sure it's capable of doing exactly what it says."

They listened for a moment. The Team's voices grew closer. It sounded as if they had found Parker. Mossman was shouting at the top of his lungs, daring the shaper to face them.

Jamie scowled. "That guy's losing it. Sometimes I think we should take him off the board."

She narrowed her eyes. "What does that mean?"

For a moment, Jamie didn't answer. He stared, his eyes so intense they might as well have been giving off sparks. "Nothing," he said. "I'll swing by Kenneth's place, and if nobody's watching it, I'll make sure he's still there."

"Text me when you're home," she said. "You know the group needs to meet, right?"

"Yeah. When we do, bring your charm. I'll tell the others to bring theirs."

With that, he flew away. Christian waited a moment, watching him soar. When he passed out of sight, she ran home along the quickest route, still wondering what the shaper had meant.

CHAPTER TWENTY-ONE

After Christian had left for the store, Micah and Bec had decided to take a study break. They had turned on Christian's PlayStation and fired up *Destroy Hell*, a *Bloodborne*-type game in which you played as an angel tasked with breaking into Hell. You had to work your way up the demonic hierarchy until you supplanted the devil and brought the realm back under Heaven's control. Micah had always found the game only slightly above average—great gameplay and graphics, cool concept, poor story logic and muddy sound. Bec seemed to like it, though. They created a character in five minutes and launched into the first mission, which involved fighting your way through a hell gate in Tuscaloosa, Alabama. While Bec murked a ton of demons with the flaming sword the character brought from Heaven—like *that* wouldn't stick out in Alabama—Micah texted with Gabby, who hadn't heard from Jamie or Christian since the original message. Gabby reported that Kenneth hadn't left his house, not that Micah gave a shit what he did.

When the front door finally opened and Christian walked into the room, she looked paler than usual. Two spots of deep red stood out on her cheekbones. If Bec noticed, they would probably believe the bike ride had done it, but Micah knew better. Only extreme physical exertion affected Christian these days. No, this was something else, probably related to the Team or this so-called shaper. Christian said hello, though Bec barely acknowledged her. On screen, the flaming sword twirled and flashed. Christian took off her sneakers, sat on the edge of the bed, and fell back, expelling air as if she were exhausted. Micah stood and pretended to stretch, catching Christian's eye. She shook her head, looking serious, and mouthed the word "later."

"Get the Coke?" Micah asked, playing along.

"On the counter in yonder," Christian said. "It looks like I missed the end of the study session."

Bec grunted. "Sorry. Just got caught up in this."

"We got all week anyway," Micah said, sitting back down.

Bec and Micah played another hour. Christian didn't want a turn. She tapped away on her phone, probably with Jamie and the others. Micah's own phone was blowing up in his pocket, but he'd check it later. Bec might look over at exactly the wrong time and see something sensitive. And he didn't want to leave them alone with Christian. Maybe that was petty, but it was how he felt.

When the games ended, Micah and Bec had maybe twenty minutes to make curfew, so they said goodbye to Christian, who was still texting the others in the vague language they had used since the Team got up on their phones. Outside, the temperature had dropped a bit more. Bec stuck their hands deep in the pockets of their black jacket—was it leather or the fake stuff or what?—and shivered. Micah thought about trying to put an arm around them, but that seemed a bit much at this point. He had no idea if they liked him that way. How could you even tell? Did you just flat-out ask? Get one of your friends to ask? Send them a DM? Those tended to wind up on the Internet if you had misread the situation. Maybe he should just chill and wait for a clear sign. He—

Behind a tree between the yards, something rustled through fallen leaves.

Micah froze.

Bec was getting on their bike. Now they paused. "What's up?"

"Something behind that tree."

"Probably a dog or a cat, yeah?"

"Probably," Micah said. He had turned up his vision and hearing. Something human-shaped moved behind the trunk. A heartbeat thudded. Something breathed.

"Bruh," Bec began.

"You might as well come outta there," Micah called, turning his senses back down as a precaution. "We know you're there."

He didn't know what he had expected, but when Agent Chip Mossman stepped out from behind the tree, still wearing his stupid sunglasses in the dark, Micah almost fell over. There was no Team vehicle on the street. Mossman's suit looked impeccable but odd—fringey? Was that a word? Like perfectly tailored shag carpet. But that might have been a trick of the light, because when the agent got closer, the effect had disappeared.

"Who's this guy?" Bec said.

"Go on home," Micah said, trying to keep steel in his voice. "I'll text you."

Bec said nothing else, but he didn't hear them leave, either.

Mossman's face was expressionless. "Why send your friend away?" he asked, his voice a bit deeper than Micah remembered. "Are you afraid of being seen as you are?"

"What's he talking about?" Bec asked.

"Go home," Micah repeated, harsher this time. "You don't wanna be here for this."

"For *what*?"

"Don't," Micah hissed at Mossman. "They got nothing to do with this."

"Being here makes one part of it," Mossman said.

Why's he talking like that? Micah thought. *He don't sound like himself. He—*

Faster than Micah could follow, Mossman dashed forward and kicked him in the chest.

Micah flew backward, crashed into something, and landed on his back. His feet flew over his head as he somersaulted and came to rest in Christian's driveway, near Ms. Frey's car. He groaned, shook his head, pushed himself up on his elbows.

Bec lay on their face, body twisted, the bike sandwiched between their knees. They must have been what Micah struck when the shaper knocked him back. Beyond Bec's prone form, Mossman stood, arms at his sides. The streetlights winked in his sunglasses, giving the impression of pupils. Or maybe it was the moon. He stepped forward, laughing.

Micah raised both hands. Fire exploded from his right, ice from his left. Both beams struck Mossman, driving him back.

The government agent only grunted.

What the hell, what the hell, what the hell—

Ice caked Mossman's legs, freezing him to the spot. His upper chest and face had darkened, but he had not caught fire or suffered the kind of awful burns Micah had expected. And now he raised one fist and brought it down on the ice. It shattered, and he stepped out of the remnants. He smiled. Behind him, a couple of low-hanging limbs smoldered.

Micah scrambled to his feet and stood over Bec. "What the hell are you? You sure as shit ain't Mossman."

The Mossman-thing took another step forward. "What am I?" he asked. "Ask that question of yourself. Does your friend know of your powers, or do you lie, as you lie to the rest of the world?"

"You're the shaper."

The Mossman-thing looked puzzled. "Shaper?"

Micah clenched his fists, ready to pour on the juice. "Shape-shifter. Skin-changer. Whatever."

Now the shaper roared laughter. When it subsided, he considered Micah a moment. "I am much, much more than any skinwalker. And sooner or later, I will be your death. Yours, and all your friends'."

The front door burst open. Something zipped by Micah, the wind spattering grit into his eyes. While he wiped at them, Christian circled the shaper, or whatever it was, raining down punches with her good hand, driving it backward a step at a time. She blazed around it so fast that she reminded Micah of those old Tasmanian Devil cartoons. Her fist must have struck the shaper hundreds of times, thousands, each blow punctuated with a heavy *thwack*.

Within the whirlwind, the shaper laughed.

Still blinking hard, tears streaming down his face, Micah reached down, grabbed Bec's arms, and pulled them toward the house. "Christian, get outta there!"

The shaper moved almost as fast as Christian, and suddenly she was arcing over Micah's head, smashing into the house, crumpling to the ground. She tried to push herself up but only collapsed again. A trickle of blood ran from her nose. She wiped it away and brushed her hand in the grass, her eyes glassy. Even her aura had only done so much good.

"You son of a bitch!" Micah shouted. He dropped Bec, raised his right hand, and shot fire at the shaper. It sidestepped the blast, which headed straight for a car parked on the street. Micah gestured, and the flame vanished. Spots played over his eyes.

The shaper laughed again. "You discovered my trick, child, and sooner than I would have thought. But I have thousands, and all the time in existence. It has been far too long since I toyed with humans. But I will tire of it soon enough."

Micah stood in front of Bec and Christian, feet spread, hands raised in what he hoped approximated a boxing stance. *Note to self: Watch more MMA with Christian.* "Come on, then. Let's see how much ice I can stuff down your throat."

The Mossman-shaper took one step, but then a strong wind buffeted Micah, whipping more grit into his face. *Dammit, Christian, quit trying to freaking blind me while we're fighting a freaking monster.*

Christian stopped beside him, trembling. The handle of a butcher knife had grown out of the Mossman-shaper's chest. "Stay away from my friends," Christian said. "If you want me, come at me, but leave them out of it."

"Jesus *Christ*," Micah said, trying not to vomit.

The creature looked at the handle curiously. Then it pulled the knife out and dropped it. In the darkness, Micah couldn't be sure, but he didn't believe he had seen even a drop of blood.

"I cannot recall the last time I brooked such an attack without crushing my enemy," the thing said. "But I have already offered you time. I will not revoke so soon. For your sake, girl, not these others'. If I could only teach you to marry your bravery with the warrior's heritage I have detected, you could help preserve the true People and what remains of their world." It looked to the sky, where the waning moon shone down on them all. "But so faint is their song within you that I will not wait long. I will return soon. As inevitable as the sunrise. As certain as death."

Christian said nothing. Behind them, movement—Bec was stirring.

"Get outta here," Micah said to the shaper. "Or I'll burn you to ash."

The shaper fixed him with a cold, calculating stare. It snickered. Then its body shimmered, broke apart, fluttered, and became a swirling mass of flapping wings and screeching beaks: a flock of blackbirds, whirling like a tornado. It flew at Micah and the others, struck them with its many wings, banked upward, and soared into the night sky, where it eventually disappeared.

Micah turned to Christian. He was holding his arms out and looking down at his torso and legs. The birds had crapped all over him. He was covered in white shit.

Christian barked laughter. Then she shuddered, stumbled. Micah caught her and helped her to the front walk, where she sat and leaned against the house. Even in her dizziness, she saw that Micah had transferred some of the poop to her. She grimaced.

Bec grunted and sat up, holding their head. "Oh, shit. What happened?"

From inside, Ms. Frey was calling Christian's name. Micah dabbed most of the remaining blood from Christian's nose. Her eyes looked glassy. How hard had the shaper struck her? How strong was it? It had bloodied her even though it seemed to *like* her. What would it do to the rest of them?

Bec hobbled over as the front door opened. Ms. Frey came out and saw them sitting there dazed. "What happened?" she asked. "What's going on?" She bent, tilted Christian's chin upward, examined her. Bec sat next to her, knees drawn up, elbows resting on them, head hanging. Even Micah, whose aura had taken the brunt of the shaper's force, must have looked stunned. "I said, what happened? And what's that all over y'all? It stinks. Somebody better answer me."

Micah and Christian looked at each other. Things were happening so fast it was hard for him to come up with a believable lie. "Um," he said.

"Um, what?" Ms. Frey said, hands on her hips.

"We got mugged," Bec muttered.

Ms. Frey's mouth fell open. "Mugged? Are you okay?"

Christian glanced at Micah again. "Yeah. Just shaken up. Don't freak out, Mom."

"You tell me you got mugged in our own front yard, and you want me to be cool? And what the hell does a mugging have to do with that crud all over Micah? If I didn't know better, I'd swear it was bird shit."

"I don't even know if 'mugged' is the right word," Christian said. "It all happened so fast."

"I guess I stood under the wrong tree," Micah added. He worked hard to keep his expression neutral, his voice even, but inside, he felt like a volcano ready to erupt. Since getting his powers, he had never been this furious without blasting something. Bec could have been killed.

"Damn it, somebody talk to me," Ms. Frey said.

Micah cleared his throat. "Me and Bec were leaving when this guy came out from behind a tree. He knocked us both silly, but I don't think he even stole anything. It was weird. Maybe he was tweaking?"

Ms. Frey looked unconvinced. She turned to Christian and Bec. "Is that right? Some man jumped you and then just … disappeared? And then Micah stood under a tree and somehow almost got buried in bird poo?"

Bec rubbed the back of their neck and grimaced. "I remember Micah getting between me and that dude. Then I woke up on the ground."

Ms. Frey narrowed her eyes. "What did he look like?"

"Old white guy," Micah said. Christian nodded.

"Okay," Ms. Frey said. "Bec?"

"I didn't get a clear look, Ms. Allen," they said. "But yeah, pretty sure he was a white dude."

"Posey," Christian and her mom said at the same time.

"Oh, sorry," Bec said. "Ms. Posey."

"Nah, the kids all call me Ms. Frey."

"Uh … okay." Bec looked confused.

Ms. Frey patted them on the shoulder. "What was this white dude wearing, hon?"

"Sunglasses and a suit."

Ms. Frey folded her arms across her chest. "Sunglasses at night. A mugger in a suit."

Bec looked her in the face. "That's what I saw."

"He *was* wearing some kind of coat and a tie," Micah offered. "I don't know if it was the kind of jacket you wear with a suit or just a regular one, though."

"I think it was a windbreaker," Christian said. "Maybe black or navy blue. Could have been dark denim."

Ms. Frey studied them. "I ran off and left my phone inside. I'm going in and calling the cops. Then I'll look y'all over myself. Unless somebody needs an ambulance?"

"I'm okay," Micah said. Bec said nothing, but they nodded and leaned against Micah, despite the poo. Their touch felt electric.

"Mom, please just chill," Christian said. "We—"

"I. Am. Calling. The *cops*," Ms. Frey said. She went back inside, leaving the door open. Her voice floated through the screen. "And y'all's parents."

Micah made a disgusted sound. "Great. Well, I hope she at least remembers to tell Baltar to bring me some clean clothes."

Five minutes later, a cop car braked in the street, lights flashing. Officers Gillan and Heck got out. For some godawful reason, Gillan had grown a pornstache since last year. Micah recognized him because the bridge of his nose was dented, its tip smashed to the right. The Freaks had spent a good deal of time speculating on what had happened to it, but none of the kids or parents seemed to know. Heck's hair had been slicked back, as usual. You could see that even with his hat on.

They split up Micah, Bec, and Christian and interviewed them separately. Basic questions not unlike what Ms. Frey had asked: Who's hurt? Who remembers what? A few minutes later, Bec's father showed up in a dark-gray Honda Civic. He unfolded himself from the driver's seat and strode through the yard. Everyone stopped to look at him. He must have been six and a half feet tall and as thick as a defensive tackle, with olive skin and a goatee as pepper black as his lustrous hair. How the hell did he even fit in that car? Mr. Villalobos introduced himself to Heck—his first name was Vicente, Vin to his friends—shook hands, and walked over to Bec. He put an arm around them. They leaned into him, still looking at the ground. Were they scared, or mad, or confused, or all three, or something else altogether? Would they ever hang out with the Freaks again? *Should* they?

Baltar Sterne drove up in Micah's mother's car fifteen minutes after Ms. Frey called him, his shaved head shining in the moonlight. He wore a black peacoat, black slacks, and black dress shoes. He carried a paper sack. After briefly speaking with the cops, he handed Micah the bag. "A change of clothes. The officers say we can go. Are you all right?"

Micah shrugged. "Got knocked around a little. No biggie."

Baltar nodded toward the tree. "The assailant came from there?"

"Yeah."

Baltar walked over and squatted down, ran his hands along the ground, stood and examined the trunk.

What a weirdo. Who does he think he is, Sherlock Holmes? Batman?

Micah went inside and changed in the bathroom, stuffing his dirty clothes in the sack. The cops were talking to Christian and Ms. Frey in the kitchen. Christian was giving the same answers. Micah walked past them and through the front door. Bec and their father were heading for the Civic. Baltar waited beside Mom's car.

The screen door banged open. Christian ran out at normal speed and caught Bec, who pulled away from their father. Christian hugged Bec and whispered something; they nodded and rejoined their dad. As Christian headed back, she caught Micah's eye and shook her head.

Micah turned to Bec, who glanced back over their shoulder and lifted their chin. He waved and mouthed the word *sorry*.

As he and Baltar got in their car, Police Chief Mark O'Brien arrived in his personal ride, some kind of cherry-red muscle job. He stopped and considered Micah and Baltar.

"Hi," Micah said.

"Hello, Micah," he said. "Mr. Sterne."

"Call me Baltar." Micah's great-uncle didn't smile, though his voice sounded warm.

O'Brien strode past them and into the house.

"Let's go," Micah said.

Baltar raised an eyebrow again. "You don't want to listen in?"

"I already know what Christian's saying. Let's just hit it. Hey, where's your Lexus?"

Baltar started the car. "I thought it prudent to leave it at home, given that the police and your government friends have likely marked it as a suspicious vehicle. I have recently protected it from their perceptions, but I couldn't exactly appear out of thin air."

Micah understood, but he didn't like it. Nobody should drive Mom's car but him, or maybe Dad. Yet he said nothing. Baltar had shown up. That counted for something. "Can we swing by Mickey D's? I'm starving."

"Certainly," said Baltar as he maneuvered around the police car.

Half a dozen folks stood on their porches or walks, huddled inside their coats, watching. "Look at those dumbasses freezing their nuts off."

"I noticed your new friend embraced Christian."

Micah's cheeks burned. "So what?"

Baltar shrugged, his voice as pleasant as ever. "Just an observation. Don't worry. You are young. You will find and forget plenty of loves before you settle down."

Micah turned in his seat and glared at the old man. "Okay, first of all, Bec ain't my *love*. Second, they're Christian's friend, too, and we just went through something. That's all that hug meant."

Baltar held up a hand. "Fine, fine. As I said, it was just an observation."

"Third, it's none of your business."

"If you say so."

Micah settled back into his seat. They rode the rest of the way to McDonald's in silence. Baltar ordered Micah a McNuggets combo meal with a Dr Pepper. On the way home, Micah munched French fries from the bag.

"Good shit," Micah muttered to himself.

"By the way, I found fur at Christian's house," Baltar said. "Both in the yard and stuck in the tree bark. Soon, I'll know the nature of the being that hunts you."

"Fire," Micah said, his mouth full. He didn't know what else to say. It was still weird talking Freaks business with a grown-up.

Baltar fell silent. Shadows and streetlight ran over his face like liquid. But what had he meant with that stuff about Christian and Bec? Had Christian made a move? Had Bec reciprocated?

I'm a freaking idiot. I waited too long with Gabby. Maybe I've waited too long with Bec.

There was also the shaper to consider. It had targeted him, as if losing his mother to a giant vampire wasn't enough for one kid. Micah still saw that night in his worst dreams—Na'ul grabbing his mother's torso and legs, ripping her apart, eating her spilled organs and blood. Those images would be burned into his brain if he lived to be a hundred. Now some other monster wanted to kill everybody Micah cared about. Well, not if he could help it.

I'll protect them, Mom. I won't just stand there and watch anybody else die. So help me, when I see anything supernatural, I'll burn the meat off its godforsaken bones.

He leaned his head against the cold glass, fogging it with his breath. Streetlights passed by. The tires hummed. The Escort's heater toasted the inside of the car. Micah fell asleep before they could reach home.

CHAPTER TWENTY-TWO

Gabby parked behind Jamie's parents' Camry and the charcoal Nissan Sentra they'd had for only about six months. Mrs. Entmann's old car had died when they were in eighth grade, but that was the year Jamie had wrecked his bike and needed surgery on his arm, so hospital bills had come first. It was good to see that space in their driveway filled again.

Despite what had apparently been a crazy night—Christian, Micah, and Bec "mugged" in Christian's front yard—Gabby had left home this morning without a government tail. Two Team vehicles were sitting on Jamie's place, though. Strangely, the Team members stood on the street, hands in their pockets or clamped to their phones, while Chief O'Brien and Officer Ralph Snead leaned against a police car, watching them with obvious displeasure. As Gabby closed her door, the curtains in the Entmanns' front window parted. Jamie and Mr. Entmann looked out at the commotion. They seemed pissed. Gabby didn't blame them. Why were the local cops here? Just to watch? To make sure the Team didn't snatch Jamie?

Huh. I wonder if the chief knows what the feds did to Christian.

Gabby glanced up and down the street. How many neighbors were peeking between their own curtains or blinds? Some of them might be spreading this story all over town, even if they didn't know the plot.

Mossman, Greenwalt, Vincent, and Kragthorpe watched her. Mossman gestured at her, or maybe he was pointing at the house. She could have enhanced her hearing, but she didn't really care what Mossman had to say. Chief O'Brien caught her eye and motioned for her to go in. And why not? If the feds wanted her, they could knock on the door like decent folks.

Jamie ushered her in and slammed the door, muttering under his breath. Mr. Entmann stood at the window, his brow wrinkled. The gray sprinkled at his temples seemed to stand out in greater relief today. Given the mess last year, he had probably started to wonder how his son might be involved in all the weird shit around here, no matter how much he trusted Jamie.

"Why's your dad home?" she whispered.

"He took a personal day," Jamie said. "It's like he smelled this coming."

Thom Entmann turned to them. "Why are all them white folks with guns having a damn parade on our street? They gonna come up in here and try to tell me you jumped your own friends last night?"

Gabby tried to keep her expression neutral, but she had always had a lousy poker face. Micah had once suggested that if their lives ever depended on Gabby lying to somebody in authority, they might as well stick their own heads in the guillotine. Just something else everyone knew she couldn't do. And how much better would Jamie be? He loved his parents with the kind of fierce, unquestioning affection other kids envied. Of them all, he probably concealed the least from his folks.

"I don't know," Jamie said, which, Gabby knew, was mostly true. Unless Jamie had listened to the feds' conversation, he couldn't know. They probably wouldn't have to wait long to find out, though.

As if on cue, Mr. Entmann grunted. "Here they come."

Moments later, someone knocked three times.

Jamie squeezed Gabby's arm. "It's cool. We didn't do nothing. We weren't even there."

"I know," Gabby said with more confidence than she felt. Jamie had left his house last night, though he hadn't gone anywhere near Christian's place. Had he used his charm, and if not, had he done enough to fool the feds' cameras and bugs? What if they tried to yank him out of the house, cuff him, stuff him in one of those SUVs? *They could take him someplace besides the farmhouse. Somewhere we'd never find him.*

But Gabby knew the Freaks wouldn't let that happen. Not after what had happened to Christian. Even if it meant exposure, life on the run, they would fight. And if it came to that, God help the Team. She would force-blast them to hell before she let them hurt her friends again.

Mr. Entmann opened the door. Chief O'Brien's voice: "Morning, Thom."

"Chief."

"Mind if we come in? These fellas need to talk to Jamie and Gabriella."

Mr. Entmann probably wanted to slam that door in their faces. Given what had happened in America since … well, since before it was even America, she could imagine, at a purely intellectual level, what Mr. Entmann must have felt when a white cop and four government agents showed up at his door and asked to see his son. He probably wondered whether he or Mrs. Entmann or Jamie might end the day on a slab, whether his lessons on how to be Black in the presence of police had been thorough enough, whether even the most deferential behavior would save lives. Plus, as far as he knew, his son had done nothing to deserve this show of authority and force. Would anything change if he knew what Jamie and the other Freaks had become? Or would he be relieved, knowing his son stood a better chance of surviving this country, this world?

"What's this about?" Mr. Entmann asked. Amazing. He sounded so calm. Gabby supposed it came from a lifetime of practice.

"Nobody's in trouble," O'Brien said. "You might have heard about what happened to Jamie's friends last night. We just want to see if him or Gabby knows anything that might help. Might be something they don't even know they know."

"That shit had nothing to do with my boy. And if you knew Gabby, you wouldn't even ask about her. She's a good girl."

Gabby's heart hurt a little. Mr. Entmann had such conviction. What had she ever done to deserve that kind of faith?

"It won't take but a minute," O'Brien said.

Mr. Entmann stood there, impassive, looking over the men Gabby couldn't see. She could imagine what they looked like, though: Stony faces, eyes hidden behind those mirrored sunglasses they all seemed to love, arms crossed or hands in their pockets, their service weapons—not the special ones but the plain old handguns—bulging under their coats.

"They'll come to you," Mr. Entmann said. "I don't want y'all in my house."

Now he did shut the door, keeping his hand on the knob a moment, eyes closed, head bowed. Maybe he was praying. When he looked at Gabby and Jamie, his eyes blazed with fury. Like he could have eaten steel for breakfast.

"It's cool, Dad," Jamie said. "It's like you told 'em. We didn't do nothing, and we don't know nothing."

"Y'all be real, real careful," Mr. Entmann said. "Men like them don't need much of a reason to do what they already know they wanna do. Sometimes no reason's enough. Be polite. Keep your hands in plain view. Eyes on the ground. If they make a move toward you, hold your hands in the air and start yelling. Say you ain't resisting and please don't shoot. Especially you, Jamie. You hear?"

"Yes, sir," Jamie said. He looked sick, even scared—probably not for himself but for his father, who had lived a life of decency and kindness and had now seen doom knock on his door, wearing a badge.

"Yes, sir," Gabby said. Her stomach flip-flopped like it always did when she went to Magic Springs and the roller coaster took that first plunge.

"I'll be coming out, too," Mr. Entmann said. "Gabby, you want me to call your parents?"

Her folks would be at work, and at this stage, she didn't want to worry them. "No, sir," Gabby said. "I ain't scared." That was a lie, but she didn't know what else to say.

"All right," said Mr. Entmann. "But if it looks like they're really leaning on you, I'm calling your momma."

"Yes, sir."

With that, Mr. Entmann took a deep breath, exhaled, and opened the door.

The whole scene lasted only minutes, but to Gabby, it felt like an hour. Mossman and Vincent corralled Jamie near the cars, with Mr. Entmann standing next to his son. Officer Snead stayed close. Jamie stared at Mossman's shoes, answered quietly, and kept his body language benign, even when Mossman glowered and postured. Mr. Entmann's voice, louder than the feds' or Jamie's, carried over a couple of times, usually something like, "He already answered that."

As for Gabby's interview, Greenwalt and Kragthorpe took her all the way across the yard. Chief O'Brien said something to Mr. Entmann and joined them. Jamie's dad watched carefully, phone in hand. O'Brien stood beside Gabby, facing the feds as if he were her lawyer.

"I want to reiterate what the Chief told Mr. Entmann," Greenwalt said. His voice was surprisingly kind. "You're not in trouble. We know you weren't at the Allen house last night."

"So what can I tell you?" Gabby asked. Then she looked away. Mr. Entmann had told her to chill, and chilling was certainly her first instinct, but she had already interjected.

"We want to make sure that this incident—mugging, assault, what-ever its precise nature—that this incident isn't related to any sort of terrorist threat. After what happened last year, we don't want to rule it out yet. And as an FBI agent, I'd like to compare these events to similar occurrences in other states. Maybe there's a pattern. Can you tell us anything else about what happened last night? Anything your friends might have said to you?"

Like you don't know what our friends have said. You're up on our phones and social media. You were watching my room, *for God's sake, until Baltar worked his magic. And an interstate pattern? Please. I was born at night, but not* last *night.*

"Not really," she said, looking Greenwalt in the face just long enough to seem sincere. She hoped. After what Kragthorpe had done to Christian, Gabby couldn't meet his gaze. Even standing in his presence brought back that roller-coaster feeling. "Christian DMed me and told me the basics. I haven't talked to Micah or the new kid yet."

"And what did Christian say?"

"That they got jumped outside her house. That they were mostly okay. Y'all got any leads?"

"We can't comment on an active investigation," Kragthorpe said. His Southern California accent made it sound like a joke.

"Then what did you come over here for?" Gabby snapped. She had to stop herself from clapping a hand over her mouth like a little kid who just cursed in front of her mother. Her face burned. Even her ears felt hot.

"Gabriella," Chief O'Brien said, his voice quiet but firm.

"Sorry," she muttered, staring at the ground. God, what the hell was wrong with her? She acted like a mouse when she needed to step up and like a wolverine when she should have been cool.

"That's okay," Greenwalt said. He moved a few inches to the side until he partially stood between her and Kragthorpe. "You've been through a lot, and I'm sure you're worried about your friends."

"Yeah," she said, hoping she sounded demure enough.

"Moving on. Have you seen anything out of the ordinary lately? Strangers in town, especially in your neighborhood or around your friends' houses?"

"No, sir."

"Any cars that don't belong?"

"Only y'all's," she said.

Kragthorpe laughed and shook his head. Greenwalt's expression didn't change. "Do you have any idea who might want to hurt your friends? Or why?"

The words *only y'all* came to mind again, but this time she kept them inside. And she couldn't exactly mention the shaper. "No, sir."

Greenwalt turned to Kragthorpe, who shrugged. "All right," Greenwalt said. He took a business card out of his inside coat pocket. "If you think of anything, anything at all, call that number. Day or night. In the meantime, be careful. Somebody who'd attack three teenagers at once won't hesitate to come after a lone girl."

She had to hold in her own sardonic laughter. Who did this guy think he was fooling? If the shaper ate her for supper and shat out her bones on Main Street, the feds would probably throw a party.

"Is that it?" O'Brien asked. He had stood shoulder to shoulder with Gabby the whole time, hands clasped at his waist. He had asked no questions and taken no notes, but his bright and lively eyes seemed to see everything, right down to Kragthorpe's microaggressions.

"That's all for now," Kragthorpe said. She couldn't see his eyes behind those glasses, but she had an idea he was staring right through her. Maybe sizing up her weaknesses for the day when they would kidnap her. Torture her. Kill her.

"Gabby, why don't you go back inside?" O'Brien said.

"Yes, sir," she said. She turned and walked back to the house, and the Chief headed back to the Entmanns, Officer Snead, and the other agents.

"Hang on," Greenwalt called. He caught up to her a few feet from the door and leaned in close. "If you know anything, you should tell me. I can help."

She glared at him. "Like somebody helped Christian? And her fingers?"

Greenwalt grimaced. "I wish that hadn't happened. But don't let your anger cloud your judgment. If you can help me find and destroy this shaper, everybody wins."

Gabby considered a moment. Then she lifted her chin in the

direction of the other agents. "I don't know what a shaper is. But Christian said *he* was the one who jumped her."

Greenwalt followed her gaze. "Him? Which one?"

"Your partner. Agent Mossman."

Greenwalt's mouth fell open. He shut it again quickly, but she had seen it. "He was accounted for all night."

"Yeah," she said. "I guess I shouldn't accuse people without proof."

She left Greenwalt standing there. Once she had closed the door, she turned up her hearing.

"Well," Kragthorpe was saying. "If I had known you'd only pitch softballs, I'd have brought my glove." God, Gabby hated that CIA piece of garbage.

"I know you and Manticore like to conveniently forget this, but she's an American teenager, and without a parent or guardian present," Greenwalt said. "Besides, we know she wasn't at Allen's place."

"Doesn't mean she wasn't involved. Or that she's as ignorant as she claims. Next time, we do it my way."

"That's up to Engineer."

"No shit."

The men fell silent. Maybe they were watching Jamie's interview. Gabby thought about listening in to that, too, but she figured Jamie would tell her about it anyway, so she returned to normal levels and sat on the couch.

After perhaps five more minutes, the Entmanns came inside. Mr. Entmann walked straight to the kitchen and puttered around, clanging pots or pans. Gabby checked her phone. It was almost lunchtime. Her stomach rumbled. "How was it?" she whispered.

"Okay," Jamie said. "I just told 'em what I know, which is nothing." He glanced at the smoke detector, where the Team had planted a camera and a bug. It had been a long time since they could talk freely in their own houses. Baltar had taken care of that much, at least.

"Me, too," she said.

"Dad's making grilled cheese," Jamie said. "Hungry?"

"Sure."

At the table in the dining area, Jamie took out his phone. After a moment, Gabby's dinged. Jamie had sent a group text:

Mumpsimus neck

"Neck" represented a new code word: "wear your necklace," the sensory charms.

Gabby put her phone away and waited for her sandwich.

CHAPTER TWENTY-THREE

Christian met the other Freaks on the walk near their pavilion. The wind had blown piles of leaves and dirt onto the slab. Several newly downed limbs lay around the grounds. The wedge of pond visible from this area was spread open like a fan, and a cold wind stirred the water. Gabby zipped her coat and stuffed her hands deep into its pockets. Jamie put his arm around her and pulled her close, wrapping that side of his brown fleece coat around her. Micah wore only a blue short-sleeved T-shirt. Christian supposed they should be grateful he hadn't completed the outfit with shorts and a sign that said *I'm the Fire and Ice Freak! Ask Me about My Powers.* That piercing wind kept blowing, and Christian kept thanking all the gods that ever were that she hadn't been born in North Dakota, or Canada, or some village on the shore of the Arctic sea.

As they waited for Kenneth, and everyone but Micah shivered, Christian kept thinking of last night's attacks. The shaper had stepped things up, but she didn't understand its motivations. First, it had lured her to this very spot, apparently intending to kill her, but then it had saved her from the Team. Not long after that, it had assaulted her again. What did it want from her? Plus, she still didn't know what it had been talking about. They needed to know more about the shaper's nature: what it was, where it came from, what it wanted, what it might do to further its goals. But so far, they were flying in the dark.

Kenneth finally rounded the bend, jogging alongside Brayden in school-logo sweats. Brayden had chosen a white headband, like something Christian had once seen in pictures of a 1970s tennis player. Micah laughed out loud. Jamie elbowed him. Kenneth and Brayden stopped beside the others, breathing hard. Brayden bent over and put his hands on his knees.

"Seriously?" Micah said.

"What?" snapped Kenneth, shooting Micah a go-to-hell look.

"Never mind him," Jamie said. "You bring your charm?"

"Yeah," Kenneth said, still panting. "But he ain't got one."

"Well, what the hell did you bring him for?" Micah asked. "Baltar hasn't whammied this pavilion yet."

"I had to tell my parents we were running the park to stay in shape, in case I decided I wanted to go back to football," Kenneth said. "And I always jog with Brayden. If you got a problem with that, step to me."

"Quit it, both of you," Christian barked. She had gotten sick of their posturing a long time ago. Micah looked like he wanted to bash her head in. He had been getting more hostile over the last couple of weeks; she didn't know why, but this wasn't the time or place to figure it out. She turned to Kenneth. "If we'd known you were bringing him, we could have at least asked Baltar for another charm. Seems like he got 'em wholesale. Or we could have met somewhere else."

Kenneth shrugged.

Jamie rubbed his eyes. "We were gonna sit under the pavilion and let the charms keep us safe. But screw it. Let's just walk. They can't have the whole damn park bugged."

"Whatever," Kenneth said.

Those with bikes retrieved them and walked them along, Jamie and Gabby side by side, Micah next to Christian, Kenneth and Brayden following. Everyone raised their voices just enough to be heard over the wind.

"Okay," Jamie said. "Last night, two feds sitting on Gabby's house had their car ripped out from under 'em. Literally. Whatever did it looked like Kenneth."

"But it wasn't me," Kenneth wheezed, still trying to catch his breath.

"We *know*," Gabby said. "The shaper did it. Even the Team knows that."

"I'm just saying," Kenneth muttered.

"Anyway," Jamie said, "when we followed the Team out here, the shaper talked to Christian."

Micah grunted. "No shit?"

Christian told the story of how Jamie got knocked silly, what happened to Parker, what the shaper had said. "I thought it was over, but then Micah got jumped."

Here Micah took up the story, from when he and Bec closed Christian's front door to the moment he stepped into his mother's Escort with Baltar. "We need to watch Bec," he said. "Maybe even bring 'em into the group."

Kenneth laughed. "Sure. Then we can build a website and tell the rest of the world."

Micah turned on Kenneth. They almost collided. "This ain't funny, you dick. They could have got killed. Besides, we put up with this little dog that follows you everywhere."

Brayden looked around, as if trying to spot the dog. Then he realized what Micah was saying. "Hey!"

"Jamie said to quit all this macho bullshit," Christian said. "If you don't, I'll carry one of you to the top of the tallest tree in Quapaw City and hang you by your underwear. Then I'll leave the other one naked on Main Street."

"You wouldn't," Micah said.

"Freaking try me."

Micah and Kenneth stared each other down. Once, Micah's fronting would have been laughable. Kenneth could have picked him up and tied him in a knot. Now, a fight might kill them both, and God only knew who else.

"Yo," Jamie said, sounding weary. "First one to throw a punch gets an ass-kicking from the rest of us. I ain't even playing."

"We ain't just high-school kids anymore," Gabby added. "Grow up."

"Just keep this gorilla outta my face," Micah muttered, turning away.

Kenneth laughed but held up his hands and backed off.

"We *do* need to keep an eye on Bec," Gabby said. "We got them into this."

Micah stared into the woods. His jawline seemed a little stronger, his shirt and jeans a bit snugger. Was he exercising more? Had his powers done something to his body? Christian's own waistline had shrunk by a couple of inches over the last year. Her muscles had grown more defined. She had assumed it was part of her natural development, the kind of thing that happened to any active teenager, especially one who had run so much last year. Now, studying her friends, she realized that all of them had changed in subtle ways: Jamie a tad more muscular, Gabby not quite as soft around the joints, Kenneth a little thicker in the shoulders. All that might have been fine, but as the shaper stepped up its assaults, as the Team grew more aggressive, as their own bodies molded themselves into sharper weapons, Micah's and Kenneth's feud was heating back up. Or maybe it had never cooled down. Maybe, in the absence of regular contact with each other, they had just gotten better at camouflaging it.

Christian flexed her left hand. The fingers Kragthorpe had zapped with that doohickey still felt numb, but now they twitched a bit, probably thanks to the healing factor the Freaks had gotten as a bonus power. Anybody else would have carried those dead fingers for the rest of their life.

"Let's get back to business," Jamie was saying. "I say we stick together like we used to."

Gabby nodded. "Splitting up didn't keep the feds off our asses. So why bother?"

"About damn time y'all figured that out," Micah said. "Let's bring that stupid farmhouse down on their heads."

"I'm down with that," Kenneth said. "We can't let 'em jump us and get away with it."

That stunned Christian. A minute ago, Kenneth and Micah had almost thrown down. Now they agreed on something. You could get mental whiplash trying to keep up with them.

"Hang on, y'all," Jamie said, holding one hand up. "We can't start killing people."

Micah scoffed. "Why not? They'd kill us in two seconds if they could."

The mood fell back into awkward discomfort, like that time last year, before they got their powers, when Micah had suggested using his father's rifle on Kenneth, Brayden, and Gavin.

"Dude," Gabby said.

"Oh, for God's sake," Micah said, turning toward the woods again. Then he started. "Hey. Check it."

Everyone followed his gaze. Christian gasped.

This is bad. Not just because they're here. Because we missed them.

Scattered throughout the woods surrounding the sidewalk, among the trees and stretching back into the park, hundreds of rabbits were watching them. Maybe thousands. Black, brown, spotted, reddish. Most fully grown, some barely older than kits. They watched the Freaks, their eyes wide, their mouths working as if chewing or talking to each other. Short ears and long ones twitched at every sound.

"Y'all," Kenneth said, "let's get the hell outta here. Like now."

"Yeah," Jamie muttered. "Yeah. Let's book."

Those with bikes saddled up. Those without jogged. And though she had to keep her eye on the ground in front of her, Christian spent much of that retreat watching the rabbits, which lined the sidewalk until the Freaks left it and headed for the street.

Once they had gotten out of the park, Gabby looked down at her sensory charm. "We didn't even use these stupid things." She tucked it into her shirt.

✳✳✳

Micah got home after dark and left his bike in the front yard. He couldn't fricking wait until he could drive. Once, bike riding had seemed like the coolest thing ever, like freedom itself. Now it felt like a little kid's activity, or a douche-jock-look-at-me-I'm-so-in-shape flex.

Leaves scraped over each other with a sound like bugs skittering on wood as the wind picked up. It struck the house and swirled around it, moaning. Tree limbs bobbed and scratched against windows. Through the living room curtains, a muted glow pulsed, probably the TV, though Micah had never seen Baltar watch it. Maybe the old man liked the light, or maybe it was just the closest thing the Sternes had to a fireplace. Gather round and warm yourself before Netflix. Throw another log on the Wi-Fi router.

Half expecting Baltar to throw open the door and command him to enter, Micah hesitated. Ever since his mom's death—and especially after his weird-ass great uncle had shown up—he hadn't felt at home here. Everything felt familiar except his own life, like he was a TV character who had been recast between seasons. Maybe Baltar's presence had rearranged the house without actually moving anything. Like if you put a tombstone in front of your math class whiteboard. Or like that poem they had read in English a couple of weeks back, the one about the jar on some hill in Tennessee.

He sat on the porch, letting the wind play over his bare arms. His nerves acknowledged the cold wood and the breeze, but he understood temperature only intellectually. He could have fallen into a frozen river or a blast furnace and come out fine. Was that how fatigue felt to Christian? He'd have to ask her. It was something he couldn't talk about with anyone else.

So was Bec Villalobos.

When Bec and Micah sat near each other, Bec seemed to make a point of keeping at least a foot of space between them, but at the same time, hadn't he felt a spark when they accidentally touched, when they talked closely while everyone else jabbered or went to the kitchen for a snack, when their gazes lingered one or two seconds longer than strictly necessary? A fluttering in the stomach and below the waist, a quickening of the heartbeat, a not entirely unpleasant feeling of extra weight on the chest? Micah had felt all that, and Bec must have experienced *something*. If they hadn't, why those lingering looks, the cleared throats and flushed cheeks?

But he had also seen Bec and Christian together. Maybe Bec was playing him, or Christian, or both. God knew Micah had no experience with this stuff. But Bec didn't strike him as the kind of person who would jerk around two people, maybe even permanently fracture a friendship. Maybe they just didn't know what, or whom, they wanted.

The front door creaked open, the screen squealing on its old and rusty hinges. Micah didn't turn. It could only be Baltar, given that Dad was supposed to be somewhere near St. Louis right now, and Mom … well, Micah didn't like to think about Mom. He hadn't visited her grave in months.

Baltar said nothing. *What, is he waiting for me to break down and cry on his shoulder or show him my journal or something?* Somebody's mixed-breed dog wandered into the yard, sniffed around a tree, dropped its haunches, pissed, continued across the grass with its nose to the ground. The neighbors' houses were covered in shadows and set behind teeth-like hedges, some trimmed, some not. A plastic kiddie pool sat in the McKluskeys' grass across the way and several houses down. Micah didn't really know the family, but he had seen a toddler playing in that pool, a little boy with blond hair and pudgy legs. Such a boring-ass street, at least when blue vampires weren't tearing your parents to pieces. Baltar didn't fit in here. It wasn't his height or his shaved head. Anybody could look like that. It wasn't even his all-black wardrobe or how he looked so much younger than his age. No, something about the guy just seemed off, alien even. Like in that movie Gabby had made them watch last year, *The Thing*. Baltar could have been one of the characters the alien replaced. He looked like a person and sounded like a person and mostly acted like a person, but something felt wrong, like he only pretended to be Baltar Sterne but was, in fact, something that might rip out your heart.

"Coming inside?" the old man finally asked.

Huh. The silence between them had seemed like a contest. Micah hadn't expected Baltar to give in. "In a minute," Micah said, which meant *when I feel like it*. He wanted to be alone.

"But it's so warm and bright in the house," Baltar said. "Safe."

That deep voice, the way Baltar's cadence rose and fell, rose and fell, like ocean waves muttering against the shoreline … it all seeped into Micah's mind. His eyelids grew heavy, as they had so often lately. He shook his head, blinked hard, slapped himself lightly. It didn't help. Why did he need so much damn *sleep*?

"I don't wanna come inside. The cold don't bother me. And I ain't scared."

"Of course not," Baltar said. "You are the most powerful being in this town, one of the strongest on earth."

"Uh-huh," Micah said, yawning. Dammit to *hell*.

"And yet a boy should be nestled safely in his room. Swaddled in his soft, toasty blankets. Dreaming his dreams."

Micah's breathing slowed. His hands and feet tingled. He slapped himself again. "I'll come in when I'm ready," he said, as forcefully as he could. Even to him, it sounded more like a toddler's impotent protest against bedtime. Defiance without real conviction.

"Come in," Baltar said, his baritone soothing. "Tomorrow, everything may look better."

"Everything's fine," Micah said, realizing his eyes were closed. He forced them open. "Just … just back off, okay?"

"Certainly," Baltar whispered. He sounded close, right next to Micah's ear. "I am here for you. On your side. Always."

"Sure," Micah said. He was standing in his living room. When had he come back inside? He blinked. Now he was sitting on the couch, the ragged fabric rustling underneath him. The room was dim and warm, only a single lamp throwing light along the floor. The kitchen sink dripped, a monotonous sound that merged with his pulse.

"You've had a long day," Baltar said from behind and above him. "Rest. I will call you when dinner is ready."

"Yeah," Micah said. "Okay." His voice sounded far away. His chin rested on his chest.

In his dream, Micah stood in a dark field the likes of which he had never seen in southeast Arkansas—farmland that stretched to the horizon, flat and fallow, tilled rows in which nothing grew. No moon, no stars. Intermittent lightning strobed behind thick clouds. A distant mountain stood against that sky, or perhaps it was some tower the nature and origin of which he could not guess. How far away was it—fifty miles? Hundreds? How gargantuan must it be, to seem that tall over such a distance?

Then, as lightning flashed again, the mountain *moved*.

The world seemed empty, yet Micah didn't feel lonely. It was like the air itself embraced him, warmed him.

My child, said a voice much deeper than Baltar's, the voice of thunder, of avalanches, of meteors smashing into planets.

What are you? Micah cried.

Untold distances away, near the summit of that mountain, two red eyes opened, their irises ringed in pulsing orange. Like fire. Another strobe, and the entity in the distance raised long and muscular arms. Its five-fingered hands flexed. Its mouth opened, revealing a long, flicking snake's tongue. When the lightning flashed again, it illuminated a head like a water monitor's, two meaty legs with hock joints like a horse's, who knew what kind of hooves or feet.

While I live, you are never alone, the voice said. *Your friends are nothing. I am all.*

What are you? Micah cried again. He should have been terrified, but that sense of being held overwhelmed him.

I am your world's master, said the voice. *And I am coming.* A bell or chime rang, high-pitched, driving itself into Micah's skull. He held his hands over his ears. *Sleep now,* the voice said, and its thunder was somehow gentle, tender. *Sleep. And, when the time comes, remember.*

Another clang. Darkness swallowed Micah, pulling him down to a place where the strobe lightning could not find him. He floated in inky nothing, eyes open, asleep.

"I'm coming," Baltar said, his voice the palest imitation of the mountain creature's. Light seeped into the void, strengthened, coalesced. Now Micah dreamed he was sitting on his own couch and watching Baltar crack the door. "Yes?" the old man said through the opening.

"Is Micah here?" A scratchy, low voice, like the owner had recently shouted a lot. Bec Villalobos's voice.

"He is not," Baltar said, flat and emotionless.

"Oh." Was Bec disappointed? "Do you know when he'll be back? We were supposed to—"

"No," Baltar said. His voice dripped with finality. "He said nothing of you."

"Okay," Bec said. "Well, if he gets back—"

"I am not a messenger service. Good night, young lady. Or whatever you are."

"But—"

Baltar shut the door. After a moment, footsteps crunched through the leaves in the yard. Baltar pulled the curtain back and watched. Then he nodded, shut the curtain, and left the room. Darkness closed in again, and Micah lay back in it, floating, floating.

CHAPTER TWENTY-FOUR

As I ate the haunch of a buck deer, I pondered how I might save the one called Christian. And that led me to ask myself why I even felt that I should. Had my vision been corrupted by my years of watching the evolution of the white world, corrupted until I could satisfy myself with minuscule and dying connections to my old life? Surely not. If Christian forced my hand, I would pick my teeth with her bones. And such might happen soon. Already I was growing weary of sharing this land with government men, with the white mass whose ancestors had driven out my chosen people so that only their names remained. Fear and hatred had poisoned the air, turned the water bitter.

Tomorrow the sun would rise on the whites' false holiday, the story of which is a greater trick than any I ever played—white invaders and the First Nations feasting together without weapons or diseases or wars. No white man demanding that the Nations forsake the gods they had long worshipped, no false promises written in ink that faded before it even dried. Every year the white world commemorated this dream that had never come true except in their own minds, a dream that undermined and, soon enough, replaced the realities of illness smashing the Nations more efficiently than any army ever could, of the invaders' triumph so complete that the Indigenous now spoke their oppressors' languages, of the brutal tribal wars that followed, of an incursion that grew into genocide.

Few of the People remain, no matter the tribe: Those from the deltas, from the mostly vanished deep woods, from the mountains, from the desert bluffs and cliffs scoured clean by wind and sand, from the swamps of the South. Imagine the face of the earth today if all those people had lived, had not succumbed to white diseases and white alcohol, had not fallen before the roar of white guns. Imagine the village where my adversaries dwelled. I had heard its name, Quapaw City, and wondered how anyone could live with it stamped in their memories, why they did not spend every moment of their lives on their knees begging the gods for forgiveness. Names have power. That is why no one knows the one I was given at the dawn of everything, why I shall never speak it. Yet the children of the invaders, of murderers and rapists and blighters, these children slept under a shadow so deep and dark that the sun can never penetrate it. Perhaps they long ago chose never to think of the past at all, lest it crush them.

I considered all this as I sat under the endless sky, as I ate meat I had killed with my own might, as I mourned the lives I would have to take. The young ones never meant to be what they had become. But that changed nothing.

The deer was excellent. I ate the meat mixed with grasses, clover, roots. If my plans worked, others could eat those delicacies in the future, long and long.

CHAPTER TWENTY-FIVE

Christian and her mom sat across from each other at their wooden dining table. Between them, buttered rolls had been piled on a plate next to a pan with their fresh-from-the-oven turkey breast. The table was a round job with room enough for four chairs if you didn't mind banging your shins against other people's. Mom had occasionally told the story of buying this table with Dad, back when he could stand to be in the same room with his wife and daughter: How they had found it at an artisan fair near Fayetteville, had wrestled it into their hatchback's trunk and tied the lid down with a rope someone had given them. They had revarnished it themselves. After Dad bailed, Mom had never remarried. There had been no more kids. So, every year since, Christian and Mom had eaten Thanksgiving just like this.

A round single-bulb glass globe hung from a chain attached to the ceiling. It cast a cone of light that almost precisely covered the tabletop. Three dead flies were slowly desiccating in the bottom of the fixture. To Christian's left, the muted TV flickered in the dark living room. Their dirt-brown sectional looked like hills seen from a distance. Behind Mom, the kitchen was in disarray—dirty dishes piled on the counter and stacked in the sink, an extra pan of rolls cooling on the stovetop, pots without lids sitting on three dead burners and containing canned corn, canned yams, instant mashed potatoes. A jar of gravy from the grocery store. In the refrigerator, a store-bought apple pie chilled on a shelf next to the remains of a homemade peach cobbler they had eaten half of the night before. Christian and Mom were drinking sweet tea from sweating glasses that rested on coasters. Neither of them had spoken much. Mom seemed exhausted, having worked a handful of double shifts in the past week.

All day, Christian had been preoccupied with matters she couldn't share with her mother—what the Team had done to her, what the shaper had said, how her body buzzed whenever Bec looked her way. Or the way a pit opened in her stomach whenever Bec paid any attention to Micah. God, what a stupid time for a crush. Sometimes Christian wished she could amputate whatever part of her controlled whom she felt attracted to, whom she might love. Or, at least, that she could find an on/off switch for times like these, when she should be focused on survival. So much seemed out of control. Sometimes she felt that she had managed to do precisely the wrong thing at the wrong time, risking humiliation and heartbreak and maybe even death.

She mopped up extra gravy with a roll. Then she took two more slices of turkey, spread a thin layer of gravy on them, and dug in.

Mom stifled a yawn with the back of her hand as she finished off her potatoes. The bags under her eyes looked purple. Her hair needed washing. Soon she stood and gathered her plate and empty glass. "You want me to bring you anything?"

"No, thanks," Christian said. "Unless you wanna get into that pie?"

"Sure," Mom said. "Be right back."

This had been Thanksgiving for as long as Christian could remember: a precooked breast or a ham, vegetables from cans with a little added salt or butter, packaged rolls, prebaked pies. Nothing fancy, little from scratch, unlike the groaning tables full of perfect dishes you saw on TV. She had never complained because she knew that Mom did her best, that money had always been tight and so had time, that what they cooked tasted fine and filled her belly and made her feel just as sleepy as those fancier meals would have. Christian and her mom would never be rich, but they still had plenty.

Mom came back and set a thick slice of cold apple pie and a fork in front of Christian. The juice had congealed in that pleasant fruit-pie way. Christian's mouth watered at the scent of cinnamon and sugar and baked crust. She ate three forkfuls in rapid succession, thinking of how she could live on pie, especially apple with lots of cinnamon, maybe some allspice, the fruit tart and firm enough to crunch. Mom sat with her own small slice and picked at it. Soon, they would do the dishes and pile the leftovers in the fridge. They would watch TV for half an hour, maybe a little longer. Then Mom would yawn again, rub her eyes, and apologize for being so tired. Soon after that, she would go to bed. It happened so often that way that it sometimes seemed they lived separate lives, like roommates who worked different shifts.

"Mom," Christian said, "can I ask you a question?"

Mom's lids looked heavy. "Sure, baby."

"How come we never really do a big Thanksgiving?"

Mom frowned. "Something wrong with the food?"

"No, no. I just wondered."

Mom ate a forkful of pie and drank a little tea. She eyed Christian over the rim. "How much have I told you about my grandmother?"

That took Christian by surprise. "Not much. I know she lived in Arkansas all her life, out in the backwoods, never had indoor plumbing. Your granddad hunted and trapped and carpentered. That's about it."

Mom nodded and sipped her tea. The heater kicked on with a puff of hot and acrid air. "Well, I'm too pooped to tell any real stories tonight."

"How about a quick fact or two?"

"Well, she was one-quarter Quapaw."

"For real?"

"Yeah. Her own mammaw was full-blooded."

"Wow." No one in their family had ever mentioned an Indigenous Peoples heritage. You would think it might have come up. Of course, if you grew up in America, chances were your family tree branched into different cultures, even if some of those branches were just stubby little twigs. But still. "How come nobody ever told me?"

Mom picked up her glass and wiped away the moisture ring it had left on the table. "I guess because those folks were long dead by the time you were born. And, I mean, my other grandmother was Scotch-Irish. I probably never told you that, either."

"That's different."

Mom yawned again. "Is it? I guess it's all so far back that claiming it would feel weird. Like posturing. Anyway, Mammaw's side of the family never celebrated Thanksgiving. You can imagine why. Pappaw was about as white as you can get, though, and his family had always celebrated. So, being a woman in that time and place, Mammaw followed her husband. Every year, they had a little dinner like we do. When we went to their place in the woods, she'd bake fresh bread and fry up whatever meat Pappaw had killed. Usually deer and squirrel, but sometimes duck or rabbit or a wild boar, maybe fish. Nothing fancy. I guess that was their compromise. A meal, but not what you'd call your average American Thanksgiving."

Rabbit, thought Christian. *Man, if her granddad was around today and wanted to kill some rabbits, all he'd have to do is hang out with me. Wouldn't even need a gun. He could just step on some.* "So this is our family tradition, from way back," she said, gesturing at the kitchen and the table.

Mom ate the last of her pie, drank some more tea, and wiped her mouth with her paper towel. "More or less." She looked sad. Mom's father, the son of the one-quarter-Quapaw woman, had died in a car crash when she was just a little girl. Her mother had passed away from some kind of rare blood disease back when Christian's parents were still together. Christian barely remembered her, but now it seemed that raising daughters alone might also be a kind of tradition.

Mom stood, picking up her saucer and fork. Christian brought her own dishes into the kitchen. They put away the food and rinsed off the plates and loaded the dishwasher in silence. Christian bagged up the trash, took it outside to the bin that sat against the house, came back inside, and fixed herself some instant hot chocolate. Mom sat in the living room, scrolling through the list of shows they were streaming.

Christian snuggled next to her and squeezed her wrist. "I really was just wondering," she said. "I love how we do things."

Mom kept scrolling. "It's almost criminal how much food some people throw away." She put the remote down and turned to Christian. "Every year when I was a schoolkid, they'd tell us that bullshit story about Thanksgiving. We'd make these headdresses and pilgrim hats out of construction paper. Kids would play Indian, doing the kinds of war dances and stuff they'd seen in the movies. We learned about Manifest Destiny. When they taught us about Little Big Horn, I got the feeling Custer was the hero. And then I'd go home and throw my headdress in the trash before anybody saw it. Our family never claimed to be Native Americans, but the least we could do was respect the Nations by not buying into the whitewashing."

"Whitewashing?"

"The official story always leaves some people out, and it warps other folks until even their families wouldn't recognize 'em. History really is a story, and somebody decides how to tell it, and they've always got a reason for what they emphasize and what they leave out. Don't forget that."

"I won't," Christian whispered, looking into her mother's eyes. Mom had never spoken to her like this before.

"Here. Let's do a *Gilmore Girls*," Mom said. They were watching the series for the fourth or fifth time.

"Okay," Christian said, wondering whether Mom would stay awake for forty-two more minutes.

She did, but barely.

After Mom had crashed and Christian's own food coma washed over her like a warm tide, she lay on the couch with the TV off, thinking about everything Mom had said. A full-blooded member of the Quapaw Nation in their family tree. The first family Thanksgiving celebration had occurred only three generations before Christian's, a muted affair that seemed like a metaphor for how those ancestors had been forced to live in two worlds while being a complete part of neither. Did all that relate to what the shaper had said?

Hell, for all you know, he's just screwing with your head.

Okay, but why? It wasn't like she had beaten it down and stood over its broken body, ready to deliver a killing strike. If anything, *it* had knocked *her* reeling, with its talk and its transformations.

Maybe that's why. To make you easier to kill.

And yet it had saved her from the Team. In the park, it had let her go.

Christian shook her head and punched the couch cushions. None of this was getting her anywhere. Besides, she had other stuff on her mind. Bec had DMed a couple of days ago. Apparently, they had gone over to Micah's on Monday for a date—not a *date* date, Christian kicked herself for hoping—and Micah had stood them up. Baltar had been rude. Though Bec had tried to laugh it off, Christian had sensed the hurt behind their words and had asked them to hang once the Thanksgiving festivities had ended.

Without a bike or a car, Christian would have to run.

She opened the curtains, turned up her vision, and looked outside. No government vehicles on the street. She went to her room and dug around in the closet until she found her duffel bag. After putting on her costume—the night-black fabric covered in barely discernable moons and stars and suns, all one piece that you stepped into and then zipped up like a HazMat suit, plus a ski mask and her stolen shoes—she zipped through the house and out the door, down the driveway, and up the street.

Bec lived on Johnny Cash Way, a half-completed residential street on the northern edge of town. The half dozen small houses out there had been built within the last two years. Christian had no idea who else lived out there or why they had come to Quapaw City, which had no major industrial or commercial businesses. Once, new people might have worked at Georgia-Pacific over in Crossett. Prices here were lower and the air was cleaner. But GP had pulled out of Crossett a few years back, and Christian doubted Bec's mom and dad had dreamed of working at McDonald's or Walmart. If she could find a way to bring it up, she would ask Bec about it.

Johnny Cash Way had only three streetlights, all on the south side in front of the houses. Across the road, raw woods stretched north, east, and west, with occasional dirt roads and access trails running through them. Christian ducked into these woods and took off and stored her costume. Another cold wind shook the trees and sent someone's yard decoration, a cardboard cartoon turkey, somersaulting down the road. Bec's place was the last one on the row. The porch light glowed and reflected off the white aluminum siding above waist-high hedges. A pickup truck and a dinged-up Hyundai Tucson sat in the gravel driveway. A hickory tree thrust its branches into the sky on Christian's right; a magnolia grew to the left side of the drive. She walked through dying grass and onto the small concrete walk. When she reached the black front door, she rang the bell.

After a moment, a woman answered. Long, silky black hair tumbled past her shoulders. Her deep-brown skin seemed flawless, her lips full, her dark eyes sparkling. Her simple blouse and jeans hugged a fit body. Christian felt as if someone had punched her in the stomach. Bec's odder, less mainstream kind of beauty, the way they carried themself, their I-am-who-I-am-and-I-don't-care-if-you-like-it attitude had attracted Christian from the start. Now this woman. How could one house contain so much beauty without catching fire?

Bec had mentioned that their mother's name was Patricia, pronounced the Spanish way, with the tongue rolling over the syllables. But Christian could not call this woman by her first name, even if invited. It would feel too much like taking some minor god's name in vain. "Hi," Christian said as Mrs. Villalobos held the door open with one hand and looked at her curiously. "I'm Christian. Is Bec home?"

That stunning smile faltered. Mrs. Villalobos looked into the yard, the woods. "*You're* Christian?"

"Yes, ma'am."

"Bec left for your house an hour ago. You haven't seen them?"

Something frigid opened in Christian's chest. "No, ma'am. I probably just missed them."

Bec's mom frowned. "Maybe. But it's been an hour. I'll call. Come in."

She held the door open. A wedge of bright light spilled onto the walk. Heat rushed out and kissed Christian's cheeks. She didn't want to go in there. If she did, the Villaloboses might expect her to provide answers, to wait around in case Bec came back or texted. Christian wanted to get out and run, scour the town, find Bec. Surely they had just gotten their wires crossed.

But she couldn't do that. It would look suspicious and wouldn't be fair to Bec's parents. No, she pretty much had to go inside. She stepped into the light, and, as Mrs. Villalobos shut the door, texted Bec. Then she waited with Bec's parents for another hour, but by the time she excused herself and ran home, Bec still hadn't replied.

CHAPTER TWENTY-SIX

Lunch at Jamie's house had consisted of fried turkey, collard and turnip greens with bacon and hot sauce, sweet potato casserole, baked mac and cheese, and various veggies. They had eaten until Gabby felt she might burst, and then Mrs. Entmann had hauled out the pies: pumpkin, pecan, chess.

Afterward, they watched football. Gabby had cut her eyes at Jamie. He had seldom spoken of sports in all the years she had known him, and when he had, it had mostly been related to the Arkansas Razorbacks basketball team. When he realized she was staring, he grinned. "I watch here and there. I think Dad wanted a ball player. Instead, he got a science nerd who reads manga."

Mr. Entmann had grunted. "Wouldn't trade you for ten quarterbacks." Jamie's eyes had moistened. Gabby guessed Mr. Entmann didn't talk like that much.

She had fallen asleep halfway through the first quarter of the first game. When she woke forty-five minutes later, Jamie and his dad had burst out laughing. Mrs. Entmann told them to quit it, that knocking out a guest sounded like a great compliment to her cooking. Mr. Entmann reminded her that *he* had fried the turkey.

Around five, she drove Jamie to her house, where she introduced him to her family food traditions: A kosher turkey set next to a dish of dressing with chorizo and poblanos, potato pancakes, pumpkin flan, latkes. She took some of everything. So did Jamie. By the time they found themselves on their second sofa after their second enormous meal, Gabby could have slept the rest of the night.

She and her friends were so lucky. Sure, none of them were rich.

Mr. Sterne and Ms. Frey worked themselves to the bone just to make do. But none of them were homeless, either, and when this holiday rolled around, they had plenty to eat. Gratitude shone inside her like a star. Did any of them deserve such good lives? In some respects, they were responsible for several deaths. But if they had done bad or stupid things, they had also tried to fix them, and that was more than a lot of people could say.

Now Gabby and Jamie sat on the Davisons' couch and watched YouTube while her parents cleaned the kitchen. Something clanked. Dad laughed. Jamie's arm, casually slung around her shoulder, squeezed a little tighter. The heater turned on. Sure enough, Gabby felt herself drifting, but then her phone sounded off, a guitar riff from some heavy metal song she didn't know. She was pretty sure Kenneth had swiped her phone and changed it during game night, but compared to the kinds of pranks he used to pull, the sort that felt more like borderline abuse, she guessed it was pretty funny.

Jamie raised his eyebrows but said nothing.

The message was from Christian.

u heard from Bec

Gabby showed Jamie her screen. He frowned. "I don't think Bec's even got my number. I know I don't have theirs."

"They've got mine," Gabby said. "But I haven't heard anything."

She replied to Christian, and they turned back to the videos. After a moment, the riff sounded again.

was supposed to meet them
no show
parents dk where they r

"Huh," said Gabby. "Think we should be worried?"

"Nah," Jamie said. "Probably just a mix-up. I'll keep an eye out when I head home, though."

"I'll text you Bec's number."

"Okay."

Gabby asked Christian to keep them informed. Christian's only response was

k

God, Gabby hated getting texts that only said "k." But Christian clearly had more important stuff on her mind.

In the kitchen, her parents finished up and turned out the lights. Their voices carried, but Gabby had turned up the TV loud enough to drown out the words. Soon, Mom walked in, her dark hair in a bun. She wore an old red T-shirt that might have been new when Gabby was born, jeans, no makeup. Even at dinner, the shirt had been streaked with flour and spatters of grease and who knew what else. Now she had splashed dishwater all over herself. Still, somehow, she looked radiant. In her weaker moments, Gabby wished she had gotten even a piece of that beauty, but she felt pretty sure it had missed her entirely, no matter what Jamie said.

"We're gonna go watch our show," Mom said. "I got a big crush on that Giancarlo Esposito." Her parents were finally watching *Breaking Bad*.

"I heard that," Dad called.

"Okay," Gabby said, ignoring this exchange. It shouldn't be legal for parents to have a romantic life. "Jamie's about to head out."

"Yep," Jamie said, sighing as he pushed himself off the sofa. "Though now that I weigh about ten million pounds, I might just roll home like a ball." He held out his hand. Gabby took it. He pulled her up, and she walked him outside, where he picked up his bike. No Team cars on the street tonight. Maybe even those dickweeds took the holiday off.

Gabby hugged him and kissed him. "Still gonna look for Bec?"

Some of her hair blew into her eyes. He pushed it away and kissed her forehead. "Yeah, as long as I can get away from my parents, I'll drop my bike at home and costume up."

"Be careful." She stepped away from him and crossed her arms. She hadn't worn a jacket.

"I'll hit you up later. Whether I find them or not." He climbed on the bike.

"I love you," she said.

He looked her in the eyes. "I know." Then he burst into laughter.

"Get outta here," she said, cackling. She couldn't believe he had Han Solo'd her.

She scrolled on her phone for about twenty minutes before she got bored and texted Christian.

bec turn up yet

Nothing for perhaps two minutes. Then Christian replied.

no im freakin out

Gabby:

dont worry someone will find them

Christian:

hope so holler if u hear something

Gabby:

ok u 2

Next, Gabby wrote Kenneth and Brayden, but neither of them even knew Bec was missing. Though the heat was turned way up, Gabby shivered again. Normally, if one of her friends missed curfew or ghosted for a little while, especially when school was out, she didn't worry. But after what had happened to Christian, she couldn't take anything for granted.

I wonder if there's rabbits outside. That might mean something.

She opened her door and tiptoed down the hall. The front part of the house was dark, quiet. A wedge of light shone from under her parents' closed bedroom door. The sound of the TV carried this far, though at normal hearing levels Gabby couldn't make out the dialogue.

Gabby opened the front door as quietly as she could and stepped into the cold. Light shone from some of the neighborhood windows. Streetlights cast their usual pools of soft illumination that made the darkness seem deeper. The street was as still as a picture. Not even a dog or a stray cat.

She felt so helpless. She didn't know Bec that well, but she hated the thought that something might have happened to them. Their poor parents must be going crazy.

Someone stepped out from behind the oak tree. Gabby yelped.

The figure moved into the starlight. Holy shit. Bec had turned up after all.

"Hello," Bec said. They sounded calm, almost amused. They wore short sleeves and no jacket.

Where had they lived before they moved here? Gabby couldn't remember but didn't think it had been a place so cold that Arkansas autumn wouldn't bother them. "Hey," Gabby said. Bec had paused with their face still in shadow. Something felt weird. "Did you know you're missing?"

Bec's hair blew in the breeze. They took another step forward. "I know where I am."

Gabby stepped forward, too. She cranked up her vision until she could trace every wrinkle in Bec's clothes, each individual hair on their head. Gabby had noted Bec's milk-chocolate eyes when they had first been introduced. Maybe the dark was affecting her perception, but Gabby would have sworn those eyes were a shade darker now, perhaps even two, more like *dark* chocolate. An alarm buzzed in her mind. "Where you been?" she asked. "Everybody's worried. Your parents are probably freaking out."

Bec moved closer. Now they were only five or six feet away. "I've been here. Waiting for you."

The alarm wasn't buzzing anymore. Now it thundered like one of those huge bells you sometimes saw in old churches. "You could have knocked," Gabby said, trying to keep her voice even. "Jamie was just here. We could have hung out."

Bec took another step, moving beyond the shadow. The moonlight and the streetlamps brought them into sharper relief. They smiled. Two front teeth protruded from their mouth. "I like it out here," they said. Their voice had deepened.

The street was still empty. Gabby backed up all the way to the front walk, her heels on the concrete, the rest of her feet still in the grass. Those front teeth had already grown longer, sharper. "You're not Bec."

Bec grinned again. All their teeth looked sharp. Their face and arms were … *fuzzy*, as if they had grown a thin coat of fur while Gabby talked. Their voice grew even deeper. "I am who I have always been."

"Where are they?" Gabby asked, trying to sound forceful. She couldn't let this thing see her fear. "What did you do to them?"

"They sleep," the Bec-thing said, and now it *grew*, legs and torso and arms elongating, thickening. Bec's clothes were sinking back into that fast-growing, deep-brown fur. Its feet stretched, widened, the boot tips becoming toes that ended in claws.

"Where?" Gabby barked. She spread her feet and balled her hands into fists, the energy inside her cycling up. Her hands began to glow white. If the shaper made a move, even if it just refused to answer, she would blast it. No way she would die in her own front yard, cowering and crying. She might be a try-hard, a half-breed, a geek, but she would not blubber like a terrified child.

The shaper laughed. Its arms had grown so muscular they seemed unreal. Its hands had become paws. "Deep in the earth," it said. "They await you there. You and your friends. Come for them if you dare."

"You piece of shit," Gabby said, her hands now glowing so bright they hurt her eyes.

The shaper laughed again and kept growing taller, wider. Its voice deepened, deepened again, until its laughter sounded like gunshots.

Gabby raised both hands and pointed them at the shaper's expanding head. *Eat this,* she thought as the energy peaked, rushing through her body and up her arms.

Then, just before she could fire, the shaper shimmered, warped. In its place, a wall of water wavered over Gabby, frothing and sloshing. In her surprise, the energy inside her largely dissipated. Still, she got off a shot as she fell backward. It struck her family's mailbox and blew it across the street, where it clattered, misshapen, into the gutter.

The water crested, smashing her to the ground. Her head barked on the concrete. Light exploded behind her eyes. She had managed to close her mouth and take a breath at the last second, but water still invaded her nose, her sinuses. It smashed her against her parents' car and buffeted her over and over, swirling as if she were stuck inside a washing machine. The sheer force of it ripped the shoes off her feet, drove the breath from her lungs, tore her shirt open and over her head, yanked her pants to her ankles, over her feet, completely off.

Then, as quickly as it had begun, everything stopped. The water streamed toward the street and down the gutter and into a storm drain, every drop, leaving the yard bone-dry. Gabby lay on the walk, aching all over. She hadn't been able to use her powers, so her aura hadn't protected her. It felt as if she had survived a tsunami. Was she bleeding? Groaning, she sat up, one hand on the back of her neck. Her soaked clothes lay on the ground several feet away. She could only find one shoe.

The front door banged open. Dad burst out, looking around wildly. "What the hell was all that noise?" he cried. "It sounded like—" Then he saw Gabby. He ran over and kneeled beside her, one hand under her head. His eyes were so wide they looked like a cartoon character's. She half expected them to accordion out from his skull with an *ah-OOO-gah!* noise. "What happened to you? Are you okay?"

He helped her sit up. She groaned, winced, leaned against the car, returned her vision to normal levels. "You wouldn't believe me if I told you," she muttered.

Dad rubbed his palms up and down her arms as she shivered. "Who did this to you? I'll rip their goddam heads off."

"No," she said. Together they stood and walked toward the house. "It was just some kids. We've been pranking each other for a couple months now. Things just got outta hand this time. No big deal."

"No big deal that they stripped you down in public and left you in this cold?" he roared.

"Dad, it's just a game," she said. "Let me get inside and get dressed."

"But—"

"Really," she said, pulling away from him and heading for her room. "No biggie. I'm good." She practically dove into her room and shut the door. Then she fell on the bed and wrapped herself in the blanket.

"This isn't over," Dad called. "Hey, what the hell happened to our mailbox?"

Gabby would have a hard time convincing him to let this go. Picking up her phone, she sent her friends a 911 DM.

✳

In costume and with his vision enhanced, Jamie patrolled the town. No feds on his tail tonight, none at Gabby's. No sign of Bec, either. Now his phone dinged, so he hovered, dug it out of his pocket, and read Gabby's message.

If he was reading the code right, the shaper had attacked her. *Son of a bitch. I'm gonna kill this thing with my bare hands.*

He turned toward home. He wanted to hear Gabby's voice but couldn't afford to hover too long, or somebody would probably video him and put it on the internet.

On the way, he spotted a familiar form coming out of the Korner Mart with two plastic bags. On a whim, Jamie zipped down and landed on the store's roof. As the FBI agent dug for the keys in his pocket, Jamie cleared his throat and tried to deepen his voice. "Agent Greenwalt."

Greenwalt looked up, did a double-take, dropped the crap he was carrying—something made of glass shattered, and one of the white bags turned dark—and yanked his service weapon from his shoulder holster. Jamie engaged his flight power and hovered a few inches above the rooftop to jumpstart his protective aura.

But Greenwalt didn't fire. He held the gun on Jamie, his jaw set. "That's a good way to get shot, kid."

The street was empty, as was the parking lot, except for Greenwalt's Tahoe. Oak, hickory, walnut, and pine trees stood guard in yards and in the lots between businesses. Quiet lay over town like a thick blanket.

"If I come down there," Jamie said, "are we gonna tussle? Or can we talk like our mommas raised us right?"

Greenwalt watched him for a few moments. Then he lowered his gun, holstered it, and looked down at his bags. He put his hands on his hips and shook his head. "So much for my iced coffee. Thanks, kid."

Jamie floated down, arms crossed. Doing this always made him feel like Superman. Still, he stopped six inches above the pavement, in case Greenwalt changed his mind. "You probably heard about what's happening," Jamie said.

"You mean Villalobos." Greenwalt fished out some packages of jerky and Corn Nuts dripping with coffee.

"Yeah," Jamie said. The Tahoe's tinted windows looked like pools of tar. "It would actually be a relief to know y'all took her."

Greenwalt frowned. Jamie could practically hear his teeth grind. "Well, we didn't. We aren't in the habit of kidnapping American citizens unless they're mutated threats to national security."

Jamie's anger flared. He knew Greenwalt was referring to Christian, and Greenwalt knew he knew. *Don't say shit about that. Just let it go.* He took a deep breath, exhaled. "I'm not gonna trade insults with you. Not when an innocent kid is missing. Surely you got enough conscience left to agree they're innocent, don't you?"

"Don't preach to me about conscience, Entmann. Not after you and your friends ripped up your own school and endangered dozens of lives."

Entmann. So Greenwalt wanted to get real. *Okay, dickweed, let's get real.* "I seem to remember somebody shooting guns in that same school. Is that how y'all keep American citizens safe?"

Greenwalt stared at the pavement for a bit. When he turned back to Jamie, he looked resigned. "I don't see the point of this conversation. Can I get back in my car in peace?"

Jamie tried to soften his voice. "Look," he said. "I didn't come here to argue. I stopped because you seem like you've got a more open mind than your homies."

Greenwalt picked up the bag that hadn't been doused in coffee. "You shouldn't assume I'm on your side. That won't end well for you."

"That ain't what I mean. Me and my friends wanna find that kid. If y'all didn't take them, maybe you'd like to help. I mean, from what I've seen, it ain't like that shaper wants to take your Team out to lunch."

"Help how? If you think my boss and my colleagues are gonna team up with you, you haven't been paying attention."

"No, no. Not them. Just you."

Now Greenwalt's eyebrows lifted. He opened his mouth, then closed it again. "Okay, so you're saying … what are you saying?"

Jamie sighed and rubbed the bridge of his nose. "I'm not asking for anything major. Just maybe run interference if we find out where the shaper's got Bec and your boss decides that would be a good time to jump us. I ain't asking for our sakes. I'm asking for Bec's."

Greenwalt looked around, as if worried that he, too, might have been followed. When he turned back, he looked a little less hostile. "That kid's probably terrified, but that won't make any difference to my people. Not when national security's threatened."

"They didn't do anything."

"Oh, yes they did," Greenwalt said, not unkindly. "They made the wrong friends. Has it occurred to you that your little band of pirates puts your friends and family in danger just by being in their lives? If Bec Villalobos hadn't started hanging with you, I doubt that shaper would have even noticed her. Them. Whatever."

Several replies formed in Jamie's mind. He rejected them all. Of course that had occurred to him. How could it not, after what had happened to Mrs. Sterne? But no one else had said it out loud, and now that Greenwalt had, it opened a deep pit in Jamie's gut. He felt nauseated. But he couldn't tell Greenwalt any of that. "Will you help us or not?"

Greenwalt laughed without humor. "If you find the shaper and the kid, and if my Team tries to take you out before she's safe—*they're* safe, dammit—I'll advocate for waiting. Only until the shaper's down or you get the kid out of there, you understand. But I'm telling you, I don't expect my advocacy to do any good."

It wasn't much, but it was still more than Jamie had expected. The pit in his gut didn't fill, but he felt a little better. Anything to give Bec a chance. "Okay," he said, holding out his hand.

Greenwalt looked at it. "Don't ask me to shake, kid. We aren't friends or allies. Sooner or later, we'll have to settle this."

Jamie let his hand drop. "Yeah. I guess we will."

Greenwalt backed up and unlocked his Tahoe. As he got in, Jamie floated up and back. He hung above the Korner Mart's roof until Greenwalt backed out and drove away. The town still slept, though it was relatively early. That deep sense of quiet held, almost oppressive, as if the place had been soundproofed. The shaper had hidden Bec somewhere in all that dark and silence. And Greenwalt had been right about this much: It was Jamie's responsibility to save them.

His phone dinged. He dug under his robe and pulled it out of his pocket.

Micah:

mumpsimus friday my house

Jamie texted an affirmative. Then he headed home. He had seen no sign of Bec or the shaper and doubted he would find them tonight.

Rabbits loitered in people's yards, groups of twos and threes watching him as he passed.

CHAPTER TWENTY-SEVEN

Gabby picked up Jamie around one p.m. and drove to Micah's. They rode in silence. Jamie seemed worried. For her part, Gabby couldn't stop thinking about Bec. The cops were searching, but they weren't trained to track and fight a shape-shifting monster, even if they had been aware that one had come to town. Of course, neither were the Freaks. Trying to think about something else, *anything* else, Gabby checked out all the cars sitting in driveways and under carports. Black Friday didn't really affect this town much, compared to what you read about online. A lot of people had probably stampeded into Walmart at midnight, but today kids played in yards like any other day. Rays of sunlight that looked solid enough to walk on shone through scattered holes in the clouds.

She and Jamie hadn't drawn a tail today, but when she turned onto MacArthur, one of the familiar black Suburbans sat three houses down from Micah's. Jamie waved when they passed the SUV.

Gabby parked behind Baltar's Lexus. They got out of the car, and she led Jamie to the front door and knocked. Micah let them in. The couch and easy chair had been pushed close together and facing each other. Kitchen chairs sat on either side of the recliner. Someone, almost certainly Baltar, had drawn a symbol on each of the walls in what looked suspiciously like blood. Beneath them, something sweet yet acrid smoldered in old bowls covered in runes and hieroglyphs. Thin columns of smoke drifted up and out.

"What's all this?" she asked. "Is Baltar doing a spell?"

"Already did," Micah said. "A little extra protection. He'll tell you why."

Christian was sitting in the middle of the couch. Her eyes were watery and bloodshot, with bags so dark it looked like someone had punched her. Her hair was greasy and unbrushed. When Gabby and Jamie entered, she didn't even look up. To her right sat Kenneth, with an expression that suggested he might have felt more comfortable tied to a chair in the Gilchrist farmhouse. On Christian's left, Brayden played with his phone.

Micah sat across from Brayden in one of the kitchen chairs, his back straight, arms crossed over his chest, knees apart, chin on chest. He seemed really out of it. Maybe Bec's disappearance had stunned him that badly or kept him up all night.

Baltar had taken the recliner. In profile, he looked like the vampire in that old silent movie.

Only one seat remained. Jamie sighed. "I'll grab another chair from the kitchen." Gabby took the empty one. Jamie set his chair between her and Kenneth.

Just as Jamie opened his mouth to start the meeting, somebody's ringtone went off—frenetic, breathless music. Christian dug her phone out of her pants. Her brows knitted, and she held up a finger to the group: *Hang on.* "Hello?" she said. She listened a moment. "Really? And they said what? Huh. Well, okay. Thanks for letting me know. Yes, ma'am. Yes, ma'am. Right. I'm glad, too. Okay, bye." She put her phone away and looked at the group, laughing and shaking her head. "That was Mrs. Villalobos. Bec came home late last night. Just decided to go for a walk. Unbelievable."

"Did she say what they're doing right now?" Jamie asked.

"Just chilling in their room," Christian said. "Why?"

"Why didn't *they* text you?"

Christian opened her mouth and closed it again. Finally, she just shrugged.

"Something sounds off," Gabby said. "Let's text Bec."

"Yeah," Christian muttered. As she tapped away, a car that clearly needed a new muffler drove by, engine blatting. The kitchen sink, a bit leaky for as long as Gabby could remember, dripped every few seconds. Micah breathed deeply and exhaled, like someone fast asleep. "They're not answering."

"I'm not sure it was Bec that came back home," Jamie said.

Stunned silence for a moment. Then everyone but Micah and Baltar talked at once, their voices raised and unsteady.

"If I may," Baltar said, his deep voice rising over everyone else's. The conversation faded. "I have gathered some of the shaper's fur from the forests. And I have analyzed it."

He paused. For dramatic effect?

"And?" Jamie asked.

Baltar's eyes flicked toward Jamie, but when he spoke, he seemed to look each of them in the face *except* for Jamie. A tendril of unease coiled around Gabby and squeezed.

"*And* we are not dealing with a mere shape-shifter. Even the gossamer tufts of fur that I collected were infused with power beyond your imagination. No, this creature is something much, much more."

Again, that dramatic pause.

"Well, what the hell *is* it?" Christian asked.

"According to my findings, we have set ourselves against a god."

For long moments, no one spoke. Then Jamie said, "*What?*"

Baltar talked for a long time, explaining that the so-called shape-shifter's energy signature and power level indicated its true identity—Rabbit, the trickster figure from the myths of Indigenous People like the Quapaw. Rabbit, known to some Anishinaabe tribes as Manabozho, to others by names as varied as Jistu, Chukfi, Teetkana. Rabbit, who once slew a man-eating monster by dressing as a woman and decapitating it in its sleep. Rabbit, who gave the deer its horns. Rabbit, who stole fire on behalf of humans. Did all these legends refer to one being, or to cousin gods, or to unrelated but similar entities?

Were some based on real-life events? Were others entirely fictional? Baltar claimed not to know.

"Okay, so what *do* we know?" Christian said. She was sitting on the edge of the sofa and leaning forward, her eyes wide, hands clasped together.

"We know this trickster shape-shifts," Baltar said. "We know he is brilliant, mischievous, devious. Scholars believe he inspired the tales of Brer Rabbit and Bugs Bunny. And we know that he is utterly ruthless when he believes it's necessary."

"Holy shit," Christian muttered. "And that's what might be sitting in Bec's house right now. God only knows what it did to the real Bec."

Jamie stared at Baltar with an intensity Gabby hadn't seen since the night they killed Na'ul. "What the hell are we supposed to do against something like that? How are we supposed to kill a god?"

Baltar favored Jamie with a smile and an expression that said, *Bless your heart; you have no idea what you're doing.* "Nothing can kill a god. Rabbit's essence is inextricably entwined with the very fabric of the multiverse. Even if you scattered his molecules to the farthest borders of existence, he would eventually reform. Or he would reshape himself into a new being. One that would still remember you."

Jamie fell against his chair. Staring at the floor, mouth open, he looked eerily like Micah.

Kenneth actually laughed. "Of course," he said. "A god. Sure. Why the hell not? Ha!"

No one else spoke for a long time.

CHAPTER TWENTY-EIGHT

When Christian ran into the woods across from Bec's place, the sun was easing toward the western horizon, casting the landscape in bright reds and oranges. These were the days when sunset seemed imminent at three p.m. and every other hour seemed like a good time for a nap.

Christian, though, felt wide awake. Every cell in her body buzzed. Something had been growing between her and Bec, a connection beyond friendship, maybe even beyond attraction. Butterflies fluttered in her belly whenever Bec smiled, laughed, touched her arm. She and Bec weren't in love, at least not yet. But it had felt like romance. And maybe lust. *Definitely* lust. So when Baltar had suggested that someone check out the Villalobos place, Christian volunteered. No, insisted. "I've got some kind of connection with this trickster," she had said. "Maybe he'll talk to me. With the rest of you, he might just rip off your leg. Besides, I've already met Bec's mom." Micah had woken up long enough to scowl, but no one argued. Christian had gone home to throw on her costume. Then checked for any sign of the Team and tore through the streets, her anxiety and anger ratcheting up with every step.

The plan called for the others to load up in Gabby's and Baltar's cars. Team or no Team, the Freaks would drive out here and wait somewhere near Johnny Cash Way. Christian had only a few minutes before they arrived, and she needed to make it count. Who knew what would happen once the shaper sensed everyone's presence?

Bec's driveway was empty. Nothing moved in the yard, not even the twelve or fourteen rabbits scattered around.

Okay, yeah. That's not spooky at all.

Christian took off her costume, wrapped it and her mask around a low-hanging limb, and stepped out of the woods. The rabbits regarded her stoically. Images flitted through her mind: The little creatures leaping on her as soon as she stepped in Bec's yard, cute little buck teeth ripping into her flesh, her body falling to pieces in their jaws. That would be a seriously stupid way to die.

Nothing happened. The fuzzies didn't even turn their heads as she passed. Like they stood guard, but not against her.

She paused before the door, willing her pulse to slow, her hands to stop shaking. She'd never been scared to stand up to bullies, and she had thrown down with Na'ul, but now only a wooden door a couple of inches thick stood between her and a hostile god.

Just turn around and get your shit and run back to the others. Nobody will blame you.

But she couldn't do that and live with herself. She knocked.

The door opened, as if Rabbit had been watching through the peephole. Maybe he had.

The form of Bec Villalobos stood before her. The trickster smiled. "I have been waiting," he said in Bec's voice. "I wondered which of you would come. Now I know for certain who is bravest."

"Are you coming out, or do I come in?" Christian asked.

"I dislike these dwellings. Let us talk under the sun and sky, as men used to do."

"I ain't no man, and neither are you." But Christian backed into the yard and chose a spot halfway to the road, making sure not to step on a rabbit. She wouldn't have wanted to do that anyway, but who knew how the trickster might react if she murdered one of his little cousins?

Rabbit-Bec left the door open and sat cross-legged in the grass. The bunnies that had been scattered throughout the yard now hopped over and nestled against him. A couple jumped into his lap. He stroked them between the ears and watched Christian with those deep brown eyes.

"You have already rejected the open hand I offered," he said with a hint of a smile. "But I still admire you. I have done since the night you destroyed the Prince of the Go'kan. As much as I can admire anyone who has embraced the white world."

Christian nearly fell over. Had Rabbit been in the park that night, assessing the Freaks? Still, she wouldn't get sidetracked, not by his bullshit or his compliments. "Where's Bec?"

Rabbit took one of the bunnies off his lap, held it to eye level, kissed it on the nose. "They sleep in my warren, warm and comfortable and dreaming of pleasant days."

Christian crossed her arms, stood straighter, tried to look serious and tough. "And where's your warren? Tell me where they are or let them go. Do anything else, and we're gonna have a problem."

The shaper threw back his head and laughed. "I fear you not, child. Nor would you be so impertinent if you knew what I am."

"I *do* know," Christian said. "You're a trickster. A god. And I still ain't scared of your hairy ass."

Rabbit-Bec's eyebrows twitched upward. "Again you surprise me. How did you come by this knowledge, I wonder? From your ancient books? Or, perhaps, from something else? I have sensed a powerful presence in this village. Not you and your friends, and certainly not those government bumblers. Something stronger. Darker."

What was he talking about? Baltar, maybe? Better play it cool. "You'll find out if you don't let Bec go."

The shaper's expression hardened. "Beware, girl. If you are aligned with the force I have sensed, more than your life is at hazard. And disrespecting me will not serve you."

Frost seemed to form along Christian's spine. She clenched her muscles to keep from shivering, from running away. When she felt in control again, she said, "I'm not trying to disrespect you. But me and my friends won't just curl up and let you kill us. That ain't a challenge. It's just the way it is."

The trickster considered this. He petted the rabbit still in his lap. "You are stone and fire. But so am I. Never forget that."

Christian had no idea what to say or do next. Even if it had been possible to kill a god, she couldn't do it alone. Knocking Rabbit out wouldn't help her find Bec. And if she got herself killed, her friends' already limited chances would plummet. She could think of only one thing to do. Just conceiving the idea nearly made her piss her pants. But Bec needed her.

"What if I took Bec's place?" she asked. "If you let them go, I'll come with you. You can teach me ... whatever it is you've got in mind. Besides, they've got nothing to do with all this anyway."

Rabbit set the bunny down, stood, approached. He and Christian looked into each other's eyes. "You continue to astound me. After all these centuries, very little does."

"So it's a deal?"

Rabbit-Bec smiled, but he looked sad. "No. You live in a world where promises mean nothing. I hear the voices of the Nations in your own, but far too faintly."

Christian laughed. "Ain't your whole deal that you lie and fool people? What's *your* promise worth?"

That stony expression again. She was pushing her luck. "I have already given you my best offer. Come with me, and you will live forever. I will teach you the limits and the possibilities of your power. I will show you the ways of honor and courage."

Rabbit-Bec sure sounded sincere. And part of Christian felt tempted. She could watch the long, slow march of the present into the future. She'd never have to worry about the Team again, or high school bullshit, or heartbreak. But accepting that offer would also mean leaving friendship behind. And family. And love. How long would it take to forget how she had abandoned the only people who had ever accepted her? How long to forget how she felt when Bec touched her? To forget her mother's voice?

Now it was her turn to offer a sad smile. "I'm sorry."

Rabbit-Bec didn't answer. Instead, he held out his hand like a businessperson closing a deal. Christian hesitated. She didn't trust this odd gesture, but if she left the trickster hanging, would that make everything worse? She steeled herself and took his hand.

Energy shot through her. Her joints clenched. Her teeth rattled. An image formed in her mind, as vivid and clear as a high-definition photograph: a clearing deep in the forest, the ground carpeted with leaves. Surrounding this area, black oaks and pines rose as high as forty or fifty feet. On the clearing's eastern edge, a fallen pine lay before two of its tallest sisters. To the north stood half a dozen stunted and gnarled oaks, looking as if they had barely survived some disease or disaster. In the middle of the clearing, a hole gaped six feet across, leading into darkness.

Rabbit-Bec let go, and Christian stumbled backward, tripped over her own feet, sat down hard. The impact jarred her spine and drove the breath from her body. The trickster loomed over her. "Come to me there, girl. After our business is concluded, I will release your friend. No tricks. Fail to find me and I will kill the child slowly."

Christian struggled for breath. "Don't … don't hurt … their parents."

"Fear not. I have no reason to stay."

Rabbit-Bec's body shimmered and flowed and became a colorless blob that stretched in many directions. Then it exploded, each fragment transmogrifying into a blackbird. The flock came together in a swirling mass, sailed upward, and flew over the uncut woods stretching between Quapaw City and the next towns over. The rabbits in Bec's yard hopped away in all directions.

Christian sat a while longer, catching her breath. A few minutes later, she rose and retrieved her costume from the woods. Trotting down the road at normal speed, she found her friends: Gabby behind the wheel, with Jamie riding shotgun, Brayden and Kenneth in the back seat. A few yards to the rear, Baltar's car idled, exhaust rising from its tailpipe in the cold afternoon. Christian couldn't see past the tinting with her vision at normal levels, but she assumed that Baltar had driven, with sleepy-head Micah curled up in the passenger seat. A lot of good that kid would do in a fight if he couldn't even stay awake.

Jamie rolled down the window as she approached. "Hey," he said. "We were listening. This Rabbit thing thinks *we're* the bad guys? Don't he know he's a kidnapper?"

Christian flexed the fingers Kragthorpe had tried to ruin. Thanks to her handy healing power, she could move them again, but they were still stiff, as if she had badly jammed them just this morning. They reminded her of how much she already knew about kidnapping. Kragthorpe had exuded hostility like an odor that night, but Rabbit seemed genuinely sad. *He ain't wrong. We built this world on genocide. On theft. On disease and addiction and the desecration of other cultures. We deserve the grave he's digging.*

She pushed the voice away. "Rabbit knows exactly what he did," she said, and left it at that.

Brayden had fallen asleep, his mouth open, a line of drool hanging from his lower lip like some weird piece of jewelry. Kenneth sat quietly beside him. He had said very little to the rest of them all year, even on the few occasions when he had hung out with them. There had been no bullying of any kind, which had resulted in an unspoken but palpable sense of relief within both the Freaks and the Quapaw City High student body. At the same time, that distance had stunted the growth of Kenneth's relationships with his former victims. Two steps forward, one and a half steps back. Yet they needed Kenneth now more than ever.

"Dude," she said to him. "Do y'all still have your four-wheelers?" She nodded at Brayden.

"Yeah," Kenneth said. "Mine needs some gas."

"Can y'all get your folks to carry 'em to the woods? We'll need a way to get everybody a few miles off the road. If me and Jamie have to carry y'all, we'll be too wore out to fight."

Kenneth looked at Brayden and closed his friend's mouth. He even wiped away the drool and then cleaned his hand on his own pants. The gesture was almost sweet. "I think so," he said. "Where should we ask 'em to take us?"

"I'm not sure. I know what the place looks like, though, so I'll take a run and find it. I'll text everybody when I know something."

"I'll help," Jamie said. "After I pick up my costume."

"Okay," Christian said. She looked back at Kenneth. "Listen, man. I know we've kind of gotten away from each other. But please don't antagonize Micah. We're probably gonna get squashed anyway, but we need all hands on deck."

She expected bluster, some offensive comment. Instead, quietly, Kenneth said, "Micah antagonizes *me*. I ain't said boo to that kid all year."

Gabby turned in her seat. "I know it ain't fair," she said, "but he's still hurting. It ain't just that he saw his mom die. His dad ain't been around much either."

"Yeah," said Jamie. "God knows I wanna wring his damn neck sometimes, but he's been through a lot. We're not asking you to take his shit forever, but somebody's gotta be the bigger person. Right now, I doubt it will be him."

Kenneth sighed and rubbed his eyes. He looked old and worn down, nothing like a not-quite-sixteen-year-old kid. "Yeah, okay," he said. He sounded as tired as he looked. "But if he tries to set me on fire, it's on."

Christian supposed that was the best they could hope for. "Okay," she said. She thumped her palm on the roof. "Y'all keep your phones on. I'll be in touch."

As she ducked back into the forest, Christian glanced at the Lexus. No one got out, rolled down a window, hailed her. If Baltar or Micah felt even the least bit curious about the conversation that had just occurred, they gave no sign.

CHAPTER TWENTY-NINE

The prisoner lay deep in my warren, dreaming their dreams, my kin nestled around them and sharing their warmth. I had brought the child there unconscious so that they would know nothing of the body crumpled deeper in the den. Time and decay had begun working their will while I was occupied in the village, but I had since arrested their effects. With his strange clothes and puny weapon and arrogance, the government man named Parker had been with me for several days. I should have secured him deep in dreams, but I had wanted him to understand my outrage. A folly. He never listened, only tried to run. In so doing, he trod on several of my small and blameless cousins, snapping their backs and necks.

I made him pay.

The other government men had abandoned their war on the children. Instead, they searched every tree and bush near the village, calling their friend's name. Soon I would walk into their lodge and show them the location of my den. If the young ones knew their government adversaries were coming for me, would they still seek me out?

I believed they would. Courage shone from their eyes like the sun. And, like the sun, it would burn them.

I had desired that the girl with the godlike speed would renounce her white heritage and join me in watching over what remained of the Nations, but it seemed to me now that the siren call of mortal friendship had overwhelmed her connections to a past she did not understand. The story of this land's devolution had been written in her very bones. I should have been able to turn my back on her, strike her down as easily as the others. What lay at the root of my hesitation? Was I that desperate to find some vestige of the Nation I once knew here on the grounds where we all once lived and dreamed and died? If so, I had two choices: cling to this girl or finish my business here and then scamper northwest until I found those to whom everything here had once belonged.

Maybe some other choice would reveal itself. Perhaps the girl would prove herself to be more than a shadow of those who had vanished.

Or perhaps not.

I thrust my hands into the earth and loosed a fragment of energy, calling the creatures of the woods, the birds, the very wind to stand alert. And then I lay down to dream. The end of this story fast approached. I would be ready.

CHAPTER THIRTY

On the side of a dirt road four miles northeast of town, Kenneth and Brayden waited for the others. Their fathers had dropped them off a couple miles away; they had ridden here on their own. Kenneth's dad and Mr. Sears had promised to return before dark or when the boys called, whichever came first. Like they'd ever get a decent signal in the woods.

Both he and Brayden wore camo coveralls, orange vests, and orange hats with drawstrings. Tied down to his ATV's ass end with bungee cords, Kenneth's duffel held his costume and mask, plus the sack lunches Mrs. Sears had insisted they bring. His Winchester .30-30 lever-action was mounted in the rack, though he had brought it only to maintain the illusion. No plain old gun would hurt Rabbit.

Brayden carried a pump-action shotgun. He seemed pretty chill, considering that Kenneth was probably going to die today. The Freaks might have thought Brayden was so calm because of stupidity or a lack of imagination. Of course, he hadn't encountered Rabbit yet, but hell, maybe they were right. Brayden would never be a straight-A student. He probably couldn't get into a local cow college. But if a practical mind meant that he could sit here without shitting his pants, well, great.

Kenneth didn't have the greatest imagination, either, but he had seen enough of Rabbit to worry about the condition of his own underwear. A single vampire had pushed the Freaks to their limits. A big-ass, super-strong, hyper-vicious vampire, but still. Now they had to fight something much more powerful. Yeah, Kenneth was scared. He wouldn't admit it, but he wished he could just call Dad, go home, and watch a ball game.

239

Rabbit wouldn't stop until all the Freaks were dead, though. Where could you hide from a god?

Ten or fifteen minutes after Kenneth and Brayden had cut their engines, two cars arrived, Gabby's and the old dude's.

"That everybody?" Brayden asked. He had found some jerky in his coveralls and tore a piece off.

"Looks like it," Kenneth said.

"That Baltar dude creeps me out," Brayden said, but not too loudly, as if he were afraid Baltar would hear.

"Me, too," Kenneth said. "I'ma go see what's up."

He got off the ATV and walked to Gabby's car, his hunting boots crunching on gravel. The woods stretched in every direction. A handful of houses were scattered along these roads, but Kenneth hadn't seen any close to this spot. Once the Freaks rode into the forest, they'd be on their own.

Shit like this shouldn't happen to kids, Kenneth thought. *Or anybody, really.*

Entmann, Davison, and Allen got out. Gabby locked the door and went around to the trunk. She opened it and started unloading duffels. Kenneth paused next to Jamie as Christian retrieved her bag and took out her costume. "Sup?" Jamie said. Kenneth couldn't be sure, but it sounded like Entmann's voice was shaking.

"We already suiting up?" Kenneth asked as Baltar and Micah disembarked, Micah carrying his own duffel. He looked more *there* than he had the last few times Kenneth had seen him. Maybe he had gotten a better night's sleep. Of course, sheer proximity to a horrible death tended to wake a guy up. As for the old man, he wore dark jeans, heavy black combat boots, and a thick black sweatshirt. He carried a bag of his own draped over his shoulder. It looked like leather that might have been new around the time Abraham Lincoln got ganked in that theater. What was it, some kind of saddlebag, like in those old Clint Eastwood movies Kenneth's dad liked to watch? Or a man purse?

"Yeah," Jamie said. "No point in sitting here and letting all this shit build up in our minds. Let's just get it done." Christian tossed Jamie's duffel over the car. Jamie caught it, opened it, took out his mask and something on a chain. His sensory charm.

Shit, Kenneth hadn't brought his. The old man had said the charms were for hiding from those asshole feds. "I left mine at home," Kenneth said, nodding at the charm.

Jamie watched him for a moment, eyes narrowed. "It seems like a good time to use anything that might keep us alive."

Baltar opened his bag, took something out, and handed it to Kenneth. Another charm. "I doubt the trinkets I gave you will do much against the senses of a trickster god," the old dude said. "But it's better to have it and not need it, yes? Besides, I suspect we'll see our government friends today."

Kenneth examined the charm while his allies—he still couldn't bring himself to call them friends, especially not with Micah around—put on their costumes. This necklace was different from the others. For one thing, the chain was heavier, thicker. The others were aluminum or silver or some shit; this one felt like stainless steel. Plus, this charm looked like a symbol, maybe a letter, though not from any alphabet Kenneth had ever seen. It was inlaid in tiny, sharp-looking jewels, all of them the same no-color. They might have been glass, except they looked denser, stronger, more faceted. If anyone else had noticed the difference, they gave no sign. In fact, nobody seemed to be paying him any attention at all.

Figured.

Brayden wandered over and stood beside Kenneth and Jamie, hands in his pockets. "What's my job? I mean, other than driving some of y'all out yonder."

Kenneth had pulled the new charm over his head and had begun removing his coveralls, because his costume wouldn't fit over them. Now he paused and took Brayden by the shoulders. "You don't got any other job, bro. Follow me out there and then carry your ass right back here. Don't stay to watch. And do *not* get involved. You hear?"

Brayden frowned. "But maybe I can—"

Kenneth shook him. "No. This kind of bullshit got Gavin killed. That ain't gonna happen to you, too."

"Kenneth's right," Jamie said as he put on his mask and adjusted the eye holes. "You got no powers, so you ought to be safe as long as you don't try to get in the fight."

"But the folks I'm carrying out, how are they gonna get back?"

"Walk," Jamie said. "Or maybe me and Christian will be in good enough shape to help. If not, you can come back once it's all over."

Everyone went quiet. Baltar cleared his throat and turned away. Birds sang in the woods. Across the road, opposite the direction they would take, something crashed through the foliage. Kenneth turned that way.

"Jesus," Brayden said. "Y'all don't think you're coming back."

"Nobody knows what's gonna happen," Kenneth said. "All we know is that this is our only play."

Brayden's eyes filled with tears, but he turned away before any could fall. "Whatever."

Kenneth nodded and finished removing the coveralls. He understood.

Baltar approached Jamie. "Best I don't go with you," the old dude said. "I shall take my own path. Perhaps the trickster won't sense me."

"Sure," Jamie said, sounding as if he didn't give a shit either way.

The charm felt frigid against Kenneth's chest. It hadn't warmed up since he put it on, nor had he gotten used to it. The old man had walked away and stood by Micah, whispering in the kid's ear. Weird-ass family. Gabby and Christian joined Jamie, who caught Kenneth's eye and gestured toward the ATVs. They walked over and stood around the vehicles.

"Y'all know anything about these?" Brayden asked.

Gabby shrugged. "What's to know? We'll just hang on until we get where we're going."

"Um, well. Yeah," Brayden said. He looked embarrassed. Didn't Gabby know he was just trying to help?

"You take Micah," Jamie told Brayden. "He won't like it, but he'll have to deal. Gabby, you mind riding with Kenneth?" She shook her head. "Good. Christian showed me the spot yesterday, so I'll lead y'all in. Christian will watch our six. Cool?"

Everybody seemed good with that, though Micah paid no attention. He still stood by the Lexus, arms dangling, staring at the ground. Half asleep, scared shitless, on heroin, whatever. With that kid, who knew? Baltar had vanished. Maybe he had already started creeping through the woods on foot. He couldn't fly, at least as far as Kenneth knew.

"Well," Christian said, "let's get to getting."

"Yo, Micah!" Jamie yelled. "Saddle up."

Micah looked up slowly, seemed to notice them for the first time, and rubbed his eyes. Then he shook out his arms. Jamie explained the arrangements to him. If Sterne resented having to ride with Brayden, he didn't show it.

Kenneth climbed on his four-wheeler and started it. Gabby got on and settled against his back, her legs dangling to either side, hands resting on Kenneth's hips. Brayden cranked up his own ride and Sterne dragged himself onto the back edge of the seat. He braced his arms on the rear rack. If Brayden had to crest some hill or struck a hole at speed, Micah would probably somersault backward and break his neck.

Kenneth smiled. He'd never be that lucky, but a guy could hope.

Christian hadn't put on her mask yet. Her eyes were wide and darting, as if she expected an ambush.

Entmann turned to Kenneth. "I'll try to find the easiest path. If you gotta go a different way, give me a wave."

With that, he floated up. When he passed the tallest of the trees, he flew forward. Gabby squeezed Kenneth's hips harder when he engaged the throttle. They bumped along, into and out of the ditch and among the trees.

✳❉✳

Brayden Dumbass Sears couldn't miss a fallen branch or a hole in the ground if he tried. The ATV's chassis kept jamming into Micah's nuts. At least the discomfort jarred him out of his stupor. He needed to get his shit together before they found this trickster. Fighting monsters while distracted sounded like a sure way to get murked. If he died today, though, at least he wouldn't have to worry about all this shit anymore. And maybe his friends would remember the good times. God knew that if things kept going like this, he would come to a bad end, and everyone would curse his memory.

He couldn't remember when he had last slept at an appropriate time. Ever since Baltar had shown up, Micah had been crashing in class, while watching TV, as he did his homework, and he always, always, *always* dreamed of that weird voice, the one that kept telling him to join it, to be raised to a high position, to rule.

He probably should have told the others about it. Jamie, at least. But every time he started to, something stopped him. He and his friends had already drifted apart. They had left him alone, gripped in the fist of a sadness the likes of which he had never felt. If he told them about the dreams, they might sympathize and offer to help. Or they might not. On the way out here, in that warm cocoon of a car, Uncle Baltar had actually tried to talk Micah into abandoning the Freaks. "You owe them nothing," Baltar had said.

Around the others, the old man's voice took on a soothing, disarming quality, like he was the best-ever reader of bedtime stories. But when he and Micah were alone, it recalled a vocabulary word Micah had learned in English a couple of years back: *stentorian*. It grew in power and depth and volume until it blocked out everything else. Micah had never heard a charismatic lunatic speak, one of those cult-of-personality guys like Hitler or that preacher who had led his followers to mass suicide, but he imagined that their voices would have sounded like Baltar's, the kind of voice that could make killing yourself or slaughtering millions of people or ditching your best friends sound logical, forgivable, right. Was Baltar responsible for Micah's brain fog after all? That voice—maybe it didn't just *seem* like it could put you to sleep. Maybe it actually could.

That was crazy, though, right? Why would Baltar want Micah half-zonked all the time?

"They're my only friends," Micah had said in reply to Baltar's suggestion.

"You can make new friends," Baltar had said. "Why put yourself in danger for a person you barely know, one who rejected you for Christian Allen? Or for so-called friends who chose Kenneth Del Ray over you?"

For a while, Micah had said nothing. His eyelids had felt so damn heavy. But he had forced them open. Looking out the window, forehead against the glass, he had let the cold ooze through the brain fog. "You're turning out to be a really shitty Giles."

"I still don't know who that is."

"Lame." *No, I won't ditch my friends,* he had thought. *I can't. Because then all I'd have is Baltar, and I'm pretty sure he's crazy.*

"You cannot defeat a god," Baltar had said. "Even if you fight it to a standstill, the trickster is immortal and can afford to wait, to try again. Can you?"

Micah hadn't replied. Now that they were driving deeper into the forest, though, it felt like they were rushing into the teeth of a hopeless cause.

If that is truly the plan you follow, that eerie voice whispered, the one that sort of sounded like Baltar, only even deeper, surer, more powerful, *then perhaps your group needs a new leader. Perhaps it needs you. Perhaps it would be best if the one you follow died a glorious death.*

Shut up, Micah thought. God, what *was* that voice? And *who*?

And maybe that really summed up why it bothered him so much—not just because of what it said, but because he truly didn't know whether it belonged to some being the group hadn't yet encountered or whether it was a version of his own voice, whispering the dark thoughts that had lain deep within him all along.

✳

As the uneven terrain made the ATV buck and shudder, Gabby had clasped her hands around Kenneth's waist, her torso against his, her left cheek pressed against his back. She hadn't bothered trying to keep up with the landmarks. A town girl through and through, she wouldn't even camp in her own backyard. All trees looked pretty much alike to her. Besides, if she had to find the road by herself, that would mean both Jamie and Christian had been killed or incapacitated. She couldn't imagine going on after that.

Yeah, right, said a voice in her mind. It sounded like Gavin. *You'll be the first one to die. You might as well borrow Brayden's pocketknife and cut your own throat before this monster hurts you worse than you can imagine.*

Shut up, Gavin. You're a douche even from beyond the grave.

Jamie had positioned himself just above the trees and twenty or thirty yards forward, arms held near his body, fists clenched. He looked like a superhero heading into battle, which he was. Gabby wouldn't let him down, wouldn't listen to that hateful, condescending voice, no matter how scared she was. She would stand with Jamie to the end, even though she felt like pissing herself.

You're a superhero. And heroes don't chicken out.

Brave words. She hoped she could live up to them.

She closed her eyes and invoked a prayer her mom had taught her, as best she could remember it.

Lord, you are Holy above all others, and all of the strength that I need is

*in your hands. I am not asking, Lord, that you take this trial away. Instead,
I simply ask that Your will be done in my life. Whatever that means, that is
what I want.*

*Jesus, hear my prayer. I know that it is not your intent to bring me to this
point just to leave me in the wilderness alone.*

In Jesus's name. Amen.

And then, from her father's traditions:

In the name of Adonai
the God of Israel:
May the angel Michael be at my right,
and the angel Gabriel be at my left;
and in front of me the angel Uriel,
and behind me the angel Raphael …
and above my head the presence of God.

Would prayers work against a god? Was it blasphemous to invoke
the protection of one deity against another? She didn't know.

The ATV droned on, taking her farther and farther from the world
she knew. The trees swallowed them.

✳✳✳

Jamie's costume flapped like it had been hung on a clothesline in
a windstorm. He thanked God for his aura, which eased the cold's
bite. If only he could have worn a jacket, but Rabbit had said the Team
would probably show up. Of course, if they found Gabby's and Baltar's
cars, no disguise would make any difference, but given all the miles
of back roads around Quapaw City and how the one they had parked
on seemed more like a dirt path with ambition, Jamie thought the cars
would be safe.

Kenneth and Gabby buzzed along below. Brayden and Micah's four-
wheeler followed maybe twenty feet behind Kenneth's. Kenneth and
Brayden still wore their orange vests, but so what? Rabbit knew they

were coming. Besides, the trickster would hear the engines, the crunch of tires over leaves and twigs. Christian was "super-jogging" behind the ATVs. It must have driven her crazy, using her powers at the lowest level, like Jamie might feel if he could only float a millimeter off the ground.

When he and Christian had first found Rabbit's clearing, Jamie had nearly wept. It lay deep in the forest, far from any possible help. Probably why Rabbit had picked it. *We're gonna die out here. I should have come alone. Maybe I could have struck a deal. My life for the others'. For Gabby's.* But no, Rabbit wanted them all. And Jamie was leading every-one right to him. They might as well have hung raw meat around their necks and gone swimming in shark-infested waters. *Micah thinks I'm a dumbass. Could be he's right. My only plan is try not to get killed.* What else could he do, though? They couldn't run from a god; it would find them. This way, at least they could die on their feet, not kicking and screaming in some hiding place. They would stand up and walk forward and do the best they could. *God, if we die today, please don't let my friends suffer.*

Maybe Rabbit believed they deserved whatever pain he would inflict, especially the white kids. Ever since Baltar had told them about the trickster's true identity, Jamie had been thinking about what had happened to the Indigenous People who had once roamed the land now called the United States. Even if you left out genocide and that Manifest Destiny bullshit and broken treaties and every single colo-nialist excess they had learned about in school—you couldn't leave any of that out, of course, but say you could—the evidence of America's crimes lay everywhere. Just look at the names you could still find here in Arkansas: Quapaw City and the Quapaw River. The Ouachita River. The word "Arkansas" itself. Throw a rock in any American state and you'd be likely to hit something named after the victims of a strategic, racist, violent mission to wipe out the Nations, their cultures, their languages. The Freaks weren't personally responsible for that, of course, even if some of their ancestors were. But maybe to a being like Rabbit, to whom time meant nothing, those distant connections were enough to condemn whoever was still alive—the Freaks and the Team. And if Rabbit wasn't completely right to scapegoat them, Jamie couldn't say he was completely wrong, either.

CHAPTER THIRTY-ONE

The child slept. My magic kept them safe, nourished, floating outside the world's currents. Should I have taken the young warriors one at a time and done the same to them? I could have destroyed them at my leisure or simply kept them buried and slumbering through eternity's long years. But even as I wondered, it felt wrong. As battle-tested fighters, they deserved the opportunity to die a warrior's death. Yes, trapping them in dreams appealed to my nature—what a trick it would be. But I kept returning to the girl with speed. The one whose blood whispered the songs of the Quapaw Nation, faintly, words and melody as gossamer as a spider's web. She felt nothing for me, did not understand. But in time, she could learn.

Even if she continued to defy me, she deserved a good death.

Fate had always fascinated me—the way relationships branch like streams and rivers, each touching each in ways no one could predict. I never would have taken the sleeping child if they had chosen different friends. If they had fallen in love with anyone else. But some path brought them to this village, intersected with the warriors' trajectories, brought them to me. Any single choice made differently might have led them elsewhere. They might have lived decades without knowing the inside of a warren, the touch of downy fur, the earthy smells. Did fate have a mind, or did it simply reach where it would like a blind creature searching for food? I had never known. Perhaps I never would.

But fate did not control everything. Choice could beggar it.

Would the government men, for instance, have discovered the children's trip into the woods if I had not gone to them? Or would those little tyrants have stayed in their lodge, tearing their hair and beating their chests? I think the latter.

The angriest and most reckless, the one named Mossman, had come outside and into the dooryard, where he paced, furious and frustrated. The way he stared at the ground and muttered to himself, I could have strolled up behind him in my true form and killed him, and he never would have known how he had died unless some other spirit told him. But I had no interest in killing him that day, so I walked out of the woods wearing the shape of his dead friend Parker.

He stopped, turned, his mouth falling open. He embraced me. "Floyd!" he cried against my shoulder. Then he held me at arm's length, the smile vanishing. "Where have you been? We thought maybe those kids had murdered you and thrown your body in the river."

"He is not in the river," I said. "But dead? Oh, yes."

Mossman moved faster than I expected for someone of his age, but I knocked the alien gun from his hand. It landed too far away for him to reach. Not that it could have done much against me, but I like pain no more than any other creature.

"You killed him," Mossman hissed. "He had a wife and kids, you son of a bitch." He threw a punch. I let it strike my face. The crunch of his finger bones sounded like one of my little cousins munching fresh lettuce. Mossman stared at his hand a moment and then began to scream.

I covered his mouth. He grunted and moaned and struggled, but I held him fast, and when he subsided, I let him go and stepped away. "You should learn to control yourself," I said. "Be still, and I shall tell you a revelation. Scream and I'll tear out your throat. Choose."

Tucking his broken hand under his other arm, Mossman glared, his face reddened and sweating despite the cold. "What are we supposed to tell Parker's family?"

"What did your ancestors tell the families of the Red Men they slaughtered?"

"You bastard," Mossman said. His expression suggested that he wanted my pelt on his lodge's wall.

"I am the spawn of the marriage of nothing and everything."

Mossman hesitated, perhaps weighing the satisfaction of striking me—with what, though?—against the rest of his life. In the end, his life won. I imagine it was close.

"We aren't done, you and me," he said.

"No. To your sorrow. But if you would bring Parker home and tend his body, come to my warren. Bring your friends and all your pretty weapons."

Mossman's eyes narrowed. "What warren?"

"Here."

I touched his forehead and seared the location in his mind. It would sit in his dreams like the blank face of a bluff in winter until I activated it. After that, he would be able to think of little else. His path to me would be as unerring as the wolf's when it stalks the deer. His wide eyes stared. His open mouth drooled. I left him that way. By the time he awakened, I had reached home.

And now, as my emissaries marked the children's entrance into the forest, I sent my rabbits to the government men's lodge. Soon enough, the one called Jeffcoat looked out the window and saw them. The men came outside, and Mossman fell to his knees, clutching his head. The path burned bright in his mind. He would lead the others here.

I left the child to their slumber and crawled into the chamber where Parker's corpse lay. He looked as if he, too, had fallen into a peaceful sleep.

The endgame had commenced.

CHAPTER THIRTY-TWO

Bec Villalobos appeared to stand in the middle of the clearing, beside a hole in the ground. But Jamie couldn't mistake that being for Bec. He hoped the others wouldn't either.

He landed some distance from the trickster, who watched him in silence. The approaching ATVs buzzed like a swarm of insects. "Sup?" Jamie said, lifting his chin, as if Rabbit was an old friend.

Rabbit-Bec smiled. "I knew you would come. Yet part of me wishes you had not. I take no pleasure in your death."

"Ain't you sweet."

The ATVs reached the clearing and flanked Jamie. He didn't turn to look at them. Better not to take his eyes off the enemy. One engine cut off. Feet crunched through leaves as the Freaks dismounted. The other ATV revved up and drove away—Brayden getting out of Dodge.

Jamie's arms dangled at his sides. He wiggled the fingers of each hand like a gunfighter preparing to draw.

"Before we begin," Rabbit said, "I have a question." He stepped closer.

Jamie held his ground. "Knock yourself out."

Rabbit cocked his head like a curious puppy. "Why do you fight alongside the whites?"

Whatever Jamie had imagined the trickster might ask, that wasn't it. "Huh?"

"You are descended from the enslaved," Rabbit said. "From their rage and sorrow and loss. The whites stole them from their homelands and bore them across the oceans in chains, dumping the sick and the weak and the dead overboard like so much garbage. Whites put your people in chains, whipped them to the bone, bred them like cattle, shattered

255

families and murdered and raped. Even after the slaves were freed, the horror continued. And continues still."

"No shit," Jamie said, gritting his teeth. "What's your point?"

"My point is that you stand with the spawn of those responsible."

Jamie's jaw clenched. "They're my friends."

"Are you sure?"

"Look, you're right. White folks got a lot to answer for. Only a dumbass would argue about that. But these kids right here? They've stood beside me my whole life. All of 'em. We've earned each other's trust. Each other's love. Can you understand that?"

Now Rabbit looked sad. "But now you will die with them. This saddens me. Your flight power seems a lesser threat to this world than the girl's energy bursts or that other boy's fire and ice. Leave now, and I will spare you."

Jamie spread his legs shoulder-width apart and clenched his fists. "Nah."

Rabbit sighed. "You have chosen your path. Now you must walk it, all the way to the end." The rest of the Freaks had encircled Rabbit. He glanced over his right shoulder, where Kenneth stood. "Surrounding your enemy is sound strategy. But today it will not help you."

Rabbit began to change.

✳✳✳

Christian's stomach turned over as everything that made Rabbit look like Bec—the height, the weight, the body type, the hair—ran like water, morphed and pulsed and bubbled, until his whole body expanded. It was like watching Bruce Banner transform into the Hulk in real life. In place of Bec stood a hunched, slobbering monster from one of those old black-and-white movies, the end product of the change she had seen only part of on that night by the pond: A more-or-less human face with long, sharp buck teeth, a mouth full of lesser incisors.

Perfectly round rabbit eyes over a human nose. No tail, but those ears, the final absurd touch.

Jamie flew straight at the trickster, one fist held out like Superman, but as soon as his feet left the ground, Rabbit's body exploded into that flock of screaming blackbirds. Some of the Freaks had seen this trick before, but that didn't help. The birds enveloped Jamie, completely obscuring him, a shifting mass of dark feathers and beaks that forced him toward Kenneth, whose eyes grew wide, his feet seemingly glued to the ground. At the last second, the birds shot upward, and Jamie smashed into Kenneth. They tumbled over and over almost to the tree line, where they both lay, stunned.

Rabbit can change and react almost as fast as I can. Two of us knocked silly already.

The flock flew near the treetops, spiraled, funneled down, and struck the ground, where their swirling mass formed legs, waist, torso, all of it fur-covered and thick. Now the bear that had saved Christian from the Team thrust its head forward and its front legs out. It roared. Then it fell to all fours and ran at Jamie and Kenneth, covering ground at shocking speed. When it reached the boys, it stood and raised a forepaw, ready to knock Jamie's head from his shoulders.

Christian broke her paralysis and zoomed across the clearing. She struck the bear, battering it with kicks and punches, dodging its blows. *Hey, my fingers ain't stiff anymore. Good timing.* The bear roared again, outraged. This attack had done a lot of good against Na'ul. Maybe it would here, too. Buy Jamie and Kenneth some time, at least. Maybe—

The bear stuck out its leg like a schoolkid trying to trip a classmate. Christian struck it and went stumbling into the woods at super-speed, glancing off trees until she fell headlong into a thicket. She rotated as she went down and managed to land on her back, but the brush clutched her costume, tore it in places, grasped her left leg and right arm and the back of her head. She came to rest partially suspended, struggling and yanking at the foliage.

The bear made a deep, throaty noise that sounded like laughter. *At least he didn't turn into a giant banana peel.*

Ice grew around him and froze him solid, like a cartoon character that had fallen in a winter river. His mouth was caught in mid-snarl. Micah had gotten into the fight.

As Christian extricated herself, Gabby helped Kenneth and Jamie to their feet. Micah walked across the clearing, pouring on the ice. The block grew thicker. The others had to back away or get frozen, too. It was the first time Christian had seen Micah use his powers since the Freaks realized that the whole Team had arrived in Quapaw City and intended to surveil them 24/7. He looked like he had on the night they fought Na'ul: Angry and aggressive and ready to freeze or burn the world.

Christian finally ripped her way out of the thicket, tearing holes in her costume where her arm and leg had gotten tangled. She trotted to the others. Kenneth and Jamie looked dazed.

"Hey," Jamie said. "Bec's gotta be around here somewhere. Maybe down in that big-ass hole over yonder. Can you—"

"Y'all!" Micah cried.

The ice exploded. Jagged chunks flew everywhere. One struck Micah in the chest. He staggered backward, sat down hard, fell over. Another grazed the side of Kenneth's head. He stumbled sideways, blood dripping from a small tear in his mask onto the forest floor.

A bear-shaped glob of water hung in the air. Then it fell to the ground, bubbled over to Micah like it was following a stream bed, and engulfed him. It forced its way up his nose and into his mouth. He thrashed and gurgled.

"It's drowning him!" Gabby shouted.

Duh, thought Christian as she sped over and jammed her arm into the water puddle. She made a circular motion at top speed, flinging water to all points of the clearing. "Micah, heat yourself up! Make it steam!"

Still caught in the panic of drowning on dry land, Micah did nothing. Gabby got behind him, put her arms under his, and held her palms over the thin layer of water rippling around his body. She sent energy pulses through the water, scattering it, disrupting its flow.

Micah finally recovered enough to help himself. He grew *red*, redder, like fire, and the water began to steam away. Gabby let him go. Christian speed-dragged him away, stopping when she reached Jamie and Kenneth, who had just stood there, helpless.

The water sprang from everywhere it had been flung, sometimes in individual drops, and coalesced behind Gabby. A shape began to form.

"Watch out!" Jamie yelled.

Christian was already moving. The water hardened, becoming green and scaly. Short, stubby legs and a head with a long, toothy jaw revealed themselves in the half a second it took her to reach Gabby. She had intended to speed Gabby away, but the alligator fell to all fours, bent, and chomped down on Christian's right leg. She flopped to the ground. The gator bore down and rolled, trying to rip her leg off. Since she couldn't run, she vibrated. If she could keep her protective aura engaged, maybe she could save her leg. But the pressure was tremendous, like someone had dropped a car onto her, and now the gator was dragging her toward that hole in the ground. Jamie grabbed her and engaged his flight powers, his hands under Christian's armpits. The resulting tug of war threatened to tear her apart. She screamed.

Kenneth lumbered toward them, his right fist clenched and raised over his head. "Son of a bitch," he muttered as he brought the fist down on the gator's head with a crunching, squishy sound. The gator let go, and Jamie flew Christian to the far side of the clearing.

"You okay?" he asked.

"Yeah," she said.

Kenneth's hand had smashed completely through the trickster. Now he raised his arm, stuck through the gator like a knife into a ham, and shook it. Rabbit's form began to shift and run again. Before anything could solidify, Gabby blasted it, her energy screaming in the air and splattering the Rabbit-blob. She held the beam steady, her feet set. Kenneth stumbled away. Micah, who had been rolling on the ground and groaning while holding his injured chest, got to his knees and shot fire at the glob of not-quite-flesh-and-bone, engulfing the whole mess. Gabby added her own destructive energy, though much of it passed beyond Rabbit and blasted trees to splinters that rained into the clearing. Dust and leaves obscured much of the sky in that direction. Jamie raised a hand in front of his eyes.

Christian got to her feet. "Gotta recharge," she called. "Be right back."

She speed-limped into the woods, looking for Kenneth's ATV and the high-calorie food they had brought. Her leg felt better already.

✳✳✳

Shielding his eyes, Kenneth watched Gabby and Sterne blast away at that weird meatball. He hated to admit it, but those two were a lot more powerful than him or Jamie, and while you might call Christian's power more versatile, she couldn't do anything like this, either. *If me and Sterne ever throw down, he might just kick my ass. Even kill me. If anybody had told me that a year ago, I would have laughed.*

The meatball contracted, condensed, and burst outward. Sterne's fire and Gabby's energy shot up and out, like they had hit some invisible wall. The meatball became a gator again as the Freaks' blasts struck the woods, setting some trees on fire and blasting others in half.

"Dammit," Sterne said, flicking his wrist. The flames went out.

The gator skittered forward, its jaws wide open. For a moment, Kenneth froze, looking down its maw, wondering how it would feel to get swallowed a chunk at a time. But as the gator tried to chomp him, Kenneth caught its jaws, one hand on the upper and one on the lower. He dug his heels in and pushed, but the jaws inched closed anyway, those terrible teeth pressing against his aura. Without it, they would have skewered his palms. As it was, his arms were on fire with the strain. Were all alligators this badass?

Kenneth's legs started to feel rubbery. Christian flitted from Freak to Freak, handing out junk food. That was what Kenneth needed: fuel for his power. He hoped he lived long enough to get some.

The alligator disengaged, backed up, and shifted. Now a full-grown tiger roared, swiping at Kenneth with one forepaw. Kenneth staggered backward. "Jesus *Christ!*" he cried, and then he tripped and fell onto his back. The tiger pounced. He got his hands under its front legs and shoved as hard as he could. It arced over the clearing and into the woods and landed on its side with a thud. Gabby, eating a Snickers, used her free hand to blast it. Sterne joined her again, shooting fire. The smell of charred flesh filled the air. Kenneth gagged.

Rabbit made no sound. Had they killed him?

The smoke merged with all the other shit they had stirred up. Visibility beyond the clearing had gotten bad, even though Sterne and Gabby had stopped shooting. Kenneth stood, his body aching, and joined the others. Somebody handed him a Three Musketeers. He hated Three Musketeers, but he ate it in three bites. They had been fighting for maybe two minutes, but everything already hurt. Still, the sugar in the candy bar charged through him, and he felt a little better.

The Freaks stood shoulder to shoulder, facing the direction where they had last seen the trickster. Kenneth stood next to Micah and, so far, neither of them had barfed or thrown a punch. Christian was bent over, hands on her knees, though she kept her gaze trained on the woods.

"Is it over?" Gabby asked. "Did we win?"

No one answered. Kenneth strained his eyes, trying to spot any sign of movement. For all he knew, Rabbit could mimic the dust-choked air itself. He sure as shit wasn't going to walk out there and kick over every log and pile of leaves until that thing turned into Godzilla and ate him.

Somewhere behind them, something moved. A squirrel barked.

Then the ground shook.

"What the hell?" Micah said.

"That's an impact tremor is what it is," Jamie muttered. "I'm fairly alarmed here."

"Quit it," Kenneth said. This was no time to geek out. The quaking grew stronger by the second, and now they could hear thudding footsteps coming closer and closer. Kenneth spread his feet a bit, determined not to lose his balance at precisely the wrong moment.

Something trumpeted. He recognized the sound from the movies. Christian must have, too. "Great," she said.

A bull elephant burst out of the debris cloud, its head shaking from side to side, its trunk knocking downed branches out of its way.

"Scatter!" Jamie screamed as he grabbed Gabby and flew straight up.

No shit, Kenneth thought as he leaped to his left and hit the ground rolling. A sharp branch jabbed him in the shoulder. Christian had vanished, but Micah was on the ground, trying to regain his feet. Kenneth had no idea why he had fallen.

The elephant tried to trample Sterne, but the kid rolled sideways. Unfortunately for him, he tumbled right into the elephant's trunk, which wrapped around him, picked him up, and slammed him to the ground. Sterne squealed like a mouse. Christian appeared on top of the elephant's head—how had she gotten up *there*?—and drummed on its skull with both fists. The trickster tried to use Sterne to knock her off, but she kept bobbing and weaving. Why didn't Micah do something with his powers? Maybe that slam had knocked him silly.

As if Rabbit had heard Kenneth's thought, he slammed Sterne into the ground again. Was the kid unconscious? Dead?

Probably. Nothing else can shut him up.

One of Gabby's beams struck the elephant in its right side. It staggered a couple of steps and turned, looking for the source, while Christian kept playing that heavy metal drum solo on its head.

Kenneth was running before he realized he was even moving. *I'm charging an elephant. What the hell do I do when I get there?*

Rabbit the elephant was tensing. Kenneth planted his feet, wound up, and threw a right cross from the waist. His fist struck the side of the trickster's head with enough force to dislodge Christian, who either landed on her feet or got up and zoomed out of range. Rabbit staggered sideways and fell over, dropping Micah in a heap. The elephant-god-thing was already getting up when Kenneth slugged him again, this time a left uppercut that snapped its head backward. And that was when Jamie swooped down, landed in front of the prone creature, and lay his palm against that big gray noggin.

Jamie's eyes rolled back. His body locked. Rabbit jerked and snorted.

Entmann had told the Freaks that he had always been an empath, someone who could sense what other people were feeling, even to the point of feeling it himself. Apparently after they got their powers, he had become even more sensitive, to put it mildly. When he'd touched Na'ul skin to skin on the shore of the pond, the two of them had mind-melded. Jamie had felt Na'ul's emotions, but even crazier, he had fallen into the monster's memories and briefly lived them. From the way the vampire had reacted, Entmann believed the experience had gone both ways. Now it looked like he was doing it again. Mind-melding with a god. Brave kid.

Can't let this chance go to waste.

Kenneth climbed on Rabbit's body, straddled his neck, and rained down punches with both hands. The elephant's head dribbled against the ground, but Entmann kept his palm flat against Rabbit's skin. Both he and the trickster remained frozen in place, their bodies locked as their minds intertwined.

Christian showed up carrying a thick tree branch and began to bash Rabbit with it. When it splintered and fell apart in her hands, she went and got another one. Gabby and Micah took positions on either side and zapped Rabbit. Sterne's fire lit up the belly and back legs. That godawful smell of burning flesh rose over the clearing again.

Micah caught Kenneth's eye and lifted his chin. *Holy shit, did he just give me a what's-up or something? We really must be about to die.*

Jamie was trembling, eyes closed. Who knew how much longer he could keep Rabbit down like this? Kenneth had to do something. Besides, whether on purpose or not, Micah was about to fry him along with the elephant. Kenneth leaped down and ran for the woods, calling over his shoulder, "I'm gonna find something to hit him with. Like a tree or, I dunno, somebody's house."

"Hurry," Gabby said through clenched teeth, still pouring on the energy blasts.

Kenneth sprinted. He got within fifteen yards of the trees before he saw the Team marching toward him in a skirmish line. Their special weapons were trained on him. He skidded to a halt.

McCreedy wasn't there, nor was Agent Parker. Greenwalt, Jeffcoat, Vincent, and Kragthorpe flanked Mossman, whose remaining hand sported a thick, clublike cast. He wore his dark glasses, as usual, and a savage smile. "Freeze," he said, his voice conversational, as if Kenneth had met him for coffee. "Federal agents. You're under arrest."

CHAPTER THIRTY-THREE

From behind Kenneth, Gabby shouted, "Ignore them! Don't let up!"

"Y'all's timing sucks," Kenneth said, keeping his eyes on Mossman but well aware of how the others were flanking him. "We've got him down. Leave us alone and we'll take him out."

The moment stretched out. The agents shuffled forward a foot at a time while Kenneth backed away. The constant sizzle of Gabby's power joined the crackling of burning foliage. Kenneth's eyes and nostrils burned from the smoke.

"Hurry up!" Christian called. "I don't know how long we can hold him!"

"Come on," Kenneth said to Mossman. "What's it gonna be?"

Mossman nodded at Vincent. "Lancer?"

Vincent held a boxy weapon that looked like a shotgun's older, meaner cousin. He pulled the trigger.

The gun coughed twice, *huk huk*. Kenneth winced, expecting to feel some sort of projectile strike him. But nothing did.

Instead, two tiny pellets floated out of the big-bore barrels. They looked to be about the size of a couple of aspirin. For a moment, they floated and swirled around each other. Then, with a whining noise that increased in intensity until it threatened to burst Kenneth's eardrums, they shot forward. They grew as they flew, from aspirin size to golf ball, then baseball, softball, basketball. They sprouted serrations, like circular-saw blades.

"Oh, shit," Kenneth said, and then they struck him.

One sliced into his left shoulder. Searing heat ripped through his body. He bellowed in agony. The other blade dug into the outside of his right thigh. Those limbs grew wet and warm even as the blades, still screaming, sliced him across the back, driving him to his knees. The blades circled him, crisscrossed in the air, and came back, slicing his right arm and left thigh, his chest. Then they circled again.

They were going to cut him to pieces.

❋

Jamie felt like he was being shredded. Every cell in his body cried out *Let go let go let go*. Someone was screaming over the frying-meat sound of Gabby's power and some sort of high-pitched whine. Raised voices blended into a low-key growl. Amid all this, Jamie fell farther and farther down a seemingly bottomless hole filled with stars, planets the color and hue of marbles, exploding suns, and cold, dead moons. Oceans formed on planetary surfaces and dried up and died. Whole forests grew and thrived and burned or decayed. One crude hut became two became a cluster became a city. He glimpsed the shadowy forms of creatures his mind could not comprehend, some bathed in the soft light of a spring afternoon, others wearing darkness like clothes and radiating furious hunger that could only be satisfied with mass death. Energy filled Jamie, a power that threatened to burst his very atoms. He could feel himself coming apart.

The darkness of space and time rushed at him, zoomed past him. One pinprick of light grew and grew until it enveloped him, and now a world revealed itself, swaths of dark green and deep blue and white breaking into individual trees standing tall against a cloudy sky. A river flowed nearby, the water impossibly clear. Fish swam in it; the smallest of them was as long as Jamie's arm. This river stretched so far into the distance that its far shore couldn't be glimpsed with human eyes. In the woods, untouched by any ax or machine, enormous animals wandered: thirty-point deer, bears that could have stood on their hind legs and leaned their forepaws on the roof-peaks of houses, squirrels the size of dogs.

This is one of the eternal places, sighed a voice in his head. Rabbit's? *They exist beside time's river, whose waters flow from the past to the future, its mouth undiscovered even by the gods. From this shore I saw you open the portal. From this shore I traveled to your world so that I could fix your mistake. To this shore I will return when you are gone.*

Jamie gritted his teeth and concentrated. Rabbit's voice faded but didn't disappear. Images bombarded Jamie, each one like a punch to the brain: the earth before life, angry seas and swirling gases and exploding volcanoes; the rise and fall of dinosaurs and giant mammals, some of which resembled creatures from a nightmare; the coming of humanity and their eventual mastery of fire and tools; the migrations; the First Nations in their glory; the advance of Europeans and the vanishing of all those tribes; chattel slavery and cultural appropriation and the death of shame; agriculture and industry and information; everything evolving, growing, the human blight spreading like ink on cloth until every patch of ground, every animal and insect bore the signature of that particular and violent ascension.

Were those Jamie's words, or Rabbit's?

See what whites have done to our land, our peoples. See whom you stand beside.

Jamie groaned, whimpered. What was worse, the physical agony of this connection or the way all these images and that voice flayed his psyche?

I don't stand beside any of that bullshit. I stand with my friends. We'll never leave each other to die alone just because we're different. We're all we've got. And that's why we'll beat you.

And now, somehow, all the pain doubled, blotting out every thought, every perception. Jamie had become a ball of raw nerve endings.

Impressive, Rabbit whispered. *But futile.*

The pain doubled yet again.

Jamie screamed.

✳

Pouring on the flame and listening to Kenneth banter with that Mossman shitbag, Micah had believed he could actually kill Rabbit if the others would back off so he could let loose. And Rabbit deserved to die. He was supernatural, like Na'ul, the mother-killer. If the others didn't have the stomach or the power, Micah would do it himself. He opened his mouth to say so, but that was when Jamie shrieked. Startled, Micah lost his concentration. His fire went out, but he barely noticed because Jamie was falling backward, his body stiff. Gabby, of all people, wasn't even paying attention. Instead, she was looking at something behind Micah. Her eyes grew wide. She stopped shooting. Micah turned. Two huge sawblades flashed around Kenneth, shredding his costume and the body underneath it. Blood spurted in mists and arcs. The air sizzled, and Gabby's beams obliterated the blades. Kenneth fell on his face, blood pooling around him.

A shifting from behind. Rabbit was moving.

Kragthorpe fired his souped-up rifle, and a green line of goop headed straight for Gabby, some of it burbling onto the ground and disintegrating whatever it touched. Micah stumbled away just as Gabby vanished. *Sometimes,* he thought wildly, *it seems like Christian spends half of every fight just moving people around.* The acid or whatever it was struck a pine tree on the clearing's edge, and much of the trunk disintegrated, the upper branches tumbling into the clearing and onto the smoking, bloody elephant that had just gotten to its feet.

"Son of a bitch," Micah hissed, sending half a dozen grapefruit-sized ice balls Kragthorpe's way. The CIA man dodged four of them, but the fifth knocked the rifle out of his hands, and the sixth grazed his temple. He fell backward and lay still.

Micah fired more ice balls at Jeffcoat and a solid line of fire at Greenwalt, who sheltered behind a tree. When it caught fire, Greenwalt yelped and ran deeper into the woods. Mossman, still grinning like an ax murderer, was walking toward Kenneth. Micah had no idea what that douchecanoe planned to do with no working hands, but that grin pissed him off. He shot a burst of flame at Mossman's feet.

"Whoa," Mossman cried as he backed away. One of his shoes had caught fire. He turned in a circle, stomping and trying to kick the shoe off at the same time.

Micah stood over Kenneth, his shoes squishing in blood. Kenneth shifted and groaned. "Use your powers," Micah whispered. "You'll heal."

Jamie had flown or been carried out of the clearing, leaving only Christian and Micah, who drew a flame circle around himself and Kenneth, raised the fire to chest height, and lobbed ice balls at Mossman. The first few battered the agent, who fled, cursing, his shoe still smoldering. Gabby's beams pressed Greenwalt and Jeffcoat, zapping the trees they hid behind. Micah wondered where she was standing but had no time to look.

Kragthorpe crawled around, probably looking for his gun. The elephant no longer lay under the downed pine. Who knew where the hell it had gone? Too much to keep up with.

Kenneth got to his hands and knees. His costume hung in rags. Blood dripped everywhere. Micah's nerves jangled; his hands and feet buzzed with adrenaline. He felt like he was in a first-person shooter video game where anything might happen. For example, you could find yourself protecting your oldest enemy, who had just fought off a god in the form of an elephant as it tried to smash you to jelly.

Then a high-intensity dizziness struck him. It felt like the top of his head was going to lift off. The world spun, then went dim. Micah staggered away from Kenneth, hands on his head. Gabby was yelling for him to help her, but he couldn't even help himself. He dropped to one knee. Darkness swirled in the sky overhead and engulfed the clearing, but before it obscured everyone and everything else, Micah saw that the others were still fighting. Whatever this was, it was happening only to him. From somewhere in that darkness, the voice returned. It sounded louder than a tornado, bigger than an Ozark mountain, and it pulsed against his temples from the inside, as if trying to burst out.

Why do you help them? They are nothing. Embrace your true self. Your real power. Burn them all until not even ashes remain. Crack their charred bones with your teeth. Do it now. Kill them. Kill them. Kill.

Every word thundered against the backs of Micah's eyes. He held his hands over his ears. The darkness swirled again, opening a path between him and Kenneth, who was clenching his fists open and closed, open and closed. Maybe letting his strength ebb and flow, charging up that healing power they all shared. Soon, if the feds and Rabbit stayed off him, he might be able to fight again.

Kill him before that can happen. Freeze the blood in his veins. Shatter him like glass. Kill. Kill. Kill.

Micah stumbled toward Kenneth, raising his fists, aiming at the stunned and bleeding kid.

A blur, and Christian stood between Micah and Kenneth. "Are you serious? You pull this shit *now*? Get back, before I kick your ass myself!" She shoved him away.

I'm sorry, he thought as Christian helped Kenneth up. They started toward the opposite side of the clearing. *I know nobody would believe it, but I really am.*

Kill, said the voice. *Kill. Kill.*

LEAVE ME ALONE!

His entire body burst into flame. He poured on the energy, getting hotter and hotter, ignoring the empty, ravenous feeling in his gut. Anything to override that awful voice and the things it urged him to do.

Jeffcoat stepped out from behind a tree and aimed a blaster at him, the one that looked like Han Solo's. Micah had no idea whether a laser could get through flames this intense. He only knew that fear and despair filled him like water in a bucket, threatening to spill over at any moment.

The hell with it. Maybe it's for the best.

Micah lowered his hands. "Do it," he said.

But Jeffcoat was yanked backward, like someone had lassoed him from horseback and took off at full speed. Greenwalt was shouting Jeffcoat's code name. What had done that? Rabbit? Uncle Baltar?

Kill those who remain. Kill them all.

Micah shook his head hard enough to rattle his brain and turned up his flame again. The ground had caught fire in a six-foot circumference around him. Now that flame bulged outward. And still the voice demanded that he murder the feds, his friends, the trickster, everyone and everything.

And, again, Micah felt himself falling into the depths from which that voice spoke. He let his flame die, turned, and stumbled through the clearing and into the woods. He ran and ran, and then he sat down, head in hands, and closed his eyes. In that darkness, a pair of red, reptilian eyes pulsed.

They grew larger, larger.

Micah tumbled into them.

✳

Christian watched Micah's retreat. The kid looked concussed, even though nothing had happened to him after the elephant slam. Maybe he hadn't recovered after all. Kenneth had managed to stand up, but he looked out on his feet. He, too, stumbled for the cover of the trees. At Christian's feet, Jamie was regaining consciousness. That left only Christian and Gabby, who still stood at the clearing's edge, firing bolt after bolt at feds. Rabbit had disappeared again.

Jamie sat up. "Oh, shit. I feel like somebody stuck my brain in a blender."

Christian put a hand on his shoulder. "Stay here until you feel better. But feel better in a hurry."

"Use your charms," Jamie said.

We forgot all about them again, Christian thought. She pressed hers to her chest and said the magic word.

"What the hell?" Mossman said.

Kragthorpe and Greenwalt fired their weapons at Gabby, but Christian sped out there and grabbed her and carried her back to Jamie. Gabby took him in her arms. "I thought you might have been in, like, a coma or whatever," she said.

"That might have been better than going inside Rabbit's head," Jamie said. "Now I know how that dude felt at the end of *2001*."

"We don't have time for this," Christian said. "Gabby, use your charm and piggy-back on me."

Gabby did it. So did Jamie. The Team cried out in surprise again and started talking to each other. Gabby climbed onto Christian's back. "What are we doing?"

Kragthorpe, Mossman, and Greenwalt were advancing in triangle formation, Mossman on point despite his having zero functional hands and no weapon. Christian had to admit that the man had courage. Or maybe just stubbornness and hate. All three of them were looking around wildly.

From the deep, wide hole in the ground, fog or smoke boiled up and spread over the clearing. It surrounded the feds, who tightened their formation and stood back to back, weapons ready. Mossman was talking, too low for Christian to make out. Greenwalt and Kragthorpe swung their barrels around, but what was there to shoot? Then the fog coalesced and spiraled into a twisting vertical column that reminded Christian of a DNA strand. The column widened and began to take a form three or four times taller than the men. It was hunched over, with a big head, short arms, a long tail.

A tyrannosaur loomed over the Team, who stood goggling at this latest impossibility.

"Aw, shit, yo," Jamie whispered.

The T. rex bellowed at the feds, who fell over each other as they tried to get away. Mossman was shouting for everyone to form up, maintain tactical discipline. Greenwalt and Kragthorpe scrambled to their feet and fired their weapons at the tyrannosaur. The acid goop and whatever energy shit Greenwalt was shooting struck it and hissed, eating away flesh that regenerated almost as soon as it disappeared. Rabbit roared again.

He could eat those guys any time he wanted, or just step on 'em. And all that shit we did to him when he was an elephant? It's like it never happened. Is he playing *with us?*

"Come *on*, Gabby," Christian said. Gabby climbed on. Christian hooked her arms under Gabby's legs; Gabby snaked one arm around her throat. "Blast anything that ain't one of us."

"I ain't stupid," Gabby snapped.

Gabby fired as they ran, striking the T. rex in the upper torso and face, knocking the weapons out of the Team's hands. Another sweep, and she hit the T. rex in the eyeball. It bellowed and shook its head.

The feds regained their guns and resumed shooting, though Mossman had started backing away, perhaps finally remembering that he was helpless. "Look at those beams," he yelled. "The kids are still out there! Shoot them, too!"

Christian couldn't wait to kick that dude's ass, but he had supplied her with a vital piece of information: Even while the Freaks were invisible, Gabby's beams weren't. Micah's fire and ice probably wouldn't be, either. And what the hell had happened to Micah anyway?

While she was thinking, something struck her, a massive jarring like a two-car collision, and the world turned upside down. Christian tumbled through the air. *His tail, he swiped us with his tail, oh shit where's Gabby.* Christian hit the ground, rolled with the impact, regained her feet, and started running again, all in a fraction of a second. Gabby was sailing into the woods, where she struck the ground and skittered away.

Christian stopped to get her bearings. The T. rex saw her—yes, she was sure it saw her, which meant that Baltar was right about the charms not working on Rabbit—and seemed to ... smile?

The situation's unreality washed over her like cold water. *I am fighting a god disguised as a dinosaur. And he's definitely having fun.*

Rabbit bellowed. His mimicry was so realistic that his breath smelled like rotted meat.

Christian tensed, ready to run.

Something struck the trickster in the side of his head. He grunted and stumbled sideways. A weird, yellowish light, seemingly generated from nowhere, surrounded Rabbit and began to pulse and crackle and contract. Each time it did, Rabbit roared, tossed his head, thrashed his tail. Another strike—energy? blunt force? something else entirely?—knocked the trickster sideways again. The yellow cloud pulsed faster and faster, grew tighter and tighter. Rabbit's roaring was almost constant. Christian covered her ears.

Jamie flew into the clearing and landed beside her. He handed her three candy bars. "Maybe we should have brought popcorn," he said as Christian inhaled a Milky Way. "You think Baltar's doing this?"

"Don't know what else it could be," Christian said, her mouth full. "It sure ain't us or those feds."

The yellow energy strobed. Rabbit stopped screaming. Was he dying?

The T. rex *exploded*.

The resulting energy wave rippled outward, knocking Christian and Jamie through the air and driving everything before it. Christian passed over ragged tree stumps, struck the ground, somersaulted several times, and came to rest. After a moment, she sat up and groaned. All her body parts seemed to be in order, her costume intact. She must have engaged her powers and protective aura on instinct. She hoped Jamie had done the same. Even with the aura, she hurt all over. The forest had been flattened in a vaguely circular pattern, the blast radius at least one hundred yards. The wave seemed to have hovered a couple of feet above the ground, based on the height of the stumps. If her friends and the Team had managed to hit the deck, they had probably survived. If not—

Forty or fifty feet to her right, Jamie stirred. More debris dust had risen above the enlarged clearing. Fragments of wood rained down. In the distance, other human figures sat or stood, wobbled, turned aimlessly as if half asleep. Christian engaged her enhanced vision and spotted Mossman, Greenwalt, and Kragthorpe, their suits torn and filthy, their faces covered in dirt. Mossman had even lost his ever-present sunglasses. His face looked naked without them. Some distance away, Micah lay facedown. His position didn't seem to have changed. Several yards from him, Gabby was trying to sit up. And on the farthest edge of the blast zone, Kenneth was standing and brushing himself off, but he swayed like a drunk man.

Rising in the middle of the clearing, Rabbit shifted into his true form.

Damn it to hell. This is impossible.

"Child," Rabbit said to Christian. His voice sounded deep and garbled. "Surely now you understand that standing against me is folly. Surely now you will take my hand."

She speed-jogged into the clearing. Maybe she could buy the others time to regroup or get away.

She stopped only feet away from Rabbit, who towered over her, those saber teeth poking out of a face that otherwise would have been … well, cute. The whole concept of a giant, carnivorous, murderous rabbit kept slipping out of her mind. It was simply too absurd. What was next, a man-eating guinea pig? But here Rabbit stood, solid and muscular and unharmed, despite the power the Freaks and the Team had unleashed against him. He smelled like rich soil.

"I can't come with you," she said. "Eternal life would be hell if you couldn't live with yourself."

A sound from somewhere nearby. Kenneth had fallen onto his ass.

Everyone that had entered the clearing, including the Team, was either unconscious or addled. She stood alone against the trickster.

"Your sacrifice will not save these others," Rabbit said. "But theirs will save you, if only you will join me."

Christian's legs shook. She looked around, praying to see someone, anyone, heading their way or making a move against Rabbit. But no help seemed forthcoming. Never had she felt so close to shitting her pants and pissing herself at the same time.

"Can't do it," she said, hating the way her voice quavered.

Rabbit sighed. The light rippled through his fur like water trickling over rocks. "I can smell your terror. You know you are doomed."

"That's right."

Rabbit examined the clearing, his gaze pausing on each human form. He looked sad, which Christian would not have believed possible for any rabbit, much less a monster one. Then, moving so fast even she couldn't dodge, he kicked her in the solar plexus. The force drove her through the air. She landed hard, gasping for air. Things inside her shifted. She hadn't been able to raise her aura. It felt like her rib cage had caved in.

The trickster stood over her, those deep brown eyes burning. It raised its leg. This time Christian managed to vibrate her right hand just enough to engage the aura, but the force of Rabbit's stomp drove her six inches into the solid ground. Her ribs screamed.

"Stop it!" Jamie cried. He was flying toward Christian. Well, floating, like a balloon in a light breeze. After several feet, he fell to the ground and landed on one knee. His head hung. Then he forced himself to stand, rise, float toward them again.

Rabbit cocked his foot. Christian engaged her aura just before he soccer-kicked her in the head, so she survived, but she was lifted high into the air. She crashed down and lay prone. The world spun. She couldn't think. She couldn't move.

"Stay down," Rabbit said.

Christian closed her eyes for a bit. She wanted to pray, but her thoughts had turned as slippery as a bar of soap.

A weak sizzling, and one of Gabby's beams struck Rabbit, but it barely disturbed the trickster's fur. He stared down at Christian, waiting.

"No," she said.

Rabbit leaped high into the air. Christian followed the arc, realized he would land on top of her, and fell backward, vibrating her hands. The trickster landed on her chest and arms, driving her into the ground. Her aura kept her from being crushed, but her jostled ribs took away her breath. Her hands fell to her sides. She groaned.

Balling her costume in his paws, Rabbit yanked her up and held her only inches from his face. Those huge brown eyes bored into her. His breath smelled like carrots. Christian burst into laughter. It was the crowning absurdity. Rabbit looked puzzled, but if he expected an explanation, he'd just have to get over it. She couldn't fight, could barely think. If he decided to rip her throat out with those teeth or tear her limbs off, she wouldn't be able to stop him.

Maybe the others can keep going. Make him pay for whatever he does to me. I'm sorry, Mom. I tried.

But Rabbit hesitated. He seemed to be looking into the deepest parts of her psyche, her soul. More sizzling, another of Gabby's beams, still weak. Rabbit didn't even flinch when they struck him.

"Let her go," someone yelled. Jamie? The voice was unsteady.

Rabbit paid it no mind. "You would truly die with this tribe rather than renounce them and save yourself."

Christian laughed again. There was a rushing in her ears, like the sound you heard in seashells. "Dude. We've been through this. Do what you gotta do, but don't bore me to death."

Still those eyes probed. "You have wagered your existence on your belief in your friends' decency. On the chance that they will learn to harness their powers in service of creation, not destruction. Would you also gamble with the very life of your planet?"

Christian looked around, straining her neck. Micah still hadn't moved. He lay forty or fifty yards away. Gabby had regained her feet and was approaching one halting step at a time. Kenneth limped forward, though he wandered off course—from overhead, his path would probably resemble a snake—while opening and closing his fists. Jamie set down only feet from Rabbit. He assumed a shaky fighting stance. Her friends, still fighting, or trying to.

"Let her go," Jamie called.

Gabby stopped near him. "Yeah," she said. "Get away from her."

From somewhere behind Rabbit, Kenneth's shuffling footsteps stopped. "You and me ain't done," he said.

Christian thought about Rabbit's last question, about Micah and Kenneth—how their lifelong hatred had settled into a stable pattern of low-grade loathing; how the recent flare-ups of their old hostility had both worried and exasperated everyone; how Micah had only gotten weirder, quieter, more isolated since his great-uncle had showed up. What if he and Kenneth couldn't coexist? What if the Freaks chose sides and went to war? If everyone's powers continued to grow, what were the chances that Kenneth and Micah would destroy Quapaw City as they tried to kill each other? What if they demolished Arkansas? Or the country? Or the world?

Jamie flew forward and snatched her out of Rabbit's hands. He set her down several yards away and looked her over. She knew she was swaying, that she might fall over. While Rabbit watched them, Kenneth and Gabby joined Jamie. All three formed a wall in front of Christian.

"You can't have her," Jamie said. Then he attacked.

"Jamie—" Christian began, but Rabbit's right arm flashed out and sideswiped him.

Jamie skidded through the upturned soil and debris before coming to rest on his back. "Ow," he said.

That sizzling sound, and Gabby's beams struck Rabbit in the chest.

She had regained enough strength to drive the trickster backward a foot or so.

"Wait!" Christian shouted, but Gabby kept firing from both hands.

Rabbit melted, swirled, flashed with some kind of crackling strobe effect. He became lightning and zapped across the clearing, striking Gabby. Sparks flew. Christian shielded her eyes. Gabby stood her ground as the bolts swirled around her. She pumped her own energy back at the lightning, the dueling cracks and flashes almost blinding, deafening, the sound of a million insects, until the whole mess exploded.

Christian closed her eyes, turned her head. The air stank of ozone. When she looked back, Rabbit had assumed his true form again, and Gabby lay propped on her elbows. Smoke rose off her like heat from summer concrete.

Rabbit raised one foot, ready to stomp on her.

Christian ran between them and caught the foot on its way down. It drove her backward; her feet dug rivulets in the bed of leaves. She bent her knees, flexed, and pushed upward. "Gabby, get outta here," she grunted. "I can't hold him!" From behind her came the sound of Gabby scrambling away.

"Stop that," Rabbit said as he shifted his body weight and increased the pressure. Then he began to grow. His head filled Christian's entire range of vision, then his face, then his eyes. The pressure increased in proportion, driving her back to her knees. She could find no leverage to get out from under him. She couldn't even vibrate. And still Rabbit grew. "Cry off before it is too late."

"Not ... if you're gonna ... kill my friends," she sputtered.

Rabbit roared like the bear he had sometimes become. It sounded so silly coming from the mouth of a rabbit that, despite everything, Christian laughed. But the pressure doubled, tripled. Black spots played across her eyes.

Then all that weight lifted. Christian fell over, gasping. Her arms and legs felt like cooked spaghetti; everything ached. What the hell had happened? She looked up.

Rabbit had backed away. He studied her, unblinking. If a rabbit could look frustrated, this one did. "You vex me, child."

Screaming Rabbit's name, Kenneth charged. The trickster turned and slashed at him with claws that had grown to the size of broadswords. Kenneth dodged, rolled, came up swinging. His fist struck those claws and broke two of them off at the quick. "Hah!" he said.

Rabbit headbutted him. Kenneth fell backward like a cut tree.

Rabbit's right foreleg grew straight and stiff, the humanlike fingers fusing together into a pointed, sharp dagger made of what looked like bone. He raised it, preparing to thrust it through Kenneth's chest.

Ignoring the roaring hunger in her gut, the dizziness, the weakness in her limbs, Christian speed-dragged Kenneth away. Rabbit's sword-arm jammed into the earth as she set Kenneth down and dashed back. Rabbit swung the arm at her. She dropped to her knees as it passed over, then stood, scurried up his back, and tap-danced on his head. Rabbit struck her with his other arm. She fell to the ground, rattled all over again. Her ribs felt better, but all that jostling nearly made her scream.

Jamie flew at the trickster, using his body as a projectile, fists outstretched. He struck Rabbit's gut, the force carrying them both back and back toward where Micah lay. Rabbit turned to mist, and Jamie passed through, flying most of the way to the new tree line before he could stop himself.

Rabbit spotted Micah and leaped, apparently planning to crush him. Christian rescued him, too. As Rabbit landed, all the crushed gunk on the ground puffed around him like smoke. Christian rolled Micah over. His eyes were still closed, squinted even, but he was breathing.

Rabbit approached. His arm had returned to its true form, but the claws at the ends of his fingers still looked like butcher knives. Machetes, even. The ones Kenneth had broken were whole again. "I can sense your fatigue," Rabbit said. "Give in. Perhaps you can make new friends. Perhaps I could be the first."

Christian met him halfway and stood to her full height. Every muscle felt as if it had been liquefied. And the hunger. God, how she needed food. "No," she said. "These kids aren't just friends. They're family."

Rabbit stared at her a moment. He seemed about to speak. Then Christian realized that the sound of a straining motor was growing closer and closer. She had been concentrating so much on Rabbit that she hadn't even noticed it until now. The trickster heard it, too. He turned.

Brayden Sears drove his four-wheeler straight into Rabbit's leg.

The ATV caught purchase in the fur and flesh and zipped upward into the torso, but Brayden flew over the handlebars, glanced off Rabbit's shoulder, and spun through the air. At the same time, Rabbit shoved the four-wheeler away. It fell onto its side. The engine died, and silence descended on the clearing. Only Brayden's groaning broke it.

Christian eyed the vehicle. In its little compartment behind the seat, she would find snacks, enough to recharge and continue the fight. *We won't last long,* she thought. *Rabbit ain't having fun anymore. But screw him.*

"Give in," Rabbit said again.

"No."

Jamie was flying this way, but he wavered everywhere, much as Kenneth had done. As for Kenneth himself, he had gotten to his hands and knees. Now he forced himself to his feet and trudged forward. Gabby had nearly reached Rabbit. White energy flickered around her hands, though her eyes looked glazed.

Rabbit turned to her. His body started to shift.

Christian gritted her teeth and got ready to move. Jesus Christ, she hurt so *bad*, and she was so *tired*.

She zoomed to the ATV and speed-ate four candy bars. Energy surged through her body. Her thoughts cleared. Rabbit watched her, whiskers twitching. "Come on, bruh," she said, beckoning him. "Just you and me." The trickster shuffled close, stood over her like a shade tree, peered into her with those chocolate eyes. Christian's heart skipped a beat, but she stood her ground. "Get it over with. Come on. *Come on!*" She assumed a fighting stance.

Rabbit cocked his head, as if he were curious. "You would truly face me alone. Even though you will die."

"*Yes*, damn it. Just come at me before I lose my goddam nerve."

But Rabbit made no move. Now the others reached this spot. Jamie landed in front of her, only an arm's length away. Gabby and Kenneth joined Jamie in shielding Christian. "You can come at her if you want to," Jamie said, and though he trembled, his voice sounded strong. "But you'll have to get through all of us first."

Rabbit looked them over, one at a time. Then he turned to Christian. "And if I let you bring the child—the one you love, the one with whom you could make a life—you would still resist me?"

"I don't know another way to say it," Christian said. "Are you hard of hearing or just stupid?"

Rabbit sighed. He looked to the sky, at the destruction they had wrought, at the government men who, some distance away, huddled together like injured soldiers. Mossman was ranting, shouting at the others, who mostly ignored him as they crawled around, probably looking for their guns. "You are true warriors," said the creature. "And therein lies much of our problem."

"We're the good guys," Christian said, shouldering her way into the line her friends had made. "But you've made it clear that don't matter. So for God's sake, *stop freaking talking and let's do this.*"

For a moment, nothing happened. Then Rabbit's body morphed, shrank. Bec Villalobos stood before the Freaks, in form if not in fact. "By all the gods that ever were, girl, you vex me more than anything ever has."

"I wish you wouldn't look like Bec," Christian said. She felt tears forming and blinked them away. "I don't want them to kill me. Please."

Bec-Rabbit stepped forward. His right hand stroked Christian's left cheek. "I will not kill you. And neither will anyone else. Not today, at least."

Christian's mouth fell open. "What?"

Rabbit-Bec turned, walked toward the hole in the ground, stood over it. After a moment, Christian joined him. The others followed. "Your friend lies down there," Rabbit said. "Retrieve them at your leisure. Your government friends should also go down, though they will not like what they find."

"They ain't my friends," Christian said.

"Another reason why I have fought myself today, almost as hard as I fought you. At first, I merely wanted to prolong the game. But watching you and your friends strive against all odds and good sense, I feel something I did not expect: hope." He turned to them and looked them over, one at a time. "When I left this plane, my chosen people had been murdered and cheated until they teetered on the brink of extinction. Only by joining the tattered remnants of the other Nations in some far-off land could they cling to some sort of life. And then even that land was stolen, given to the whites who had already claimed the world. Despair throttled my better nature, and I abandoned the Nations as surely as the encroaching whites had forced my people to abandon their ancestral lands." He gestured at the Freaks and seemed to smile. "But now look. You are young. One day soon, the world will be yours. And you have already learned to stand beside each other in the very shadow of agonizing death. You embrace the differences in your skins, your beliefs, your histories, where humans of the past might have gone to war. Even now I find this plane filled to bursting with the forces of dissolution and fear and indifference. Yet if two whites can fight beside a scion of slaves and the offspring of blended cultures, then perhaps this world's future can be different from its past. Perhaps I can still hope."

That same emotion flared in Christian's heart, too. She tried to ignore it, knowing she couldn't survive this kind of inner turmoil for long. If Rabbit was doing this to her on purpose, it was the height of cruelty. "So what now?"

"Now I leave you. The magics that kept my burrow intact even during our battle will not last long in my absence. I suggest you collect your friend now." Rabbit-Bec's smile faded. "But know this. I hold you responsible for your friends. If any member of your group poses an existential threat to this world, I will return. And at that point, I will not be interested in a good fight, or second chances. Everything you know and love will wither before my wrath like a flower in fire. Do you understand?"

"But—"

"No," Rabbit said. "This is the best I can do."

Christian looked back at the others. She couldn't see their faces under their masks, but their eyes looked exhausted. She held Jamie's gaze for a moment; he nodded. Christian turned back to Rabbit. "All right," she murmured.

"In that spirit," Rabbit said, "beware the one called Micah. I sense a deep darkness there. And not just inside him. Evil clings to him like flies to a corpse. It speaks to him. And he listens."

"Wait," Christian said, reaching out as if to grab Rabbit-Bec's shoulder. "What do—"

"Monster!" someone shouted from behind them.

Christian and Rabbit-Bec turned. Kragthorpe stood fifteen or twenty yards away in his dirty, ruined suit, his face covered in grime. He aimed the goop gun at Rabbit. In the distance, Mossman was supporting Greenwalt as they shuffled toward the Freaks.

"Little man," Rabbit-Bec said, "put your toy away and run."

"Nah, dude," Kragthorpe said. He pulled the trigger.

In a split second, Rabbit's body turned liquid, flowed between Christian and the fed, and solidified in the form of a boulder twice her height. The goop struck it and hissed, spat, sizzled. Then the boulder liquefied, too, and flowed straight at Kragthorpe. It swirled around his gun and yanked it from his hands. In half a second, the blob of undifferentiated flesh resolved into Rabbit-Bec again. He handed the gun to Kragthorpe. Its barrel had been bent and tied in a bow.

Just like in Bugs Bunny, Christian thought. *Which makes Kragthorpe Elmer Fudd.*

She burst into laughter as Kragthorpe took the gun and stared at it, his expression dull and unbelieving.

"Pray you never see me again, white man," Rabbit-Bec said. "And thank these children for your miserable life."

Then he shifted into his true form and backhanded the CIA man, who fell. Rabbit bounded away. He passed Greenwalt and Mossman, who watched him go but did nothing. Maybe they had finally wised up.

A low, barely perceptible rumble, and hundreds of bunnies boiled out of the hole, climbing and hopping over each other. They stampeded Kragthorpe. His outraged cries were muffled under all the furry little bodies.

Christian jumped into the hole and landed on the warren's dirt floor. Bec lay nearby, still unconscious, eyeballs twitching under their closed lids. Christian picked them up and, thanking God that the chamber was big enough to stand in, ran up the slope. When she and Bec emerged, Kragthorpe sat there sputtering. The rabbits were dispersing into the woods. Mossman and Greenwalt stared, open-mouthed, and Christian realized they must be seeing Bec floating along, unconscious. How much longer would the cloaking spell last? Several feet away, Brayden was righting his ATV and cranking it. The collision didn't seem to have damaged it—or him—much. Christian carried Bec over and put them on the seat. Brayden climbed on behind them, holding them up with one arm, steering and working the throttle with the other.

"Get them back to the cars," Christian said. "The rest of us will be along in a minute."

Brayden nodded and drove off.

Kenneth had never engaged his charm. He walked over to

Kragthorpe and kicked dirt in the CIA agent's face. "Asshole," Kenneth said. Kragthorpe cursed and wiped at his eyes.

From the woods came the sounds of birdsong and buzzing insects. The world was already moving on. "Let's get outta here," Jamie said. "I'll bring Micah. Kenneth, can you give Gabby a lift again?"

"Yep," Kenneth said, watching the feds limp their way. "If my four-wheeler's still in one piece."

Jamie flew toward Micah, who was finally beginning to stir. The dickweed had missed half the fight. Kenneth and Gabby speed-walked in the direction of Kenneth's ATV. Christian stood alone over Kragthorpe, who had cleared out his eyeballs and was struggling to his feet. She gripped her charm and said the magic word. Kragthorpe started, his eyes widening. "The shaper told me your friend's down the hole," she said. "Y'all need to get him quick, before the tunnels collapse."

"Where the hell did you come from?" Kragthorpe asked.

"My parents," she said. Then she turned and speed-jogged through the woods, heading for the cars.

CHAPTER THIRTY-FOUR

I scampered northwest. In that direction lived the descendants of those I used to know. Those I once tricked in the unspoiled forests of a vanished world. I looked forward to sharing this plane with them for a time. Many of my cousins ran with me, and though I eventually bid them farewell, I sent them love and my wish that they might live long and peaceful lives. After that, I traveled alone, as I have since time began. When the next human road appeared, leading to another white village, I became a hawk and took to the skies.

For the first time in centuries, I did not understand myself. I had vowed to lay the young warriors low. Then, once the battle began, I did little more than exercise muscles and abilities I had not used in years. Their mutual love, their embracing of each other's differences, had disarmed me. Had I truly made the right decision? Had they somehow tricked me? Or had I tricked myself? These were mysteries to ponder in the coming days.

So few of the First Peoples survived. Whites had herded them onto tiny scraps of wastelands, had built a new nation on the bones of the vanished. Whenever I thought of this, anger and despair clutched my heart like the talons of a bird afire. Genocide, hatred, the loss of ancient languages: these were among the legacies that dominated this continent. I could never forget that, nor could I forgive. But perhaps those child-warriors had earned the chance to become something better than the world that produced them.

Time would show me how well I had chosen, or how poorly. It always did.

In the distance, a gunshot echoed through the woods. Curious, I investigated and found three men with guns standing over the body of a buck. They seemed pleased with themselves, as if they had won a fair contest. I swooped down some distance behind them, became myself, and found their strange vehicles, the same kind that the young warriors had ridden into battle against me. I squatted over each of these transports and defecated on the seats. It was a fun trick. Much better for them than what would have happened if they had ventured a few miles to the south, where slumbered the traveler of wings and scales and fire. And it occurred to me that if the young warriors encountered her, they might soon wish I had killed them quickly.

But that was not my concern.

I took to the skies again and rode the frigid winds northwest.

CHAPTER THIRTY-FIVE

On the last day of November, Bec hadn't returned to school, so Christian asked Gabby to drive her to the Villalobos house. Gabby kept shifting in her seat and grimacing. She had told Christian that something had happened to her lower back in the fight, though her healing power had taken care of the worst of it. Christian was still sore, too, and she was also smarting over Juana's most recent texts. Too stiff and tired to hang, Christian had begged off one too many times, and Juana had finally stopped sending or receiving any texts or DMs. Apparently being a Freak had cost Christian a friend. What would it cost her now?

Gabby waited in the car while Christian knocked on Bec's door. Bec answered. Their eyes were dark and swollen, their movements furtive, as if a step in the wrong direction might lead them to another hole in the ground. They leaned against the door frame.

"Hey," Christian said.

"Hey. Come on in." Inside, the heat was blasting, so Christian took off her coat. Bec was still holding the door open and looking out at Gabby's car. "She not coming?"

"I wanted some time alone with you."

"Okay." Bec closed the door and led Christian into the living room. They sat on the couch together, perhaps a foot apart, Bec with their hands in their lap.

"So," Christian said. "How are you?"

Bec glanced at the floor, then back at Christian. They seemed troubled. "Making it. Mom and Dad won't let me go back to school yet. Today is the first time I've been alone since ... well, since I woke up in bed on Saturday night. Dad's at work. Mom needed to run to the store, and it took me an hour to talk her into going without me. I'm mostly staying in my room."

Ever since they'd laid Bec in the front yard, honked Gabby's horn, and hauled ass out of the neighborhood, Christian had thought of little else. Sitting in class, eating dinner with Mom, riding with Gabby, listening to the Team, her mind had been here, in this house, gazing at this face, into those eyes. She liked Bec, and not just as a friend. "How are you *really*?" she asked.

Bec shrugged. "I don't even know what happened. Mom and Dad say I went missing for days, but I don't remember anything. I was here. Then I woke up in my room to find my parents guarding me like a prisoner."

"I'm sorry."

"Why? It's not your fault."

Christian couldn't argue with that unless she was prepared to tell Bec everything. She wasn't. Neither were the other Freaks. "Listen," she said. "Before all … this, you and me were hanging out. Like, a lot. And. Um. I mean—"

Bec took her hand. Christian's heart leaped. "It's okay," Bec said. "Just say it."

Christian closed her eyes and took a deep breath. If anyone should understand what this moment was like, Bec would. As a gender-fluid female-as-assigned-at-birth who liked girls, Bec had almost certainly experienced misery, uncertainty, a nagging belief that every person you met had set a trap that would snap closed anytime you made yourself vulnerable. In this world, did any queers come out of the womb automatically comfortable in their own skin, ready to take romantic leaps like so many straight people did without a second thought? Each moment could lead to trauma that struck years from your future. Any careless word might be the one that ostracized you, that ripped the foundation out of your life until you either found a way to live in the world or you died. Christian had never experienced such a moment, not in terms of her romantic heart. But now this gorgeous, self-assured person had come into her life, and Christian wondered if she had the guts to take the risk.

"Um," she said.

Bec leaned closer and looked into her eyes. "Anything," they said.

A lump the size of a golf ball had formed in Christian's throat. She felt overheated. "God, you got a glass of water or something?"

"Yes. But I think you just ought to say it."

Christian squeezed Bec's hand. "Look, I've ... well, I don't really know how this works. I mean, I *know*, but I don't *really* know. You know? This town ... it ain't exactly known for flying rainbow flags or throwing Pride parades."

"I've noticed," Bec said.

"So I ... well, I never had much chance to do this before. Any of it." She ran a hand through her hair and sighed. "Jesus Christ, I'm screwing this up."

"You're doing fine."

Christian closed her eyes, breathed deeply, opened them again. "Every time I've showed any real part of myself, kids have lined up to spit on it. But I think you're different. I think *we're* different."

Bec scooted closer. "I think so, too."

"What I'm saying is, if you want to try this ... I mean the more-than-friends thing, you and me, like, together ... then I guess I, well, I'm down. I mean, unless, you know, I misread the whole situation or whatever. I probably did, right? I thought there were signals. But if I'm wrong, just forget I said anything, okay? We—"

Bec leaned forward and kissed her on the lips, and every conscious, coherent thought in Christian's head evaporated. She felt flushed, trembly, like when she used her powers too much, except that this felt *good*, as if parts of her were awakening for the first time.

Bec broke off the kiss and booped Christian's nose. They took both of her hands. "I've wanted to do that for a long time."

"Well," Christian said, breathy and more than a little stunned, "I'm glad you did."

Bec kissed her forehead. "Me, too. Wanna do it again?"

✳✳✳

Micah had taken his bike some distance into the woods and set it behind the thickest tree he could find. Then he had come back to the forest's edge, where he sheltered behind a pine and turned up his vision. Gabby's car had turned onto Johnny Cash Way before he could talk himself into walking over and knocking on Bec's door. Gabby hadn't gotten out. Her car still idled in Bec's driveway, the tailpipe pluming in the cold air.

Micah hadn't turned up his hearing, so he had no idea what was being said in the house. Not that he hadn't been tempted. He hadn't seen Bec in several days, unless you counted the glimpses of them when they were leaving the woods, and they had been unconscious then. Before all that shit happened, though, he had gotten closer to them. At least he had thought so. For the first time since his puppyish crush on Gabby had shriveled away, the longing for another person—their presence, their laughter, their body heat, the little crinkles in the corners of their eyes when they grinned, everything—had opened inside him, spilling out a kind of chill that made him shiver at odd moments. So today, he had slipped out of the house while Baltar napped. He had biked over here. And then he had watched Christian get out of Gabby's car and go inside. Ever since, he had been waiting for the other two Freaks to leave.

Now the door was opening. Micah leaned on the tree trunk, the rough bark digging into his shoulder.

Christian exited. Bec followed, leaving the door open. The two of them were holding hands.

Micah's stomach leaped into his throat.

Bec escorted Christian to the passenger side of Gabby's car. There they paused, hands on each other's faces. Bec said something. Christian laughed. Bec smiled. Micah called himself a coward for not listening in. And at the same time, he nearly burst into tears from the relief he felt at not having to hear what they said.

Christian and Bec kissed, long and deep, like people did in the movies.

Bec stepped away. Christian got in the car. In a moment, she and Gabby were gone.

Bec went back inside and shut the door.

Micah staggered deeper into the woods and vomited.

When he straightened up, he felt dizzy. Pinpricks of light shot into his eyes, his brain. The top of his head felt like it might burst open.

Never forget this, a voice whispered, the one that had so often spoken in his dreams, the one that now thundered inside him every time he felt wronged, alone, miserable. *Your friends laugh behind your back. Without me, you are alone.*

"God, shut *up!*" Micah shouted, hands over his ears. "Just leave me alone!"

Come with me when I ascend, and no one will ever laugh again. Women will lie at your feet and beg for the chance to kiss them. And your enemies—oh, how they will cower, flee, plead for their lives. You will look down on them before they are destroyed. Then it will be your turn to laugh.

"Leave me alone," Micah whimpered. He leaned against another tree, slid down, curled into the fetal position. "Just stop."

Come with me. I will raise you on high.

"Stop it!"

Micah fought that voice for a long time. But he was losing.

CHAPTER THIRTY-SIX

Bundled into his jacket, hands deep in his pockets, Jamie stood in his yard and waited for Gabby. The year's cold, dark days had truly arrived. Mom had finally let him and Dad turn up the thermostat, which she usually guarded like a dragon hoarding treasure. It also seemed to get dark about half past noon. He had never really understood why daylight saving time was still a thing, but even the early darkness and the cold seemed like gifts. He had not expected to survive the fight against Rabbit. As they had driven back toward town that day, he had nearly burst into tears because he felt so glad to be alive. Every leaf, every rock on the road, every piece of litter some self-involved shithead had dumped in the ditches took on a kind of brilliance, like they were generating their own light. That giddiness hadn't subsided yet.

When Gabby reached his house, he got in her car. "Hey," Gabby said.

The heater blew hot air into his face. He adjusted the vent. "Hey."

"Still wanna go to Kenneth's?"

"No," he said, slipping out of his coat. He had already begun to sweat. "But I guess we gotta." He glanced into the side mirror. No tail again. He had seen few signs of the Team since they'd left Mossman, Greenwalt, Kragthorpe, and Vincent in the woods. Their absence made him more nervous than their presence ever had. Jamie liked an enemy he could see. Maybe he and Gabby should ride out to the farmhouse and look around. Kenneth might even want to come with them.

When they pulled up in front of the Del Rays' house, Kenneth came outside. He moved slowly, grimacing. Jamie rolled down the window.

"Hey," Kenneth said.

"Haven't heard from you since the other day," Jamie said. "How about you take a ride with us?"

Kenneth shrugged. "I guess." He opened the back door.

As Gabby drove away, Jamie turned and looked into the back. "You good?"

"That saw-gun shredded me," Kenneth said. "I think I could only move that day because of adrenaline. Now it feels like I worked out too hard. Everything hurts. But it's a little better every day."

"That's good," Gabby said.

"I guess. I told my folks I hit a big hole and got thrown off my four-wheeler. I think they believed it."

Awkward silence descended. After a while, Jamie said, "Hey, you wearing your charm?"

"The new one," Kenneth said. "I found the first one in my closet, but this one's badass."

"Good. We're heading out to Grisham's Loop. See what them feds are doing."

When they got there, Gabby parked ten or twelve yards deep on a little unpaved trail heading into the woods. Keeping inside the tree line, they walked the remaining five hundred yards to Jamie's and Christian's usual spot. They all reached inside their shirts and touched the charms, saying the words Baltar had taught them. There was a *poof* sensation, as if a burst of air had struck them.

Kenneth fell to his hands and knees, his head hanging. He grunted.

Gabby kneeled beside him and put a hand on his back. "You okay?"

"Oof," Kenneth said. "What the hell? I feel like I just played a whole game against a pro team. By myself."

"Meaning what?" Jamie said.

"Everything *hurts*," Kenneth said, groaning. "More than it already did. And I'm tired. Like, wore slap out."

They waited a bit. Jamie had no idea what to do: Abort and carry Kenneth back to the car? Keep going? Call for help?

Kenneth finally stood. "I feel better. That was weird."

"Yeah," Gabby said, her hand on the small of his back.

They sat on the cold ground. Jamie closed his eyes and turned up his hearing, focusing on the farmhouse. Soon he had filtered out the ambient noise. Only the voices came through, each one distinct, all of them sad and angry.

Mossman: "I'm telling you those mutated freaks killed Doberman. We should implement Scorched Earth right away, before they get even stronger."

Greenwalt: "We've got no evidence those kids killed him. We found him in the trickster's burrow."

Mossman: "They could have stuffed his body down there to throw us off. Frame the bogey. And anyway, the trickster's vanished. We can't get to it. But we can reach the brats."

Other voices muttered in the background. Kragthorpe sounded as if he agreed with Mossman, but the other voices, Jeffcoat's and Vincent's, sounded skeptical.

McCreedy: "The last time we took one of those kids, Manticore, a bear ate your hand. If a rendition seems like our best play, we need a foolproof plan. And I am nowhere near prepared to implement Scorched Earth."

Mossman: "But—"

McCreedy: "This isn't a discussion."

No one said anything for a long moment. Then Mossman muttered, "Yes, sir."

McCreedy: "Good. I'm leaving for Washington in the morning. While I'm gone, do not engage. Keep monitoring them remotely, but stay off their streets. No contact. Do you hear me, Manticore? *Do not engage.*"

Mossman: "Yes, sir." It sounded like he spoke through clenched teeth.

The men dispersed, but Greenwalt must have hung back. "Thank you, sir," he said. "I hope you know that if those kids killed Doberman, I'll be the first one to put a round in their skulls."

When McCreedy replied, his voice had lowered almost to a whisper. "Keep an eye on Manticore. He's taking this personally."

Greenwalt lowered his voice, too. "I'm worried about him too, sir. This mission ... well, he hasn't seemed himself. Not since the bear."

"I know. We'll deal with him when the time comes. *If* it comes."

"And if he disobeys your orders while you're gone?"

Another pause. "Stop him. Do what you have to do."

"Yes, sir."

Once the conversation turned to what to eat and whose turn it was to pick which football games to watch, Jamie lowered his hearing to normal and nudged Gabby and Kenneth.

"That Mossman guy really hates us," Kenneth said, huffing as he stepped over a tree branch on the way back to Gabby's car.

"Did it sound to you guys like McCreedy's ready to replace him?" Jamie asked. He was panting, too, with the effort of dodging briars and holes in the ground, with keeping his balance on the wet and slippery bed of leaves covering the forest floor.

"Maybe even kill him?" Gabby said.

"We ain't that lucky," Kenneth grumbled.

Jamie understood how he felt. Sometimes it seemed like the entire world had built a united front against the Freaks. In those moments, he almost missed the days when their biggest worry had been dodging three teenage bullies who liked to punch people in the arms.

After they had taken Kenneth home, Jamie and Gabby sat in the Entmanns' driveway, the car idling, the music off. Already the light was draining from the day. Soon they would have to worry about what else might be out there in the dark. Jamie took Gabby's hand and gently squeezed it. She turned to him and smiled. He brushed a lock of hair behind her ears.

"So what do you wanna do with the rest of the day?" she asked.

"I can think of some things."

She looked away. "I'm not ready for that."

"No, no," he said, swiveling until he could face her. "No pressure. I just meant maybe we could do ... aw, hell, I don't know what I meant."

For a while, neither of them spoke. Jamie turned the music on low and listened to the song, some new mid-tempo pop-R&B hybrid. It seemed to him that it had been playing when they got back in the car and hadn't stopped, one long song with a thousand verses. Or maybe he just wished his life had better background music, something like a movie's score that could tell you what you were supposed to feel, what you needed to do.

"Look," Gabby said, her voice low. She still wouldn't look at him. "I'm not against taking things to the next level. It's just ... well, I don't know what that should mean."

A wind kicked up, bending the trees' branches. Grit skittered over the windshield. "It's okay," Jamie said. "We've got plenty of time to figure out our shit."

"You mean that? You'll be patient with me?"

He squeezed her hand again. "Always." Finally a different song came on, this one faster, with a banging beat. He turned it up, and they bounced their heads to the music, hummed it under their breaths.

We made it, Jamie thought. *We've fought a vampire and a god, and none of us died. Maybe I can do this leader shit after all.* Of course, Christian had pretty much stared down Rabbit by herself. *With Na'ul and Rabbit, we reacted. From now on, I think we gotta take the fight to the bad guys. Active patrols. Contingency plans. Training.* The Freaks needed to become the proverbial well-oiled machine, and they needed to do it now. Who knew when they might have to fight for their lives, or their town, or the whole world?

He and Gabby listened to half a dozen songs. Then Jamie kissed her goodbye.

✳✳✳

On the way home, Gabby kept one eye on the road and one on the rearview mirror. The feds' bugs were still active, so she would have to keep things benign, but she intended to spend a lot of time in front of mirrors, telling herself what she needed to hear until it stuck. No more backsliding.

"You're strong," she said to her reflection. "You're worthy. You're not a worthless half-breed and you never were. Get over that shit and leave it in the past."

She repeated those words all the way home. *I'm never going to be that scared-of-her-own-shadow girl again,* she thought. *Never.*

CHAPTER THIRTY-SEVEN

The sun was setting. Bundled into their coats, Kenneth and Brayden sat on a park bench overlooking the pond. They had biked over just to get out of the house. Kenneth wanted to breathe some fresh air and look at the water. Since he had nearly died in that clearing, those blades buzzing around him and slicing deep into his muscles, scraping his bones, he had tried to see the good in each moment. If Mom got on his nerves, he still nearly burst into tears because he could hear her voice. When Dad made him go outside and clean up the dog shit the neighbors' mutts kept leaving in the yard, Kenneth couldn't stay mad. He had never really paid much attention to how the outdoors smelled: that clean, fresh scent that practically burned your lungs in the cold months. Or the way the clouds scalloped across the sky. It was all so damn pretty. Even that old, rusting dishwasher somebody had dumped in a ditch near Grisham's Loop had looked like a freaking work of art.

Of course, Brayden hadn't felt any of that. Kenneth understood. Brayden hadn't been seriously injured. Even the other Freaks might not get it; none of them had come so close to death. They had saved him, though. No matter what had happened in the past, no matter the future, he could never forget that. Right now, he couldn't even stay mad at Micah. At one point, it had seemed like Sterne was going to burn Kenneth to bones and ashes; at a different point, he had protected Kenneth like they were old friends. Who knew what to make of that fool? But damn, life was too short to sulk. If Sterne wanted to hold onto old grudges, that was his trip. Kenneth had better things to do.

"That move with your four-wheeler?" Kenneth said. "That was pretty badass."

Brayden wore a Razorbacks beanie that made the top of his head look like a strawberry lollipop. He laughed. "Dude, I think I pissed myself."

"Maybe. But you stepped up. You may not have powers, but you got balls for days."

Before Brayden could reply, someone walked up behind them. They both turned to see who it was. Agent Drew Greenwalt stood a few yards away, hands in his pants pockets.

Kenneth and Brayden leaped up.

"I'm unarmed," Greenwalt said "And I'm not looking for trouble."

Don't say anything that proves you're one of the Freaks. Just chill.

Kenneth forced himself to relax, though he positioned himself between Greenwalt and Brayden. "I don't know what you're talking about, mister," Kenneth said.

Greenwalt scoffed. "Right. You know exactly who I am."

"Whatever. We're just here to look at the pond."

"Mind if I join you?"

"It's a free country."

Greenwalt came forward and stopped two or three arms' lengths from the bench. He wore jeans, sneakers, an overcoat, a gray sweatshirt. A featureless black ball cap covered his red hair. Brayden backed away, giving Kenneth plenty of room to swing if the agent made a move. But Greenwalt just stood there and looked past them. Kenneth glanced back over his shoulder. A flock of blackbirds flew down and perched on the bare limbs of a tree and sang to each other. The wind whipped up some small whitecaps.

"Nice place," Greenwalt said.

"What do you want?" Kenneth asked. Greenwalt hadn't fired the blade gun, but he had been there. If Kenneth had died, this guy would have been almost as culpable as the one who pulled the trigger.

Greenwalt sat and patted the bench. When Kenneth only glared at him, he shrugged. "I've got a proposition."

"You shouldn't proposition kids in a park. That shit can get you arrested."

"I'm glad you can still joke. But I'm afraid things have gotten pretty grave."

Kenneth kicked a pine cone. "They've been grave since Jake Hoeper died. How'd you know we were here, anyway?"

Greenwalt looked around, making sure no one was nearby. "We always know where you are, even when we're not watching. But that's beside the point."

"What *is* your point, bro? I'd like to get back to my day."

Greenwalt looked Kenneth in the eye. "My colleague Floyd Parker's dead. So maybe you want to give me five minutes without the smart mouth."

"I don't know anything about that."

Greenwalt glared at him. "I don't think you or your friends had anything to do with his death. If I did, I would have come heavy. But even with the way we found his body in the trickster's den … it isn't enough for some people on my team. Some of them want your heads."

Despite himself, Kenneth trembled. He clenched his fists and jaw, willing himself not to show fear, but when somebody on the street honked their horn, he jumped. "I hadn't even heard that anybody died until you just told us," Kenneth lied.

"We're not publicizing it," Greenwalt said. His voice betrayed a bitterness that made Kenneth even more uneasy. "But that's not the point, either. The point is that certain colleagues of mine are out for blood. And they can't take it out on a bogey that's effectively disappeared."

"So they're gonna take it out on a bunch of teenagers," Kenneth said. His face burned. At least it was from anger, not fear.

"Maybe," Greenwalt said. Now he glanced at Brayden. "Unless someone can give us a specific target. Maybe the teenager most likely to have murdered an NSA agent."

"Hey, bro, I didn't do nothing," Brayden said, raising his hands.

"Not you," Greenwalt said. "You're nobody."

"Eat me," Brayden said, giving Greenwalt the finger.

"Shut up," Kenneth said. Then he turned back to Greenwalt. "Look, stop screwing around. Just lay it out."

"You can buy yourself some time," Greenwalt said. "Maybe even save most of your little rock band."

"Oh yeah? How?"

Greenwalt looked him in the eye. "Help me get Micah Sterne."

Kenneth nearly fell over. Instead, he sat down, elbows on his knees, looking at the ground. This was crazy. What was he supposed to do? Just like Greenwalt had a team, so did Kenneth. And whether he liked it or not, Micah was part of it. They had fought side by side, twice, against things that shouldn't exist. They might not like each other—they probably never would—but experiences like that changed things. He couldn't flip on Micah. Could he?

"You're saying I can trade Sterne for the rest of us," he said.

"I'm saying you can trade him for time. If we give my team something, I think I can get those loud voices to quiet down. Then maybe we can figure something out to *keep* them quiet."

Now it was Kenneth's turn to scoff. "That ain't much of an offer."

"No," Greenwalt said. "But it's the best you're going to get." He pulled a business card out of his shirt pocket and handed it to Kenneth. "Think about it. But don't think too long. We're all on the clock." He stood, turned, and made his way back through the park.

More light had slipped out of the day. Soon Kenneth and Brayden would have to go. The park closed at sunset, and if the cops saw them, there would be trouble. For now, though, Kenneth stayed put, listening to the sounds from the street. Soon, school would let out for Christmas, and then a new year would start. Who knew what it would bring? It might even be the last one of his life.

"Dude," Brayden said. "What are you gonna do?"

For a long time, Kenneth didn't answer. Then he shook his head. "I don't know."

Brayden zipped his jacket and shivered. They stood there until it was almost too dark to see, and then they made their way back to their bikes.

EPILOGUE

Elvis Schott puttered along in second gear, watching for deep holes. He had to wipe his bleary, watering eyes every minute or so. The cool, strong breeze blew directly into them, though his third beer of the day, held tight in his left hand and resting on the ATV's grip, didn't help. He should have eaten before he left, but he had wanted to get the hell out of the house as soon as possible. The wife had been nagging him lately—*You drink too much* this, *I can't do everything around here* that—and weekends in the woods were his only chance for relief. Plus, his daughter Marla, once his little sweetheart who could create whole lives for her dolls and get Daddy another beer with equal enthusiasm, had turned into a smart-mouthed little shit. Elvis couldn't wait until she graduated and he could pack her off to college. Maybe by the time she got out she'd be a decent human being again.

In the meantime, Elvis would keep putting on his orange and loading the four-wheeler into his Chevy and "maintaining the lease." The other members of the Twisted Pine Hunting Club had been glad to hand over the chores to him. His responsibilities mostly consisted of keeping the signage posted and readable, dragging any carcasses off the land, and shooing away anyone who shouldn't be there. That third job hardly ever needed doing. People around here were pretty good about keeping to their own lands. In fact, he could have done everything in an hour if he had wanted to. But then he would have had to go back home.

It ain't like I got a drinking problem, he thought as he crested a hill, maneuvering the ATV between trees. *I just like to take the edge off. You'd think I had killed somebody, the way everybody carries on. I—*

As he reached the bottom of the hill, the ATV struck something.

307

If he had been going any faster, he might have broken his fool neck. As it was, the four-wheeler's ass end reared in the air and pitched forward, crushing Elvis between it and whatever he had hit. Pain flared in his back and neck even as the front part of his body smashed against something as solid as iron. Elvis cried out and slid downward—but against what?—as the ATV fell sideways, sputtered, and died.

Groaning, he turned onto his back. Above, the trees swayed in that same cool breeze. The Sunday sky was overcast but bright. He squinted, feeling more of those tears spill down his face and into his hair. Nearby, his still-intact beer bottle lay on the ground. He was pretty sure it had spilled all over him, and wouldn't the wife bend his ear about that?

Grunting and wincing with effort, the pain radiating up and down his outraged spine, he pushed himself into a sitting position and looked around. The ground in front of him was clear—no stumps, no big limbs, no deep holes. He had been approaching a little clearing maybe forty feet in diameter, so the nearest trees in front of him were still quite a ways off.

"What in the blue hell did I hit?" he asked himself.

In the open space before him, something shifted. He could see the indentations of something big on the ground. Then whatever it was snorted like a horse, if the horse stood about three stories high.

Elvis crawfished backward, eyes wide, breath ragged. Something moved, something *breathed*, but he was alone here, nothing to see, nothing to touch—

The air before him shimmered, and a long, serpentine form seemed to emerge from it, like the shell of a turtle breaking the surface of a river. It was a neck, long and twisting and covered in scales the size of Elvis's chest. And at the end of that neck, a head the size of his truck, purplish, some kind of fringe around it, and the eyes, the eyes—

When it snorted now, blazing hot air struck Elvis in the face. Those eyes bore into his.

The air shimmered again, and Elvis sensed movement, a shifting, a turning, and then the ground thudded over and over as whatever he had seen bounded away, jostling the trees and knocking limbs to the ground.

He sat there for several minutes, waiting for his heart to slow down. When he felt he could breathe again, he stood up and righted the ATV. It cranked on the first try, and he turned it toward the road where he had left his truck. The beer bottle lay where it had fallen, and it would stay there forever if he had to come back for it.

You didn't see nothing, he told himself as he drove. *And you're gonna knock off the drinking.*

He shifted into fourth gear, reckless and almost panicked, until he reached his truck. Then he loaded up the ATV and headed home. The woods had gotten too weird.

ACKNOWLEDGEMENTS

Thanks to Kalene Westmoreland, the love of my life. You're the best. Thanks to Shauna, John, Brendan, Maya, Nova, and Luna. You keep me going.

Thanks to Cookie, Nilla, and Tora for making every day fun.

Mark Sedenquist, Megan Edwards, and every single member of the crew at Imbrifex Books—you believed in this story. I cannot express enough appreciation for everything you do. I love being part of the Imbrifex family.

Thanks to Maya Meyers, editor extraordinaire, for making this book stronger than it otherwise would have been.

To keep in mind the story of Thanksgiving from a non-Eurocentric point of view, I often read Claire Bugos's November 2019 *Smithsonian Magazine* article, "The Myths of the Thanksgiving Story and the Lasting Damage They Imbue." The article features an interview with David Silverman, author of *This Land Is Their Land: The Wampanoag Indians, Plymouth Colony, and the Troubled History of Thanksgiving*. I thank both authors for their work.

Thanks to Catholic Online for the text of Gabby's Catholic prayers, which I have altered to avoid repetition.

Thanks to *Jewish Prayers, Psalms, & Readings for Comfort, Hope and Support* for Gabby's Jewish prayer. I know it's for protection at night, but since Gabby is only half Jewish and not the strongest practitioner, I thought it might be a prayer she would turn to under these circumstances.

Thanks to God, without whom I am nothing.

And to you, reader, whoever you are—thanks for sticking with us on this ride. It's always my honor. May you find your own team. May they always stand by you.

ABOUT THE AUTHOR

Brett Riley is a professor of English at the College of Southern Nevada. He grew up in southeastern Arkansas and earned his Ph.D. in contemporary American fiction and film at Louisiana State University. His short fiction has appeared in numerous publications including Folio, *The Wisconsin Review*, and *The Baltimore Review*. He has also won numerous awards for screenwriting. Riley's debut novel, *Comanche*, was released in September 2020. *Lord of Order*, a dystopian novel set in New Orleans was published in April 2021. *Freaks*, a superhero thriller featuring dangerous aliens and badass high school kids was published in March 2022. The second novel in this series, *Travelers*, was published in August 2022. Riley lives in Henderson, Nevada.

Connect with the author online:

🌐 OfficialBrettRiley.com

🐦 @brettwrites

📘 @brettRileyAuthor